SHATTERED SECRETS

KRIS BUTLER

❀ Created with Vellum

blurb

I came here to find the truth, but it might actually shatter me to pieces instead.

Someone had tried to kill me. *Again.*

I'd come to TAS for answers, but I never expected to uncover the hornet's nest I fell into.

Conspiracies. Kidnapping. Secret identities
I was scared of what I'd learn next, if I was honest.

My instincts screamed to run away, disappear, and never look back. But I couldn't bring myself to leave TAS despite knowing the Council was dangerous. They wanted me for something; I just didn't know what.

Usually, I'd drive myself bonkers obsessing over it, but a perk of dating six people meant limited time to worry about the looming threat over your life. Score!

Except the Council wasn't backing down, and I didn't have it in me this time to be the 'sit on the side-lines' kind of girl. I just hoped the next attempt on my life failed because there was no doubt there would be another. If they couldn't use me, they would ensure no one else could either, and I couldn't have that.

Between my evolving love life, new family, and an

emerging career on the line, I suddenly had a whole lot to live for, and I wouldn't go down without a fight.

foreword

This book has sexual scenes meant for adults. It is a why choose romance that has MM. The steamy scenes are steamy, and apparently insta love on some levels. If that is not your thing, then this book is not for you and that is okay. That is the great thing about books, there are many different kinds and we can all find ones we love.

It has been mentioned that this book may make you laugh out loud, so be careful when reading while drinking or eating or it may cause spewing accidents.

This book highlights mental health in a positive light and the characters have positive coping skills that they will use from counseling. While they may be helpful, this is not a self-help book and if you feel you need help please reach out to someone you trust, or you can find some help here at https://www.samhsa.gov .

content

- Medium burn
- Explicit language (the f word is used a lot)
- Multi-Pov
- Found Family
- Bi-awakening
- Threesomes
- Grumpy/sunshine
- Sex positive
- Mental Health rep
- Queer rep
- No third act breakup, just some angst and mild anxiety about the status of the relationship
- Male virgin
- Second chance
- Friends to lovers
- Enemies to lovers
- He falls first
- A cute dog
- Voyeurism
- Exhibitionism
- Face sitting
- Pierced peen
- Tattoos galore
- Winter sports
- Lots of ice skating
- A fierce bestie

- LOL moments #codeorange
- A FMC with no filter
- Not your average skater, body inclusive
- Twists and turns
- Roomates/forced proximity
- Group Scenes

sensitive topics

- 'God, Jesus, Hell, Damn' used casually or in a sexual context
- PTSD/panic attacks
- Depression/anxiety
- Alcohol recovery
- Self-doubt
- Negative thoughts
- Sexual abuse (past)
- Parents murdered
- Lied to about birth parents
- Family death
- Past suicide attempts
- Grief
- Human trafficking
- Drug abuse
- Kidnapping
- Jealous ex
- Past trauma

For all the times you've felt shattered and broken lying on the bathroom floor, you're not alone. Let's Rise Up and be the Queens we're meant to be.

prologue

TWENTY-TWO YEARS AGO

THE BABIES' wails were deafening as they ricocheted off the wall of the hospital operating room. The mother laid on the operating table, looking exhausted. Twenty hours of labor had resulted in an emergency C-section for the two newborns she'd carried for eight months.

The father of the children spoke with the doctor in hushed whispers as the babies were delivered. It was said that the nurses overheard snippets of conversations, "You will do this, the girl has died," and "Don't cross me."

While he was the father of twins, it appeared he was only interested in the female baby. The nurse took the girl out of the room after a nod from the doctor, and the father trailed behind her, not letting her out of his sight. The remaining staff shifted uneasily on their feet.

The mother heard a commotion but wasn't able to

see anything despite straining her neck to glimpse sight of the baby girl before she disappeared out of the room. The doctors continued to work on the mother as she fretted about her daughter. When she returned from the recovery room, the nurses placed the baby boy upon her chest, smiling down at her.

"Where's my husband?" the woman asked. No one made eye contact, not wanting to be the bearer of bad news. Her stricken face pulled on the heartstrings of the gathered nurses, and one brave soul stepped forward to answer.

"He left. I'm sorry, ma'am."

"Oh, okay. Thank you." She nodded, wiping the shock from her face. "He's an important man," the mother justified, but no one knew if it was for the nurses' sake or her own.

The nurses demonstrated how to get the newborn to latch on for breastfeeding. He latched quickly, and soon he was full and ready to return to the nursery.

"Where's my daughter? I haven't fed her yet," the mother asked, looking over in expectancy for someone to walk in with the baby.

This time it was dead silent; no one wanted to answer. They avoided eye contact as they hastily cleaned up in the room. The uncomfortable quiet rose, and in the end, the same nurse answered the woman.

"Again, I'm sorry, ma'am, to be the one to have to tell you this, but your daughter... she didn't make it. The nurses attempted to resuscitate her for fifteen minutes, but there wasn't anything else for them to do at that point. I'm sorry. Would you like me to get the doctor for you?" the nurse asked with kindness.

It took a few moments for the information to penetrate the woman's mind, but once it did, the most haunting, shrill sound was heard in those halls that night. The young mother sobbed uncontrollably for an hour until she eventually had to be given a sedative to calm down. Pity shone in the nurses' eyes as they cared for her and the newborn boy.

The father never returned that night, nor any nights his wife and son were in the hospital.

The doctor who signed the death certificate conveniently transferred hospitals the following week.

The woman left a few days later via a chauffeured car with only her one bundle instead of the two she'd planned. One birth certificate and one death certificate sat in the bottom of her bag, where they remained to this day.

Asa Orson Abernathy (Walsh) was born to parents Orson Abernathy and Isla Walsh Abernathy on October 10, 1998, at 4:12 am.

Abigail Olivia Abernathy (Walsh) was born to parents Orson Abernathy and Isla Walsh Abernathy on October 10, 1998, at 4:15 am.

Abigail Abernathy died due to complications from a premature birth on October 10, 1998, at 4:30 am. No autopsy was performed per the request of the father.

A small funeral took place two days later, where a

tiny casket was lowered into the hard earth. The mother sobbed throughout the ceremony, while her husband sat stoically, with no trace of emotion on his face. The baby boy was quiet throughout as the nanny held him, subconsciously grieving for his twin.

A single white rose was left on the tombstone, and a new one appeared every year on October 10th, but from whom was unknown.

The father left the mother two weeks after his children's birth and sent divorce papers in the mail the following month. He was uninvolved in his son's life and only allowed him to visit on occasion.

During those visits, the boy spent more time with his father's assistant than his father, who was nothing but a stranger to him. When the boy was about ten, these visits stopped altogether, much to the boy's delight.

The mother never spoke of the child she lost, and until this day, the boy never knew he had a sister. He grew closer to his mother but came to despise his father.

The boy often wondered why his mother would have both tears and smiles on his birthday, but eventually, he quit celebrating it at all, not liking to see her sad.

one

oliver

"HELLO?" the undistinguishable voice on the other end sent a wave of chills through me. I'd avoided making this decision my whole life by ignoring it and sticking my head in the sand like an ostrich.

I was never involved with the family business, and I'd assumed it was enough to just stay out of it. But now I was going to have to pick a side and take a stand, one way or the other.

All because a beautiful girl had made me feel I was worthy.

"I'm ready," I said, my voice steady. My whole body relaxed with the decision being made.

"Good to hear, Mr. Windsor-Latimer. We'll be in touch."

The sound of the phone clicking off reverberated in my heart. It was done. There was no turning back now. For the first time in my life, I was committing to something instead of staying in the neutral zone, playing it safe. Oddly enough, stepping across that line hadn't been as difficult as I'd imagined.

Sitting on the bench in the locker room, I placed my phone beside me, bracing my head in my hands. Tugging a little on the strands, I pulled some of the tension out of my body. Fixating on the floor, I focused on the tile squares as I took several deep breaths to quell my racing heart. The buzzing of my phone brought me back to the present as it made the bench vibrate.

Grump: Oliver, it's time you tell me what's going on. Meet me at the bar in town in a few hours.

I'd wondered how long he'd give me, and quite honestly, I was surprised he'd lasted this long. No point in avoiding the inevitable now; the ball was already in motion.

ME: I'm ready to talk. I'll be there.

I still had some time to kill before speaking with Rhett, but I wasn't ready to face the house just yet, so I headed to town. Perhaps I could get ahead of some of the shit about to come down the pipeline. At this point, it was all I could hope for.

rhett

The sound of the pencil scratching against the paper soothed me as I sketched the garden where Sawyer and I had our first date. I wanted to add it to the canvas I'd given her, but time kept slipping away from us. The fairy lights were almost completed when my alarm went off. Sketching was the only activity I lost time while doing.

Tonight, I had plans to have dinner with my sister and mother. It'd been a while since I'd made it home, and I missed them. I couldn't wait to tell them about Sawyer, and hopefully, they would understand my dating situation. My family was important to me, and Sawyer was it for me—the one. I just knew it.

Heading up to the main floor, it seemed no one else was home either. Sawyer had mentioned she was heading over to Aggies' house, but I wasn't sure where the others were. I pulled out my phone to check the group chat and wondered if Oliver had changed the name today. Except when I thought about that, I realized he hadn't done it in a few days. That was the biggest red flag to show he was hiding something.

Oliver might've presented to the outside world one way, but he'd always been open with us guys. It was time to push him before he did irreparable damage to himself and his relationships. I cared too much about him to let him do that without at least trying to help. Thankfully, he responded to my text, and I didn't have to go and track his ass down. He probably knew that, too.

Oliver: I'm ready to talk. I'll be there.

It was more than I'd hoped for when I sent the text, progress.

Family Affair:
ME: I'm headed to Mom's. Check-ins.

It took a few minutes for them to respond as I made my way to the garage. Luckily, by the time I'd buckled up, most of them had replied.

Elias: Home. Working on lesson plans.
Soren: Late practice. Home later.
Rey: Finishing up a routine and then skating for a bit.
Mateo: Mentor night for me. How long does this typically last?
Baby: Just got to Aggies. I'll text when I head out.
Soren: What activity do you have, Mateo?
Mateo: Concessions and Meet and Greet.
Rey: Raw deal, dude. Concessions are heinous. Good Luck. You may be awhile.
Mateo: Ugh.

Soren: *thumbs down*

Elias: Where is Oliver? Anyone seen him lately?

Satisfied with everyone's answers, I figured they could figure out the Oliver situation on their own. I locked my screen and put my phone away as I pulled out of the drive. My mom lived close by, making it a quick drive there. I should spend more time with them since they were only fifteen minutes away. They were both busy as well, and lately, my life had become consumed with a certain blonde who'd stolen my heart.

My mom had started a themed bed-and-breakfast after Rowan had been diagnosed with lupus; hard to believe that was seven years ago. Rowan was now in her twenties and had stayed close to home. She helped mom out at the B&B with graphic design and social media marketing. Since she'd stepped in, it had helped the business soar. Rowan was taking online college courses in advertising and marketing, but was conscious of not stressing herself out too much. I was proud of all she'd accomplished and the path she was weaving for herself.

Parking around the back of the B&B, I made my way through the side door. The part where they lived was more of a carriage house in the back that consisted only of bedrooms and bathrooms, so we utilized the kitchen and den in the B&B.

Rowan was sitting at the counter, staring at her computer, when I entered the kitchen. Her dark hair was down and a mess from hours in front of the computer. She was always pulling her hair up and taking it down over and over when she was working on something. Her focus was intently on her screen, and she didn't seem to hear me enter.

"Hey, pipsqueak."

Her head popped up, brown eyes meeting mine at the sound of my voice, a smile spreading across her face, effectively warming my heart. There had been a time when I questioned if I'd made the right choice to stay closer to my family, but every time I saw my sister smile, I knew that I had.

"Rhett!"

Jumping from the stool, she rounded the island and barreled into me with her hug. She was tall as well, coming up to my shoulders, allowing me to squeeze her tight as I relished her hug. The threat of losing her made me cherish each one now, they were a true gift.

"About time you visited us! I was telling mom that it seemed like ages since we last saw you. What's been going on? Is the school year stressful already?" Rowan asked, concern lining her voice.

Shit. I knew I'd been away for too long, and now I was going to have to come clean. My cheeks did it for me, though.

I had to give it to my face. It was used to communicating things for me without having to say any words.

"Shut up!" She slapped me, beginning to jump up and down. "You met someone! When do I get to meet her? What's her name? What's she like? Tell me! Tell me! Tell me!"

"Sis, calm down, or I won't be able to get any words out," I huffed, but the smile that followed gave me away.

"No way! You really like her. Oh my god, does mom know? I can't wait to see her face. This is priceless. Finally met someone who meets your standards, huh?" she asked, observing me.

Lifting my eyebrow, she eventually calmed herself enough for me to speak without her constant interruptions.

"Her name's Sawyer, and I met her at school. She's a new instructor. Mom doesn't know yet, and I think you guys will get along great. I'm not sure when you'll get to meet her. Did I leave anything out, Nosey Rosey?" I grumbled.

Rowan just stuck her tongue out, but seemed appeased by my answer.

"Well, I feel sorry for her then if she's stuck with you, and actually, I should question her sanity!"

"Ha, Ha. You're so funny. Don't make me tickle you again; you know I always win."

"That's only because you have bigger hands!"

"Sure, if that's what you want to believe."

"I swear, no matter how long you two are apart, within five minutes, you revert to acting like children," my mother, Rhonda, said as she entered the kitchen. Feeling chastised, I walked over and hugged her.

"Hey, Mom," I said, kissing her cheek.

"Hey, honey, I've missed you. How are things at the house? School going okay so far?" Mom assessed me, a look of concern crossing her face. Before I could open my mouth to share anything, my sister butted in as sisters do and blasted my news, putting me on the spot.

"He met someone!" Rowan shrieked, resulting in our mutual cringe and covering of our ears at the sound.

Once her high-pitched voice lowered, mom was able to understand her words, turning to me with a look of hope in her eyes. The blush reappeared on my cheeks, giving me away for the second time before I could open my mouth.

My mom embraced me in a tight hug, infusing me with her love. Moms must take a class on how to hug this way because they were seriously the best. Drawing back, she looked into my eyes, and something there must've eased whatever worry she had as her face softened.

My mother's features were a little different than Rowan's and mine. Unfortunately, we inherited most of our dark features and height from our father's genetics. Our mom was petite, in her forties, and had light brown curly hair that sat on her shoulders. Her eyes were more hazel than ours, but I liked to believe we obtained our kindness, laughter, and smiles directly from her.

"Come on, dinner's finished, and you can fill me in on this girl." Her teasing tone didn't escape me, but I was too enamored to care. I wanted to tell them about Sawyer. She'd brought the laughter back into my life that I hadn't realized had faded.

Following my mother and sister into the dining area, I was happy to see she'd made one of my favorites for dinner, lasagna. The smell alone was making my stomach grumble.

"Ah, Mom, you're the best!" Her simple smile told me she was pleased with my appreciation.

"So, how are the students this year?" Mom asked, letting me know she was starting easy. We all took our seats and began to dish out the food.

"They seem to be committed. No issues so far." I shrugged.

"Well, I don't care about his students. I want to know about the girl! Tell me more about Sawyer," Rowan pleaded, giving me her puppy dog eyes.

"She's everything I've been looking for, all wrapped up in a small, feisty package." It flowed out of me effortlessly, not even having to think about it.

"That tells me nothing, jerk! Give me details. I need details!" Rowan begged, causing me and mom to laugh at her exuberance.

"Sawyer has blonde hair, green eyes... she's just beautiful. She's sassy and smart, but also awkward in the best ways. I've laughed more in the past few weeks than I have in the past few years. She makes me want to want, and I hadn't realized how long it's been since I've wanted something honestly," I professed; the hope in my voice wasn't lost on either woman at the table if their smiles indicated anything.

"Squee! When can I meet her? What's she doing here?" Rowan quizzed as she rapidly fired questions at me.

As we ate, I was open and honest with them as I

disclosed our relationship's true nature. I shared my feelings about Sawyer and how the house's dating situation occurred, with us all realizing our feelings for her.

"You mean... you're *all* dating her?" Rowan asked as her face scrunched up in thought.

"I know it's not common, but it works for us. We've created a family together, and we all feel strongly about her and this relationship."

"But don't you get jealous?"

"Surprisingly, no. I was worried, but I saw her kiss one of the guys, and it didn't bother me in the way I thought it would, and that's how this whole relationship started. I trust the guys, and it's not some weird free for all. It just works for us, and that's hard to explain if you don't see it, but it's the choice I've made. I hope you can support me in it."

It was quiet for a while as they gathered their thoughts.

"Son, if you feel that strongly about her, then we'll accept your relationship. You aren't a rash person, so I know if you've decided to open your heart to someone, then it's serious. Could we meet her?" my mother asked with a look of apprehension on her face, almost as if she thought I would say no.

"I was hoping you'd say that because I really want you all to meet. Thank you for understanding and accepting my choice. Your support means everything to me."

They both seemed to brighten at that, and the rest of the dinner was spent catching up on the B&B, Rowan's classes, and their marketing for the alumni exposition coming up next month. It was always a big draw for tourists and alumni for the school.

I'd been expecting mom to ask me more questions, so once Rowan was away, I wasn't surprised when she cornered me as I rinsed the dishes.

"Are you being careful with your heart, son?"

"Yes, Mom. If anything, my heart is beating more than it has in five years. Through everything with Rowan's illness, dad leaving, and Molly... well, Molly breaking my heart, I started to block out the world. I was merely biding my time, and I hadn't realized that until it lit up around her. I know it's soon; I get that. And the relationship we're in isn't typical, but I'm happy." Drying my hands, I turned to address her for the rest.

"I care for her a great deal, and I think once you meet her, you'll understand that. I've smiled more, laughed more, hell, even talked more in the past few weeks. I feel excited in the mornings to see her, and I look forward to spending time with her. For once, I'm thinking about my future beyond this town."

She studied me for a moment, taking in the words I'd spoken, the emotion swimming in my eyes, the joy in my voice. When she nodded, I knew she accepted my decision fully this time.

Pulling her towards me, I embraced my mother in another hug. She held me for a little longer before squeezing me and letting go. Stepping back, I was halted before I could say anything else by Rowan entering the room, cutting me off.

"Bro, Elias called the mainline. Said he's been trying to text you but hadn't gotten a response. Something about having to go to the medical center, but to meet him at the house." She shrugged, grabbing some cookies off the plate mom had set out.

"Did he say anything else?"

Fear clawed at my chest. Not again. I prayed it wouldn't be anything serious.

Thoughts of Sawyer and the guys raced across my mind.

Shaking her head, Rowan ate her cookie while scrolling on her phone, oblivious to the impending doom she'd cast on me. I began to pat my pockets for mine when it dawned on me; it was still in the car.

Turning toward Mom, I kissed her as she urged me out the door. Rowan might not remember how her illness affected me, but Mom did. I saw the concern in her eyes for me, but I couldn't focus on that at the moment. Needing more information to calm myself, I rushed out of the B&B and headed to my car.

The force I yanked the door open with wasn't lost on me, but fear was pumping through me, causing my adrenaline to race. Frantically, I searched for my phone, wondering where it had gone. Remembering I'd placed it in the middle compartment while driving, I wrenched it open. I sighed when I spotted my phone sitting there innocently. When I touched it, I had ten missed calls and just as many missed text messages.

Immediately, I hit redial to call Elias, but it went straight to voicemail. Scanning his messages, my heart dropped the more I read.

Fuck.

Putting the car in drive, I zoomed out of the driveway as I headed back to the house, completely forgetting my meeting with Oliver.

two

rey

"TRY to add more extension with your arm on that last move. You want to extend through the whole count, or the judges will deduct a point."

"Like this, Coach Rey?"

I watched Phil and Jill, yes, their names were funny, but they were good students and skated well together. Jill did her turn and nailed the extension this time, but Phil was still only going through the motions. Stopping the music, I skated toward the pair as they caught their breath.

"Jill, that was spot on. You nailed it and are free to go. I'll see you tomorrow in class," I said, praising her before turning toward Phil. When she was off the ice, I questioned him.

"What's going on? You've been off your game today

and half-assing movements the whole session." He hung his head, and I knew I'd been right. Something was going on with him. "What is it, Phil? I've known you a few years now, and this isn't you. I know something's going on, unless you suddenly decided not to care. I'm here if you want to talk about it," I said, trying to reassure him and squeezed his arm to offer him support.

He seemed to deflate at my words and began to spill, his tears falling down his cheeks. In that moment, I identified with him more than I'd imagined. Sympathy and concern filled me as I listened to him, but something was missing. There was more to this story, and I would need to be mindful to check back in with him when he was ready to tell me everything.

I'd skated hard for an hour after my conversation with Phil. My mind was racing with my own failings and memories. Dripping with sweat, I finally headed to the locker room for a shower. It was late now, so no one else was in the facility. While that was kind of creepy, it was also nice to just be free to walk around naked if I wanted.

I chucked my clothes off at my locker and grabbed my towel and phone. My phone was flashing, indicating I had messages, so I checked them as I walked toward the showers.

Sorbet: Hey, I'm finished. Want to grab a late dinner? When's Sawyer supposed to be home? Want to see if she wants to join?

ME: I'm taking a shower, but dinner sounds good. I'm not sure how long she planned to be but check with her. It'd be good to get some time together.

Sorbet: Shower… eh? So, does that mean you're naked? Can I see? *winky face*

ME: I'm not falling into that trap. Lol. I would end up sending it to my sister. No thanks. I'll see you at the house in a few.

Sorbet: You're no fun. Fine, I'll just have to use my imagination. I want to talk to Sawyer more anyway about things from last week, so hopefully, she is free. See you in a few.

The water rushed over me, and I started to relax under the spray. I loved the water pressure here, and how it worked over my muscles. Humming a song under my breath, I missed the sound of the door opening, so when arms snaked around me suddenly, I jumped back, letting out an admittedly high-pitched scream.

"Ahhh!"

My attacker chuckled, pulling me closer, and I was met with a firm chest as his arms banded around me tighter.

"Surprise! Sorry, I scared you; I thought you heard the door."

"Fuck, Sor. I think I almost had a heart attack. I thought you were here to off me or something," I panted as I tried to regulate my breathing.

"Well, I can off something if you'd like," he purred, "I wanted to surprise you. Did I ever tell you about the scorching kiss I had with Sawyer here a few weeks ago?"

"No." I swallowed, already forgetting my panic as I became aroused by his voice and touch. "You didn't mention that."

As I talked, his hands began to move lower down my stomach toward my erection that had already taken notice of the naked body pressed against me. Soren nibbled on my neck as he recounted his story.

"I surprised her, just like I did you, but I was standing outside against the wall." His breath started to quicken as he began to nip along my earlobe. His hand was now on my cock and he moved it slowly up and down, causing me to chase him as my hips moved.

"Tell me more," I rasped out, dropping my head back onto his shoulder.

"Oh, you like hearing how I turn on our girl, huh?" Soren teased.

"Yes," I moaned. Mercifully, Soren obliged as he started to move his hand faster on my cock. I could feel his dick pressed into me from behind as he bucked his hips harder, rubbing his piercing against my ass crack.

"First, I grabbed her by the hips and pulled her into me; as I felt her body against mine, it started to turn me on. She feels so good, doesn't she? I kissed her like I needed her to breathe, and the whole world fell away. We probably would have stripped-down right there if two of her students hadn't walked by and catcalled at us."

"What more would you have done?"

"I really wanted to taste her. Kind of like how I want to taste you right now."

He released my cock, only to grab my hips and yank me around. Immediately, I felt bereft as his body pressure left mine, but when he dropped to his knees before me, I soon lost all train of thought. Soren took me into his mouth as the water cascaded down around us. Grasping his hair in my hands, I tightened my grip on him. His hair was down now, and I could tug more than before. He took me deeper at my pull, making my head fall back against the shower wall.

"Sor," escaped me in a moan as I rocked into his mouth. His hands were on the back of my thighs, and he moved one to my virgin hole and began to use the water to help him enter me with his finger.

The sensation was odd initially, as my ass muscles clenched around him, not used to the invasion. He continued to press further in and inserted his finger more. Soon, I wasn't even focused on the discomfort, as my mind was lost to the feeling of my cock in his mouth with each suck and twirl of his tongue. As he hit that magic button I'd always heard about, I was a goner and erupted down his throat with a moan of ecstasy.

"Oh, Fuck, Soren."

He didn't stop until every last drop was sucked from me. As he stood, licking his lips, I couldn't help but fall more in love with him. Grabbing his face, I smashed my lips hard against him as I passionately kissed my best friend and lover. Every time our lips met, a part of me settled back into place. Almost like Soren was a magnet pulling me home, back to my center.

Drawing back, I gripped his wet strands between my fingers, cupping the face of the man I loved. The darkness from last week still lingered in his eyes, but his golden orbs were clear as they captured my soul with his penetrating stare. How I missed the obvious love shining in them for a year was beyond me.

Depression was a fickle mistress, though, feeding you with doubts and hiding the truth from you. The fog of despair that had surrounded me for months, well years, had finally vacated, allowing me to see the real truth. Smalls returning to me had a large part in it, but the man standing in front of me had just as much impact.

"I love you, Sor. I'm here with you, and we will fight the monsters together. You, me, and Smalls. I dare them to try to take that away from us."

"How did you know what I was thinking?"

"Because I've been there. I've lived there, and it's not you. We aren't only strong when we keep standing after we get knocked down. We're strong because we have people holding us, supporting us, and keeping us from even falling to begin with. You don't have to heal from the bruise you never got. It took me too long to understand that. But every time I looked up, you were standing there, stretching out your hand. Don't forget the strong person you are because, frankly, learning the truth doesn't change what happened or how you think about your mom. Those are fixed things in your history, and they only reinforce the truth you already knew. You are Soren. Someone who is pure light, genuine, and one of the loves of my life. Don't let Pamela take anything else from you. She's not worth it, but you are. You're so worth it, and I hope I get to spend the rest of my life reminding you of that."

Tears filled his eyes, but none threatened to fall down his cheeks. Placing a tender kiss on his forehead, I pulled back as I tried to gauge how he was receiving what I'd just said to him. As he started to talk, the tears broke free, making tracks down his face, allowing me to wipe them away one by one.

"Thank you, Rey. I avoided thinking about how it made me feel, which only led to me feeling worse. I'd started to believe you and Sawyer would be better off without me. That I was damaged goods."

Sobs wracked him as he finally gave in to his emotions, his doubt, his fear, his self-loathing. His head fell to my shoulder as he cried out his pain. I held him tightly to me as I smoothed down his hair, attempting to infuse him with the strength he always gave me.

"Shh, babe. It's okay. Let it out. I'm here, and I'm not going anywhere. Shh," I cooed over and over as he broke down in my arms, finally letting out his pain and allowing me to comfort him. When his tears slowed, he pulled back, his head lowered.

"Sor, don't you dare feel shame. That was one of the sexiest things you've ever done." He stared at me intensely for a moment, deciphering my comment.

"I hate the things that happened to me; they honestly disgust me to think about them. You don't see them, though, do you? I can see that now. When I look in your eyes, all I see is acceptance and love. Thank you for letting me be vulnerable, providing me the safety and strength I needed. You've reminded me that it's not always about the steps you take to get somewhere, but where you land. You're my landing space, Rey, and I don't think I even realized that until just now. But you are. You're my shelter in the storm, and Sawyer's the light pulling me forward. Together, you both show me the way to my truth."

He took a deep breath, gathering his thoughts. I could see pain written all over his face, but there was a light now in his eyes as he shed some of the shame he'd been carrying around.

"You're right. Learning those things about Pamela doesn't change the fact it happened. It doesn't change the fact that she's a horrible mother. I knew those things. But maybe… it will help lead us to who is behind this and to the Council. The demons of my past will pay, and we will fight to stop this from happening to anyone else. Those are things I can control. I need to choose them. Come on, the water's running cold, and I have a sudden urge to see our girl. I need to tell her what she means to me."

His smile wasn't as bright as usual, but it was a real Soren smile, and his dimple made the briefest of appearances. Kissing his nose, I turned off the now cold water as he handed me my towel. We dried and dressed quickly, anxious to see Smalls and spend some time with her. With any luck, her meeting with Mrs. Monroe had gone well, and we might have somewhere to start looking for answers.

Soren grabbed my hand as we made our way out of the ice rink, and the sensation still surprised me each time. My phone buzzed in my pocket, alerting me to a new text. Pulling it out with my free hand, I saw I'd missed a call and had a few messages.

Calls: Stinky Sister

Stinky Sister: Where's Sawyer? I've found something.

Stinky Sister: Why is no one answering their damn phones? I'll be over at 9 pm. then to share with everyone. Have something I need to do first. Tell everyone to be there—time for another family meeting.

As I was starting to reply to Fin, a new text came

through, stopping me in my tracks as I clutched the phone so tightly my knuckles went white.

> **Elias:** Anyone home? I just got a call from the medical center. Sawyer was in an accident. I'm headed there to pick her up. Meet us back at the house.

three

. . .

sawyer

A FEELING of awareness followed by a sense of déjà vu tickled at my subconscious. Where was I? Why did my body feel like a giant bruise? The familiar smell of antiseptic pierced my mind, and I realized I must be at a hospital. There wasn't any beeping, so not too critical then, I decided. Detached logic was my friend at the moment, as I tried to remain calm and gather the facts.

Managing to open my eyes, I squinted as the bright fluorescent light shined down on me. Gingerly, I tried to turn my head to investigate if anyone was in the room with me. My neck seemed to be functioning as I turned in both directions, taking in my surroundings. The room seemed to mirror most medical offices, with nothing sticking out to indicate my location.

Sitting up, I assessed the rest of my body. Nothing seemed broken, and only a few scratches littered my skin. My outfit was a mess with several rips in it, but overall, it appeared I'd survived reasonably unscathed. A breath I hadn't known I was holding rushed out of me at this realization. Things were moving forward in my life finally. I'd hate to have to go back to Iowa now.

The toe of my shoes stuck out on the chair next to the bed, pulling my attention. Cautiously, I moved my legs over the edge one by one. Tensing at the soreness my body felt, I slowly placed my feet on the floor. Nothing was broken, but everything still felt like I'd rolled down a hill, hitting every rock.

Ah, yeah. I had. Guess I wasn't as funny when injured. Welp, we all had our skills; a comedian in a crisis wasn't mine.

I'd just finished lacing my shoes when there was a knock on the door. It must've only been a courtesy one because before I could answer, the door opened, revealing a man in a white coat. Oh, yippee, my favorite kind of people. Cue the eye roll.

"You're awake. How are you feeling, Miss…?" The doctor looked down at the chart he was holding to verify my name.

Way to be prepared dude, I bet if you took thirty seconds to let me answer your knock, you could've read my name, jackass. Apparently, injured Sawyer was a bit of a sassy bitch.

"Sullivan, is it?"

I nodded my head, not trusting myself to speak yet. Hospitals made me anxious, especially when I randomly woke up in them. Which unfortunately was an all too common occurrence in my life. I needed to remedy that, as it wasn't something I wanted to be known for. 'Sawyer-the one who woke up in random hospitals.' Nope, definitely didn't have a ring to it.

"You were brought in an hour ago, Ms. Sullivan, by ambulance. Since your injuries appeared minor, the ambulance diverted to the medical center here on campus instead of making the trek into the city."

My body relaxed at the information. I wasn't far from the house or people who cared about me. Bonus, my injuries hadn't been more severe. Though, I was getting really tired of being run off the road. So. Not. A. Fan.

"Do you remember how you ended up here?" the doctor questioned.

I swallowed, testing my voice, and realized it was quite dry. The doctor noticed and grabbed water off the side table, handing it to me. The coolness of the liquid instantly refreshed my parched throat, and I sucked it down.

"Um, sort of," I said, wiping my mouth. "I was returning from visiting a friend, and then I think a car swerved. Honestly, I don't remember much after that as I tumbled down the hill."

The cup in my hand stole my attention as I started to tear the rim off. I'd done this as a child when I was uncomfortable and would see if I could rip the styrofoam into a perfect curly piece without breaking it. The doctor noticed my unease and began to go over my injuries.

"Fortunately, a bystander saw you go off the road after the truck swerved at you. It seems the truck intentionally came for you per their report, pushing you off the road and then hightailed it out of there. They called 911 instantly after they saw you dive off the scooter. I'm sorry to report your scooter didn't fare as well and is currently being pulled out of the small stream. Some of your belongings survived the crash and will be sent to you once they finish the investigation."

I sucked in a breath. Oh no, the box Mrs. Monroe had given me. Where had I put it? My anxiety spiked, and if I'd been attached to machines, my pulse would be skyrocketing. The panic took me fast, and I was pulled into flashbacks before I could do anything.

"Little bird, I have something for you." Flashes of a man's shoes, toys strung along the floor, a broken crayon on the ground swirled through my head.

"Hush, dear. It will be okay. Your imaginary friend will travel with us, you'll see," cooed my mother as she rubbed circles on my back as I curled into her chest.

"Do you think her skating is the best idea?" a vaguely familiar voice asked from the kitchen. Peeking around the corner, I could see my father and the back of a man's head I didn't recognize.

"It's what she wants. Her name's changed, and there's no way they could connect her. We're safe, Samson. We are her parents; we know what's best for her."

"You're not the only one who cares for—"

"Sawyer! Henry and Finley are at the door for you. Go out and play, sweetie," my mom said from the hallway, a strained look on her face. The voices in the kitchen stopped at the sound of my name, so I skipped off, forgetting about the man in the kitchen.

Glass breaking, tires squealing, the smell of burning...

Hands bracketed my face, pulling me from my memories. A voice was calling to me in the distance, and it sounded familiar. My vision started to return, shapes came into focus, and I could make out the face directly in front of me. Chestnut brown hair with a slight curl, short stubble, and whiskey eyes peered back at me as my brain digested the information.

Elias. Elias was here. Why was Elias here? I must've made a face or even voiced my thoughts out loud because he answered me.

"The house was called when you were brought in. I tried to get a hold of the other guys, but no one seemed to be answering or around. The thought of you waiting did not sit well with me, so I took a chance and came. I hope that was okay."

Elias sounded so unsure, but I could hear the sincerity in his words. Elias always seemed to be rescuing me lately, like some unsung hero. It conflicted with the version of the man I'd met that first day. I was beginning to believe he hadn't been making excuses, and his behavior actually was out of character for him.

Besides, having learned about his past with Queen Bitch, I could understand his reaction that night, and while it didn't excuse the things he'd said, I was learning there was more to him than just the pompous asshole he showed.

Not to mention, anyone who'd put up with QB was clearly a saint. I'd have to give him the benefit of the doubt, especially if he continued to rescue me white knight style. There was only so much resistance a girl could withstand. I hadn't forgotten those forearms.

"Thank you." I nodded as I breathed in his rich sandalwood scent. That's when I noticed his hands were still clasping my face. They felt warm and comforting. I must've hit my head harder than the doctor thought.

Wait, did he tell me my injuries? Elias must've realized he was still touching my face because he dropped his hands quickly and stood up, turning toward the doctor who'd been watching our encounter. Creeper.

"Are you feeling okay now, Ms. Sullivan? You had a panic attack. But I wanted to go over your injuries and care so I can release you to this gentleman."

I just nodded. I didn't think I could form words right now, not until I knew which of my mother's things had survived the wreck. Not wanting to fall into a panic again, I focused on what the doctor had to say.

"You have a few small abrasions on your arms and legs, likely from the debris on the ground. Nothing appears to be broken, but if that changes, please come in for an x-ray. Your previous injury on your knee may feel more tender over the next few days, but it doesn't appear to be affected other than bruised with the rest of you. We don't want you to train injured, though, so take it easy over the next few days. Mostly, you're just bruised and will have sore muscles. You'll need to take a few days off before you can go back to full active duty. You may have a slight concussion, so we ask that you're monitored tonight as a precaution. Take a soak as well for your muscles. Do you have any questions for me?"

I shook my head and then immediately regretted that decision as the room swam. Otherwise, it wasn't anything out of the ordinary I hadn't dealt with as an athlete.

"Wonderful. I'd like to see you back in for a follow-up in three days just to verify there aren't any long-term repercussions. The nurse has your belongings, some paperwork to sign, and an appointment card for you."

The doctor left, and it hit me that he never stated his name. Weird. I couldn't contemplate it for too long because as soon as the doctor left, the nurse entered, almost as if she'd been sitting outside waiting. She passed my belongings off to Elias and handed me the clipboard, motioning to where I needed to sign. My hand shook as I gripped the pen, but I was able to manage a signature.

When I returned the documents, she presented me with a card that had a date and time for my next appointment. At least the follow-up would be convenient since it was on campus. This school was its own functioning town.

Elias grasped my elbow, pulling my attention back to him. "Do you need any assistance walking, Sawyer?" he asked.

"I'm not sure. I'd only made it to my shoes when the doctor came into the room. I'd like to try, though."

He nodded, but kept hold of my elbow as I stood. My legs were wobbly, but it seemed I would be able to walk out on my own, which did a lot for my pride. Elias kept hold of me the whole way to the car, only letting go when I was secured with my seatbelt.

I wanted to question his motives, but I was also too tired to think about it at the moment. Glancing at the dashboard, I saw it was almost 7 pm. It'd been an emotional day even before the crash. I never expected my mom would be the first significant lead I would find. I couldn't think about it right now, but I hoped her box had survived the crash.

If it hadn't... I might shatter all over the floor.

four

elias

WHEN I'D GOTTEN the call that Sawyer was at the medical center, a sense of panic had rushed over me. Was she okay? What had happened? Would she be taken from me before I ever got to know her? It was the last question that lingered in my soul, urging me to make changes so I could prove I wasn't a tosser.

Walking into the room and seeing her frozen in a panic attack undid something in me. The first time I'd seen her like that had been because of me, but this time I was able to bring her back and ground her. It felt good to be that person for her for once.

It set my heart racing to think maybe, I was redeemable and worthy. Voldemort had made me doubt myself, causing me to lose my sense of worth. It wasn't until that moment when I saw appreciation in her eyes that I realized how true that was.

"Do you need anything before we head back to the house?" I asked, starting the car.

She had allowed me to touch and assist her to the vehicle, either due to her pain or fear. I wasn't sure which one was the reason, but I also didn't care, since the outcome was still the same. But now, she was quiet, and I felt awkward and wanted to reassure her.

These urges were foreign to me. Typically, I didn't feel out of sorts because of girls. It had always been obvious what my role was before. Show up, smile, look good next to them, compliment them, and make sure they were happy. Unfortunately, it didn't seem I was good at that either, but I knew it was expected with my family.

"I don't think I need anything. Thank you for coming to get me and helping me back there when I panicked, Elias."

"No thanks are needed, Sawyer. I know our first encounter wasn't ideal, and for that, I do apologize. But I'm not the guy you met your first week. I hope you can continue to see me for who I am. That is my hope."

I sounded like such a wanker! No wonder she thought I was standoffish, but my upper-crust upbringing kept flowing out of my mouth every time it opened. Sawyer turned toward me, slowly this time, mindful of her injuries.

"I'm starting to see that, Elias. While I don't commend your behavior, I understand how we can say and do things at times and not mean it. I'd like to get to know the real you."

Her small smile sent my hope soaring that I might not have screwed up completely. Joy crept into my mind, and for once, I let it stay, stopping myself from dismissing it. I was tired of expecting the worst-case scenario, because you only saw the worst when you always envisioned it.

I pulled into the driveway, skipping the garage so we could be closer to the door. Hurriedly, I made my way around the car to her side. Sawyer looked awful, and I was worried about how the others would react when they saw her. I was hoping I could get her inside and into the recommended bath before anything else happened.

Despite my wish, things did not go that way.

As we made our way up the walk to the front door, it was flung open, almost slamming into the side of the house. The sound and movement caused Sawyer to tense, and for once, I was the one leveling a glare at my housemates.

"Stop right there. You lot crowding Sawyer and demanding things is not helpful right now. I will share what I know once I have her inside safely. Now, please, kindly move out of my way."

If this hadn't been a dire situation, I would have wished I had a camera to capture the look of shock on both Rey and Rhett's faces. Rhett's, especially. His ordinarily stoic and impassive face hung wide open at my demands. Or perhaps it was the fact Sawyer hadn't contradicted me and instead seemed comforted by my presence. I didn't blame them for their shock; I almost wanted to pinch myself.

They silently moved back and out of our way as we made it up the stairs. Lucky sat at the door, waiting patiently. It amazed me at his ability to understand emotions and know when he needed to be calm, and when it was okay for him to be his crazy puppy self. Dogs were geniuses, I swear.

Sawyer gave him a soft smile when she saw him waiting for her, setting his tail wagging. I was no longer under the pretense he was waiting for me, oh no, he had entirely replaced me, but it didn't feel as detrimental to me anymore as it had.

As we made our way through the house, we seemed to gather an entourage. It was the slowest parade in history with the weirdest headliner, but it seemed to have gathered my housemates as we went. Funny how they were all here now.

The stairs were difficult for Sawyer, but I saw the determination in her eyes, making me force down my need to swoop in and carry her. She needed this, and I would not take it from her, no matter how much my best friend grumbled about it behind me.

Her squeeze on my arm told me I'd assumed correctly. She wanted to prove to herself she could. I understood that more than she probably knew.

We made it to her room with the quiet trail of men behind her. I immediately led her to the bathroom, much to their dismay if their rumbles indicated anything. I sat Sawyer down gently on the toilet and began to prep the tub of water, with her watching me curiously from her perch.

Sawyer had lucked out with this bathroom since it was the biggest one in the house with a dual-head his and her shower and a separate garden jacuzzi tub big enough to fit four to six Sawyer sized people.

Once I had the water started, I searched the cabinets to see if any Epsom salt had been stocked in here. It was common enough for athletes to use, and I figured I had a good chance of finding some. As luck would have it, under the sink, I found a tub of lavender Epsom salt. Jackpot.

I poured in a handful as I tested the water temperature again. I'd rolled up the sleeves of my button-down shirt to start the water, so when I turned to grab her some towels, I noticed Sawyer fixated on my forearms. I was unsure if she was zoning out or if her gaze was purposefully fixed there.

Deciding to test out this theory, I flexed one forearm deliberately as I grabbed an extra washcloth. Her breath hitched, and she licked her lips, making me feel all kinds of aroused. *Sawyer was checking out my forearms.*

Huh, guess I wasn't as behind as I had assumed. Focusing back on my task, I finished preparing the bath and turned off the tap.

"Do you want my help, or for me to grab someone else?" Somehow I managed to get that out without falling all over my words in the process.

"I, um, I think I can manage on my own, actually.

Thanks, though." Her cheeks tinted red, and I was curious what the minx was thinking.

"Unfortunately, I have to disagree. You heard the doctor, you might have a concussion, and in good conscience, I cannot leave you to undress on your own in case you were to fall. So, I can turn my back, grab one of the others, or help you. It's nothing I haven't seen before, Sawyer. Don't make this a big deal. Your safety is more important."

Well, that was clearly the wrong thing to say, and I soon ate my words.

"Oh, you've seen breasts before, have you? No problem."

Despite her injuries, she stood up and whipped her dress off her head so quickly I was unable to do anything more than stand there and gape at her. Fuck!

Her indignation caused her breasts to heave up and down with each breath she took. I tried not to stare, really I did, but it was hard, so hard, and soon so was I.

Turning quickly, I deflected, trying to throw off my arousal and reaction to her. Bloody Hell, the woman was a menace to my blood pressure, though.

"Sawyer! What the hell, woman! I did not mean right then. Fuck. Please be careful and allow me to help you into the tub, and then I will leave you be. You are a difficult patient."

"Maybe you're just an inept nurse. Did you ever consider that, Mr. Perfect? Huh? No. I bet not. Well, you can take your bloody forearms and get the hell out of my bathroom. Thank you for picking me up, but you can let one of the others take over now."

If I had still been looking at her, I was relatively confident steam would be coming out of her ears. Her little huff was adorable, but I would not be sharing that with the tiny monster. I also think she'd just made fun of me, but was not confident without seeing her face. At least I had been right about my forearms.

I exited the bathroom, latching the door firmly behind me, to come face to face with four guys, all attempting to hold in their delight for my dressing down. Glad I could be your entertainment, fellas. Their animosity rose the longer I delayed in telling them what had happened. Relaying the information I'd gleaned from the doctor, I left her bedroom to put some distance between me and her intoxicating presence.

While I had not wanted to cause another fight with her, I had to admit her spitfire personality was what got my blood pumping. Plus, in a weird way, it allowed her to control the situation, and I couldn't fault her for that. I was glad we seemed to be turning over a new leaf and that the tiptoeing around one another would be ending. This type of interaction was much preferred, in my opinion. It was real, and I knew where I stood with her.

Hopeful that progress was being made between us, I headed to my room to take care of the rigid appendage in my pants. Sawyer's breasts would forever be burned into my memory, not that I was complaining about it. If I was lucky, they wouldn't just be in my memory. As I stripped out of my clothes, I couldn't help but picture her as she lusted after my forearms.

With that thought, I fisted my hard length as I stood in front of the mirror. Watching myself, I quickened my pace on my dick, as her breasts, with their pebbled nipples, made their appearance again in my mind. Fuck, those were beautiful breasts.

Her reaction to me, combined with the visual she left me with, had me pumping my cock faster up and down as I gathered the bead of pre-cum from the tip. Sooner than I had imagined, I orgasmed hard as I sprayed ropes of cum over the sink.

Catching my breath, I had to admit to myself I was more than just curious about her. I stepped into the shower, and the water washed away the evidence of my lust, and I realized Sawyer was slowly pulling me into her web.

The problem was, I didn't want to leave.

five

rey

PACING BACK and forth in Small's bedroom, I shoved my hands in my hair again and yanked hard. I was sure by this point, my hair was standing up after the damage I was causing it, but I didn't care. It was all I could do to express my current frustration that didn't involve hitting a wall.

I really wanted to hit a wall, but as Soren kept reminding me, it wouldn't be productive. I was about to punch his face if he said that to me one more time, though. Turning to make my trek back across her room, I paused when her voice echoed out from the closed door.

"Maybe you're just an inept nurse. Did you ever consider that, Mr. Perfect? Huh? No. I bet not. Well, you can take

your bloody forearms and get the hell out of my bathroom. Thank you for picking me up, but you can let one of the others take over now."

Her sass at Elias filled me with hope. I had no clue what she was talking about, but I couldn't help but want to laugh at Elias' pain if it meant a little of her fire had returned. She'd appeared so forlorn and lost when she entered the house. Hearing her quips to Elias, though, showed she was still there to some degree.

Laughing as Elias exited the room, I couldn't help but revel in his uncomfortableness with Smalls. I think the fact he couldn't charm her was more puzzling to him than anything. When he just stood there, offering no information on what was going on, my agitation returned.

"Well?" I questioned, throwing up my hands. I knew it wasn't helping the situation, but I felt too out of control to stop myself. Especially when he still didn't answer me.

"What's going on? What happened? Tell me!" I demanded.

Elias glared at me like he had all the time in the world, and I guess he did because he knew what was going on. *Asshole.*

I'd been waiting for the past hour after I'd gotten his text to learn anything. It felt too much like last time when I'd lost her, and my thoughts were spiraling.

It was my fault.

I should've gone with her. Instead, I was off fucking around with Soren. So, while I was getting my cock blown, Smalls was lying on the side of the road. Her body lying there broken, kept repeating in my head. *Over and over.* I was about to strangle the answers out of Elias when Rhett spoke up, saving me the trouble.

"Elias, *speak.*"

I had to give it to Rhett. He got his point across in the littlest amount of words possible unless he spoke to Sawyer. He seemed to have all the words for her, not that I could fault him for it. Elias dropped his righteous act and began to share what he knew.

"All I know is a passing car saw a truck run her off the road. She was on her Vespa, so when she veered off Pearcrest Grove, she swerved toward the stream. The witness reported she didn't use her brakes, which to me means they weren't working. Her speed increased as she made her way down the small hill toward the stream, and she realized she had a choice of jumping off or crashing into the water. She chose to jump off. Fortunately, her injuries are minor. Scooters aren't known for being fast, and so her speed was low when she jumped, resulting in mostly small abrasions, bruises, and a possible mild concussion. She will mostly feel sore and bruised for the next few days and will need to be monitored tonight for a concussion. The doctor prescribed some pain medication and suggested numerous baths, hence her current location. If that is all, I do have papers to grade."

Elias stalked off, looking uncomfortable and irritated with his report, but I wasn't sure why precisely, unless he was just upset about having dealt with Sawyer. No one stopped him, so I guess none of us had any more questions. It was a better outcome than I'd anticipated, and at the news of her condition, my body deflated all the pent-up nervous energy I'd been carrying around.

Soren approached me, but I couldn't look at him. A tremendous amount of guilt and shame was pooling in my belly, and I felt sick. I needed to see Sawyer.

Brushing off his tender touch, I tried to ignore the hurt expression on his face as I headed to the bathroom door. Rhett had beaten me to it and was already inside talking to her. I couldn't focus on him, though; I was her oldest friend, and I would assert my right to that position if I had to in this situation.

The door was ajar, so I poked my head in the door. Rhett's giant frame was bent over the tub as he delicately washed and rinsed her hair. Smalls leaned into his touch and appeared to melt under his ministrations. The moment was tender and intimate in a way that made me blush.

Suddenly, I felt like the intruder in their moment and quickly backed out of the room. Smalls' eyes caught mine in the mirror as I shut the door, but I couldn't explain the emotions I saw there. I'd never seen her eyes look that way before.

Feeling even more confused, I pivoted on the balls of my feet and exited her room. It suddenly felt suffocating in there, and I needed to escape. Dashing across the hall to mine, I shut the door behind me. My heart thumped loudly against my chest, and as I peered around my room, all I saw was disgust and filth everywhere.

What was I even doing with my life? What was the point? I wasn't suitable for anyone. All I did was bring despair. Sawyer didn't need me. She had Rhett and the others. She would be fine. I was sure of it, now more than ever. Soren didn't need me, either. I would only hurt him. I'd proven that a few minutes ago. Earlier in the shower had been a fluke, and it only demonstrated I wasn't good to be around. People always got hurt around me.

My eyes caught on all the clothes still littering the floor, and something inside of me snapped. Rushing around the room, I grabbed them and began frantically shoving things into my hamper. Deciding it was time to change the sheet, I ripped it from my bed and balled it up, cramming it down into the hamper as well. My mind was frantic, my movements manic, but I couldn't stop. Everything my gaze fell on, I would immediately pick up and shove it somewhere else.

Somewhere in this process, Soren entered my room and watched me scurry about the place. I didn't notice him until he grabbed my hands as they reached for a pile of dirty clothes I'd shoved under my bed.

"Rey, stop! Focus on me. She's okay. It's okay. Breathe with me now. In. Now out. In. And now, out. Good. Again."

His calmness washed over me, and I momentarily forgot I wasn't supposed to love him anymore, that I wasn't supposed to need him. Needing people meant I had the potential to be hurt, to be left alone again. I couldn't go through that. Today had been the wake-up call I'd needed. They would be better off without me—

"No, Rey. Focus back on my voice. Don't listen to your thoughts. They're lying to you. Just breathe, for now, then we'll figure everything else out. I promise."

Soren's voice lulled me back to him, and I was able to ignore my thoughts for a moment and breathe. My heart calmed, my body relaxed, and my brain cleared. I'd heard once that when we were at our angriest, we were at our stupidest because when we experienced intense emotions, we cut off oxygen to our brain, not allowing in the oxygen needed to think. Deep breathing, while simple, allowed oxygen to return to our brains, and then thinking became clearer.

I hated to admit it was true. As soon as my breathing slowed, I ignored my thoughts and could see through the haze. Mostly, I could see into Soren's eyes. His eyes were my beacon, and this time, I was swimming in them.

"It's not your fault, Rey. You couldn't have prevented it from happening. It didn't happen because you were happy, either. It doesn't work that way. It just happened. You're allowed to be happy, Rey, to want things... to be with me. Remember your own words from earlier. I can be your strength now, and we will fight the monsters together. Don't push me away, please. I'd be lost without you."

Soren's voice broke a little at the end, and his eyes had a glossy film to them. Peering into his golden gaze, I knew I was being stupid, but the fear had been real, allowing the doubt to eat and consume me. I wanted to be the man he saw me as.

"Thank you."

I leaned forward and gently placed my lips on his in the softest kiss we'd ever shared, but one of the most intimate. This kiss represented me choosing to ignore my demons and choosing to be happy instead. Because that was what it was, a choice. I would probably always struggle with these thoughts, specifically when triggered. But I didn't have to allow them to win. I didn't have to become a mess each time and self-destruct. It would take time and effort, but I had the best reasons, and the first one was for me—to believe in myself.

"Want to try again and go back and check on our girl?" Soren asked soothingly. He still had my face between his hands, so when I nodded, his hands moved with it, causing us both to laugh.

"Yeah. Let's do that."

We made our way back to Smalls' room, and I relished in his words. Every time he said "our" girl, the dream of us solidified and caused a shiver down my spine. Walking into her empty room, I felt more in control now. The bathroom door was shut again, so I knocked this time, not wanting to interrupt her moments with others.

"Come in."

Her voice beckoned to me, even in her despondency. It amazed me how something as simple as her voice caused a visceral reaction in my body to react every time. Stepping into the bathroom, I was ready to be the man Sawyer and Soren believed me to be—that I believed myself to be.

six

sawyer

THE FIRE I'd felt a moment ago quickly fled me as the door shut behind Elias. Every ounce of energy had been used just then, leaving me wrung out. Turning, I stepped into the water and instantly felt the soothing warmth wrap around my sore muscles. Elias had done well with setting up my bath, as much as I hated to admit it.

I didn't want to accept he was growing on me more and more. My feelings regarding Elias gave me whiplash, and I was at the point where I couldn't think about it. I laid my head back, my eyes closing, and I tried to relax in the water.

Not even a minute alone, and there was a knock on the door before it opened.

"Baby, can I come in? Do you need any help?"

His gentle question made me tear up. So I promptly

shut it down and shoved my emotions far away into the back of my mind. Those would have to wait.

Nodding my head at Rhett, since I didn't trust my voice, he entered the rest of the way into the bathroom.

"I know you probably don't want to talk, so I won't ask. But I needed to see that you were okay. Would you," he paused, swallowing, "let me wash your hair?"

He'd squatted down at the side of the tub, and yet still towered over me. The softness in his features was strange, but it was what I needed—to be wrapped up in comfort and protected against all odds sounded like the perfect place to escape to.

Not trusting my voice again, I nodded my head before turning back to stare at the wall. He moved me forward and poured water over my head tenderly, soothing something in me. Rhett always gave me space. No demands or expectations; he simply wanted to be near and take care of me. I rather liked that about him.

I was still waiting for his ugly toe to appear, though, because he seemed too perfect. Remembering that metaphor brought up memories of my mom. She joked with Fin and me how even the most perfect of people had an ugly toe. We might not always be able to see it, but we all had some sort of an ugly toe feature. It was her way of reminding us no one was perfect, even if they presented as such on the outside.

My dad had one with his snoring and body twitches, making him a bear to share a bed with. A small smile graced my lips as I remembered the memory. Rhett's ministrations soothed and lured me into a state of peace making me lean into his hand. A flash in the mirror caught my attention, but by the time I looked up, the door was shutting and I was alone.

My head was gently placed back against the tub as cool lips touched my forehead. Now that I was calm, the events of the last few hours began to replay.

Victoria Draven.

My adopted mother's real name was Victoria Draven, and she'd been an ice dancer.

There was a part of me that felt betrayed by her lies. All the years we'd had together, and she'd never shared that with me. I knew it was irrational, but I'd always valued our closeness compared to other girls and their mothers. This discovery was shattering my belief in our bond. What else hadn't she told me? Was anything we shared or felt even real?

The last of my shock dissipated, and fat teardrops fell down my cheeks. Turning, I placed my arms on the side of the tub and quietly sobbed into them. I hoped no one outside my bathroom could hear me, but my pain was drowning me too much to care.

This moment, in this room, was mine. In here, I could wallow in the overwhelming grief and pain that flooded me without having to shield it from others.

Five years might have passed, but it didn't diminish the pain. Day to day was bearable, but in these quiet moments where I missed my parents, it felt as all-consuming as it had that morning in the hospital room. I wanted nothing more right now than to feel my mother's arms around me, soothing me through her presence and gentle touches.

That was the most challenging part of grief for me, the absence of touch. Their memories would live on in my mind always, but the feel of their hugs, the warmth of their embrace, the comfort of their kiss on my forehead would forever be gone. It was unfair; I had to do this without them.

I wasn't strong enough—I really wasn't.

Faking it had become so natural that I presented to the world as having it all together, but inside… inside, I was still that scared sixteen-year-old girl rocking in a corner, hoping someone would come and save me from this nightmare. My tears slowed as I laid on the side of the tub, staring into empty space. That was what I was, empty space floating in the nothing.

The water grew cold, but I didn't notice since I could barely feel it. A knock at the door drew my attention, and I briefly remembered Rhett left. My voice was unfamiliar to me as it came out in a robotic sound, devoid of emotion. "Come in," I called out as I continued to stare off into the nothing.

The nothing was safe; it was empty, and it allowed me space to cast off the grief that threatened to suffocate me. Faint noises in the background seeped through, but I couldn't focus. The only thing I wanted was to float here. Because in the nothing, I didn't have to worry. I didn't have to make choices, and I most certainly didn't have to pretend.

Floating along, enjoying my bliss, I was abruptly

pulled out from the safety of my escape as ice-cold water splashed over my head. Goosebumps erupted over my flesh as I sputtered water out of my mouth and nose. Blinking, I tried to make sense of what had just happened.

"What the hell?" I screeched, looking up to see who'd rudely made me return to this place.

"Sawyer! You weren't responding. I'm sorry, but it was all I could think to do outside of slapping you. Are you okay? Are you back with me?"

The fear and panic in Henry's voice registered as the haze I'd fallen into began to evaporate around me. The bathroom came into focus again and my surroundings transmitted to my senses. The goosebumps on my flesh were noticeable now as my body finally sensed the water temperature.

Looking down, I noticed my hands were pruney, and all the bubbles had disappeared. Glancing up, I took in Henry standing over me. He was fidgety and worried as he focused on me and how I'd responded. The moroseness of earlier began to lift as my actual circumstances infiltrated my mind, reminding me this wasn't the same as last time. I wasn't alone anymore, but instead, I had several people who cared about me. This wasn't pretending. This was real.

The breath left me as I relaxed into that truth. Tears filled my eyes again, but this time for a different reason. Grief had clouded my judgment earlier and made me unable to see what was right in front of me. *Love.*

My parents were gone, but love wasn't. My life was full of love again.

"Henry." His name wavered out of my mouth, causing my lip to tremble. Immediately, he swooped in and held me in his arms as I cried on his shoulder, soaking his clothes with my wet body. His touch reassured me, his embrace strengthened me, and his words affirmed me.

Henry held me perched over the tub, rocking and petting my head until my tears stopped, never once mentioning how uncomfortable he had to be in that position.

Love wasn't always the words expressed or the good feelings one felt. No, most of the time, love was the everyday things someone did for you, despite how it affected them. There in the bathroom, dripping wet, a boy declared to a girl his love.

"Shh, Smalls. It's okay. I'm here. I'm here."

Over and over, he cooed this to me as my tears dried, and the sobs quieted. He kept rocking me in a soothing gesture until I pulled back. Soft touches smoothed the hair away from my face, wiping the tears on my eyelashes.

"Smalls, you're not in this alone because I'm never letting you go again. So, if you need to borrow my strength until you regain yours, it's here for the taking. I will hold you up until you don't need me, and then I will stand beside you, reminding you that you're not alone. No matter what, you will always have me. I've lived the version of my life without you, and it was second-rate to the real thing. I love you beyond measure," Henry said.

The emotion in his words rang true and took root in my heart, dislodging the poisonous lies I'd kept believing.

"I love you too, Henry. Thank you."

My voice was small, but the honesty shone through, reassuring Henry to whatever he'd debated in his mind. Releasing me, he stepped back and grabbed a towel for me. Draining the water from the tub, I stepped out into his waiting arms.

My limbs felt heavy, and I wasn't sure if it was from the accident or the all-consuming emotions. Each movement was slow and strenuous as I dried my body, making me pant and feel slightly dizzy from it all. Leaning against the counter, I tried to catch my breath. Exhaustion filled every part of me, but I knew I wasn't allowed to sleep yet. Concussion protocol sucked donkey balls.

Henry took pity on me and assisted me in dressing in the clothes he'd gathered for me. They were my comfiest leggings and what appeared to be one of the guys' shirts. Raising my eyebrow at the top, the blush and shrug of his shoulders clued me in on who it probably belonged to. It was cute to see him embarrassed for his sweet behaviors when the big ones came so easily to him.

"I'm sorry about earlier. I'd gone into an empty space, I guess to escape everything, but I never meant to scare you." I hung my head, feeling ashamed.

"It's okay, Smalls. I get it, I do. More than you know. I'm just glad you seem to be back with me now."

"I am." I leaned into his chest, his heartbeat reassuring. Drawing back, I looked up. "Um, who's all out there?" I asked, motioning toward the door. I wanted to be prepared for what I was walking into.

"It was Rhett and Soren when I came in. Elias had gone to his room, and I heard the shower running. Oliver isn't back yet that I know of, and I'm not sure where Mateo is, to be honest."

Two of them, I could deal with that. The mention of Soren reminded me I hadn't checked in with him for a few days. He'd been more withdrawn after the photo had been leaked, causing me to be concerned.

"How's Soren? He hasn't said much to me the past couple of days. I don't want my stuff to overshadow him because his stuff is just as important."

"He's doing okay, we talked earlier, but I know he wants to talk to you about it as well. I think he's feeling a little lost at the moment," answered Henry.

Grabbing my hairbrush off the counter, I braced myself to exit the bathroom. Stepping out the door, it was just as Henry had reported, and only Soren and Rhett were in my room. Soren sat on my bed, his face showing relief as he took me in. My heart jumped at the knowledge, accepting he cared.

Rhett leaned back against the wall, his legs outstretched, and crossed over one another. He straightened as I exited and took me in from head to toe, calculating each bump and scrape, no doubt. Smiling softly at both of them, I crossed the room slowly to Soren, hoping I could bring us both some comfort.

"Hey, Chilly Willy, can you do me a favor, please?" I asked him, giving my big eyes to say yes, offering up my best puppy dog look.

"Did you just call me a cartoon penguin?" Soren asked, pouting in an attempt to hide his laugh.

"You know it, captain! I'm still on the hunt for your nickname."

"You're too cute; you know that? What can I do for you, sweet pea?" Soren flirted back, and it felt good to see him smile, his personality returning. While I didn't relish getting hit by cars, in fact, I loathed it, but if I was rewarded with a Soren smile, I could bear it, I suppose.

"Would you brush my hair for me?"

My question was soft, and it seemed to have shocked Soren, as he stared at me for a few seconds before he took the hairbrush. Grinning, I turned to sit on the floor between his legs. Henry had taken my cuddle chair while I'd been talking to Soren and gave me a thankful look as I sat. My insides warmed at the feeling that I'd accomplished something good.

We all sat in the quiet as Soren brushed my wet hair. It was soothing and allowed me to ground myself more in the movements. A knock at the door brought me out of my meditative state. Rhett moved toward it to let in whoever it was.

I was surprised when it was Elias. His hair was wet, and he now wore lounge pants. It was his t-shirt that took me by surprise, and my brain to mouth filter was apparently not functioning in my semi-concussed state, and my knack for blurting random things struck once again.

Code. Fucking. Orange.

"*Fuck me*, of course; you're a Ravenclaw! Shit, I didn't mean it that way. I just meant, of course, you would be Ravenclaw with your pretentious personality. Fuck a duck, I mean, with your penchant for knowledge. I'm going to stop talking now. Remember, I have a concussion." Cringing, I ducked my head to hide my flaming red cheeks.

Now, I'd known Elias for almost a month by this point, so I was expecting him to retort some nonsense back at me as per usual in our dynamics. So the laugh that boomed out of him caught me by surprise, and well, the rest was a catastrophe of epic proportions.

At Elias' laugh, he scared not only me but Lucky, who he had been carrying when he'd entered my room. Lucky sprang from Elias' arms in a jump so impressive he managed to land right on Henry's lap. More specifically, his balls. His. Fucking. Balls.

Henry curved in on himself as he attempted to save his precious family jewels, groaning out and somehow flinging Lucky across the room toward me in the move. At the same time, I managed to jerk my head up, nailing Soren.

Yep, I head-butted Soren. He'd leaned over with me when I'd ducked down in my cringe, since he still had my hair in his hands.

My head flew back with such force, I nailed him in

his beautiful nose, causing it to explode in an outpouring of blood. And boy, did it bleed. My semi-concussion was becoming more concussion-like by the minute with the head-butting of the century.

Soren grunted while holding his nose; I cussed while holding my head; Henry moaned while he grasped his balls, and Lucky, well, he was being hurled toward me like a flying missile.

During the few seconds this was all occurring, Elias realized his dog, I mean *my* dog, was on a crash course straight for me.

Neither of us saw the other, so as we both attempted to catch Lucky, we only ended up colliding with each other instead. Elias' sculpted abs landed on top of me as he dove, effectively knocking the breath right out of me with a big aplomb. Miraculously, Lucky landed on top of Elias' back, saving himself from the impending doom he was headed for. That dog should be on a game show as he personified his name.

As I laid there struggling to breathe with Elias on top of me, the only thought floating through my head was, *his eyes have a bit of gold around the edges.*

Clearly, I'd been hit in the head one too many times today since I seemed to have forgotten this was *Elias.* Off-Limits *Elias.* Incredibly sexy with an accent *Elias.* I was having a hard time remembering why he was off-limits as his hard body pressed into mine. He must have been struggling with the same shock because he remained on top of me, staring into my eyes.

Through the whole scene that could only be

described as a kerfuffle, Rhett had remained by the door he'd just opened and watched everything play out.

But did he help a girl out? Nope. You know what that giant did instead? He laughed. He fucking laughed so hard he was practically rolling on the ground, unable to breathe, tears streaming down his cheek, snort laughing.

Evidently, it was contagious, as we all eventually joined in the laughter. It almost made me forget a hot guy I often loathed was laughing while lying on top of me. We both seemed to remember this fact simultaneously, as our bodies pressed against one another more.

seven

finley

MY FACE WAS FROZEN as I gawked at Asa after he'd revealed his little piece of information. How was this possible?

Realizing I didn't want to freak out and scare the boy I liked by staring awkwardly at him, I did the only thing I could, I faked a bathroom break.

"Uh, one second, I need to use the restroom," I blurted, jumping from my desk chair. Darting into the bathroom, I quickly shut the door, bracing myself against it.

Holy fuck, holy fuck, holy fuck.

My thoughts raced as I patted my pockets, looking for my phone. I sent a text message to my brother and Sawyer, but there were no responses after a few moments, so I put my phone away to tackle Plan B.

Hurriedly, I flushed the toilet and fake washed my

hands so Asa wouldn't think I was in here pooping. I found him propped back on his arms, looking all delicious on my bed. I stopped, taking him in for a minute before remembering what I'd learned.

Seriously, this was the worst time to discover *that* truth bomb. Epic fucking fail.

Anxiously, I started to fidget, and it eventually alerted Asa to my presence. His smile made me go all gooey, and I forgot to think for a moment. He was just so damn pretty and nice. Asa beckoned me to the bed, and I slowly dragged my feet there.

"Everything okay, Fin? You just seem," he shook his head, looking at me. "I don't know, unusually nervous suddenly. I was hoping we could talk about something, but if this is a bad time, I can leave."

Emotions had shifted on his face from concern to doubt and appeared to land on disappointment, causing me to stumble and fall forward in my anxious state. I couldn't have planned it better if I'd tried because, low and behold, I fell right into his arms.

"You okay?" he asked as he stared down at me. His grip was firm, and he'd clasped his hands around my back. I'd somehow fallen dramatically into his lap, lying across his legs as I stared up at him.

"Yeah. Thank you," I rasped out.

Asa's stare was intense and out of place on him as his eyes bored into mine, searching for something. Whether from me or in general, I didn't know until he started to descend to my lips. His eyes stayed open for a moment; I assumed to gauge my reaction.

When I didn't make any movement to stop him, his eyes closed, and he pressed his lips hard into mine. The kiss engulfed me as fireworks erupted throughout my body. This was the kiss I'd been dreaming about my whole life.

But as happy as that made me, it didn't feel right. As I came back down from the high, I knew I couldn't kiss him anymore while knowing this massive secret about his life. Retreating, I tried to mask my feelings.

"Wow." Smiling, I stared at him, still amazed he'd kissed me.

"I agree. I've wanted to do that for a while, honestly, but always kind of chickened out."

"I'm glad you didn't this time because I've also wanted you to kiss me for a while." My blunt honesty caused us both to laugh. I realized I was still in his arms, so I moved to get up, but he tightened his grip to keep me there.

"I like you right here. It's easier to do this." Asa started to lower for another kiss. Crap, I couldn't do this; I would hate myself.

"Wait!"

Abruptly, he stopped, and I wasn't sure whether it was worry, or possibly pain, that filled his eyes as he peered back, assessing the situation.

"I thought…"

"It's not that, I want to kiss you and kiss you and kiss you until I can't breathe," I paused, "but I just can't right *now*."

His arms fell from around me, allowing me to sit up

this time, but I was still somewhat in his lap. That fact bolstered my resolve, and I pulled off the band-aid to get out what I needed to—time to be brave, girl.

"There's something I need to tell you, but it would be best if I told you and Sawyer together. I know it sounds weird, and you probably have a lot of questions, but I do really like you, Asa. I would like this to be more, and I hope we have a future together, but I can't start anything with deception in my heart. It would poison us before we even started, and that's not the love story I want." He was quiet for a few minutes before nodding his head.

"I trust you Fin, and I know the type of person you are, so if you say it needs to wait, and it's important, then that's what we'll do. Any idea on when that will be, though? It's going to be hard not to kiss you now that I've had a taste of sunshine."

Be still my heart; how was he real?

My experience with guys over the years hadn't been stellar. My bad attitude as a teen didn't really drive them toward me, and my inability to not nerd out at times usually sent them running as an adult. We wouldn't even go into my dark years.

Asa had been the first guy I'd met who got me and accepted me—weirdness and all. So, you could bet your bottom dollar I was ready to climb that man like a tree. Glancing at the clock, I saw it wasn't too late yet. Pulling out my phone, I sent another text stating I was coming over. It was my preemptive coitus-interuptus attempt to not walk in on any sexy shenanigans I could never unsee.

"Come on. I don't want to wait any longer, either. We've spent a year dancing around each other, so, no more. Let's see if Sawyer's home yet. If you still want to date me after, which I'm hoping you do based on that kiss, we could talk about it then. You know, have that whole DTR thing, but first," I stopped when I found him staring at me. "What?" I asked, placing my hands on my hips, waiting.

"You're adorable when you start to ramble, and words are flying out of your mouth faster than I can process them." He placed his hands on my shoulder, halting my progress as he addressed me. "Yes, Finley Reyes, I would like to date you very much. So, let's go find Sawyer if that's what we need to do before I can kiss you again. Come on, Finster, I'll drive."

The smile on my face was real despite the big ole truth nugget I was about to drop on them. I was hoping it wouldn't change things between us; it wasn't like I kept it from him; that was the opposite of what I was doing. So hopefully, those lips would still be open for business after he learned the truth.

sawyer

"Would it be possible for you to get off me now?" I squeaked as I tried to suppress my urge to kiss his stupid face—his stupidly handsome face. Gah.

"Oh, yes, absolutely, erm, just let me." Elias fumbled as he tried to figure out how to get up without squishing me more.

"Fuck's sake, you two are ridiculous. Here, let me help," Rhett interjected, finally seeming to have come to his senses and helped his best friend off me.

The cold air rushed me as Elias and Lucky, who apparently had stayed propped on his back, were finally removed from me. Pushing aside the emptiness I felt at that, I sat up and adjusted my top, that had gotten a little twisted in the commotion. My sore body screamed at me from the weight it had been under, almost as if it just remembered all my injuries. Elias had that effect—he made you forget things.

"Apologies for the fiasco. I was merely bringing you Lucky to see if you wanted him for a bit. I know you two have a bond, and he always makes me feel better."

Well fuck, I couldn't be mad at him if he was going to be all nice and shit. I couldn't have that. I needed to restore my footing.

"Thank you, Elias, for returning *my* dog."

Oh, my goodness, his face. The kicked puppy look was not becoming on him. Not at all. Unable to handle his dower expression any longer, I gave in.

"Fine," I grumbled. "We can have joint custody. I

appreciate you bringing Lucky. That was very thoughtful."

Taking my dog from him, I snuggled Lucky in my arms and gave him kisses for being the best doggo in the whole world. Looking around, I found that while Elias had been suffocating me, Henry had recovered from his ball shot and retrieved something for Soren's nose. He was now sitting next to him on the bed, helping him clean up. They both smiled at me as I returned to the floor with Lucky now in my lap. I was hoping Soren wasn't too injured and could continue to brush my hair, because it had felt wonderful.

Unfortunately, that didn't occur as Finley stormed into my room on a rampage with a confused Asa trailing behind her. I felt a little awkward being half-dressed with him here, but I also had a concussion, survived a scooter accident, and had a giant bomb dropped on me today. I was officially out of fucks to give. It wasn't like I saw Asa that way, anyway.

"Why am I the last to know Sawyer was nearly killed?" Finley screamed at the room, causing me to wince in pain.

Holding my hands up in a placating gesture toward my best friend, I pleaded forgiveness. "No clue where my phone is and chill it on the volume, concussion here," I stated, pointing at my head.

She relaxed at my tone and took a few deep breaths, calming herself before addressing the room again. "Sorry, Sawyer. You're forgiven. My ire is mostly toward my brother, anyway." She gave a dark look toward Henry, who only looked slightly sheepish at her. Finley rolled her eyes before she continued, "I found something I need to share, but now," she paused, looking at me and then Asa, "I'm not sure if it's the right time."

Her whole body changed, and she began to shift on her feet as she wrung her hands in a nervous gesture. Asa stood behind her, looking perplexed as he tried to put the pieces together. I wasn't sure why he was with her, but it did seem as if things were progressing with them, which made me happy. No one spoke up, which meant I had to.

Thanks, guys—cue the eye-roll.

"I don't think there's ever a time that's better than another at this point, Fin, but is this something you should be sharing," I paused, moving my head toward Asa, "you know, in front of everyone?"

Fin stared only at me and nodded her head. It seemed whatever she had to share was a big deal. Sighing, I realized I might as well get it over with. Then I could pretend not to go to bed. It was still early in the evening, but I didn't care. This day had been very overwhelming and exhausting already, and it looked like it wasn't entirely done with the surprises.

"Let's have at it then. I'm ready for some sleep. Getting run off the road really takes it out of you." No one laughed at my lame attempt at a joke. Well, okay then, people, be that way. I was sticking out my tongue at them all in my head.

"Well, I, um, this information will affect you and Asa, which is why he needed to be here."

Again, I nodded, since it seemed she was waiting for my approval. At her words, Asa turned and looked at me like he was trying to solve a math problem. Good luck with that, buddy, unless you spoke quantum Fin.

"Earlier, I was researching our project when Asa arrived. I didn't think anything of it, but he saw the name I had in the search bar, *Abernathy*. Do you remember that?" she paused and looked to Asa in question.

"Yes, and I asked why you were researching my father."

At his words, the air in the room went cold, and my blood stagnated in my veins. I turned toward him and began to assess his features through a new lens. His golden hair was eerily similar to mine. The familiar green eyes were a shade, unlike any other I'd seen, except reflected back at me from a mirror. The sense of connection between us I hadn't been able to define. Holy shit.

"You're my brother," I whispered. Asa turned, shock written all over his face as he looked at me.

"What? That's impossible. I'm an only child." He turned back to Fin, addressing her. "What's going on here, Fin?"

She ignored his questions as she looked at me, and I knew that wasn't the only thing she had to tell me. She gulped a big breath before letting out the last bit I hadn't anticipated at all.

"Not just your brother, Sawyer, but your... *twin* brother."

Gasping, my brain stuttered and stopped before it took off racing. What? But that meant... My memory pulled the conversation with my father, and it clicked.

"Latimer informed me he could make me a father, that he knew of a couple who were expecting and weren't able to keep the baby girl."

"He said, 'baby girl.' It was literal," I mumbled, my eyes flicking up to Asa. He appeared as shocked as me, apprising my features and coming to the same conclusion; Fin wasn't wrong.

"I need to sit down," he croaked, before falling into the empty cuddle chair. Fin sat next to him, taking his hand in hers.

Henry got up from the bed and sat with me on the floor so he could put his arm around me. I realized I was somehow in Soren's lap, as well. I wasn't sure when that had happened, but Lucky didn't seem bothered as both Henry and Soren comforted us in their arms. Looking up at a shell-shocked Asa, I opened my circle of trust to include one more.

"Looks like we have some things to share with you... brother."

eight

soren

THE POUNDING in my head was only increasing as the night dragged on. The incidents over the past two hours had fried it. Surprising Rey in the showers had been fun, but having him comfort me had been every-thing. I felt lighter than I had in almost a week since we'd gotten the texts from the unknown number.

Everything Rey had said resonated within me. He was absolutely right, it didn't change anything. I'd already known she was a horrible mother, and the events had already occurred. Learning she was connected to the reason it happened did nothing but give me more justification to stay clear of Pamela Stryker. My life was good, and I didn't need her to take any more joy from me. She'd done enough.

Receiving the text saying Sawyer had been in an accident scared me. My feelings for her were growing fast, and I hadn't realized just how invested I'd become until she was almost taken away from us. Grief was written all over her face when she exited the bathroom earlier. It was evident something profound had occurred with her and Rey based on the heaviness they carried within themselves.

Despite her struggles, she smiled and attempted to cheer me up, only solidifying my feelings for her more. How something as simple as brushing her hair could be intimate, I didn't know, but the task had connected me to her in a new way. Perhaps it was the simple act of taking care of her that thawed some of the ice around my heart; ice I hadn't even realized was encasing it.

When Squish entered the room dropping the bomb that Asa was Sawyer's twin brother, I immediately dropped to the ground and scooped her and Lucky up into my lap. She didn't even notice until Rey joined us on the floor, and we held her together.

At Sawyer's words, "Looks like we have some things to share with you… brother." Asa looked up, questions in his eyes.

"How is this possible?" His voice was thin and reedy as he attempted to process everything.

"What I'm about to tell you, it's pretty shocking and may change everything you've known about your life. Are you sure you want to know this?"

Sawyer sounded strong despite the news and was trying to give him an out, even if it might hurt her in the end. I admired Asa as he held her gaze, coming to a conclusion.

"If you're my family, my sister, then I want to know. I want to know *you*."

Sawyer's body deflated, almost as if she'd prepared herself for the final blow that would've crushed her for good.

"When I was born, I was given to my parents by their boss, Jayce Latimer. Does that name mean anything to you?" Asa shook his head at her question, hanging on to her words.

"Well, when I was about three, Latimer returned to my father, who I knew as Scott Brennon, and told him he owed him a debt—that he would have to give me back when I was of age. The adoption had been a ruse to make me more "desirable" for his human trafficking ring. Apparently," her voice filled with disgust, as she swallowed to get out the next part, "Latimer had found that girls who'd grown up in good homes with loving parents were more fun to break, and would, um, therefore, go for more money."

I rubbed soothing circles on her hand, reminding her I was there, and that she wasn't alone in this. It seemed to help as she gathered herself to continue.

"My dad was understandably outraged and disgusted this had been the plan all along. He didn't agree with it, so he took my mom and me, and we ran in the middle of the night. We moved to Indiana, where I met Finley and Henry. Everything was great until I was sixteen and we had a visitor."

She paused as she recounted that night in her

memory, presumably trying to find the right words to share the worst memory of her life.

"The man only introduced himself as R, and he was sent to retrieve me. After his creepy introduction, he left me to pack with a guard. He had another errand to run, but said he'd be back in the morning. R acted like he was doing me a huge favor by allowing me to pack and say my goodbyes," Sawyer huffed. "I wasn't on board with that plan, and neither was my dad, so we ran again that night, but they caught up to us. Our car was hit, and we swerved off the road. I barely escaped the wreck before my parents were shot. My father had told me to run, so I did but I passed out in the woods. Fortunately, someone found me and delivered me to the hospital."

Sawyer shifted again, her anxiety rattling her body.

"From there, I went into foster care and have been living under the name of Sawyer Sullivan ever since. My father told me before he was shot to come to this school and look for Abernathy. That it would lead me to my biological parents, it wasn't until last week that I recovered another memory, one where he said to find my brother. So that brings us to now, I think. Well, not exactly, I uh, found out some more information before the accident." Sawyer trailed off, hanging her head.

We all looked at her in shock. It seemed this day wasn't done with dropping bombs on us, and it was only 9 pm.

sawyer

The longest day award went to this day. If I wasn't living it, I would've thought this was a sick joke or some crazy plot in a book.

But, nope, this was real. It was so fucking real.

When they all turned to look at me, I didn't know if I could handle anything else and dropped my head. "I literally have nothing left in me. So please, can we revisit this tomorrow, or I don't know, next year at this rate? I've been run off the road, landed on, and found out I have a twin brother. I'm not capable of anything else tonight. I need sleep before I can dredge up more painful memories, and with my possible concussion, I can't even get that."

Soren squeezed me tighter around the waist, and I melted into him. This day could go fuck itself; I was done.

What should be a happy moment of finding my brother just felt empty. Maxed out on feelings, I couldn't even pinpoint what I did feel at that moment.

"Absolutely. Can we return tomorrow, maybe lunch?"

God bless Fin; she knew when I'd hit my limit and gave me the time I needed to process everything.

"Yeah, that works, I'm off the next two days per the doctor's orders anyway, so I'm free."

Fin nodded and stood, grabbing Asa's hand. He followed along with her, but it didn't appear he was present anymore, either. I could understand that notion, considering we'd just changed his life by laying a significant piece of new information on him and then added a helping of shit on top. He stopped before the hallway, turning back to look at me.

"Sawyer, it's been a bit of a mind-blowing hour, but I'm not upset about discovering you're my sister. I would like to get to know you more. I've always felt something was missing, and now I guess I know why. Talk tomorrow?"

I couldn't help it. Tears filled my eyes at his kind words. I'd worried he wouldn't want to know me, that he would hear my drama and run. It would be the sensible thing to do, but he hadn't. He wanted to know me and had felt my presence missing from his life. It was the answer I needed to hear, so holding the tears at bay as best as I could, I nodded and smiled.

"I'd like that a lot, actually."

Something on my face made his brotherly instincts kick in because the next moment, he charged across the room and pulled me, and a miffed dog, from Soren and Henry's embrace.

"Fuck it. You're my sister, and I just want to hug you."

We held each other for a few minutes with a squirmy dog between us, just breathing in one another. He felt like home, but different from Henry. Asa felt like a part of my very core, a part of me I never realized I was waiting for until this very moment.

Seamlessly, our sibling bond clicked into place and filled me with the strength I would need to continue this fight. Earlier, I'd entered into 'the nothing' to escape, but now it was time I faced reality. This wouldn't be easy, but I had people in my life. I even had a fucking brother. Silent tears ran down my face onto his shirt, but he only hugged me tighter as his tears hit my hair as well.

After a few minutes, we pulled apart, and a sense of rightness solidified between us. He squeezed my arms lovingly before turning and walking out of the room with Fin. She smiled and gave me a nod before taking his hand to leave. The tears in her eyes didn't escape my notice.

Registering the guys in the room, feelings of bashfulness washed over me. Shuffling on my feet, I glanced around the room and realized Oliver and Mateo were still missing.

"Where are Oliver and Mateo?"

Rhett momentarily looked panicked at my question before he grabbed the phone from his pocket, presumably to check the time.

"I'm supposed to meet Oliver, and well, I'm late. So, I better head there. Will you be okay tonight? Do you want me to check on you when I return?" Rhett's tone was solemn, and I wasn't sure what was going through his head at the moment.

"I'd planned to stay, so we can keep an eye on her,

but feel free to come and check when you return," Henry replied.

Rhett nodded before exiting the room, but stopped and turned abruptly, heading back toward me. A look of pure purpose was written on his face. Every time he kissed me, I was amazed at his gentleness. Softly, he brushed my hair behind my ears as his fingers grazed my cheek, causing my body to respond.

"I'm glad you're okay, baby."

A soft kiss was placed on my forehead, and I melted —puddle on the floor of goo, melted. Clean up on aisle one.

My eyes fluttered shut at his kiss, and when I opened them, all I could see was Rhett. His dark chocolate orbs shone with an emotion I was scared to identify. He took one last look before retreating out of the room for good this time, leaving Elias, Henry, and Soren with me. Elias shuffled on his feet before stealing my awkward hand wave move and left the room.

"Let's get to bed, Smalls. We'll take turns making sure you're okay. Since you've been alert and holding a conversation, it's safe to assume you don't have an actual concussion—"

"Thank fuck!" I interrupted, not caring. "I'm exhausted. If I had to stay up, I was going to suggest some very creative ways to keep me awake," I joked.

"Well, it never hurts to be cautious. I'm sort of hating myself for telling you that you can go to sleep now, but do you need anything, like water or pain meds?" a disappointed Henry asked.

I'd spent all my words, so I shook my head before crawling into the bed with Lucky and snuggled down under the covers. Henry joined my front, and Soren took my back, officially making me a sandwich. I couldn't say I was complaining, though; it was definitely the best kind of sandwich. I could eat it all day.

I was asleep quickly as the events of the evening caught up to me. The guys woke me a few times to check I was still coherent, but I slept for the most part. At one point, I think Mateo and Rhett came in, but I wasn't sure if that was a dream or reality. Oddly enough, I dreamt of house elves, floating bubbles, and sandwiches. My imagination was a weird place.

nine

oliver

RECHECKING MY PHONE, I still had no messages from Rhett. It wasn't like him to be late, so I was starting to get worried. Something had obviously happened. Was I already so far outside their circle that I wasn't even included?

It stung, but I could only blame myself. I should've shared with them what was going on from the start. Instead, I'd run like a coward. Motioning for the bartender to settle my tab, I was almost jolted out of my chair as my phone vibrated on the bar top.

Rhett: Sorry, there was an incident. I'll explain.
On my way now. 10 mins.

Despite hating I'd been right, the knowledge he was on his way soothed me. When the bartender walked over with my tab, I ordered another one instead. It would only be my second, but two was more than I usually had on a weeknight. My anxiety had called for one for what I had to tell Rhett, but it seemed a second one would be needed to hear what had happened.

My time in town hadn't gone well earlier, and now I was even more concerned. The bartender handed me my bottle, and I decided to move to a booth where there was more privacy. Picking one that was secluded, I made my way across the bar, avoiding eye contact with the people scattered around. My reputation was well known, and tonight wasn't the time to get hit on.

Rhett's tall frame entered the door, and I examined his posture, trying to find any hints about what had happened. Rhett's face was grim as he spotted me, but it didn't give any clues. His face always looked that way—except with Sawyer.

"Hey, Sorry. Got sidetracked with Sawyer's accident—"

"What! Is she okay? What happened?"

He held up his hand, stopping my questions. My heart raced, and I needed to know or I might explode. Logically, I could guess she was, or he wouldn't be here, but my brain wanted to hear the words. Delivering me a classic Rhett look with his raised eyebrow, I took in a few breaths to stop the barrage of questions on my tongue.

"Sawyer's okay. She got a few bumps and bruises, a possible mild concussion. Mostly she was scared, but nothing broken or serious. According to the eyewitness, a truck purposefully ran her off the road, and her brakes didn't work. The Vespa is being pulled out of the creek and will be investigated to see if foul play was the cause."

Shocked was putting it mildly with how I felt. It was already happening. They'd already tried to come for her. I waited to see if he would say anything else before I spilled my dark secrets.

"Ollie, I've been trying to give you the benefit of the doubt, but I need to know if whatever you're hiding is going to blowback on us, on her?"

Stoic as ever, Rhett stared at me, no emotion on his face as he waited for me to answer. Swallowing hard, my grip on the bottle tightened as I faced the realization that everything could hinge on this secret.

"I don't know. That's the truth. When she told us that night about her father and what had been planned for her, I freaked. I haven't had to think about that name in a while or the legacy that came with it I thought," I shook my head. "I thought I'd escaped it, but there it was, coming out of the mouth of the girl I liked. I've been debating all week how to approach it and what the repercussions would be for either choice I made, because it is a choice. One I've been avoiding for years."

I trailed off at the end, scared to look up. Sometime during my confession, I'd dropped my eyes to the bottle in front of me, peeling the label from it. Knowing I needed to face this last part, I took a deep breath and met Rhett's eyes. Everything I would need to know about my housemates, my friends, my brothers would be reflected back in his eyes in a few seconds.

"The company her father worked for, Latimer Industries, well it's owned and operated by none other than Jayce Latimer."

Rhett looked at me quizzically, knowing I was leaving something out, but the words felt trapped on my tongue.

"Yes, Sawyer said as much. But what does that have to do with you? With this choice you have to make?"

"It matters because Jayce Latimer is my uncle."

At first, nothing registered on his face, but as he processed my words, the emotion I'd been dreading never appeared—disgust. No, it was worse. Because instead, Rhett landed on sadness, and I wasn't sure if it was because he felt sorry for me or he knew it meant nothing would ever become between Sawyer and me.

My family being responsible for killing her parents was something I could never change.

"What's this choice you had to make, then? You're talking to me and telling me, so I'm hoping that means you're siding against them?" Rhett appeared panicked, showing me how much he cared for Sawyer.

Taking a steady breath, I exhaled as I began to share with him my phone call earlier.

mateo

Lying awake in my bed, my mind raced as I tried to calm it. Nothing seemed to work, and everything spun out of control. Throwing back the covers, I marched down the hallway to Sawyer's room. I knocked softly on the door, not sure if anyone would hear me. So, I was relieved when Rey opened it a crack.

He took one look at my face and exited the room, shutting the door quietly behind him. Grabbing my arm, he pulled me into his room across the hall. My breathing was rapid at this point, and I was almost past the point of no return. Lights and sounds were no longer registering, and I prepared myself for the panic attack to take over.

"Mateo, breathe, it's okay. I know, believe me, I know. I freaked out earlier, too, at the thought of losing her, but she's okay. She's going to be okay. Hey, can you tell me five things you can smell right now?"

Confused at his weird question, I just shook my head.

"Okay, how about five reasons why Marvel is better than DC?"

My brain stuttered, only five, I could name a hundred.

"Pftt… First, the stories are just better. The universe is larger creating, more diverse characters. Third, Captain America, enough said. Also, Guardians of the Galaxy. Not to mention the movies and caliber of actors are far superior, in fact—"

"Hey, Mateo?"

"What? Don't tell me you're a DC fan?"

"No, I was just going to mention you aren't panicking anymore."

My thoughts stopped, and I realized he was right.

"Thank you, I, uh, didn't know what to do, but you had said to come to you, so it was all I could think at the moment."

"I'm glad that you did. I meant it too. Anytime." His smile was warm and reassuring, which alleviated my anxiety.

"So, she's okay? Truthfully? I wanted to see her, but when I got home, she was already asleep, and I talked myself out of disturbing her, but then all I could do was lay awake in bed thinking of all these worst-case scenario situations, and the panic overwhelmed me."

"Come and see for yourself."

Rey grabbed my hand and pulled me back through his door and across the hall. Gently, he opened Sawyer's door and dragged me in the rest of the way. Soren sat up against the headboard, reading. Sawyer and Lucky were snuggled up to his side, both softly snoring. He glanced up as we approached, smiling softly at me.

My anxiety dissipated as I took in her sleeping form. Finally, I could see for myself that she was safe, whole, and here. Dropping my shoulders with relief, my entire body sagged with me. Bending over, I placed a soft kiss on her cheek, needing her to know I was here.

I walked out after thanking Rey and Soren, and it

occurred to me this was the first time in my entire life I'd cared for someone else other than myself. That thought was profound. It also slightly terrified me, and I worried I wasn't strong enough to handle the responsibility of caring for someone else.

My hand rested on my doorknob as I debated returning to my room. If I went into my room, the doubt would suffocate me, and I would talk myself out of this relationship. No, what I needed was to be more present and start making more of an effort to step out of my comfort zone. Sawyer saw me as the person I wanted to be all the time, so I needed to be that version of myself.

If I blended into the background, it would only be my fault. This moment could be me taking a risk, not just with my future like coming to TAS had been, but riskier—with my heart. Because when I really asked myself where I wanted to be, it was with Sawyer. Hands down, no doubt at all, with zero hesitation, and that was the answer I needed to assure myself.

So, I turned around and walked back into Sawyer's room. Rey and Soren looked up but said nothing as I walked in, grabbed the blanket off the chair, and curled up in it.

Here I would place my heart with a girl who shined so brightly she illuminated us all. Sawyer cast out the shadows that lurked and highlighted my strengths. So, why would I want to be anywhere else? It might be safer on the sidelines, but I hadn't won my medals playing it safe; why start now?

Amazingly, I fell asleep quicker in that chair than I had for the hour lying in my bed.

Wetness on my face awoke me the next morning. Opening my eyes, everything was blurry as I blinked and rubbed the crusty sleep boogers from the corners. I always wondered why they were called that. Kind of gross, wasn't it?

As more of my surroundings came into focus, I realized where the wetness was coming from. Lucky stood on his haunches, propped on the chair, and licked my nose, allowing me to conclude he was the reason for my early morning awakening.

Sitting up, I grabbed my glasses from the spot I'd placed them on the windowsill, and the rest of the room came into sharp focus, granting me a view of a laughing Sawyer in the middle of her bed, trying to hold in her giggles. The sight of her laughing brought me immense joy, and I knew I'd made the correct choice for myself last night.

Depending on someone was scary, caring for someone terrifying, but being alone was unbearable. Plus, some of the most dangerous things in my life had been the best if I thought about it. Skiing down that hill for the first time, telling my parents I no longer wanted to compete, and admitting that my incident hadn't been an accident like I wanted to believe.

"Hey Dulzura, how are you feeling this morning?"

"Oh, you know, like I've been stabbed by a hundred angry rocks, but other than that, peachy."

"Well, as long as you're peachy, I guess there isn't a reason for me to worry or make you breakfast. Guess I'll just head back to my room." I faked getting up to see if she would react and when she did, my heart soared.

"Wait, let's not be so quick to make those decisions. I'm sure I could benefit from some breakfast in bed from a cute guy. Puh-lease." Her cute puppy dog look gave me all the tingles. Damn, she was so cute.

"Of course, Dulzura. It would be unfair not to treat you to the Mateo Special."

Naturally, I spoke out of my butt as I didn't know how to make anything, but she didn't need to know that part. Getting up for real this time, I headed to the kitchen to see what I could fashion together for some breakfast in bed.

Lucky trailed after me, and I figured he needed to go out, so I detoured to the backyard first. He was well trained and quickly went out to the grass and did his business. He pranced back in, looking at me for something as he sat at my feet.

Dog, you are cute, but I don't speak dog. Going to need more direction.

Oh man, I was talking to myself in my head to a dog, not even out loud. Shaking my thoughts away, I headed back toward the kitchen, where I found Rhett and Elias. Perfect, I was hopeful they could help me out.

"Good morning. Could I ask for your help with something? I wanted to bring Sawyer some breakfast, but I can only make cereal."

Rhett watched me for a minute before nodding and turning. He started to put together a smoothie for me, and I relaxed.

"I have noticed Sawyer tends to drink hot tea, so perhaps you could make her a cup?" Elias offered.

Blinking at him, I was shocked to learn he'd noticed that about her. Nodding at his suggestion, I grabbed a mug out of the cabinet and filled it with water before sticking it in the microwave.

"Wait, wait, wait." He held his hands up, looking at me in disgust. "Please tell me you are not heating water in the bloody microwave?" he asked, exasperation in his tone.

When I turned to him, he had his hand on his forehead, almost as if it pained him to think of water in such an inadequate way.

"Um, how else would I get hot water?"

"Bloody Hell. Here, I shall show you."

He pulled a red kettle out from under the cabinet and filled it with water before placing it on the stove. Elias lit the burner, and I watched him meticulously, cataloging each movement into my memory. This was something I could do for her, so I would learn to do it the best possible way. I busied myself making some toast, a bowl of cereal for myself, and grabbed the smoothie Rhett had finished. The dilemma of not having enough hands hit me in my face as I tried to juggle only the three things I currently had.

"Well, shit."

At my utterance of the cuss word, the guys broke out into laughter. Why was it so funny when I cursed? I didn't understand it, but I supposed it didn't matter in the end as long as I was funny. My cheeks heated a little, though, so I kept my head lowered just as the kettle started to whistle. Turning to grab it, a tray appeared under my nose, offering me a way to carry the items without having to grow a third arm.

"Thanks, man."

"No, problem. Get everything sorted, and I will show you where the tea and things are since we don't know how she takes it yet."

Nodding at his reasoning, I placed everything on the tray as Elias gathered the tea supplies. Feeling confident now, I glanced up and nodded my thanks to the guys. Friendship was a new concept to me, but these guys made it easy, and I enjoyed developing these bonds with them.

Heading back up the stairs, I balanced the tray very precariously as I took each step. When I'd finally made it back to her room, I found myself panting from the exertion it'd taken to carry it without spilling anything. Waiters got no respect.

The door was open from me leaving, and I found Sawyer no longer in the room, but her bathroom door was closed. Deciding a picnic on the floor would be the best option, I had everything set up just as she exited.

"Ah, this is the sweetest. Thanks, Mateo."

"I have to admit, I don't know how to make anything other than the toast. Rhett made the smoothie and Elias the tea. Actually, he yelled at me when I started to heat water in the microwave."

Her cringed face told me Elias had been correct, and the kettle was the better option. Picking up my spoon, I dug into my Cheerios as she ate her toast. It was quiet but comfortable as we ate our picnic breakfast on her bedroom floor.

"Sawyer, I was scared when I heard what happened because it made me realize how much I care about you. I just wanted you to know. I'm not the best with words or expressing how I feel. It's something I'm having to actively try harder with, but I am working on it."

"Mateo, you don't have to feel bad about not being good at something. I think it's braver when you can say something you're not good at, honestly. But I'm also sorry you were worried. Not that it was controllable, but I don't like people to worry about me. There's a tiny part of me that's doing backflips because the cute boy in front of me just admitted to caring about me."

"Well, I do care, Dulzura."

"I'm glad you do because I care about you, too. Will you," she blushed, meeting my eyes, "tell me what Dulzura means now?"

"I guess it's only fair. It translates to 'the sweetness' but it's the equivalent of sweetheart in Spanish. Is that okay?"

"It's more than okay. I love it."

"Since we're on this truth-revealing train this morning, can I offer one more truth, um, something I've wanted to tell you but have been scared to say out loud?"

"Absolutely, I'm here to listen to anything you want to share because I want to know you, Mateo."

"Hopefully, that's still true after my story."

Somehow sensing my impending distress, she scooted over and held my hand, giving me that natural support she was so good at doing. Taking a deep breath, I turned so I could peer into her eyes as I shared. This wasn't the time for me to hide. I needed her to see my vulnerability.

"My siblings had no problems following the path set out for them by my parents. They both excelled at school, but I was never one to do well. So, when I was introduced to skiing by my friend, Samuel, it was something I had for myself. It was wonderful initially, but my parents started putting pressure on me when they realized I was good. Do more Mateo, strive harder Mateo, practice more… more, more, more. Winning my medals at the Olympics didn't even appease them. They still wanted more. It made me feel as if I would never be enough for them."

I swallowed, needing a moment to finish the next part. Sawyer squeezed my hand and I knew she was with me.

"I was with the team, and my parents were pressuring me as usual, and I just couldn't take it any longer. I was taking caffeine pills to stay awake so I could practice more. I hadn't slept in three days at this point, and it was equivalent to speed in my body. I took some more before my race, and they think the tiredness and caffeine-induced hysteria caused me to take too many, which led to me collapsing in the snow. But the truth, Dulzura, was that I knew. I knew how many I was taking, and I wanted it to end. The pain, the pressure, the unworthiness, it all piled on me to the point it was crushing me. When I collapsed in the snow, in a weird way, I felt free for the first time."

Tears were on the edges of my lids as I tried to hold them in. The whole time she'd held my gaze, never wavering.

"Waking up in that hospital bed was both the worst and best thing. Part of me felt I'd failed again, I couldn't even get killing myself right, but the bigger part of me was relieved because I didn't really want to die. I just wanted the hemorrhaging of my heart to stop."

Sawyer swiped a tear off my eyelashes, her own eyes filled with warmth and compassion.

"The team had me do some psychological testing, and I had to do mandated therapy, but it was the best thing for me. I learned skills to cope and was able to talk to someone who listened. Coming here was a way for me to regain my love of skiing without the pressure to win medals. I see now it's also been a chance for me to trust my own choices, and that includes you. Caring for you scares me because I've never cared for anyone before, but it's so worth it because you make me feel strong, and that's how I want to see myself."

"Mateo, you see who you already are. It has nothing to do with me. I'm flattered you think that, but you are so much stronger than you realize. You've shown me this quiet strength that resonates within you. I've seen you stand up to these guys and make them listen to you. That's not me, hun, that's you. I'm just reflecting who you already are."

Her smile was radiant, and something inside of me recognized what she was saying. It was hard to grasp it entirely, but it was getting clearer.

ten

sawyer

MATEO'S STORY sat heavy in my gut. There had been so many times I'd come close to making the same choice. Handed blow after blow, sometimes it felt as if that was it; this was the time I wouldn't get back up. Striving to be perfect and always failing, I often wondered if it was even worth it. I understood Mateo in a whole new way now.

Nobody in my life had cared; not the foster families, my peers, or the teachers who only saw me as another foster kid statistic. The day-to-day tasks wore on your soul, and you got to the point where you managed to keep breathing, but the pain sliced just a little bit harder every time.

Henry and Fin had been my beacons of light through it all. Knowing there were two people out in the world who cared about me, thought about me, and shared good memories with me… it helped remind me there were things in life to keep getting up for.

Mateo was at the height of his career, and most people would perceive him as having the whole world at his fingertips. They would assume he had nothing to feel depressed about, but depression didn't quite work that way. He had been alone, so alone and drowning in his pain.

Dropping his hand, I pulled him closer to wrap him in a hug. His head nestled into my hair, and I felt him relax at the contact. I needed to hug people more; damn, it felt nice. We held each other for a few minutes before we pulled back.

His face was so close, and I couldn't resist placing a kiss on his lips. Mateo eagerly returned it, and it seemed he was growing more confident in this area as well. We continued kissing for a few minutes, my body really wanting to take it further, but I knew he had a session soon, so reluctantly, I pulled back.

Peering into Mateo's eyes was fast becoming one of my favorite things. The blue was soothing, reminding me of an ocean and holding a multitude of emotions in its depths. They were slightly dilated this morning; trained on me with a steadfast devotion that gave me all the right kind of tingles.

"What time is your first class?"

"It's at 10 am., so I should get going, but I'm glad I got to spend breakfast with you."

"Me too, I loved it. Thank you for my bedroom picnic."

My face couldn't help but smile around him. His purity was refreshing. How he managed to save that part of himself with all the darkness he experienced spoke of who he was as a person. I was glad I was in his life now to help remind him of the brightness he had to share.

We cleaned up the remainder of breakfast, stacking it on the tray, and headed downstairs together. Oliver and Rhett were in the kitchen when we walked in. They seemed to be having an intense conversation that abruptly stopped when we entered. Not suspicious at all guys, carry on.

"Good morning," I said, looking between them.

"How are you feeling, baby?"

"Better. I think I even managed not to get a concussion, so I can't be mad about that." Shrugging, I grabbed a stool, but wasn't surprised when nobody agreed with me. Oh well, I thought it was fortunate. Concussions weren't fun and affected things for a while. If I had to roll down a hill, at least my helmet did its job.

"Sawyer, do you have time today to talk with me? You know, the conversation I've been avoiding?" Oliver asked, sheepishly. He seemed nervous and unsure of what he wanted my answer to be. I didn't know what I wanted my answer to be either, to be honest. Things had shifted so far left with us that I had no clue where I even stood with him.

"I'm meeting my brother for lunch, but after that, I could be free if it's important. Otherwise, I think your silence has spoken for you."

Oliver seemed to go from shock to hurt at my statement, but I didn't know what he expected when he'd avoided me for almost a week.

"Brother?" asked Mateo.

I realized then, neither he nor Oliver were there last night and obviously hadn't been given the latest update on the 'Sawyer Drama.' Hmm, I wonder if my life would be interesting enough for a soap opera? *Sawyer's Rink* had a nice ring to it, or maybe it just sounded similar to my favorite '90s teen drama.

"Oh yeah, sorry, you guys were missing from that particular news bomb of information last night. I figured out who my brother is, or Fin did. I have a twin brother, actually, and it turns out it's Asa."

"My teammate, Asa?" Oliver asked.

"Yep, that's the one."

"Wow," Mateo replied in shock, disbelief on his face.

"I know. I'm still trying to wrap my brain around it all. So much has happened, and I'm not even sure I'm keeping up with it. You know what we need? One of those whiteboards with strings. Do they sell those as kits? If they don't, they need to get on that." They all chuckled at me, but I was being serious.

"Well, it might be good for Asa to hear this as well, then. It kind of involves him now. Do you want to meet here, or were you meeting somewhere else?"

"I think it was here, but I was out of it last night, so I'm not 100% accurate on the details."

"Asa and I have practice soon, so I can tell him if that's okay?"

Oliver sounded considerate and solemn, and it was weirding me out. It was nothing like the jokey flirty guy I'd met that first day who wanted to get in my pants. This Oliver seemed resigned to be rejected, to be unaccepted. It made me fear what he had to share if he was already assuming I'd want nothing else to do with him.

"That works. I need to get Asa's number anyway. Thanks."

He turned and walked out of the room after I'd answered, leaving Rhett and Mateo with me in the kitchen. He didn't even say goodbye. He just left. I didn't know what was more upsetting; our upcoming talk or him leaving like that. Either way, I had a feeling my heart was going to be trampled on.

"I don't have a good feeling about this," I muttered out loud, staring at the now empty space Oliver had left through. When Rhett didn't contradict my statement, absolute dread filled my body. Fucking fantastic. What was it going to be this time? At this rate, I would need to rent space at the Smithsonian to house all these skeletons we kept uncovering.

Not being able to do any of my regular activities due to 'medical protocol' made me fidgety. The anticipation of lunch with Oliver and Asa consumed my mind with a million outcomes. I needed to do something. Realizing I never checked where my stuff had ended up last night, I went to see if Elias was available.

I decided to try his room first, so I headed down the hall and knocked on the closed door. When no response came, I decided to check the rest of the house. Most of the guys were out training students, but I wasn't sure of Elias' schedule. Rhett had said someone would be home with me throughout the day in case I needed anything, so it was a process of elimination of who I found.

After clearing the main floor, I remembered he often trained in the fitness room in the morning and decided to check there before I had to actually text him. For some reason, I wanted to avoid texting Elias. Something about texting made it feel more casual or, dare I say, intimate. Keeping him at arm's length would be better for me. I was too confused and twisted over him to know my feelings. Something about Elias made him riskier than the other guys. I could see heartbreak written all over his beautiful face.

When I reached the bottom of the steps, I knew my search was successful. Part of me wasn't sure if that was good or not, though. Granted, I didn't have to text him, but now I was forced to stare at his sweaty, glistening, tattooed, muscled chest.

Forced, I tell you, straight up, fucking forced.

How did I keep forgetting that under his proper button-down attire lay an incredible landscape of tattoos? They were breathtakingly beautiful, and I hadn't even seen them up close yet. That visual just might kill me, but oh, what a way to go.

Taking a deep breath and thinking about smelly feet to dislodge my lust, I prepared myself to enter the room. Surprisingly, classical music played over the speakers as I entered and I stopped in the doorway as I listened to the piano and violins. It was oddly soothing and enticing at the same time. Music had always spoken to me in ways words often failed. This music was emotional, a bit aggressive, but also compelling. It was such a strange concept, but it worked and suited Elias better than anything I'd ever have picked for him.

His movements as he struck the punching bag with his feet and hands were hypnotizing. Elias was really good at whatever he was doing. I didn't know the names, but the motions were graceful and powerful, and that was something I did understand—identified with even.

The music switched to a slower song, and he turned, presumably to start his cool down. He froze when he caught sight of me. I stood half in the door and half out, having stopped when my mind faltered at the perfection that was Elias Turner. My rogue hand decided she'd missed too much fun lately and did her awkward wave thing.

Seriously, if you're going to go all rogue and do embarrassing shit, couldn't you make it more badass, hand? You know, a middle finger here or there wouldn't hurt. Geez.

Elias remained frozen in a stare-off with me while I scolded my hand in my head. Which was still waving.

What the fuck! Grabbing it with my other hand, I lowered them both down.

Sheepishly, I smiled at Elias and swallowed to wet my suddenly dry throat. I'd been prepared to ask him about my stuff, but all words had left the building as I stared across the room at him.

"Did you need something, Sawyer?"

"I, uh, what?"

The sweat was mesmerizing as it trailed down his abs, glistening on his ink, tempting me to follow it down or even lick it. *Hello, new addition to my list.* My earlier attempt to stop lusting after Elias by thinking of feet was clearly not working.

Dirty diapers, vomit, onions.

My mind cleared finally as I flooded it with disgusting things.

"Oh, hey, Elias. Fancy meeting you here." I leaned against the door, acting casual as I berated myself in my head. Why did I even open my mouth? Seriously, the most idiotic things always came out. Based on his smirk and confused expression, he apparently thought the same. Something about that smirk stabilized me, and the lust dropped away.

"Actually, I was looking for you. I was wondering if you'd heard anything about my belongings?" My terseness erased his smirk, and polite Elias returned. The hint of arousal I swear I saw disappeared too, leaving me to believe I'd imagined it from the beginning.

"There were a few things they had in a bag at the medical center. I believe it was placed on the dining room table last night. The police have my number and will call once they have finalized their investigation and return your other items. I will relay that message when I receive it."

"Perfect, thank you. And Elias," I paused, turning out of the door, looking over my shoulder. "Thanks for yesterday. I know I'm not your favorite person, but you still came and rescued me from the medical center. Waking up in a room again, well, it hadn't been my favorite place to wake up. So, your help when I was vulnerable, that meant a lot to me. I just wanted you to know that."

His shoulders relaxed at my sincerity, piquing my interest in what had made him tense. I turned to leave but stopped, looking back at him one last time.

"I don't know what you're training for in here, but you're amazing at it, whatever it is. I just thought you should know that. Plus, I'm kind of digging the music."

My words landed, and I swore that boy swelled with so much pride; it was almost as if no one had ever told him 'good job' before. My heart broke a little at his expression. It was harder to hate him when you could identify with his pain. I needed to get out of this room before I fell back into my stare-off with his abs. A girl could only suffer through a certain level of temptation in one day before she finally caved.

Racing up the stairs, I prayed the box from my mother would be with my stuff.

Please be there, please be there, please be there. I chanted it over and over in my head, hoping my pleas would miraculously make it appear. If I was ever going to develop some magical, supernatural powers, now would be a great time!

There was a bag on the table, but I stopped, unable to move any further. I wasn't sure now if the crushing disappointment would be manageable if it wasn't.

Please, fate. It would be cruel to give me something from my mom after five years and then have it destroyed before I could even open it.

And all because someone tried to kill me.

Whoa. They had tried to *kill* me—again.

The realization hit me in the gut, and I sank to the floor. Too much, too damn much had occurred in the past 24 hours. It was official. I was calling it. Sawyer overload had just been met.

The tears fell before I even realized I was crying. The splats sounded on my bare arms as my tears made their presence known and alerted me to them. Time disappeared, and I wasn't sure how long I sat in the middle of the floor crying before someone found me.

Arms wrapped around me, pulling me into their lap as they began to rock me. Soothing sounds hit my ears as a hand brushed my hair back. The rocking felt nice, but my sobs were uncontrollable, and I couldn't do much but grasp the arm that held me close, inevitably drenching us both in the liquid representation of my pain as the memories overwhelmed me. The darkness came for me, and I accepted it this time. I kept thinking I was strong, but I was lying to myself, and soon, everyone would see that as well.

. . .

"No one likes you, Sariah. Henry only tolerates you because he has to skate with you. I'm going to ask him to go out with me and then you'll see. You're weird, ugly, and look like a boy. Better to realize this now, ugly duckling."

"Come here, little lamb, I won't bite. I promise you will like it. Just give me a peek; it's the only thing you foster kids are good for."

"Don't get comfortable, brat. I run this house, and if I don't like you, they won't like you. Watch yourself."

"Hey weirdo, do they not let you take showers? You stink. How old are you, anyway? You look like you're twelve!"

"You thought I loved you? Classic. You were a bet, darling. See who could sleep with the new foster kid in school first. Thanks for the $50 bucks for that crappy lay!"

"Tiny dancer, you are brave beyond belief. Trust in yourself."

eleven

elias

THE DOOR SLAMMING CLOSED REVERBERATED off the walls, leaving me standing in the now quiet room, stunned. Lately, every moment with Sawyer felt like a tornado of emotions. One moment, I was annoyed with her and wanted to go head to head with her over linguistic barbs. Then, with a look, she set my body alight with desire. But this… this feeling of being appreciated and acknowledged for something I had accomplished felt foreign.

It was a welcome feeling that filled me in a way nothing had before.

Typically, the praise I received was empty, generic, and those obligatory responses people often gave. Sawyer was not someone to mince words and did not answer to social norms. Plus, my behavior had not earned that luxury with her. She literally owed me nothing. So, to hear her say I was good at something felt like everything at that moment.

The suddenly quiet room announced loudly that my playlist had ended, and I hurriedly finished my morning routine. Thursdays were my slow days, but I did have a few students to meet. My schedule varied with mid-morning, lunch, and afternoon tutoring to work around practices and training sessions. Occasionally, I had some evening seminars, but that was only typical during exams with the older students.

Cresting the top of the stairs, I found a distraught Lucky who had been attempting to scratch at the door to garner my attention. Picking him up, I assessed him to see what was wrong. Perhaps, he needed to go relieve himself and couldn't find Sawyer.

Heading toward the door, I heard the sound of utter heartbreak. Instantly, I knew it was Sawyer, and this was what had caused Lucky to be upset. He had been trying to get me to help her, the sweet pup. Setting him down, I followed him to the sound of the weeping that was piercing my cold, dead heart.

Sawyer sat in the middle of the floor, curled into a ball as her sobs wracked her body. The bag of her belongings lay untouched on the table, so I assumed it wasn't related, so the cause of her distress was unknown. Nothing else appeared to be around, causing worry to fill me about what might have happened.

Pushing away my own reservations, I immediately reacted and scooped her up into my arms. Sawyer didn't seem to be aware of my presence as she curled into me, soaking me with her tears. My body started to naturally rock back and forth as memories of a nanny comforting me this way replayed in my head. It felt odd, but Sawyer seemed to be okay with it as she grasped my arm around her.

We sat there on the floor, with me rocking and offering words of comfort for a while. I did not dare move to check the time, but the numbness of my bum indicated it had been for a while. How many tears did girls have? I was sure she would be out by now. They had started to slow as she began to tire. The soft snore confirmed it a few minutes later, and I realized she'd fallen asleep, drained from the emotional onslaught she experienced.

I debated whether to move her and wondered how I would accomplish that when the front door opened, filling me with immense relief. When Rhett came around the corner, amusement and then worry crossed his typically stoic face before he rushed over to me. Rhett had grown so much in the weeks since Sawyer had been here, and I was happy my best mate had found happiness.

"What happened?"

"Ssh, mate. Care to help me up first?"

Thankfully, he realized she was asleep and gathered her up in his arms. I kind of hated him right then, though. Not only could he pick her up like nothing, but he also took her from me. Logic was not working since I had asked him to, but my body was angry about losing her heat, the closeness, and her smell it had grown accustomed to.

Stretching as I stood to alleviate some of the muscle tightness, I followed Rhett to her bedroom. Once she was tucked in with Lucky watching over her, we exited the room, and Rhett turned to me for answers. His patience was clearly up as he placed his hands on his hips, looming over me with his stern eyebrows—he meant business.

"I'm unsure of what happened. She came down and asked me about her belongings. I told her they were on the table. When I was heading for my shower, I found her like that," I gestured, needing him to believe me, "crying in the middle of the floor, so I reacted and comforted her. She eventually fell asleep, along with my arse, mind you. So, you can stop giving me the death glare. I didn't harm your girlfriend. Well, this time," I huffed out.

Here I was doing the right thing, and I still received flack about it, but as I spoke, his sternness lessened, and he seemed relieved as he dropped his hands.

"Sorry man, I've just been a mess since yesterday, and both times she's needed someone, I'm not there, and well, you are. Guess part of me is feeling inadequate. I'm good at taking care of people, being the steady one, and I haven't been able to be that, so I feel lost. Someone I care about is hurt, and it's just bringing all the stuff with Rowan up," Rhett said, hanging his head.

Seeing him like this softened my own exterior. Rhett

was steadfast, and I often forgot it served a purpose. His steadiness offered him control and direction.

"I hadn't thought about you feeling that way, mate. Do you want to talk more about it? Or punch something? I need to see if I can salvage my schedule, but I can be available for you."

"Thanks, Elias. Yes, let's spar later. We need to increase your training, anyway. I think there's an amateur match you could enter in a few months if you were interested."

My heart sped up at that thought, but was it possible? My family had drilled into me the importance of appearance, and being an MMA fighter was not proper, at all.

"Can I think about it? I'm interested, but I need to sort some things out first."

"Of course. I better text Oliver and let him know she won't be making lunch Thanks for looking after her when you didn't have to."

"You act as if I am some horrible, tacky person. I made mistakes with Sawyer, but I genuinely like her and want the best for her. So, of course, I would help her. My upbringing demands it for one. A man does not leave a lady in distress. I do hope someday we can be actual friends."

"Pfft. Okay, dream big there, man."

Rhett patted me on the shoulder as he made his way past me. I was kind of offended. Did he not think I could be friends with her? Now, I just wanted to prove him wrong.

Heading to my room finally, I checked the time on my smartwatch and realized if I hurried, I might be able to make it to my next tutoring session and only need to make up one. Rushing through a shower and quickly getting dressed, I grabbed my satchel and headed out the door. I had about ten minutes to make it across campus to the tutoring hall.

As I climbed into my car, my phone pinged with an incoming message, but I was too preoccupied, so I left it. Making it to the faculty parking lot with a few minutes to spare, I headed into the classroom, forgetting all about the text message.

rhett

Sawyer was still asleep when I entered her room with a glass of water an hour later. I'd tried to keep it together on the outside, but inside I was fumbling around in a panic. Stability had been the foundation of my life since Rowan's illness. My life was predictable, but that meant it was consistent.

Stable was manageable. Stable was comforting. Stable was safe.

Sitting on the edge of her bed, I watched her sleep like a creeper. My thoughts spiraled out of control because a person I cared for, *loved* even, had danger lurking around every corner. How could I protect her if I didn't even know who her enemy was?

Pulling out my phone, I sent off a few quick texts to Oliver and Fin so they'd be updated on the lunch cancellation, and then one to the whole group.

Oliver and Fin:

ME: Sawyer can't make lunch. Reschedule with Asa, please.

Family matters:

ME: Sawyer had a breakdown. Don't know more. Don't crowd her when you get home.

I turned it on silent, so I wouldn't have to deal with them while I was feeling this way. But I needed to do something; the anxiety was eating me alive. Pulling out my phone, I ignored the notifications and dialed.

"Rhett, honey? Is everything okay? How's Sawyer?" she asked immediately.

"Mom, I'm scared. I don't know how to keep her safe. Someone tried to run her off the road. How can I protect her from that?"

"Oh, Rhett, honey, that sounds terrifying! Is she okay? Do you need anything?"

"She's doing okay, just some minor things. But what if next time it's not? What do I do? How can I stop it?"

"Sweetie, you can't protect everyone from every-thing. It's just not feasible, even for you. All you can do is be there for her when she needs you. Give her the solid base to land and steady her. Is it going to be scary? Hell yes. Life is scary. Nothing is guaranteed. *Nothing.* But that doesn't mean you shouldn't live. And honey, you were right; you've been treading water, barely making waves these past years. Selfishly, I let you because I wanted you here, and I needed you. But Rhett, honey, it's time to step out of that comfort zone like you were saying last night. Otherwise, it will drag you down and suck the life out of you if you're not careful."

"But what if I fail again?"

The fear I'd been hiding behind hit me square in the chest at my admittance. I thought I had a handle on my feelings, managing the relationship I had, and even to some extent controlling the guys, but I was really just protecting myself. Giving myself an out in case things fell apart as they did before. If it was a shared relationship, I could blame it on that and not have to bear the responsibility.

Shit, I didn't want to be that type of man. I didn't want to be half in this relationship, only allowing vulnerability when it was easy. The truth had hurt, but now that I'd voiced it, I could see it was only my feeble attempt at control, but it was still an illusion.

Illusions were pretty, but they weren't real. I wanted the whole thing.

"So, what if you do?" questioned my mom. "Now, I haven't met this Sawyer, but the change I saw in you last night was real. Son, you were smiling on your own accord. You were happy and light. I hadn't seen that version of my son in years, so long I hadn't even noticed he'd been gone until I saw him again. You were right, and I realized how long it'd been since I'd heard you laugh and interact with your sister in a playful manner. That, to me, said everything I needed to know about her. I think you know this too. She's not Molly. I haven't even met her yet and I see the difference."

Taking a deep breath, I loosened my grip on my phone—everything she was saying resonated and solidified the truth in me.

"Thanks, Mom. You're right, I have been safe, and it's been boring as hell. Sawyer makes me feel, and I hadn't realized how much I was missing until I started feeling again. I think this is why I'm panicking. She means so much to me, and I just want to protect her."

"All you can do is be there. You can't fight her demons for her any more than she can fight yours for you, but what you can do is hold her hand, tell her how brave she is, and give her a port in the storm."

"You are a wise woman, Rhonda Taylor. I'll bring her by soon, I promise. Love you, Mom."

"Love you too, son. Tell the boys hi for me."

"Oh, wait. There was one more thing. Do you have any old pictures or newspapers from when you were a teenager? Or does the name Abernathy mean anything to you?"

"Hmm. It sounds vaguely familiar. I'll look through some boxes and get back to you. Call anytime, son. Bye."

"Bye."

Hanging up, I stayed staring at my hands for a few moments as I processed everything my mom had said to me. She always gave the best advice.

"Your mom sounds sweet," a soft voice said, causing me to whip my head up to see a barely awake Sawyer. Shit, I should've taken this out in the hall.

"Sorry, did I wake you? And, yes, my mom is the best. She wants to meet you, Rowan, too."

"I would love that."

Her smile called to me, so I reached over and clasped her hand. Her touch was soft and warm as I brushed my thumb across her palm.

"I don't want you to be scared for me."

Crap, she'd heard my phone call.

"It's not that, baby. I mean, I am worried for you, but I was using my fear to protect myself and allowing it to control me. I do want to protect you, but I realize now I can't, not from everything. I can be here, though. I can be your strength when you need it. So, can I, baby?"

"You already are, grumpy bear. From day one, you've been that solid and quiet strength filling me with assurance. I can't tell you how much that has meant. I don't think you understand how effortlessly you give yourself to everyone around you. This house, these guys," she shook her head, smiling. "They're the way they are because of you, grump. You're the glue, the mother hen, and the strength we all seek."

"You really see me like that?"

I was floored. I didn't do anything special. I was just here. She sat up, keeping a tight grip on my hand.

"That's what I'm talking about. You do it so effortlessly you don't even see it as a skill or a strength. We would all be a mess without you. I would be a mess without you. This might be the exhaustion talking, and frankly, I'll deny I ever said this if you bring it up, but damn, grump, you're the whole fucking package."

She moved up to her knees, clasping my face between her hands before she continued.

"Rhett, you are sexy as hell, but somehow not conceited. You're a romantic and not a playboy. You're caring, you listen, you love your mother and sister, and you take care of everyone without even being asked. I don't know where you got it in your head that you're inferior to everyone else, but it's wrong. I mean yeah, you don't have gold medals like some of the others, but well, neither do I. And okay, Soren's abs are better than yours, but yours are still nice to look at." She smiled and my heart soared.

"You did not just say that!"

She exploded into giggles, and I tackled her onto the bed. This right here, this was everything. Sawyer was right. I didn't need to do all the things in my mind I'd built up as needing to be worthy. There were skills I was naturally gifted in, and while it didn't seem like a huge thing, it was to those who weren't good at it. Taking care of the ones I loved was a huge task, and I'd never thought about it that way. It was just something I did, but seeing myself through her eyes, helped me know we all had a part to play. No one was more important than the other, and together we worked seamlessly. That was the reason why I didn't care about being in a relationship with them. It wasn't from fear, but from trust.

Lightly tickling her as I loomed over her, I got lost in her eyes. They were alight with mischief, and whatever she'd been plagued with earlier seemed far away now.

"Thank you, baby. I've never thought about it that way. How is your head feeling?"

"No issues, thankfully. Seems I was able to miss out on the concussion part."

"Elias said he found you earlier. Do you want to talk about it?"

"Not yet, but I will. I promise. I just want to be here, with you, in this moment right now."

"Oh, well, I could think of some other things that may help."

I started kissing her collarbone and down her neck. Instantly, she arched her back to allow me more access. Kissing Sawyer had become my favorite thing. She tasted like honey, and the sounds she made ignited my need for her every time. The self-imposed drought I'd been in had soon been replaced by Sawyer, and I wanted to consume every inch of her.

Just as I was about to run my hands under her shirt, a knock at her door halted them, especially as it was followed by the door opening. Dropping my head to her chest in frustration, I let out a groan at the interruption.

Sorry dude, I guess we weren't going to be getting our feel of her after all. I swear my cock just gave me the middle finger, not caring there was now another person in the room. Sawyer chuckled at my distress, the vixen.

"Oh my god, gross, you guys! I don't want to see any of this. Is it safe? Tell me it's safe, please!" Finley cried out, officially causing my boner to deflate instantly. I might be contemplating exhibitionism or whatever, but not with Finley in the room. Some lines you just didn't cross.

Groaning louder this time, I rolled off Sawyer and helped her sit up. Lucky barked at us from the floor, wanting our attention. Guess he'd jumped down off the bed when I'd launched my tickle fight earlier.

Fin picked him up on her way to us, plopping down on the opposite end from us with him in her arms. Lucky jumped out of them as soon as she'd sat and jumped into Sawyer's lap.

"So, is 'can't make lunch' code for sex now? Hmm? Is that why we had to reschedule? Seems a bit rude, guys," Fin huffed out, arms crossed as she waited for us to respond.

"Oh crap, what time is it?" Sawyer asked in a panic, frantically searching for her phone.

"Baby, I rescheduled because you fell asleep after Elias found you. Figured you had hit your emotional limit for the past few days."

Her smile of relief let me know I'd made the right call.

"Someone explain now, please! I'm tired of being the last to know anything."

I kicked Fin with my foot to lose the attitude. My eyebrow raise had her quieting for once in her life. Sawyer didn't need the guilt.

"I'll leave you; let me know if you need anything, baby."

Kissing her forehead before I got up, I headed out of her room. Turning before I closed the door, I smiled, seeing her and Fin talking in hushed whispers. Their friendship was obvious, and I was glad they'd found one another again. Fin needed her in her life, just as much as Sawyer did.

Mom's words settled in me more as I closed the door behind me. Fear would only cripple me, and I was tired of letting it. Sawyer deserved the best version of me, but I also deserved the best for myself. For the first time, the thought of unpredictability excited me.

twelve

. . .

sawyer

"SO, what's the verdict, Doc? Can I return to my normal daily program?" I snarked. I didn't want to be here anymore than necessary.

"Well, Ms. Sullivan, it seems you're cleared to return to regular activity. Be mindful of your head though, you will be more susceptible to concussions," he confirmed before walking out.

I'd never been so thoroughly dismissed, and he still hadn't introduced himself.

Wanker.

I was borrowing that from Elias. It seemed to fit the situation the best. In all honesty, though, I wasn't too upset about his behavior since I hadn't wanted to be here anymore than he did, apparently.

The past few days had been miserable as I waited

for this appointment. I was prepared to bribe him if he hadn't released me from my restrictions.

Sighing in relief, I redressed and headed out of the medical center. Soren was waiting for me in the lobby, since he was my lucky escort for the day. When he saw me, he jumped up and strolled toward me, a big smile on his face at the sight of me, making his dimple show.

Soren had rebounded back, mostly, to his jovial personality after my accident. I wasn't sure if it was because of it or something else, but I was glad to have my sunny, Chilly Willy back with me. This fact was emphasized when he picked me up and swung me around, causing me to laugh as I wrapped my legs around his waist.

"How do you know it was good news?" I asked, staring down at him.

"Your face is an open book, sweet pea. Plus, you weren't stomping and cussing out the doctor, so I figured it was a good guess." He chuckled, breathing into my neck.

His breath on my skin caused goosebumps to form, and I tightened my arms around him. He gripped my ass in his hands as he walked out the automated doors.

"Are you going to carry me the whole way to the cafeteria?"

"Yep," he retorted, popping that 'p' like it was his day job.

"You remember that part where I said it was good? I don't need to be carried."

"Oh, I remember all right. I just like to do it. I get to

put my hands all over you on campus, and no one will even bat an eye," Soren stated in a very suggestive tone, doing naughty things to my insides.

"I highly doubt that, Sor."

Chuckling, I gave in and laid my head down on his shoulder. It was kind of nice, and I got his clean scent all up in my nose this close. I wondered what he tasted like, smelling that good. Tentatively, I snuck my tongue out the briefest bit to see if he would notice. When he didn't react, I stuck it out some more, licking his neck with more of my tongue. This time, I felt him suck in a breath.

"Sweet pea, if you keep doing that, we won't make it to lunch."

"But you smell amazing. I just wanted to see if you tasted as good. You can only blame yourself, Chilly."

"Why do you keep calling me that freaking penguin, babe?"

"Because it fits you. Duh. The penguin is the cutest, but also chill and loves the snow. Ergo, Soren."

"Did you just use ergo in a sentence? Sweet pea, you're full of surprises."

We both laughed and were in a fit of giggles by the time we made it to the cafeteria. There wasn't enough time to go off campus for lunch, but I was desperate to hear what Oliver had to spill. It had been a couple of days since he'd asked, but with the emotional drain I'd felt, we'd all decided to wait until Saturday after I had my appointment.

Asa was going to be here too, and while I was

excited to see him again, part of me was nervous now. What if he had changed his mind over the past few days? What if he didn't want anything to do with me now?

I was a lot. I knew that. The shit in my life was enough to make any sane person run. What if Asa had figured that out? Being rejected by him would shatter my heart into a million pieces. Apparently, Soren could feel the dread in my body because he sat down on the rim of the fountain instead of entering into the cafeteria.

"Sawyer, what's going through that mind? You went quiet on me."

His hands caressed my face, and it felt like he was trying to read my soul with his eyes. How did his eyes make me want to confess my darkest fears?

Soren Stryker was dangerous in all the right ways. He made you believe you could trust him, and he wouldn't waste it. If there ever was a sure bet in life, it was that Soren, my Chilly Willy and cuddle monkey, had a pure soul. Despite all the horrors and darkness he'd faced, he'd managed to step into the light and wrap it around himself.

"What if he doesn't want to be my brother anymore? I'm too much, Soren. I know this. Everyone around me leaves eventually, even if not by their own choice. I've been alone for so long that discovering I have a twin brother just seems too good to be true, you know?" I shrugged my shoulder. "I'm scared." I tried to hide my head, but he wouldn't let me escape from this.

"Even if he decides that, which he won't, but even if

he did, Sawyer, you're not alone anymore. You have Rey and me always, and I know the other guys feel the same. I'm not letting you go, sweet girl. Can't you see you've captured me completely?"

I blinked. "Wow."

Soren smiled sweetly at me as my brain was stuck on what he'd just said.

"Come on now. I just gave you my best there, and all I get is a 'wow.' I want a redo. Now, try that again, but better."

This guy. I smiled, I couldn't help it. Even when he was sweet, he made it fun, reminding me who I was. Sticking my tongue out at him, I gave my best dramatic performance for my cuddle monkey.

"My stars, that's the sweetest and most romantic thing I've ever heard. Be still my heart!" I fake swooned in my best Southern Belle impression, falling into him in a fit of giggles, his hair tickling my nose.

"Much better. I feel properly appreciated now."

"You're such a dork, but thank you. I'm happy to have met you, even if you have a habit of picking me up. Now, come on—time to face the music. You're right, I'm not alone, and he'd be crazy not to want to be my brother despite all my drama. Come to think of it. He probably is crazy; he does like Fin after all," I said with a deadpan expression. I'd seen her approaching and knew she'd overhear me.

"Hey! You're the crazy one!"

A bout of laughter came over Soren and me as we

struggled to contain ourselves at my hilarity. At least Soren appreciated my comedic genius—about time.

Turning around on his lap, I realized that while I'd seen Fin, I hadn't taken in my blind spot to know she was holding the hand of Asa, my twin brother. Instantly, I sobered my expression as I took him in, trying to gauge his reaction.

"Hey, little sis!" Asa exclaimed. He pulled Fin along as he embraced Soren and me in an exuberant hug, almost causing us to fall back into the fountain. Soren overcorrected, causing us to all land on the grass instead.

"Oops." Asa chuckled as we all untangled ourselves, causing us all to laugh hysterically again. Relief washed through me at the realization he was excited to see me again and appeared to be just as much of an awkward klutz as me.

"How I never realized you guys were related before blows my mind! Seriously, you guys are eerily similar." Fin laughed as she brushed off the grass from her clothes.

"Well, you must like it since you've attached your-self to both of us, dork!" Fin and I stuck our tongues out at each other in a show of love.

"We ready to do this?" Soren questioned, sobering the mood.

"Yep. Let's see what bombs will explode today, shall we?" I quipped sarcastically, but felt it was likely an accurate prediction.

We walked into the cafeteria together as a united

front reinforcing in me I truly wasn't alone anymore. Bracing myself for whatever Oliver had to tell me, I was ready this time to face it.

Bring it, bitches.

oliver

The past few days had been the longest days of my life as I waited to share my family's past with Sawyer. Once I'd decided to tell her, I needed it to happen immediately.

Pacing back and forth in the small meeting room I'd reserved; I shoved my hands back into my pockets. I would keep pulling my hair if my hands were free, and I didn't want to look any more rumpled than I already felt.

My contact had already responded to me, and I was given clearance to share with Sawyer. It was cute that they thought they could control what I told her at this point. I owed her the truth, and she would get it all.

Just as I was about to pull my hands out of my pockets to tug at my hair again, the door opened, and Soren, Sawyer, Asa, and Finley entered, carrying take-out boxes of food. For once, I hadn't grabbed any, afraid I would throw it up before I finished talking.

Smiling timidly at Sawyer, I watched as she sat down and began to lock her emotions away. I couldn't blame her, but I hated to see her shut me out from her feelings or feel she had to protect herself because of me. That truth dagger hit me square in the chest, and I prayed she wouldn't hate me after I shared all this with her.

"Hey, guys."

"Hey, Ollie," chorused throughout the room in both male and female voices. Debating if I should sit or stand, I awkwardly crouched down, which only made it more uncomfortable.

"For fuck sakes, Ollie. Just sit down. You're making me anxious with all that anxiety rolling around," Finley shouted.

Flipping her off, everyone laughed as she responded by sticking her tongue out at me, which oddly helped lighten some tension. Deciding to man up, I sat across from Sawyer and stared at her. Asa sat on one side of her and Soren the other. Finley was close as well, all ready to comfort her or kick my ass; it was a toss-up which way this would go.

"Whatever it is, Ollie, I promise to listen and not explode. Did you, ahem, did you meet someone else? Is that what this is about? Or do you not want to be with someone who's got too much baggage? Whichever reason, I understand and promise to be nice to them."

Shock filled me, my jaw dropping open. I stared in stunned silence at Sawyer. That's what she was worried about? Fucking hell, I was the biggest asshat. I'd only been thinking of myself and not considering how my behavior might've been perceived or made her feel.

Shit. Snapping my mouth shut, I adamantly shook my head no.

"No, pretty girl. None of that. What I have to tell you has to do with my family. Do you remember that day I baked you cookies, and we talked a little about our families?"

"Yeah, you said you were the black sheep because you followed hockey instead of going into the family business or something." Her nose scrunched up as she tried to recall the conversation.

"Yes, exactly. What I didn't mention, what I failed to realize the importance of, was when I went to college and the NHL, I had to change my last name. If I wasn't going to carry on the family legacy, I hadn't earned the use of the surname. My mother's family name was Windsor, that was what I took as my own, but before that," I paused, clearing my throat and took a deep inhale of breath before I revealed my dark secret. Looking directly into Sawyer's eyes, I begged my emotions to convey the truth I spoke.

"Before that I was Oliver Latimer. My uncle is Jayce Latimer."

Stunned silence followed my declaration as I continued to hold Sawyer's gaze. A single tear fell down her cheek, and I wondered if my secret had irrevocably shattered something with no hope of repair.

"Holy shit, dude," Soren bellowed, breaking the moment between Sawyer and me as we both turned to look at him.

"What does this mean?" Asa questioned. He looked

to be holding Sawyer's hand, but it was hard to confirm from my position. Her face was blank, and I wasn't confident she was still listening at this point.

"I learned about the family business when I was a teenager. One summer, I was required to do an internship to see what branch of the business I would fit in. I was disgruntled before it even started because I was missing hockey camp. My family didn't understand my passion for hockey, which was part of the appeal; it was away from them." I took a deep breath, needing a moment.

"Even before I knew the horrible things my family was balls deep in, the toxicity rolled off them, and I avoided it as much as possible. There was a pretty significant age gap between my older siblings and me, so I was often left to my own devices, which suited me just fine, to be honest. That summer, I was assigned a two-week rotation at each branch of the company. There are four divisions, and they all deal with imports and exports due to the business's shipping aspect. Human trafficking is the largest, followed by drugs, weapons, and counterfeit goods. They can control a lot of the shipping manifests and pay off people in areas where they can't."

Taking a sip of water on the table, I didn't care whose it was. I needed it. Sitting it back down, I evaluated everyone's reaction. They were all staring at me with a mixture of horror, sadness, and pain. The pain was mostly reflected in Sawyer's eyes. Not sure what to do with it; all I could do was continue at this point.

"When I was being scouted by colleges, I'd already been blacklisted by my family and was in the process of emancipating myself. One night after a game, I thought a scout was waiting for me, but when he approached me, I could tell he was a scout of a different nature. Fear filled me, thinking I was about to be taken out. But then he introduced himself as Agent B and would only tell me he worked for 'the Agency.' That night he didn't disclose much, just that he would be in touch and that there was another way. Over the years, he's contacted me and checked in to see if I was ready."

I stopped, needing a moment to gather myself. Recalling these things was difficult. I'd buried them long ago, and pulling them back up was requiring more effort than I'd known, and I wasn't sure it was worth it if Sawyer was going to hate me.

"Ready for what?" asked a small voice, causing me to lift my head I hadn't realized had dropped. Sawyer stared at me, appearing to have digested everything despite the faraway look in her eyes. Swallowing, I hesitated before delivering the last thing—my final truth.

"To stop my family."

"That sounds like a good thing. Why do you seem so hesitant?" Soren or Asa asked. I wasn't paying attention to the others. I had all my focus on a pair of green eyes —on the girl who'd made me feel worthy for just being myself and nothing more.

"Because in order to stop my family, I have to join them and then kill them before they kill me."

thirteen

. . .

sawyer

SITTING THERE, listening to Oliver, had left me feeling bereft. Yep, fucking bereft. Why did these people keep popping up at times to ruin my life? First, right before World's, and now, just as I was getting answers and finding people I connected with, they were trying to sabotage my relationships.

What. The. Fuck.

I was over these douchecanoes. They could take a ride off a deep cliff for all I cared. So, when Oliver delivered his last statement, I didn't respond the way he'd anticipated.

"Because in order to stop my family, I have to join them and kill them before they kill me."

Laughter erupted out of me suddenly, causing Fin to squeak in alarm, which, unfortunately, only made me laugh even louder. No one joined in with me, though, making my laughter ring out through the small meeting room. Eventually, I caught my breath, wiping the tears away from my eyes as I gathered myself.

"I'm sorry. But you're a fucking idiot, Ollie."

His jaw dropped, and he stared at me in shock as my words registered. Pushing back from the table, I stood and walked around to him. Ollie was so stunned he didn't even notice when I pulled; well, I tried to pull his chair back. The big brute weighed too much, and I fell into his lap from the recoil. Soren and Fin chuckled behind me at my display. Go ahead fuckers; I'll remember this. Of course, now they laughed when my ass was in the air.

"Welp, not how I'd intended to get here, but all the same."

Shrugging, I sat up and straddled his lap instead of laying in it. Much better position for a conversation. Not that I wouldn't want to have a conversation with his dick, but my brother and best friend were in the room, and I wasn't about that level of sharing.

My clumsiness was good for one thing at least, as it seemed to have shaken some of the shock away from Ollie's face. He stared at me with a confused expression before a small grin lifted his lips. Grabbing his face between my hands, I forced him to look at me.

"Ollie, you're an idiot because you kept this to yourself for too long. Does it give me the creeps to think that the man who wanted to sell me is your uncle? Of course. But it doesn't change who you are to me or what I think we can have. That's why you're an idiot."

I rubbed his cheeks with my thumbs in soothing circles, trying to comfort him. I could see a lot of pain in his eyes and maybe some doubt, whether it was about me, the situation, or himself, I wasn't sure, but it was there, all the same.

"You're also an idiot because if you think for one second I would ever let you put yourself in danger, then you have another thing coming. I just met you, Oliver Windsor, and I don't plan to lose you already. I think you need to be reminded of something I'm learning as well. You're not in this alone—not anymore. Besides, who's going to bake me all the things? Hmm?"

Some of his sadness melted away as I'd switched from rubbing his cheeks to squeezing them and squishing them together. Nothing like a good cheek squish to turn the mood.

"You're really annoying, you know?" mumbled out of Ollie's mouth as I continued to squish his cheeks.

"I'm sorry, did you say, I'm really wonderful? Why, that's so kind of you. I do think I'm pretty awesome."

I grinned big as I dropped my hands, and he finally granted me his classic Ollie look. This fucking boy with his cocksure smile, making my heart go all pitter-patter. A throat cleared behind us, reminding me that no, we were not, in fact, alone. Whoops.

Turning in his lap, I faced the rest of the group, who were all smiling at us. Ollie's arms wrapped around me from behind, holding my midsection, offering me support in his lap. Scooting back, I felt him tense as he tried to stop me from moving around too much, and when I felt the hard outline of his cock against my ass, I understood why.

Oops. You know what, nah, I liked that I had this effect on him. It helped validate my own desire.

When I looked up, Soren's lifted eyebrow caught my attention, and I just knew he'd seen that little move play out. Shaking my head, all I could do was chuckle. Looking over at Asa and Fin, I saw Fin's knowing grin and amusement as well. Guess, everyone saw the effect I was having on Ollie. I started to smirk until I noticed how uncomfortable Asa appeared.

Oh yeah, it was probably weird finding out you had a sister, and then she was groping your teammate. Straightening, I pulled myself together, wanting to help ease some of my twin's discomfort. It was strange thinking of someone that way, but also nice to put someone else first. Soren, in his magic, saw the moment for what it was and took the lead to transition us into a new topic.

"So, where do we go from here? What's next now that we've all decided Ollie was dumb?"

"Hey!"

"What? You were bro!"

"Fine," he grumbled behind me. Ollie pulled me closer to his chest, dropping his chin on my shoulder. His spice scent surrounded me, and I was happy I'd chosen to sit in his lap. I think we both needed the reassurance of touch, currently. I was finding out more and more I was a touchy-feely person when it was with people I liked. I'd missed his fun personality as well, and it helped that his big mouth often got him in trouble as much as mine did.

"Anyway, focus. What's this Agency and who is this Agent guy? Anyone else feel like we entered some bad TV drama?" Fin mumbled. Chuckling at her comment because it was true, I focused back on the deep rumble I could feel as Ollie talked.

"I don't know much, just what I told you. But he's here in Utah. I met with him the other day."

"Do you think he would meet with us?" Asa asked. His concern radiated through his words, and it filled me with a sense of belonging to know we were family. This was what I'd been searching for my whole life— connection.

"I can always ask." Ollie shrugged, forgetting he was wrapped around me, causing me to move with his movement. More giggles erupted out of me as I felt his stubble rub against my neck. The smile on Fin's face, and even Soren's, helped me relax more into Ollie's embrace. We would figure this out—together.

I was itching to get back on the ice after a few days of nothing, so when Ollie asked if I wanted to skate with him, I jumped at the opportunity. It would feel nice just to skate and not train for a day too.

We stopped by the house so I could change and grab my skates. I had two pairs, but the others were in my locker in the skating rink, and Ollie wanted to show off the hockey rink. Not really caring where we skated, I happily agreed to just spend some time with him. The past week had put space between us that I wanted to remedy quickly.

"So, what's so special about the hockey rink? Huh?"

"You'll see. It's not something you can explain. It's definitely a 'you won't believe it unless you see it' thing." Ollie chuckled, and I realized how much I liked the sound.

"Okay, but you do remember that not only did I work at an ice rink where you know, hockey was played, but I also dated two hockey players in high school. Right?" His look of outrage caused me to laugh again for the millionth time today. Gah, I missed this with him.

"First, and no offense, but this is not a rinky-dink public ice rink, and second, I can't believe you just admitted you have a thing for hockey players. I knew I was your favorite. It's okay. I often make girls shy." He beamed, winking, and laughed as I stared at him in shock.

I took it back. I didn't miss him. Nope. Nuh-uh.

Slapping him on the chest, I slammed my mouth shut and stormed off like I was upset—that would teach him to pick on me. Before I was even two steps away, I was lifted from behind by the behemoth.

"Eek!"

His arms wrapped around me and lifted me up high.

"Put me down!" I shouted as I smacked the arms around me, which, unfortunately, only caused him to laugh more. Jerk.

He continued to carry me, bag and all, as he walked the rest of the way to the rink. It probably made quite the picture with my tiny frame squirming in his big man arms. Eventually, I hung there as deadweight to see if it had any effect, but alas, it didn't appear to have made any impact except to make him snicker at me more.

Awesomesauce—cue eye roll.

Hanging in his arms, I felt like a petulant child in trouble, so I pushed out my bottom lip in an exaggerated pout, folding over my arms.

Finally, the rink loomed in front of us, and he set me down on my feet. Gently, he turned me by my shoulders, but my head was lowered as I avoided his gaze. My arms were still crossed, and my pout game was strong when he lifted my chin delicately. I wasn't expecting the look I found on his face when I finally looked at him.

His eyes were crossed, his face screwed up in a weird expression, and his tongue was sticking out. Immediately, I burst out laughing, breaking the fake pout facade I'd had going on. Ollie, fortunately, joined me in laughter as we held onto one another's arm for support. After a few minutes, we started to gather our breath again, and he wiped some of my tears that had leaked out. His touch was gentle and stilled me in place.

"I'm sorry I shut myself off from you and created this space between us. I'm not used to people caring about me or believing in me to be more than the screw-up. So, when I heard your story and how my family was connected to it. Well, I just saw another door slamming in my face. Another reminder of how much my family has taken."

His pain was evident on his face, and my heart broke a little for him. As upset as I was for him pulling away, I got it. When people always told you that you were nothing, it was hard not to believe it, even when the evidence suggested otherwise.

"Ollie, what matters is now. Believe me, there are a million mistakes I've made and a million more I'll still make. Owning our flaws and committing to ourselves to do better is what I care about. So, let's make a pact to hold one another accountable to quiet the voices. "

"I'd like that, Sawyer."

His smile was one of the sweetest I'd seen on his face. Pure and simple, with no agenda.

"Now, let me show you around."

Taking my hand, Ollie led me through the automated doors. The guard at the front nodded at Ollie in respect, and it made me realize how revered he was here. How did Ollie not see it? I think we were blind to the positive things in life when we were only used to all the negatives.

Ollie pulled me along as I took in the hockey rink. He was right, this wasn't an ordinary ice rink. It was an ice rink on steroids. It was something that would be featured on MTV Cribs. The entrance and concession areas were more upscale than most professional rinks. It was bananas!

"The JV team is finishing up a practice, but by the time we get skated up, it should be almost over."

Entering the locker rooms, I was left speechless for a minute. The figure skating locker rooms were nice, but these were incredible. Dropping his hand, I twirled around, taking in all the extravagance. Each locker had its own mini area with a leather chair, small desk, and then varied with mini-fridges, beanbag chairs, and gaming systems. They could almost stay here and never leave if they had a bed.

Ollie watched me as I soaked it all in, my mouth hanging open as I discovered the wall of TVs surrounded by several leather reclining chairs. It was crazy cool and had sports and news on from all over the world, including every hockey game that was televised. They even had a kitchen area that looked state of the art with an onsite chef. As I kept walking, I found a barbershop and a full spa area down the corridor.

"Damn. This is like the athlete epi-center here. I'm suddenly wishing I played hockey."

"This isn't even all of it."

"You're kidding, right? What else could you need? Seriously, I'm starting to think figure skating is the stepchild of this school," I declared mockingly.

Ollie showed me over to the staff area, and we stored our gear in his locker. Lacing up my skates always filled me with mixed emotions, as there wasn't a moment of skating that didn't remind me of my parents. Still, there was also a lot of joy, strength, and confidence that accompanied me.

That was something I was learning. Something might cause sadness or pain, but I didn't have to avoid it. Most things in life had both experiences, and it didn't discount the good ones just because something also made you sad. Both things could be true.

Walking out of the locker room together, the sounds of skates, stick slaps, and grunting filled the air. I could see the team on the ice as they practiced drills. Hockey was an intense sport that required an equal balance of grace and aggression, and I loved it.

Something about the rush of the plays, and the strength of the players always drew me in. The hot guys that played didn't hurt either. I never thought I had a type, but thinking about it now, it seemed athletes were definitely my type, which was useful when I spent the majority of my time around them. I could make out a few students as they huddled around their coach.

"Is it okay to warm up on this end of the ice?"

"Yeah, go ahead. They should be heading off soon."

Stepping out onto the ice, I skated to an empty area and began to warm up my muscles by skating around and stretching my arms. The sound of the whistle blowing caused me to glance over as the hockey players huddled up. Ollie had skated over to them and was standing with the other coach, talking with him. The students all patted Ollie on his back as they headed off the ice, once again showing me how respected he was by these guys.

Ollie saw me looking and waved me over to them. I could make out dark blonde hair that was short around the ears but long on top with some curly wave to it. He was leaning on his hockey stick as he talked, and I couldn't help but appreciate the way it made his butt pop out. Realizing I was staring at his butt, I pulled my eyes up, only to discover Ollie had caught me if his smirk was any indicator. Crap.

I'd almost reached them when the guy turned and saw me. Shock, surprise, and happiness crossed his features in rapid succession, which probably mirrored my own. Somehow, I'd stopped when he'd turned, frozen in my tracks, so when he skated toward me, I wasn't prepared.

"Sawyer!" was exclaimed, before I was picked up, again, I might add, and spun around.

"I can't believe it's you, that you're here. How is this possible? I've missed you so much!" It was all rushed out at me before he leaned down and kissed me. That was right, kissed me.

Fuck me. How the hell was this possible? It was starting to feel like anyone from my past was bound to be at this school. Because the man who was kissing me as if he might never stop, well, that was none other than my friends with benefits partner, Tyler Matthews.

The worst part, his kiss had never felt this way before. Guess my Altitude Delirium was back in full force, the hussy bitch.

fourteen

. . .

oliver

"SAWYER!" I yelled at the petite blonde who skated so fast I almost thought she was a speed skater.

She kept skating and didn't look back as I called out after her. My heart raced as I watched her go. What the hell had just happened? I thought I was bringing her here to skate, to do something we both loved together, and now she was skating away from me.

This past week had been Hell, and I wanted things with us to move forward, but nothing in my life seemed to be that easy. Turning toward Tyler—my longtime friend and teammate—I looked at him in a state of shock.

"What the hell just happened? How do you know Sawyer?" I asked him, my brows raised in question.

"Better question, how do *you* know Sawyer?" He placed his hands on his hips, staring at me.

He looked pissed, and I didn't know why. Guess he wanted me to answer first.

"She's my roommate. The girl I was telling you about, that called me out on the first day."

He relaxed, shoulders slumping forward, looking defeated looking now. I knew I wasn't the brightest guy, but I really seemed to have missed the plot here. Finally, he looked up, sorrow in his eyes.

"You remember in high school when we attended hockey camp?"

"Yeah, of course."

"Well, do you remember how my Junior and Senior year I would talk about the girl I was in love with, but who only saw me as a friend? Who I had a 'friends with benefits' arrangement with Josh?"

"Yeah." I stopped, not liking where this was headed. But also, not wanting to admit it out loud.

"Well, that girl was Sawyer, and I haven't seen her in a few years." He stared at me, trying to communicate something important, but again, I think my brain had stopped.

Tyler was a few years younger than me, but we attended the same camps each year and had become best friends. When he made the same college team as me, we'd become even closer. He was a true friend to me, and I remembered him talking about a girl and how amazing she was, but how she wouldn't take things further.

At the time, I thought he was an idiot. A hot girl

sexing you up and didn't want commitment—sounded perfect.

But now that I knew Sawyer, I could understand his frustration. She was someone you'd want more with despite the scariness of commitment; she was someone who made commitment worth it. I just didn't know where that left us now. My shoulders deflated too. We stared at one another, misery and uncertainty reflected on both of our faces.

"Want to grab a beer in town and talk?"

"Yeah. That sounds like a good idea," he sighed.

We headed off the ice, our movements slow and steady as we both seemed to be dreading the conversation about to occur.

"What can I get you, boys?" the waitress asked as she placed two coasters on the booth we were sitting in. Neither of us had said much on the way over, almost as if we needed the alcohol to talk.

"Two of whatever's your special," Tyler responded. I was thankful he'd taken the initiative because I wasn't sure I could even remember beer brands. Though, to be fair, he didn't appear to either by ordering the special. Snorting, I looked up at him as the waitress walked away.

"What? Does it really matter what it is?"

"No, I was just thinking I couldn't remember brands

and was thankful you'd ordered, but then I realized you didn't either. I guess that means your head is just as confused about all of this as mine."

Tyler watched me for a minute, almost as if he was trying to read my mind. His shaggy, dark blonde hair hung in his focused green eyes. Ever since I'd known him, he'd been this easy-going guy, who got along great with all of his teammates, and worked hard. His only downfall in hockey was that he wasn't aggressive enough to make it professionally. But his usual smile was nowhere to be found, and I felt I might be seeing a side of him few ever had. I just wasn't sure if it was a good thing or not.

"Do you have feelings for her?" Tyler finally asked.

"I'm not sure if that matters, but yes, I do."

My answer confused him as he scrunched up his brow and nose. Before he could ask a follow-up question, the waitress returned and set down our pints. She tried to capture both of our attention by leaning over and placing the menus in the middle, making her boobs practically spill out of her top. Typically, I'd be all over her, but it didn't interest me anymore.

Once I'd quit hiding from my past, it'd become evident I used sex as a way to distract myself, and I was done avoiding it. Tyler never even wavered his focus, only cementing him in my mind as a good guy. I had to believe his feelings were real, and even when I thought back to college, he hadn't been one of the typical hockey guys plowing any girl that threw themselves at him—unlike myself.

"There's more going on that I can't tell you about, but for now, just know that I do care for her. It's just," I sighed, shaking my head. "I'm not sure if, and I can't believe I'm saying this out loud, I'm good enough for her. I have a lot of shit I need to deal with. I'm working on building trust and proving to myself I could be the man she needs."

"I can respect that. So where does that leave me?"

"Pftt." Blowing out some air, I wavered on how much to tell him. He wasn't part of our group, but he was Tyler. Pulling out my phone, I wasn't sure why I hadn't thought of this first.

ME: We have a situation. Another guy with a history with Sawyer.
Rhett: Explain.
ME: It's too hard over text. I'm at the bar now with him. Meet us?
Rhett: 5 mins.

"This is more complicated, believe it or not, than just two teammates liking the same girl. There are, I guess, six of us, maybe, that like her."

"What the fuck, Oliver?"

"Just let me explain. It's not what you're thinking. You see…"

I filled him in on the housing placement and dating situation we'd all found ourselves in with Sawyer, making sure to leave out anything about her history before he met her, or mine for that matter. That was

Sawyer's decision to make if he was to be brought into the trust circle.

"So, what," he paused, blinking, "you're all dating her?"

Interestingly enough, he wasn't outraged or disgusted, bonus points for that. He wasn't giving much away either though, so I couldn't tell if he was going to run from the table, effectively ruining all of our reputations, or laugh at us all and our stupidity. Swallowing down half of my beer in one gulp, I wiped the foam off my mouth with the back of my hand.

Tyler appeared to be thinking still as he stared at me. About what, I wasn't sure, and the more it went on, the more uncomfortable I became. His gaze was calculated now, assessing me. Squirming in my seat, my heart started to race under his gaze, and I weirdly wanted to know what he'd found. Was I enough?

Just as I was about to cave and ask him what his look meant, Rhett walked up to the booth.

"Hmph," was grunted at me, my clue to move my ass over. Rolling my eyes, I picked up my beer and scooted in, thankful we'd picked one of the bigger booths; otherwise, Rhett's giant ass wouldn't have fit next to mine.

"Tyler, Rhett." I indicated to both as I swallowed more of my lukewarm beer. Wincing because it tasted like shit, but I drank more just for something to do.

"So, what's the situation?" Rhett asked after giving his best resting asshole face to Tyler. Mad respect for

Tyler, though, who didn't even flinch. He had balls of steel; perhaps he would be worthy.

"I'm not sure how much Sawyer has told you about her past, or even what happened today, but Tyler was one of her friends with benefits during high school for a couple of years. So, when I took Sawyer skating, this numbnuts saw her and then kissed her. Sawyer freaked out, skated off the ice, and then we talked, and I realized he wasn't some random guy, but someone with a history to her. I've known Tyler for years, and he's always talked about a girl he was in love with, and apparently, that's our Sawyer. So," I raised my hands in front of me, "I'm not sure where that leaves us, but we all agreed to talk about things, so here we are, talking."

More exhausted after rehashing that, I swallowed down the remaining dregs of my beer and contemplated stealing Tyler's that still sat untouched on the table.

"What are your intentions?" Rhett demanded, laying it out there.

I swear, some days, you couldn't take Rhett out of the house. Coughing up the drink I'd just swallowed, I turned to Rhett and gave him a strange look.

"What?" Rhett barked when he looked at me. Shaking my head because sometimes, this guy was fucking clueless.

"You sound like her father when you say shit like that. Listen, I told him the score. We need to talk to Sawyer before you go and start making dowry arrangements. Come on, let's just go back to the house. We're not going to get anywhere here."

Pushing him on the arm to get out of the booth, I pulled out some cash as I waited and tossed it down onto the table. Tyler, surprisingly enough, followed suit. Rhett looked at me oddly, until giving himself a nod, and finally moved out of my way. Time to find Sawyer, and hopefully, this time, she wouldn't run from me.

fifteen

. . .

mateo

MY AFTERNOON WAS FINALLY open since I'd completed my volunteer hours. However, it was more like voluntold hours since it hadn't been a choice. At least, I had it out of the way for a while. The concession stands had been the absolute pits. It was enough to make a person question attending here. Not because they were messy, but because the kitchen manager was a Gordon Ramsey wannabe. If I wanted to be yelled at while selling hot dogs, I would work in a kitchen. It was hot dogs, for crying out loud. The man was mental.

Stepping into the house, I found it empty, which was surprising with as many people who lived here. I didn't remember having a moment to myself since I'd arrived. Not that my time with the guys or Sawyer had been awful, the opposite actually. But being an introvert, I hit my limit of people at times. Wanting to take the opportunity to unwind, I decided to watch my favorite movies.

It was a guilty pleasure and something I did in secret. Spending hours on a charter bus for training and competitions, I found a way to kill time since I didn't want to talk to the other athletes. I'd messed around with coding for a while, but eventually got bored of it. One night, one of my teammates was watching a movie on their computer and while I was annoyed at first since they hadn't turned the volume down, the words had spoken to me in a way I never expected.

I know what you're thinking—a teenage hormonal boy alone on a bus watching movies, must be porn. Sorry to disappoint, but I was a die-hard Mousehead and D23er.

With Netflix at my fingertips, I fell headfirst in love with Disney movies. From *Frozen* to *Fantasia*, I loved it all.

Settling in, I queued up my most recent favorite, *Onward*. I popped in my earbuds and relaxed back on the bed. Just as the bad guy was about to get his dues, my door flew open, followed by Lucky racing and jumping on my bed. I was so shocked to be pulled out of my movie zone that I was slow to react to the intrusion. Quickly, I sat up and shut my computer, not at all suspicious, nope. Sawyer was talking and looking at me weird when I realized I still had my earbuds in.

"Sorry, I didn't hear you. What did you say?"

"I was asking what you were up to. I knocked but

didn't hear anything. When I was leaving, that guy nosed his way in the crack, so sorry about that."

Sawyer shuffled on her feet, her awkwardness standing out, and I couldn't decide if I should ask about it or let it go. Sawyer saved me making the decision in the end, but I kind of wished she hadn't.

"So, you don't have to be embarrassed about watching porn. It's natural and all that. I don't want you to feel like you have to hide things."

Stunned by her statement, I stared as she bit her lip. Slowly, the words penetrated my brain, causing my face to flame red.

"Um, uh, no, that's not, I mean, IT'S NOT PORN!" I shouted, before I realized my volume.

"Really, Mateo, it's okay." She held her hands up, looking at me with concern.

Vigorously shaking my head no, I stood up with my computer in one hand as I walked toward her.

"Here, let me show you. It's not what you think. Still embarrassing, but not *that*."

Grabbing her hand, I pulled her toward the desk and sat her in my chair as I placed my laptop in front of her. Taking a deep breath, I slowly lifted the lid. I was standing off to the side, so her face was visible to witness her reaction.

At first, she almost looked as if she was cringing because she expected porn to pop up. Then, she seemed confused as the movie played, unsure what she was seeing. But once recognition flitted through her head, a smile stretched across her face.

"See, not porn." Proving my point, I shut my computer, hoping she'd leave it at that, and sat on the bed with it in my hands.

"I'm sorry, your reaction just made me think it was something else. Is there a reason you're embarrassed?" she asked, watching me, her face wrinkled in concern.

I wasn't sure how to respond. So, I sat there for a few minutes, gathering my thoughts before I answered her. "I don't know. It's just not something people accept, I guess, especially because I'm a guy. I'm just used to being judged, and I've always hidden it for that reason."

She nodded, moving closer to me. "I can understand that, but you don't have to feel that way anymore, Mateo. One thing I'm learning here is to trust myself and the people around me. No one in this house will judge you, but it's also your choice, and don't feel pressured to share something if you don't want to. That's the other side of it. Sometimes, trusting people means trusting them even when you don't know all the details."

Something about what she said made sense, and I wondered if there was something in her own life she was referring to. Understanding and acceptance trickled through me, and I realized Sawyer was right. I wasn't living in the past anymore. By embracing who I was, I wouldn't have to hide my interests or fear persecution for liking something different.

Okay, that might be a little extreme, but part of me would always feel like the loser baby brother to my successful older siblings. It was hard not to constantly compare myself to them, but something I would work on.

"You're right. It's just been something I didn't talk about for so long that it didn't even seem odd not to share it. Would," I stopped, clearing my throat, "would you want to watch it with me?"

Her answering smile let me know I'd asked the right question. We snuggled back on the bed, and I hit play on the laptop. Cuddling with Sawyer was perfect, and I soon found myself watching her more than the movie. Her expressions at moments were far more entertaining to me than the movie. Her little gasps, smiles, and coos drew me in like a moth to a flame. I was so captivated by her I wasn't even aware the movie credits were rolling until she turned to me.

"Mateo?"

"Hmm."

"Were you watching me instead of the movie?"

"Yeah, actually. I found you to be quite entertaining."

I wasn't sure where the purr in my voice came from, but the heated look in her eyes told me she liked it. Taking a moment to remember to breathe, I bent down and kissed her lips. Softness met mine as I captured her mouth in a gentle kiss. Turning more, I followed her down to the bed until I was lying over the top of her. Kissing Sawyer had become my new favorite hobby, and I was determined to get a gold medal.

sawyer

After Tyler had kissed me, I'd acted like a chicken and booked it out of there so fast I was sure they were still eating my skate ice dust. I hadn't even gone back to the locker room, just grabbed my skate guards and walked out of the rink and ran home in my socks.

In September.

In Utah.

Yeah, not my best idea, but my freak-out meter was on high alert. Hard to think logically under those conditions.

When I arrived at the house, I immediately went to my room and changed. I was headed to the fitness room when I'd noticed Mateo's door ajar. Lucky nosed his way in, and I was glad for it as we made out on his bed.

Mateo's kisses were soft and passionate. Each time we kissed, it felt more and more intimate. He put so much emotion in each graze I could almost feel his longing with each swipe of his tongue fueling me with his passion.

His body weight settled on top of me, and my pent-up sexual frustration returned with a vengeance. It had been a few days since the accident, and my vagina was not happy about that, apparently. She wanted Mateo, and she wanted him now.

Locking my legs around his waist, I pulled him

closer to me, allowing the parts of us that wanted to be together to, well, be together. I could feel his hardness through his jeans and pulled him into me more. Breaking away to catch some air, I started to kiss down his neck, nipping his earlobe as I went.

The moan that my sweet boy let out showed me just how naughty he could be. His hands began to travel up my shirt, swirling circles on my belly. He seemed hesitant at first, but as I continued to kiss his neck, he became more frenzied. Mateo's hands reached my breasts, and he pushed my bra up over them as he began to rub my nipples.

"Yes, that feels good. Touch me all over."

He complied by pushing my shirt and bra up and over my head. He stared at me for a minute, almost as if he was debating something. Mateo must have decided quickly, because before I could say anything else, he took my breast into his mouth and sucked on my nipple. For someone who was still new to this, he was picking it up quickly. Grabbing his ass, I pulled him closer into me as I ran my hands up his back, pushing his shirt up in the process.

"Best movie ending ever," I joked as we continued to ravish one another.

His chuckle was deep and sexy, and I loved seeing this side of him. Wanting to show him something more, I twisted my hips and propelled us over, landing with me on top, straddling him. His dazed expression at first made me want to laugh, but then his grin at being manhandled set me on fire.

"That was hot."

"I'm glad you liked it. I want to show you something new if you're up for it."

I didn't think words were capable of coming from him as he nodded his head vigorously. Starting with kisses on his chest, I began to make my way down his body. Licking and nipping as I went. His moans and hips lifted, demonstrating he was enjoying the work my tongue was doing.

When I got to his jeans, I popped the button and slowly pulled the zipper down, brushing his cock with my fingers as I did. His corresponding groan was music to my ears. Pushing his boxers down, his cock sprung forward, and I finally got a good look at it.

Last time I hadn't been positioned well enough to see what I was working with, so now I took a moment to drink him in. His dick had a perfect bellend with thick veins along the ridges. Lowering down, I began to lick around the tip, swirling my tongue.

Grasping the base of him in my hand, I pumped the lower half as I licked from the top down until I met my hand. Mateo's moans were sinful, and I think he was enjoying the attention. Tentatively, he placed his hands in my hair, more to hold onto, than direct me.

Taking him in my mouth this time, I sucked him down to his base as I swirled my tongue down his length. His dick hit the back of my throat, and I was able to swallow him down a little more before my gag reflex kicked in. Lifting back up, I sucked the tip again, taking in the precum that was now leaking from him.

His hands gripped my hair tighter as I continued to lavish his cock with sucks and tongue swirls. I could feel his muscles tightening up, and before he even had time to tell me, I felt him start to come into my mouth. Swallowing it down quickly, I licked him up and down one more time before popping him out.

Looking up through my eyelashes, I took in his expression. Serene bliss covered his face, and I took that to mean a job well done. Female pride rang through me as I sat back on my haunches. Lightning quick, he sat up and tackled me back onto the bed, erupting giggles out of me that soon turned into moans.

That afternoon I introduced Mateo to the art of cunnilingus. Let's just say he was a quick learner, and my pussy was appeased with the three orgasms he gave me, all in the name of practice. Hot damn!

sixteen

. . .

sawyer

BUZZ. *Buzz.*

Something was buzzing against my leg, effectively waking me up. Shifting, I moved closer to Mateo and wrapped my arm over his naked chest. His arm banded against me as well, keeping me firmly in place. Falling asleep after our steamy make-out session hadn't been the plan, but I wasn't in any hurry to get up. The things I had run away from hours ago would still be waiting for me outside this room.

"You keep buzzing," mumbled a sleepy Mateo.

"I know. I'm avoiding," I mumbled back into his chest.

"Sawyer," he said, his voice stern, and I knew he wouldn't let me keep hiding.

"Ugh, not you too."

Hiding my face under my hair, I tried to block out

the light. I didn't know why I was acting this way. Tyler and Oliver didn't deserve my two-year-old avoidance tactics. Plus, this wasn't who I was anymore, but something about the situation terrified me.

I think I was scared of what it meant, and if I took a closer look at my feelings, how would things change? Didn't I have enough change already?

Deciding that I did, in fact, have enough shit to deal with, I burrowed further into Mateo.

"Sawyer."

I knew he was trying to be stern, but that authoritative voice he used made me hot and bothered again. Eventually, he gave up getting my attention and rolled us over, capturing me beneath him. Now, I had to either look at him or be a jackass and keep my eyes closed, pretending I couldn't see him. It wasn't my finest moment.

"Open your eyes, Sawyer. I don't go away just because you can't see me."

Damn, he was onto me. Sticking out my tongue, I slowly peeked one eye open and then the other. Momentarily taken aback by his beauty, I stared into ocean blue eyes. His glasses had been removed when we fell asleep, and his eyes always seemed more intense without a shield covering them.

"Hey."

"Dulzura, what is it? Did you get some news? Did someone try to attack you again?"

Sobering realness settled in me at his statement. Fuck. I was being a wuss for a lame reason. I needed to pull up my big girl panties and woman up. Releasing a slow breath, I centered myself.

"No, nothing like that. Thank you for reminding me I have bigger things going on and that I can manage this. Pfft," blowing a raspberry at the end, I realized what I needed to do.

"Sawyer, whatever it is, you don't have to do it alone anymore. You are so much stronger than you see yourself, you know."

I swear he winked at the end of that.

"Why does it sound so much better when you say it?" I asked, laughing.

It bubbled out of me, causing Mateo to grace me with a rare smirk on his handsome face. Yep, he'd definitely winked earlier, the saucy boy.

"Maybe it's the accent? Or maybe, it's because deep down, you know I'm right but don't want to admit it."

"Mmm. Nope. That can't be it. Definitely, the accent. Yup, going with that."

I shook my head dramatically, causing Mateo to move with me. Mateo's smile lit up his face, and his hair cascaded down around him. His eyes shone with humor, distracting me from his real intention.

Swooping down, I assumed he would kiss me, so I closed my eyes in preparation for his lips. But instead of feeling lips meet mine, I was met with a slight wetness followed by vibration on my stomach—he fucking raspberried me. A high-pitched squeak escaped me as I bolted up, causing Mateo to fall over the side of the bed from my momentum.

The commotion must've been loud because before Mateo could even get off the floor, the door flew open. Mateo and I were already laughing from the incident, so we turned to see who'd entered his room. Standing in the doorway with his chest heaving, stood none other than Elias. I couldn't make out his expression, though. He was staring open-mouthed at me, frozen to the spot.

"Do I have something on my face? Did you slobber on me?" I asked, turning to Mateo. But when I glanced down to check for slobber, the realization hit me square in the nipple. Yep, I was topless. Fuck! Covering myself quickly, I dived off the bed as well, landing between the wall and mattress.

"Oof."

I didn't know if I should laugh or cry at this point. Elias had just seen my boobs again! Openly stared at them this time, actually. Peeking over the edge of the bed, Elias appeared to have come out of his stupor, finally.

"Sorry, I, um, heard a noise, and um, we've been looking, and then you, um, boobs." His face was bright red, and I didn't think I had ever seen Elias so out of sorts.

In fact…

"Did you just use a contraction?"

My brain was stuck. Elias had, in fact, used a contraction. What did that mean? Did it mean something? My brow wrinkled in thought as I tried to figure out this compound equation.

"What are you talking about?"

Elias' brow wrinkled up in confusion. Seemed I was breaking everyone. Feeling stupid for hiding, I stood up and began to look for my clothes.

"Bloody Hell, woman."

"Oh, stop. You've already seen them at this point, twice in fact, so no sense in me hiding away like I'm ashamed of my body."

Mateo was still laughing on the ground at Elias, and probably me, as I looked for where my pants landed. Finding them under the desk, I bent over to grab them, which was not the right choice to make because somehow, we'd gathered more people. Fun times.

"What the fuck does her underwear say?" Oliver barked, closely followed by Soren answering him.

"I think it says, careful—fart loading." Soren's voice was full of disbelief.

"Why are we all standing in Mateo's room? What's going on…" Henry trailed off as he made his way to the Sawyer freak show—at least it felt that way at this point.

I was stuck frozen under the desk, ass up in the air. I literally did not know what to do at this point. This had escalated from something funny to utter mortification.

"I think I'm just going to live under this desk now. Bring me food and water, okay?"

Which only caused them all to laugh more. Dick-weasels. The new profanity list I found was going to come in handy, especially if any of them thought they were getting sexed up after this. Well, they had another thing coming—or not coming, heh.

Sighing, I slowly backed out from under the desk, my pants clasped in my hand, and stood. My eyes might have been closed as well; okay, they were definitely closed. Cringing, I started to peek open an eye just as a bellow rang out through the room.

"Out. NOW!"

Rhett glared at all the guys who had been unabashedly hanging out to watch the 'Sawyer makes an ass of herself' show. I was starting to think that soap opera might have a chance.

Opening my eyes fully once I heard the door shut, I sighed in relief at the empty room. A sheepish Mateo was still on the floor, looking up at me with remorse in his eyes that I couldn't quite work out.

"What's up, honey? Why do you look like your puppy just got kicked?" I asked as I started to get dressed. Mateo hung his head before answering.

"I should've done what Rhett did, but instead, I sat here and laughed with the other guys, clearly disrespecting your privacy. I'm sorry." Walking over to Mateo, I sat down in his lap, straddling him.

"Mateo, I didn't see it that way. At least not at first when it was just you, me, and Elias. Everything escalated from there, but I don't blame you for that. Not even the other guys, really. Nothing was done out of ill intention or malice, at least I don't think. So, let's both get dressed and go face the music together? I think it's time."

"I hope you know how amazing I think you are," Mateo whispered before kissing me lightly, making my heart swoon.

Jumping up, I finished getting dressed. Otherwise, I would start kissing him more, inevitably removing the clothes I'd just put back on. Once we were both presentable, Mateo grabbed my hand, and we headed out of his room together.

He was right. I needed to remember I wasn't alone anymore. With my newfound confidence, I walked hand in hand with Mateo into the lion's den, or you know, the living room, whatever.

seventeen

rhett

TODAY HAD BEEN busy from the get-go. My mom had needed help around the B&B. Then the police department had notified us that Sawyer's possessions were ready to be released. She'd asked me to take over managing her police case after her panic attack. I was proud of her for asking for help and gladly accepted.

It was when I was leaving the police station that I received Oliver's text. Thankfully, I was already in town, so it was a quick drive over to the bar. I didn't know what to think about Tyler. I'd gone straight into problem-solving mode, but I hadn't stopped to think about my feelings.

To be honest, I wasn't sure what I was feeling. I needed to make sure I didn't lose myself in this relation-ship—scratch that. I would only lose myself if I didn't follow my heart. Sawyer was my heart—end of subject.

Feeling resolved and ready to see my baby, I took off to find where everyone had run off to when returning home. At the top of the stairs, I found the guys congregating in Mateo's room. Confused, I headed in that direction, but when I saw my baby standing awkwardly, eyes clenched closed and holding a shirt to her chest. I lost it. These assholes were just standing there gawking at her instead of offering her the privacy she deserved. It fucking enraged me.

"Out. NOW!" I shouted, glaring at all the guys. My voice seemed to break them out of their stare-off with Sawyer's boobs, and they all turned and fled quickly. Yeah, I would, too, assholes.

Pulling the door behind them, I leaned back against it; I needed to calm myself before I erupted all over and punched my roommates—my best friends. After a few minutes, I felt more centered and calmer. As I descended the stairs, the doorbell rang. Assuming Tyler was here, I headed toward it to let him in. Unfortunately, it was none other than Voldemort herself standing on our door stoop.

Her sneer at me didn't go unnoticed, but I didn't care; my face screamed the same back to her. Not even allowing her to utter a word, I slammed the door in her face, locked it, and turned back toward the living room. Damn, that had felt good. The doorbell continued to ring as I walked away, my smirk growing with each step.

The guys looked up in question at me when I entered the room. Some had looks of remorse, while others had embarrassment etched all over their faces. Shaking my head, I wasn't answering them or getting into anything until Sawyer was present. I took up my post on the wall to wait for her. The doorbell finally ceased as she and Mateo entered, hand in hand.

The sight of Sawyer holding hands with another guy should've infuriated me, but every time I saw her happy and cherished by them, I felt the opposite. Assurance flooded me, and I wanted to slap myself for even questioning earlier. This family we were building was special. It wouldn't be easy, but I had a feeling it would be worth it tenfold. They took a seat together on the oversized chair, and I swear I got a little misty-eyed thinking about how much they'd both already grown.

"So, what's up?" Sawyer questioned.

Ding, Dong.

The doorbell cut off my response, and my heart rate spiked at my ire. Why did this bitch continue to interrupt things?

"Elias, you need to go deal with that," I huffed, rolling my eyes. Sawyer caught the motion and covered her laugh, but the sound of her chuckle was a balm to my irritability, allowing me to smile back at her. I hadn't noticed Elias leave, so when he returned seconds later, the expression on his face confused me.

"I already told her to fuck off when I slammed the door in her face. Your turn."

"Yeah, I think you might be referring to someone else, mate, because I don't know why this bloke would be here to see me."

I was momentarily stunned at him using a contraction, which by Sawyer's laugh she'd caught too, so my brain was slow to connect what he'd said. So, when Elias stepped aside and didn't reveal Voldemort, but Ace, I was more confused. Was I stuck in some weird Twilight Zone episode? My brain was struggling to make sense of things.

"Ace!" Sawyer jumped up and ran to give him a hug.

"Hey, hot stuff. Just came to check on you since you've been ignoring my texts." He was trying to give her a stern look, but he wasn't pulling it off very well, and it set them both into giggles. I didn't understand their friendship, but I accepted it. He seemed like a decent guy, and Sawyer needed trustworthy people in her life.

When the doorbell rang for the third time, I'd officially lost all the calm from earlier. Stalking to the door, I ripped it open to reveal Asa and Fin.

"Going to let us in there, Rhett?" Fin asked when I didn't immediately move from the doorway.

My brain was officially working at the speed of molasses. What in the hell was going on? Was there a party at our house I didn't know about? What was with all of these people infiltrating our space suddenly?

I was already over it and had met my people quota for the day. I just wanted to cuddle up with Sawyer. Turning on my feet, I didn't reply back to Fin, but stomped back to the living room.

Sawyer was still talking to Ace animatedly, but I didn't care. I picked her up and threw her over my shoulder before moving to the couch. Glaring at Oliver and Soren, they quickly moved over, allowing me space to sit down, bringing Sawyer down with me.

She squeaked when I'd first picked her up, but as I sat and brought her down, she quietly stared at me as she settled into my lap.

"What's going on, Grump? You seem grumpier than usual."

Only huffing, I burrowed my head into her neck, breathing in her pear blossom scent. Sawyer started to stroke my hair tenderly, and my calm started to return. She kissed my cheek, and I realized that I just possibly had a freak-out moment in front of a room full of people. Shit. Although at that moment, with Sawyer in my lap stroking my hair, I didn't care much.

"We can talk more later, okay. But I need to turn around now?" she whispered to me, her breath tickling my ear. Grunting my answer, I didn't want her to move, but eventually, I lessened my grip so she could turn. As long as she didn't leave my lap.

"Hey, hope it was okay I let myself in. The door was open…"

Tyler, who I'd expected three doorbells ago, finally walked into the room. Everyone else stopped mid-conversation and turned to stare at him, confused who he was or why he was here. He'd been gesturing toward the door when he spoke, so when he stopped mid-sentence, his arm was raised in the air, pointing behind him. He was probably as confused as me with all these people in one room.

Sawyer tensed at his voice, but I rubbed slow circles on her belly with my thumb, settling her back into me.

"Tyler," Sawyer said in a breathy tone.

If I needed an answer, her voice right there sealed it for me. At the sound, Tyler turned and beamed when he found her. Oliver rushed to help out his friend by jumping up and motioned for Tyler to join him on the couch he was sitting on. Tyler looked torn, but followed after him.

"Matthews, what are you doing here? You know Sawyer?" Asa questioned. He was probably voicing the question the rest of them had to be wondering. Looking around, I took in all my roommates, Asa and Fin, Ace, and now Tyler.

The room was full of people who cared about the precious girl in my lap. Something about that realization made me feel better knowing she had people in her corner. Thankfully, Oliver spoke up for Tyler, inevitably saving me from having to unburrow from my Sawyer cocoon. I was being selfish, but right then, I didn't care. I needed my girl.

"Actually, I invited him. I wasn't expecting all the extra guests, though." Oliver rubbed the back of his head, not sure what to do now.

"Um. Well, I… hmph. Tyler and I know each other from high school. I guess you could say we dated. We ran into each other today, and when he saw me, we um, we kissed. There, I've said it." Sawyer fell back after her verbal regurgitation, covering her head in my embrace.

"Wait, what?"

"What does that mean, exactly?"

"When you say, kiss, what kind of kiss are we talking about here?"

"I guess welcome to the family is in order."

"Are we just letting in anyone with a penis at this point?"

Sawyer withdrew her head from my arms, but appeared to have her hair still covering her face, hiding. I didn't like seeing her this way. Turning her, I gently placed her into Soren's lap next to me on the couch. Making eye contact, I communicated that he needed to take care of her or death. He appeared to get the message as he nodded back, reassuringly wrapping her in his arms.

Rising to my feet, I used my height to my full advantage as I glared around the room at all of these knuckleheads. Crossing my arms, I waited until they all got the message. Eventually, they'd shut up, and I took my moment to make a statement.

"Stop and think for one second what your words are doing to that amazing girl right there. You all claim to care for her, yet here you are talking and making judgments without taking a moment to ask her anything. This isn't how we do things. I'm going to assume that if you're in this room, you at least care about her in some capacity. So, do better. Start acting like it. This is an untraditional relationship, but it doesn't mean it has to be harder. Earlier tonight, I reminded myself that we were creating a family here. We have the chance to make something extraordinary that I think we all need in our lives, all want. So—"

My sentence was cut off when I felt a small hand on my arm. Looking down, I saw Sawyer staring up at me. She had tears on her eyelashes, but her eyes were swirling with a tremendous amount of emotion; I couldn't decide if they were sad or happy tears. Wiping one off with my thumb, she momentarily leaned into my touch. I didn't want to get my hopes up, but it almost looked like something profound; something real emanated from her eyes just then.

"Thank you, Rhett. I'll take it from here. You reminded me who I am and what I'm striving for. It's time I made that clear."

Right before my eyes, I watched as Sawyer transformed from a beautiful girl into a strong woman, allowing her beauty to shine through her very essence. It was one of the most magical moments I'd ever experienced. My breath caught, and for a moment, I saw it… saw the vision of what our life could be like, and I'd never wanted anything more in my life than I did right then.

I'd entered this room as a boy, standing in front of a girl, just asking her to love me. But I would leave it, firm in my place at her side, as a man—a man who was wholehearted and stupidly, crazy in love.

Take that, Julia Roberts.

eighteen

. . .

sawyer

I THINK my brain was officially malfunctioning from the number of curveballs I'd avoided all day. Today had been the weirdest day. At least, that was what I kept telling myself. Mostly, for all the moments of weakness, where I curled in a ball and hid away.

But Rhett's words had ignited a spark in me, and it was building into an inferno. Standing as tall as my five-foot-two frame allowed, I faced all the people I'd collected since arriving on this campus. This place had accepted me more than anywhere else in my life, and I just needed to remember my courage.

"Rhett reminded me that we were a family, or at least, creating one. That's something I've wanted for a while now. This week has been all over the place, starting with the accident, and I didn't stop to think how that might affect me. The grief from the first crash flooded me, and it made me forget who I've become. I'll catch you up on the cliff notes version later for those who don't know what I'm talking about."

Exhaling, I tried to slow my racing heart as I fidgeted with my hands.

"Something my therapist once told me makes sense now. She said in times of significant trauma, 'our body keeps the score,' it was a book, actually. So, while we might forget and the memory fades, our body doesn't. So, when I went through that crash again, my mindset reverted back to fifteen-year-old me in some ways. That fear, the uncertainty, and confusion all poured through me, making me doubt and feel alone. But when I looked around this room just now, it was like cold water dumped over me. Those emotions don't belong here; they aren't the truth."

Gesturing with my hands, I was getting passionate about what I was saying. Everyone in the room remained frozen to their spots, listening.

"This here, with us all, this is real. I'm going to keep fucking things up; heck, we all will. It's natural and inevitable. The difference, though, is how we handle it. If we're serious about this life we're carving out, then we all have to be on board. Allow space to mess up and recognize it before we all start demanding answers. We've all had hard stuff in our lives, so we're going to have different things that are more sensitive than others. I feel like I'm getting on a soapbox now, and I don't want it to be like that. So, I'm going to just say this last thing."

This was it, my moment of truth.

"Every single person in this room is important to me in some way. I want you to be part of my life, whatever that looks like. I need you all to hear that, please. The kinks are definitely still being worked out, like how I need to not ignore my phone and our need for privacy at times. I also need to balance things better. At the end of the day, these are the relationships that matter, and together we are stronger. Fighting amongst ourselves only advances their agenda. We have enough outside forces pushing against us; we don't need to add to it."

They all stared at me as I finished and I realized I wasn't done yet. They were looking at me, so I needed to provide direction.

"Ace, can we get coffee tomorrow?"

"Absolutely, girl. Our usual time? I'll let Chloe know." At my nod, he stood and offered me a tight embrace. He really was a great hugger.

"I'm glad you want me to be part of your life. I'm glad I met you, Sawyer." Smiling as he pulled back, he took my coffee date as the cue it was meant to be and headed out the door. I decided to do a 'Sound of Music' style send-off after that. Or at least that was how it sounded in my head as I dismissed them along to the tune of "Goodbye, Farewell…"

"Fin, join us for coffee? Asa, would you like to grab lunch with me tomorrow when I go to see Aggie?"

For some reason, I was really nervous he would say no. I didn't know why I kept fearing the worst from him when he'd done nothing but the opposite every time.

They both stood this time, hands clasped, and I smiled wide at them. I was happy for my best friend.

"Wouldn't miss it, bestie." Fin kissed my cheek and walked past to say something to her brother so I could have a moment with, well, my brother. Still so weird to think I was a twin.

"Sis, why do you always seem so scared I'm going to run from the room screaming?" He gave me a look, calling out my earlier fear. "I'd love to have lunch with you tomorrow. I might have a surprise for you as well. If you're up for it. I invited Fin and Rey too. Felt it was appropriate."

Loving his use of sis, I was curious about what he had planned as I hugged him back, relishing in his comforting embrace. We might not have grown up together, but there was something to be said about the familial bond. I could just feel it with him down to my core, almost feeling like some part of me was returning. He kissed the top of my head before backing away. Fuck, he was going to make me cry.

"Mateo, movie night later this week?"

At his blush, I was confident he knew what I really meant. Surprisingly, he walked over and kissed me on the lips in front of everyone before heading toward the kitchen. Fucking sweet boy. Turning back to who was left, I was about to say the next name when Elias spoke up first.

"Sawyer, I was wondering if we could set aside some time together, perhaps on Monday? I received a text the other day, and I'd forgotten about it until they sent me a reminder asking when I would be by to pick up the yearbooks. They are here from storage, so whenever you are free to go through them, I thought it was something we could do together?"

Breath caught in my throat at the mention of the yearbooks. Finally, we were going to get answers. I felt it.

"Monday works. I'll check my planner and text you a time later if that's okay with you?"

I realized we were back to being our polite selves in mixed company. Why did I miss the insufferable asshole thing he had going for him at times? I wasn't right in the head. Duh.

At his nod, he walked past, squeezing my forearm, lighting up all the nerve endings as he did. Fucking fuck. Momentarily dazed, I glanced around at who was left, now. Five guys sat before me, and I wasn't sure where to start with any of them. Rhett walked over, saving me again. He was such a dreamboat at times.

"The police station called me earlier. They released your belongings, and I stopped by and picked them up. I think you should open the box with someone just in case you need support." He talked low and carefully since Tyler was still in the room and wouldn't know all the details.

"Thank you. Did you need to talk to me after? You seemed upset earlier. Everything okay?"

"I'm good now, baby. Watching you embrace yourself and what you wanted in life emboldened me too.

How about we have dinner, though, on Monday? My mom and sister would like to meet you."

"Really? I would love that. Yes!"

My smile spread wide at his news; I was ignoring the comment about my possessions. That needed to stay in a separate place for the moment. Leaning down, Rhett kissed me deeply, leaving me breathless when he pulled away. Winking, he too made his way to the kitchen. Looking at the time, I guess we had missed dinner. Turning back, I was now down to four. At least this was easier.

"Henry and Soren, would you grab my things from Rhett, and then I'll meet you in one of our rooms?"

Jumping up, Soren practically skipped to me. "Of course. We'll be in your room. Take your time." Soren kissed me lightly on the lips before leaving me with Henry. He nodded, leaving me with a lingering kiss. Something was up with him. I watched him walk away, wondering if he would tell me later. Touching my lips, I watched as part of my heart walked away. Oh, Henry.

nineteen

. . .

sawyer

TURNING BACK, I glanced between the two hockey players who remained. Two hockey players who made me feel dangerous things. I think I needed to have their conversation together after the events of the afternoon. For starters, I owed them both an apology.

"Ollie, can we all go and talk in your room? I think it would be more private." Acceptance for what I had to do settled in me—I had to let Tyler go. We could still be friends, but I couldn't start anything else with him. Our time had passed, and I'd have to accept that. I understood my choice, but an overwhelming feeling of despair sat heavy in my gut.

"Of course, Sawyer. I'll grab some snacks. I'll meet you two up there."

He gave me a wink, and I realized he was giving me a few moments alone with Tyler. Bless that man. He really did have his moments. This would be hard enough; I didn't need an audience.

Smiling, I turned and offered my hand to Tyler. I avoided looking at him, though. I had no idea what he thought after he heard all the things I'd said earlier and then watched all the guys kiss me. For a moment, it didn't seem like he was going to take my hand, but just as I was about to drop it, he reached out, grabbing it, lacing our fingers together.

Electricity ran up my arms at his touch, causing all my arm hairs to stand on end. Sucking in a breath, I finally looked up at him. Liquid heat blazed in his green eyes, setting my heart racing. Turning, I pulled him along behind me to Ollie's room, afraid if I stayed there staring at him, I wouldn't get out the words I needed to say first.

Thankfully, Ollie's room was at the top of the stairs, and I quickly made my way in. I was still just as impressed with the cleanliness of his room as I'd been the first day. Ollie's spicy scent was strong here, permeating the room, and I took in a deep inhale once I was inside, sending shivers through my body. It still smelled as amazing as it did the first time.

"Sawyer, before you break my heart, I need to say something."

Confused at his statement, I turned back toward Tyler. He'd been a true friend to me during those years when I didn't even know what a friend was, so lost in my own pain. Nearly every good memory I had from

Iowa, though, included him. I never thought about it like that. Was I making the right choice?

"I—"

He stopped my words by placing a finger over my lips and cocking his head, telling me to shush. Pouting, because who liked to be shushed—no one, that was who.

"Please, Sawyer. I've waited years to say this, and I just need to get it out," Tyler pleaded. True desperation hung in his voice, and I wanted to do anything to comfort him at that moment.

When I remained quiet, he dropped his finger from my lips, leaving me feeling sad at losing his touch. Get it together, girl. We couldn't have them all. It wasn't Pokémon.

"I know our relationship started as one of convenience, a way to not develop feelings, but it was never that way for me. Well, that's a partial lie. I thought you were a cool chick from moment one and enjoyed hanging out with you, talking hockey, and debating who was the better skater. I was gearing up to ask you on a date when you started dating that douchecanoe Hunter."

We both made faces remembering him. Yeah, dude, I hoped you got every STI known to man someday, you dickweasel.

"Yeah, well, after your thing with Hunter ended, and you realized he was just in it for that stupid bet, we made that silly pact. Friends with benefits—all the benefits without the obligations of a relationship. It seemed like a dream come true. I didn't even care that Josh was included. We all hung out, and I think at first I assumed it was just one of those late-night proclamations, one made after a few beers. But you were serious, and the first night you came to me and started stripping in my room, I about had an aneurysm."

"I remember that, actually. Your face looked frozen for a solid minute, and I thought you were having a stroke." I chuckled as I recalled it.

"Exactly." Tyler laughed with me before continuing. "Sawyer, it started out how we planned—physical pleasure. But the more we hung out, the more things we did outside of sex, those were the moments I started to look forward to, actual moments with you. My feelings for you became real."

My heart raced, and I wasn't sure what to do anymore. This wasn't what I thought he was going to tell me.

"That summer, when I went away to hockey camp, I was certain they'd go away. Instead, they only intensified. You were all I could think, dream, and talk about. I basically got on everyone's nerves because I wouldn't shut up. When I got home, I was worried you'd have met someone or be tired of our arrangement. I told myself that if you came to me, I would tell you how I really felt."

"But that night, I showed up and talked you into a threesome," I whispered, remembering. My voice was despondent and heavy with regret as it pulled in my belly. Had I wasted something real? His laugh at my statement pulled me out of my emotional downward spiral.

"Yeah, you showed up in that damn trench coat with nothing under it. You hadn't expected Josh to be there, I'm guessing, but that night, fuck, that was hot. So yeah, I chickened out, mostly because I was confused about what it meant for me. I liked sharing you with Josh. I think I even kind of liked Josh a little, but I wasn't secure in myself back then to recognize it. I made some stupid mistakes that year, but the dumbest one was leaving for college that fall and letting you think I felt nothing but platonic feelings for you. Somehow, I convinced myself these past few years that nothing with us was real, and I'd only imagined what we had."

He stopped for a minute to swallow, and I wanted to hit him for leaving me hanging on what he would say next. What did this mean? Was he saying what I thought he was saying?

"Sawyer, when I saw you today across the ice, I was certain I was hallucinating. Then you skated, and I knew without a doubt it was you. Your form is etched in my memory from all the times we skated together at Charlie's rink. I didn't even think. I just took off, and before I knew what was happening, I was kissing you. And you were kissing me back. Please tell me I'm not wrong because the kiss today felt more passionate than any kiss we've ever shared before. I have to think that's because of you. My feelings haven't changed. They slammed back to the forefront the moment I saw you, reminding me how stupid I was to think anyone else carried a glimmer to what we shared."

Wow. My heart and brain melted.

"You're not wrong, Ty. I did kiss you back, and it did feel different for me today. I think that was why I ran." I started to pace, trying to get everything out I needed to say. "I, um, there's a lot about my past I've had to hide for the past five years to protect myself. An unfortunate consequence was that I shut off all my emotions, and in avoiding the bad ones, I inadvertently shut off the good ones. Even if you had told me back then, I'm not sure what would have happened honestly. I probably would've freaked out and ended our arrangement because I wasn't ready to hear those things back then."

Tyler sucked in a breath, and I hated that it made me feel good, but it couldn't mean anything. It just couldn't.

"Does that mean you're ready to hear those things now?"

"It's more complicated now, as you probably figured out downstairs. It's not just an answer I can give you. It doesn't just matter what I feel."

His forlorn look was too much to bear. Why did this hurt so much?

"What… what do you feel?"

His words were soft, barely audible, and my own throat dried as I debated how to answer his question.

"I'm still sorting through everything. I, uh," my nose twitched, and I switched the subject. "Did you say something about feelings for Josh? Are you two?" When you couldn't admit the words, deflect, deflect, deflect.

"Ha, no." He shook his head, a soft smile at me. "He never saw me that way, and it's cool. We still grab a beer if we run into each other after games. He was just the first sign that I wasn't 100% straight. It's not something I've explored a lot since then. And if I'm honest, I think because you weren't part of it. There was just magic between us three, and I tried to recreate it but never got close. There's a guy now that I kind of like more than a friend, but I don't think he sees me that way, and I'm fine with just being friends because I value his friendship more. Fuck, I'm doing it again, though, aren't I? Playing it safe."

"Ty, your version of safe is so far past the not safe line that they had to make new measurements. I'm not sure if that even makes sense, but you're not safe, Ty. You gambled your heart, and that's the riskiest thing you can do. I think you're brave, much braver than me."

"Fuck, Wildcat. I've missed you. But don't play down your own behaviors. The girl downstairs earlier wasn't just brave; she was fucking badass."

His use of an old nickname for me had my panties disintegrating from the level of heat and desire that was currently wreaking havoc in me. I could stand here and lie to us both that I didn't have real feelings for him, but what would that prove? That I could hurt someone I cared about? That when it came down to it, I caved and took the easy way?

I didn't want any of those things. No, if I was

brutally honest with myself, I wanted to kiss the fucking daylights out of him.

There was just one problem. I'd expected to say goodbye; I'd thought it was the only choice. But what if it wasn't? Except, now I'd forgotten that one tiny detail before sending everyone away—to talk about the elephant in the room.

Our whole relationship was built on trust and communication, and I'd already fucked up once today by kissing him and running. I couldn't do it again. It wasn't fair to Tyler, or the guys. I needed to talk to them first, and not just because it was the right thing to do, but because I respected and cared for them deeply.

Everything in me needed Tyler to join our weird relationship. Because when I looked into his eyes, there was no denying my feelings for him, or his for me, for that matter. Promises were promises, though. They were hard enough to keep on their own. I didn't need to break one when I could remedy it by taking the time to actually talk to them. Stepping back some, I saw hurt flash in his eyes, and it killed me.

"I've missed you too, and I hadn't even realized it until I saw you today. It's just that I have to—"

"Sawyer, if you don't kiss him, I'm never baking anything for you again."

Ollie cut me off from the doorway he was perched in with a fierce look on his face. The tray of food he held out like a waiter.

"Harsh, but—"

"Stop making excuses and kiss him already before I start singing 'Kiss the Girl.'"

"Are—"

"Eh. Nope."

"Ol—"

"That's it, woman! Sha la, la, you better kiss the girl…" Ollie sang, way off-key, I might add. Laughing at him, I turned back to Ty, whose grin had returned.

"I would listen to him, Wildcat. He once sang the entire soundtrack to *Dear Evan Hanson* in fake accents on a bus trip. He means business when he breaks out the show tunes."

My lust had quelled some at Ollie's antics, but stepping forward into Tyler's embrace, I found I still very much wanted to kiss him. It was something I'd done hundreds of times in the past, but for the first time in forever, I was nervous.

"It's still me, Sawyer. You and me. That hasn't changed just because your eyes are open."

Trusting that he was right, I leaned up on my tiptoes and kissed a boy who'd been part of my past, but I hoped would become part of my future.

twenty

oliver

"RHETT, I'm sure it's going to come up in a minute when I go upstairs, but Sawyer forgot one tiny detail named Tyler. Where do we stand? What's our position?"

Leaning back against the counter, I crossed my arms as I waited for him to respond. He was rummaging around in the fridge and ignored me for a full minute until he had the stuff he needed to make a sandwich.

"You have a phone. Use it."

Rolling my eyes at him, because really, he could have said that sooner. I pulled out my phone and sent the guys not in the kitchen a message.

Family Matters:
ME: Tyler, yay or nay?
Rey: I need more info. What are you asking?
Soren: Yay

Rey: Soren, you're supposed to be on my side.

Soren: I'm on the side of love, boo bear. It's clear there's something there. I love you, but if you removed your head from your ass, you'd see that. Instead, you're worried she's going to forget you or replace you.

Soren: I'm assuming you know him from hockey, and he's a good guy Ollie. Otherwise, you wouldn't have asked. Is my assumption wrong?

ME: He's the best kind of person. He's actually kind of a combo of you and Rey now that I think about it.

Rey: Fine. You're right, Sor. I'm scared, but that's my bullshit. If you vouch for him, Ollie, it's a yay for me. But I feel like we need to get to know him. I want more info.

Elias: ...

Elias: Do you guys ever think it is more hurtful for me to be included in this discussion?

ME: No, because if you got over yourself, you would see she cares for you even when you're an asshat.

Elias: Harsh. I could say the same to you, brother.

ME: Fair.

Elias: Fine. Yay.

Pocketing my phone, I looked up at the two, eating in quiet solidarity. Mateo shrugged his shoulders, and Rhett grunted. I took both to be yays. Piling up a plate of sandwiches, veggies, and cheese, I grabbed some water bottles and tucked them under my arm before heading to my room.

The door was slightly ajar when I arrived, and I heard voices inside. I hadn't planned to eavesdrop, promise. But it sounded relatively intimate, so I was trying to give them space to work out their shit. When Ty admitted he wasn't 100% straight and liking someone, a weird feeling coursed through me. I wondered who he was talking about and if I knew them.

The level of longing I heard in their voices hit me in the feels as I listened. When I heard Sawyer retreating, I decided I'd peeped on their conversation long enough. Stepping into the room entirely, I cut Sawyer off just as she was about to deny herself a kiss. Not on my watch, pretty girl, you deserved all the kisses.

Fortunately, my rendition of Little Mermaid was enough to push her over the line and actually kiss him. When their lips finally pressed together, I was fangirling so hard on the sidelines for them and a sense of longing filled me as I watched them together—I wanted that.

Adjusting my hard length in my pants, I was surprised to find I was so aroused by a sweet kiss. Needing to break up this sexual tension before it escalated too far, I stepped in again. They should give me the tagline, "Ollie, always saves the day." It had a nice ring to it.

"Who's hungry?"

Setting the platter of food on the bed, I plopped

down, making an exaggerated noise as I did, making Sawyer chuckle. Job well-done, self. I was on a roll tonight. Baring my conscience really did something for me.

"So, what did you want to talk about with us bite-size?"

Purposefully, I used the first name I'd ever called her as I took an exaggerated bite out of my sandwich. Sawyer rolled her eyes but grabbed some food along with Tyler. They sat facing me on the bed, the platter between us. Their familiarity was obvious and made me envious. They naturally leaned into one another, and Tyler kept casually touching her.

"Well, part of it was the past with Ty and me that I wanted to discuss. And I guess what it meant," Sawyer replied around a mouthful of turkey and cheese. Why did that look so sexy? Fuck, I had it bad if random wait-ress boobs in my face did nothing for me, but my girl eating a turkey sandwich had me almost creaming my pants.

"I also wanted to apologize to you, Ollie. I acted like a coward today and ruined our fun afternoon skating. I'd like to make it up to you, though, if you'll let me."

Her voice was filled with sincerity, and I had to swallow some of that envy I was feeling earlier. Sawyer truly was capable of having a multiple-partner relation-ship. She didn't pick favorites and seemed to naturally understand when someone needed her. It was foolish to think I was separate from that. Regardless, if we never moved past friends, she would be the best friend I could ever want. But fuck, I hoped it would be so much more.

"Absolutely. I prefer back rubs or the occasional foot massage if you need ideas."

"You brat!" Sawyer huffed out in a chuckle. "And don't think I missed you saying bite-size earlier. Don't forget what I said would happen."

She tried to be threatening, but really she was like a tiny poodle—all fluff and no bite.

"Oh, I remember, something about your mouth near my manhood. Yes, please. Sign me up!"

"That's not what I said!"

"Tyler, did you know she was such a liar? I can't believe this, Sawyer. I am deeply hurt by this." Mock outrage filled my voice as I acted affronted, bringing my hand to my chest.

"Oh, I'll show you hurt, mister!"

"Bring it. *Bite-Size.*"

At my words, she dove over the platter of food, tackling me. Or at least she tried. Quick on the drop, I rolled out of the way and hopped up on the bed. Instantly, Tyler moved what was left of the platter as Sawyer lay panting below my feet from her efforts. Tyler watched us in amusement, laughter written over his face.

"Whatcha going to do now, short stuff?"

"You're going to regret that!" she huffed out, blowing her hair with the force.

"Did she always have this temper, Tyler?"

My mistake was being too cocky. Taking my eyes off

her to snark at Tyler had given her an opening. Sawyer dived-bombed my calves while I was distracted, causing me to fall forward like a giant tree. Not having time to brace myself, I fell face forward, right into Tyler's crotch. And when I say crotch, I mean that my face hit him directly on the dick. It was a cockstrophe—a real dick move.

That was until he jerked up from the impact, hands, and knees failing. And where was my face? That's right, in the middle of all those limbs, meaning not only did I get a black eye from his dick, but a bloody nose.

Rolling off him, I attempted to cover my nose to staunch the blood flow. Sawyer stood up on the bed now in complete shock. I honestly think I broke her as her mouth hung open, no words escaping. She swiveled her head back and forth from the two moaning guys on the bed—and not in the good way.

"Mates, could you close the door..." Elias stopped mid-sentence as he took in the scene unfolding in my room. Tyler groaned and covered his dick. Me hunched over, one eye squinted with my hand cupping blood. Fortunately, Elias only froze for about three seconds and then jumped into action, saving us from any other catastrophes, dick or otherwise—at least for the night.

Elias, *my hero.*

sawyer

Once we had Oliver cleaned up and some ice for both of them, I made my exit, not wanting to cause any more injuries tonight. At least the first half had gone well. Smiling as I walked to my room, I couldn't believe that Tyler was here, and he had feelings for me. Glancing at my watch, I saw it was already 10 pm. Shit, this day had gone by fast with the million things that had occurred.

"What has you all smiley smiles?" a voice questioned from inside my room. Gasping, I grabbed my chest at the sound, forgetting Soren and Henry were going to be waiting for me there.

"Holy shit, Soren. You about gave me a heart attack!" Henry and Soren both chuckled at my outburst.

"Well, are you going to tell us?" He lifted an eyebrow, waiting.

"Oh, just that I gave Ollie a black eye and a bloody nose, or well, Tyler's dick did." They both stared at me, not quite sure if I was serious or not. Sadly, it could go either way.

"So, how do you guys feel about things? I feel like I haven't seen you two in ages. Is everyone really okay with Tyler? Ollie said it was okay, but now I'm starting to wonder if he wasn't screwing with me."

I joined them in the middle of my bed, situating myself in Henry's lap. He looked surprised for a second before curling me up in his arms and pulling me tight to him. Ah, I think I knew what was going on with him now. Nuzzling under his neck, I placed a kiss, attempting to offer him assurance.

"That does sound like something Ollie would do, but no, we all talked and agreed he could have a chance if that was what you wanted."

"Okay, that makes me feel better, but you didn't answer all of my questions. Don't think you can avoid it."

"I'm good, Smalls." Henry chuckled. "Better now that you're here. I think, well, I know, I've just missed you." He nuzzled down into my neck as he spoke, and I could feel his lips brush my skin with each word. Knowing I needed to get out some words, I stifled the lust that was building. Raising my head, I peered into his eyes as I laid out my heart for him.

"Henry, every moment of every day I'm not directly in your presence, I miss you. Don't for one second doubt that, Henry Alexander. You are the blood in my veins, the marrow in my bones. There is no Sawyer without Henry." He exhaled slowly, dropping his forehead down to mine, bringing our faces even closer.

"Thank you. I don't mean to be an insecure asshole. It's just with everything, I guess I've felt out of sorts and didn't realize it. I promise to talk to you about it next time instead of stewing in it."

"Promise?"

"Promise."

"And I promise to kick both of you when you do."

Laughing, I turned to Soren, reaching out to grab his hand, linking our fingers.

"Oh, Sor, don't you see, you're the sunshine that lights our darkness."

"No, Sawyer. That's you."

His face had lost all signs of joking, and I could tell he was sharing something profound with me. Nodding, I accepted what he was offering—a truth, his truth. Clearing my throat, I sat upright in Henry's arms.

"Well, I don't see how things could get worse. Let's go through my stuff to see what survived. Rip the band-aid off and all that."

I'd shared with the guys earlier in the week what Aggie had told me that day about my mom, the letter she sent, and the box. Thus, at my words, Soren hopped up and walked over to my desk. I hadn't noticed it earlier, but there, on top, sat an old rain poncho I kept in my under-seat compartment, a pair of fuzzy dice Charlie gave me as a joke, and the box.

Tears lined my eyelids as I held them back. There was still no guarantee anything was salvageable, but just the fact it had survived somehow made me feel less broken. Soren placed the box in front of us on the bed, and we all stared at it, almost as if we thought it would come alive and do something.

It looked the same as when Aggie had given it to me. But how was that possible? Hesitantly, I reached out and touched the surface of the box as I ran my hands over it. The outside was made from some sort of hard plastic. Maybe it was indestructible?

The box had a keypad on the front I hadn't noticed before, but to be honest, I'd been so preoccupied, details hadn't been my main priority. The fact my mother had attended school here, on top of having enough foresight to send this, had blown my mind. It was almost as if she knew they would be gone, and I would need whatever was inside.

"Did the letter have a key code in it?" I questioned quietly as I thought back through what the letter had said.

'They have returned, and we're no longer safe. If my plan works, she will be safe. She is what matters. One day she may find her way to you. She will need to know to be safe and perhaps do what I was not able to. The Council must be stopped. Thank you for your kindness. It has often helped me push through the fear and pain to do what I must. Help her if you can. She is going to need it. Look for the tiny dancer.'

"Tiny dancer..." I mumbled to myself as I recalled the letter. The name had me reaching for the necklace my mom had given me that day. The one I now knew was a gift from Aggie.

"Do you remember anything?"

"Tiny dancer. My mom had said to look for the tiny dancer. She'd meant this necklace. But I feel like I've heard it before. It's there at the edges of my memory, but... I can't seem to grasp it."

Shaking my head, I needed to focus on what I could do right here. I thought about what the key code could be. Rolling the numbers, I settled on 101098—my birthday. I clicked the lock, and amazingly enough, it worked. Well, that was kind of anticlimactic.

With shaking hands, I lifted the top of the box. A seal breaking sound hissed out as I lifted it. I realized then the box had to be made out of the same material as one of those fireproof ones. Wow, mom had been prepared. But come to think of it, she hadn't been wrong. The box was the size of a notebook lengthwise and as thick as one of those metal lunchboxes.

The first thing I saw was a pink blanket on top. Touching it softly, I was rewarded with a vague recollection of it. Pulling it out, I glanced over it, stopping at the embroidered AA on the bottom right corner. Fingering the stitches, the movement released a memory.

"This was my baby blanket. One day, I had to be about three or four because the memory is very vague, but I think I asked what the letters meant. I was in that questioning phase. My mom told me it was the name I'd been born with. When I asked her what she meant, she tried to explain to me about adoption. She said I hadn't grown in her belly but her heart. I'd come into the world as an Abigail, but I would live it as Sariah because I was her and daddy's princess."

Tears fell down onto my hand as I stroked the As. It solidified everything I'd been questioning. I couldn't pretend it was all a dream or a weird misunderstanding. No, this was actual proof.

Placing it next to me on the bed, I gently refolded it, being careful with the material. Once that was done, I reached in for the next item. A stack of pictures sat on top of a leather journal. Grabbing them both, I flipped quickly through the photos. Some of them were of my parents and me growing up. Henry and Fin were even in a few.

Turning into Henry's chest, I let out the sob I'd been holding back. Seeing their faces again after all these years was both happy and painful. I clutched them to my chest as I cried.

"I thought I'd lost all my pictures of them. That I would never see their faces again," I sobbed as tears cascaded down my face. I wasn't sure if he understood me through the sobs, but he just kept rocking me as he smoothed my hair down my back.

"I know, Smalls. I know. Ssh. It's okay. You've got them now."

Henry repeated that over and over, helping to ground me in my happy memories. When my tears slowed, I realized Soren was at my back and had been the one actually patting my hair. Turning, I looked at Soren, and the anguish on his face surprised me.

Throwing my arms around his neck, I hugged him to me as we held one another in a tight embrace. We were all hurting in one way or another. We just had to take the time to look.

twenty-one

. . .

rey

LISTENING to Sawyer cry made me want to vanquish anything that would dare make her upset. But when it was her dead parents, how did one slay that dragon?

Looking at the photos with her had hit me more than I'd expected. Kyla and Scott had been my neighbors and my best friend's parents for over ten years. There were a lot of memories there, and I realized I'd never grieved them. I was so caught up in losing Sariah and the disbelief that it was happening. I'd shoved down the vital fact that two people I cared about had died as well.

And now, I felt so lost. Wasn't I supposed to know what to do? How to make this better? My girlfriend was upset, grieving even. Should I make her a warm beverage? Get some chocolate? I was so out of my depths here.

Pulling back from the hug, I looked at my phone and debated texting Fin, but it was already after 11 pm. Knowing her, she'd rush over here and end up only creating more drama. No, I could do this.

The contents of the box were strewn across the bed, so I gathered them and placed them back for safekeeping. They might not be worth a lot monetary wise, but they were priceless possessions to Sawyer, and I would do everything in my power to help her keep them.

It made me thankful for my own parents, in a way. They weren't perfect, and I still didn't know the extent of their involvement with Sawyer's family and the Council. But when I thought about never seeing them again, or not having any pictures of our life together… well, that put things in perspective.

Walking out of her room, I crossed the hall into mine. My room was still in disarray, but I'd started to organize. It seemed chaotic at the moment, but I could see the effort I was making, which settled my self-hatred to a degree. Taking a deep breath, I grabbed the two things that might help take Smalls' mind off things for a bit.

Soren and Sawyer still embraced on the bed. Her head was lying on his chest, and he had his head down as if he were kissing her hair. They didn't seem to hear me when I returned and might not have even noticed I'd left.

Sitting in her desk chair, I opened the notebook and flipped it to a page. My heart began to race, but I needed to be brave for her and a little for me. Taking another deep breath, okay, more like five deep breaths, I sat the guitar in my lap and began to strum some chords to warm up.

I kept my eyes focused on the paper as I sang the words my heart didn't know how to say.

Your eyes capture me, pulling me into your orbit
Every time I try to walk away, you smile, and
I'm sunk
Girl, don't you ever quit
You're the light that pulls me from my funk
The breath that fills my dreams

Every day with you is a dream come true
But I'm scared you'll float away
Leaving me battered and blue
How do I make sure you stay
Right here with me, always

Love is a scary thing, but you make it easy
Love is a scary thing, but you make it easy

I want to fight your battles, slay your dragons
Be your knight in shining armor
But you're no damsel, fighting with your own passion
Your strength is your weapon, no sword is sharper
My love is yours to wield

Love is a scary thing, but you make it easy
Love is a scary thing, but you make it easy

Together, we make sense
Together, we stand through it all

Realizing at some point I'd closed my eyes, I slowly opened them as the last chord was played. Blinking as the light returned, I was stunned to find the bed empty. What? They'd left.

Dread filled me. I'd put myself out there, and it had been an utter failure, a complete fucking disaster. Dropping my head, I debated whether to rip up my notebook or slam the guitar against the wall. Maybe I would do both.

"That was beautiful, Henry."

Turning at her soft voice, I was surprised to find her and Soren standing behind me. My face must've asked the question because Sawyer offered me an answer at my stare.

"You thought we'd left, didn't you? Henry, when are you going to see how amazing you are? If you had your eyes open, you would've seen me perched right there on the edge of the bed the whole time you sang, but when you ended, I wanted to be closer to you so I could do this."

Smalls kissed me, and I accepted it greedily like a man starved.

Soren took the guitar from between us, and I had to thank him in my head for it; it was much easier to kiss her without something on my lap. Smalls must've agreed because she straddled me in the chair, bringing our bodies closer together.

The kiss quickly turned passionate, and I realized how much we all needed this. We needed to feel connected, to remind ourselves we were here, alive, and like I had sung earlier, together.

Standing up, I walked around her desk to the bed and laid her back on it. We broke the kiss, and Sawyer scooted back, allowing me to hover over her fully. I felt another body to my left and recognized Soren was joining us.

Turning my head, I was greeted with his lips. His kiss was hard and demanding, punishing me for doubting him. Bodies started to move, and clothes disappeared quickly as we all gave in to our passion for one another.

Sawyer was between us, flat on her back, offering us both a side to devour. Looking Soren in the eyes across her body, we silently communicated which direction we were both going. He started kissing her passionately, and I just watched for a few minutes. I almost got as much enjoyment watching the two people I loved together as I did being the one to experience it. Almost.

Deciding it was time to get in on the action, I settled between Small's legs. Her pussy was dripping already with her desire, and I was ready to consume it. Slowly, I licked up her folds to her clit, flattening my tongue, giving a little pressure. Her moan filled me with pride as I started to circle her nub harder with my tongue and sucked.

Taking one finger, I began to tease her entrance as I pumped slowly in and out of her wet channel, building the friction. Smalls' head was thrown back when I glanced up, and she had her hand in Soren's hair, holding him to her breasts as he lavished them. The sight itself was intoxicating, and it spurred me on.

Adding a second finger, I increased my speed, swirling my tongue around her clit. My fingers slipped in smoothly and were coated in her juices. She smelled and tasted divine and I eagerly consumed her. My dick was rigid against the comforter as I rocked against the bed to garner some friction. Sawyer's moans increased as I sped up the pumping of my fingers, feeling her cum cover my face.

It was sexy, the level of arousal she had for us, and part of me was basking with masculine pride. An idea overcame me, and suddenly it was the only thing I could think about. Plunging in a third finger, I felt her begin to tighten around them seconds before she spasmed in orgasm, releasing a long, arduous moan.

My fingers were nice and wet now, coated in Sawyer's cum. Slowly, I drew them down to her rosette and began to circle it, spreading it over the hole. Her moan at my ministrations made me confident to keep going.

"Smalls, how adventurous are you feeling tonight? Would you… would you want to pop a cherry with me?"

They both stopped and looked at me, processing my question.

"What… huh?"

The orgasm seemed to have fuddled her brain. Smiling, I took pity on her. "Want to lose your anal virginity with me? If you let me take yours, I'll… let Soren take mine."

Again, they both stared at me for a hot second, before Soren was moving so fast I wasn't sure what was going on as he shouted out, "Hell, yes!"

"I'm so game for this, yes! Henry, I'd love to have this first with you." Sawyer's voice was full of love. Leaning up on her elbows as she looked at me, the vision she painted was breathtaking. Her bare breasts, orgasm glow, and seductive smile had me dazed.

Soren returned mere seconds later, breaking my stare with Sawyer's boobs. I realized he'd run across to his room to grab a bottle of lube. Looking over his state of undress, he merely winked at me in response. Fuck, he was cute.

"How do we want to do this?" Sawyer asked. Thinking through the logistics and what would work best, I flipped her around in a smooth move.

"Get on your knees and show me the goods."

Smirking, she did as she was told at least, and popped her ass up in the air. Soren eagerly squirted some lube onto her and mimicked what I should do.

"Use your fingers to loosen her up now."

He squeezed some more on my fingers before reaching down and coating my cock in lube as well. He stroked me a few times, the heat in his eyes lighting up my insides, pulling a moan from me. Kissing me quickly, he moved behind me as he started the same process of lubing me up. Focusing back on her, I inserted a second finger into her tight hole and started to stretch her more. Her moans encouraged me that she was enjoying this and not just going along for me.

"Are you ready, Smalls?"

"Yes," was breathed out in a moan.

Slowly, I replaced my fingers with the head of my cock. The lube allowed me to slip in easily. The tightness was unlike anything I'd imagined, causing me to let out one of my own sounds of pleasure. I felt the barrier as I went deeper and grabbed her hips to pull her closer. Pushing forward, I felt her muscles tighten around me as I became fully seated in her.

"Fuck," she moaned, with me seconding it with my own.

"Fuck indeed. God, you're so tight. Does it feel okay?"

"Oh, god, yes. I feel so full."

Using Sawyer as my distraction, Soren started to rub his cock against my ass before pushing himself into me. Tilting me forward, he grabbed my hips as I bracketed Smalls on the bed. The sensation was mind-blowing as his piercing rubbed against my walls. As he got closer to the magic button, I had to focus to not come, as my eyes rolled back into my head.

"Fuck, Rey. You feel incredible. Are you doing okay, though?"

Words were not possible right then; nodding, I let out a long moan. The vibration of my voice reverberated into Smalls as her body trembled with desire.

"Okay, slowly," Soren ordered as he pulled out a

little, and his commanding voice was doing things for me. I was in sensory overload as he started to fuck my ass; I almost didn't move as I enjoyed what was occurring, but Smalls was impatient and started to push herself back onto my dick.

Falling into a rhythm, we were all able to increase our pace as we chased the building sensations. Working in tandem, Soren and I were able to find a rhythm for us all. Reaching down, I was surprised when I felt Sawyer's finger already on her clit.

"That's hot, Smalls."

She moaned in response, and I took that as an acknowledgment. Slapping skin and moans filled the room, and I knew I wasn't going to last much longer.

"I'm close, guys."

"Me too," moaned Soren.

Sawyer moaned louder again, and I assumed she was too, deciphering her moans was fast becoming my second language. Pulling her tight to my chest, I wrapped my arms around her more as I moved deeper in her before I felt my balls tense and my orgasm took over.

Holding her body to me, Soren used the tension to gain more of his own friction and started to fuck my ass with exuberance. His piercing dragged against my walls with each thrust, lighting me up inside. Just as I thought I might actually orgasm again, I felt him tense up and erupt inside me. Panting, we all dropped onto the bed, a sweaty and cum laden mess, too blissed out to care.

"That was amazing," cooed a sleepy Sawyer.

"Uh-huh," was the last thing I remembered before pulling her into my chest as Soren wrapped his arms around us both.

Bliss was right. This was my real always.

twenty-two

sawyer

FOLLOWING Fin inside the coffee shop, I muffled my yawn with the back of my hand. Fin caught me and leveled me with a knowing grin.

"Late night?" she teased.

"Oh, yeah. You know how it is. Henry just goes all night long," I said exaggeratedly.

"Ew, gross, you bitch! Blegh. Brain Bleach. Stat!"

Gagging, she smacked me on the arm, making me laugh at her reaction—always so dramatic.

"Don't be mean then!" Sticking my tongue out at her, I finished making my way to the counter to order my chocolate fix for the day.

"Just you wait, Sawyer Sullivan. There will be payback!"

"Uh, huh. Bring it, Finley Amelia! I got thick skin."

"First, no fair! I don't know your middle name. And

second, just wait until it's your brother and see how thick of skin you have then. You're going to need that brain bleach." Full body shudders ran through her body.

Laughing, I focused on the menu, like I wasn't going to order the same thing I always did. Her words did give me pause, though, and I realized I didn't want to hear about her and my twin. Ew!

Okay, maybe I owed her an apology. It was weird thinking of a sibling now. It was still too new to feel natural, but I found comfort in the knowledge I had a brother.

"The usual? Sawyer, right?" the barista asked.

Damn, he already knew my order. Though, come to think of it, I'd gotten different things each time. That wasn't creepy or anything.

"Um, well. Yes, my name is Sawyer, but what do you mean by my usual? I've never ordered the same thing..." my voice trailed off. Curiously, I watched him, trying to observe his response.

"Ah, well, I was referring to your muffin addiction. Two chip toppers, right?"

My cheeks heated at his answer. Now, I felt embarrassed for two reasons.

"Oh, um, yes, that'd be great. I'd also like a Salted Caramel Hot Chocolate."

Why did I feel so awkward now? He smiled and walked away, leaving me filled with embarrassment. I had like four boyfriends, maybe five; I mean, who was even keeping count at this point? Not me, apparently, but I got all tongue-tied around this guy every time—facepalm moment.

At least I'd spared him and myself from a real code orange. There was at least that, small mercy. Fin laughed at my awkwardness as I walked to the other end of the counter. Giving her big doe eyes, I begged her to drop it, fearing she would use this to get me back. Maybe I should rethink the whole prank war we seemed to have started. Fin was brutal.

Thankfully, Fin didn't make a scene, and we grabbed a spot while we waited for Chloe and Ace to arrive. I'd briefed Fin on the box update and the Tyler situation on the drive, so she was caught up on the telenovela my life felt like these days. That soap drama would be a reality soon.

Sawyer's Rink. Coming at you this fall!

"How's Charlie handling your accident? Did he freak out?"

At her question, an overwhelming feeling of panic hit me. "Fuck."

"You didn't tell him about your accident, did you?"

"Nope." Popping that "p" I placed my head on my arms, sulking.

"He's going to kill you!" she singsonged.

"Shut up. He probably will. Shit, I better do this now."

Standing up, I snuck over to the book area to make the call. It barely rang two times before he answered. Shit, he had to know something, or he wouldn't have answered that quickly.

"Sawdust," growled a deep voice. Oh yeah, he was pissed.

"Hey, Charlie! How are you? How's the rink?" I feigned nonchalantly. I hoped it would buy me some time. I should've known better.

"Don't 'hey Charlie' me, Sawdust. I've been waiting four days for you to call me. That Elias kid phoned me the day you were injured. Glad to know where I rank now," barked the voice over the phone. Yep, he was mad, and I think even a bit hurt. My heart sank.

"That's not it, Charlie, and you know it. You're my person. Don't ever think you're not. Things have just been crazy here. There's a lot of things going on that you don't know about, and I can't really get into it over the phone. I'm sorry. I didn't mean to make you worry." Regret filled my voice, and I hung my head. I'd fucked up. I was doing too much and forgetting people. I didn't want him to feel like I'd replaced him because I hadn't. He was the only Charlie.

"I'm going to make it up to you, and I will do better, I promise. I got tickets and a room for the Expo next month. I'm going... to be skating." I pleaded with him to understand and forgive me.

"Hm. Is that so? I guess I could get that O'Malley kid to look after the rink for a weekend. But Sawdust," he paused, swallowing, "I was scared and worried. Can you do an old man a favor and make sure I'm called on the important things moving forward? I know you don't need to, but I do worry."

"You big lug, now it's you who's being ridiculous.

I'm going to blame it on the partial concussion, but there really has just been a cluster of epic proportions to deal with. I miss you, old man, and I'm grateful every day to have you in my life."

"Now, girl, stop that. You're going to make my eyeballs leak. Let's not have that. Now, tell me about that Windsor kid. What's he like in person? And is the nice kid who called me your boyfriend?"

"Umm…"

I trailed off as I tried to explain things to Charlie. I updated him on the life stuff that I could, and we talked a little longer about the logistics of the expo weekend. Once we had everything scheduled, we said our good-byes with promises to have weekly updates.

Returning to the cafe area, I caught something shift in my peripheral, but when I turned to look, it was empty. Shaking my head, I continued back, but I had a feeling paranoia was going to drive me crazy.

"We need to schedule that sleepover we talked about soon. We can binge chick flicks and eat junk food," Fin suggested as we cleaned up.

We'd spent the morning hanging out with Ace and Chloe, but now I needed to meet Asa. He'd texted earlier saying he would pick me up here since I still didn't have my baby back. Ace had looked uncomfortable all morning, and I couldn't figure it out, so I decided to just directly ask him. I had too much shit going on to be worrying about if I'd done something to piss off a friend.

"Just let me know the details, and I'm game. I'm going to wait for Asa outside, but Ace, I was wondering if I could talk to you for a minute."

He looked surprised at my request, but agreed. The girls both promised to text over details as Ace and I headed out the door.

"You need something, Sawyer?"

"Yeah, I wanted to know what's up with you? You've seemed cagey all morning. Did I do something wrong?" His face dropped, and my insides tightened. Was I about to lose a good friend?

"I don't know how to say this, but," he sighed, "shit, this is hard, ugh." He started to pull what little hair he had as he paced back and forth.

"Ace, just tell me. I value your friendship, and I don't want to do anything to jeopardize that."

"Oh, beautiful girl, it's not you. It's me."

"What do you mean?"

"I'm… I'm… I'm…"

Fear started to fill me. What could be so hard for him to tell me? Pleadingly, I stared at him to just say it.

"I have feelings for Tyler." He dropped his hands, his eyes scared as he watched me.

"Huh? Okay..." That wasn't where I thought this was going. I tried to retrace our conversation from earlier, but nothing was standing out. Had I mentioned Tyler?

"Yeah, I uh, I've had a crush on him for years, and

just seeing you and him last night, it made me jealous. But it's clear you guys have history, so I'll get over it. I've just been feeling sorry for myself today. I didn't mean for you to find out."

At least that explained how he knew, but something didn't add up, didn't quite ring true with what he was saying.

"I'm sorry about Tyler. I didn't purposefully set out to hurt you. We actually kind of dated in high school, so yeah, there's a history there."

"I know, which is why I said don't worry about it. But look, I need to go. I'll talk to you later, okay?"

"Okay... but is there anything else? Just, I don't know. It felt like something more was going on?" I questioned as I urged my friend to be honest.

"Everything's great. Gotta go. Later."

"Yeah, sure," I mumbled as I watched him walk away. I was trying to not focus on how he'd avoided my direct question. On the surface, things had resolved I suppose, but nothing felt resolved inside. I didn't like this, a feeling of unease settled in me.

I would give him more time to come to me and be that friend for him. The beep behind me scared me enough to jump. Turning, I saw Asa laughing at me from the driver's side of a Jeep. Rolling my eyes, it seemed brothers were always a nuisance no matter how long you knew them.

"Very funny, nerd."

"Thank you. I did think it was hilarious."

I couldn't stay mad at him though; he was just so

earnest. He was like a golden retriever who chewed up your shoes but looked at you with absolute delight, and you couldn't help but reward him, slobber and all. That was Asa to a tee.

"Thank you for going with me. I'm hoping Aggie can help us out."

"No problem. I'm looking forward to just getting to spend time with you, you know."

"Me too." I smiled over at him.

"If you want to ask me anything about my life, you can. I'll answer what I know. Now that you've had some time for it to settle, have you thought of anything?"

"What's... she like?" I asked, fidgeting.

"I'm guessing you mean, Mom?" At my nod, he continued. "Well, she's petite, like you. We get our blonde hair from her, and probably our love of skating. She was a skater for many years until she married and retired. I don't think she knew you were alive. I mean, she's never mentioned or talked about you, and on my birthdays, she would always be both happy and sad. I could never work out why, but I guess now it makes sense."

"That's kind of a relief to hear. As cruel as it might sound, if she didn't know about me, then maybe she didn't have a part in giving me up?"

"Oh, Sawyer, I can tell you without a doubt that she had no part in that plan. That was all Orson. No doubt. When I finally was able to quit visiting him, it was the best day of my life. He's barely a person. He constantly worked. Everything is about power and position with him. He only tolerated me because I gave him status. But once it was clear I didn't want to pursue hockey professionally, well, he hasn't talked to me in five years."

"Wow. He sounds like a real keeper. Is it wrong to say I'm glad I didn't grow up knowing him then? My life was sucky at times, but my parents were amazing, and I never doubted their love for me."

"No, it's not wrong or bad. I'm glad that you had a good family too. As much as I hate that we grew up apart, I'm glad you had love in your life. I'm just sorry they were taken from you."

"Thank you, me too." I rested my head against the window, needing some space after all the emotional shit we'd just shared. As I looked at the window, I realized where we were. The same curve I swerved off the road. Sucking in a breath, a memory hit me hard.

A black truck zoomed around the curve and headed straight for me. I didn't notice it until it was almost on top of me. Swerving, I jerked the handlebars away and headed off the road toward the creek. The driver flashed through my mind for a split second. I'd caught a glimpse of him as I'd briefly looked up. Black sock cap, red beard, aviator glasses, and a black sweatshirt. But on the upper left side of the windshield was a very unique sticker. It was a TAS staff parking pass. Turning back toward the hill I was careening down, I realized my brakes weren't working. Someone had tampered with it, and since they'd worked on the way there... it had happened while at

Aggie's house. There was more than one person involved in this accident.

"Holy shit!" I yelled, sitting up.

"What! What is it? Is everything okay? Sawyer, talk to me?" Asa asked, looking over in fright.

"Sorry. Yes, everything at this moment is fine. I just remembered something from the crash. When we went around that curve, it triggered it. I remember the driver, Asa. And there was a sticker! And my brakes didn't work. Do you know what this means?"

"Slow down, sis. Start from the beginning."

And so, I did.

When I was done, his face held a mixture of excitement and fear. We finally had a lead, but it meant someone on our campus was part of this and more than one person was after me. On top of that, they could very well be connected to the house we'd just pulled up to. Yup, the cluster just got fuckier.

twenty-three

...

sawyer

"MS. SULLIVAN, so happy to see you're doing better. She's waiting for you in the drawing-room," Alfred, the butler, informed us after we'd rung the doorbell.

Something about his statement felt off. Or was my new friend paranoia making me question everyone? Asa followed me as I trailed behind the ancient butler. There was no way he had cut my brakes, right? He looked like he could barely bend over.

"Sawyer, so good to see you, dear. Please, have a seat and introduce me to your friend. Alfred has already prepared our tea for us."

Aggie patted the seat next to her, so I sat with her on the couch. Asa chose the wingback chair next to me. Close enough to offer me support and keep a watch on his Jeep through the window. He was a smart one; I hadn't even thought of that. I went to pour some tea when I noticed how badly my hands were shaking. Grabbing it with the other one to stop the shake, I decided it was best to wait on the tea for now.

"Aggie, I've made some, um, discoveries since our last time together. This is Asa," I paused, "my twin brother."

The clanking of her teacup hitting her saucer made me jerk my head up. When had I lowered it? Fuck, I needed to be more in the moment.

Aggie's eyes were huge as she glanced from me to Asa. My brother sat stoically in the chair, gaze strong with hers, as he waited to see what she would say. I hadn't planned for this meeting to go this way, but I guess this was par for the course in my life. Plus, my mouth always seemed to have a way of changing my plans.

"Oh my, that is some development." She kept glancing between us, almost as if she were watching a tennis match. When it clicked for her, it was evident on her face and soothed something in me. Aggie might be holding onto some secrets, but she wasn't malicious. Her secrets were hers; I could understand how it felt to share them after keeping them to yourself for so long.

"Your Isla's son, no?"

"Yes, she is my mother."

"And… she married that awful man, what was his name… Orson Aber..." Aggie trailed off as she started to make the connections. She peered back up at me with what could only be described as pity in her gaze.

"I knew the name sounded familiar when you'd

mentioned it, Sawyer. At the end of the school year, when most of the students were going off to college, there was a bit of a scandal. Victoria just disappeared one night. The Dravens offered a reward for any clues about her whereabouts, but nothing was brought forward. A few months after her disappearance, there was an announcement in the paper, the engagement of Isla to Orson. It was quite shocking, now that I think about it."

Aggie took a few sips of her tea before continuing her story. Asa and I both seemed to be holding our breath as we waited. This could be important.

"It was strange, a few years later, Victoria returned to the scene, but no one ever knew where she'd been those years. It was quite the gossip for a while. I'm surprised I'd forgotten. My memory seems to be fading more and more, unfortunately," she finished, sounding resigned.

"Draven?" Asa asked, his voice strained, his hands tight on the armrests of his chair.

"Yeah, my adopted mother's real last name. I never thought about it until Aggie mentioned it, but my parents would've had to change their real identities when we went on the run that first time."

My answer didn't seem to comfort Asa. The more I'd filled him in, the more the color had drained from his face.

"What is it, Asa?"

"The Dravens are business associates of Orson."

Fear filled his eyes, along with some sadness, I

assumed for me discovering the news. But no, it couldn't be.

"But that doesn't make sense."

Was my mom part of the Council and fooling us all? No. I refused to believe that until I had proof. My mother had loved me and cared for me. She loved my father too, and it was real between them. They'd both risked their lives to protect me.

"No, there has to be a reason. She disappeared; maybe she was running from them." Turning to Aggie, I began to recall our last conversation.

"Aggie, you said she was scared and changed her name. Maybe she wanted out of her family. In her note, she talked about someone coming. Maybe she meant them?"

"It's possible, Sawyer. I'm sorry I never asked her for more details."

"Don't." I shook my head, attempting to dissolve her guilt. "You couldn't have known. Besides, you've given me more information than I've been able to gather in the past five years alone. Not to mention, you were able to return some very important memories to me. I'll never be able to repay you for that." Sincerity rang through my voice, and some tears threatened to escape, but I held them back. Finally, feeling calmer, I set about making myself a cup of tea. Aggie must have sensed my need to change the subject, so she began to inquire about Asa.

"So, Asa, do you teach at the school?"

"Yes, ma'am. I'm part of the hockey coaching team."

"Please, call me Aggie, dear. Just don't tell Rhett, or do," she paused, smiling, "and rub it in his face. I quite like giving him a hard time."

We all chuckled at her statement. It was true. Rhett was fun to poke fun of. Sipping more of my tea, I relaxed back into the sofa as Aggie continued to talk with my brother.

"You know, hockey was one of my late husband's passions. I've sat through many cold games but loved every minute of it."

The small smile on her face warmed my heart, and I realized I needed to ask her more about herself. It seemed I was always monopolizing her time with questions about my past. Determined to do better, I spent the next hour getting to know Aggie more. She entertained us with stories of her travels and promised to make us some baklava on our next visit.

Aggie clued us in on her love of the gardens and how it had started with her family. It was fascinating, and I was glad I was getting to know her more. Her family had a long history with the town, and it was interesting to see how the school grew and changed over the years.

"Madam, it's time for your other appointment," Alfred informed us as he popped in, nearly scaring us all.

Aggies' face fell a little, and I wondered if it was at our time being up or regarding her visitor. Taking our cue to leave, Asa and I stood and gave her a hug. Squeezing her tight, I felt comforted in her embrace.

She smelled of gardenias and tea, a perfect combo for her.

"Thank you, Aggie. Tea again soon? I'll even bring Rhett next time."

"Please do, dear. You're always welcome here. I do enjoy your visits."

"It was a pleasure to meet you as well, Aggie. I will take great pleasure in giving Rhett a hard time," Asa said.

"The pleasure was all mine, young man. I'm so happy you two have found one another. Twins shouldn't be separated. It's so cruel, really. I hope you cherish the bond you two will have."

With her cryptic statement, we made our way out the door. As we approached the Jeep, I realized I'd forgotten to bring up someone tampering with my brakes here.

"Do you know how to check if your brake line has been cut?" I jested, but meant it in all seriousness. I was really tired of being chased off the road. Asa looked at me in thought before dropping down onto the pavement. I loved that he didn't question me or think my suspicions were crazy, but just did what he could to find an answer.

I dropped down too, because why not? Asa used his phone flashlight to look under the car, but nothing seemed to be hanging down or dripping, so it appeared we'd been spared this time.

Climbing up, I dusted off my clothes before getting into the Jeep. Simultaneously, we turned toward one another and shrugged, causing us both to break out into laughter. The more time we spent together, the more I liked him. Part of me wanted to be pissed at Orson for depriving us of our relationship, but that anger would only tarnish me. I had enough things in my life already wanting to do that, I didn't need to invite in anymore. Instead, I would focus on the joy of finding my twin.

As we pulled away, I was certain I saw Alfred watching from the window, but when I glanced back, only the flutter of the curtain remained.

A knock at my door brought me out of the daze I'd fallen into as I stared into the mirror.

"Come in."

"You about ready, Sawyer?" Henry asked, stepping into my room.

Looking at the makeup job I'd attempted, it was a foregone conclusion I was worthless at it. Especially when compared to the masterpiece Fin had performed on me last week.

"Yeah, I guess so." I shrugged, giving up.

Standing, I took Henry in and was momentarily speechless. He was wearing gray dress pants paired with a royal blue button-up shirt with his sleeves rolled up. Henry's hair was more tamed, but his curls still sat on top of his swoop. He looked mouthwatering.

"If you keep looking at me like that, Smalls, we

might not make it out of this room, and that would be a shame with how delicious you look in that dress."

He stalked forward until he was inches from me, placing his hands on my hips. Having to look up into his eyes now, I soaked in the man Henry had become.

"Smalls," he growled, only that had the opposite effect from what he'd intended.

"Sister, incoming, make sure you're dressed. I don't want to be scarred. I barely have time for the therapy I already need," shouted Fin from the door. She stood in there with her hand over her eyes, serious about avoiding us. She was so ridiculous sometimes, but I cherished it all.

"Fin, we're dressed. You can remove your hand. Geez, how do I put up with you?" Henry scoffed, rolling his eyes at his sister.

"Because I'm fabulous, duh."

Turning toward me, Fin's face scrunched up, obviously agreeing with my earlier acknowledgment.

"Oh no, this will not do. Good thing I came early. Henry, out. I have work to do and little time to do it."

"Thank god, I realized how crap I am at this. Please help me, Fin! I don't know what we're doing, but it seemed important to Asa."

She smiled softly at my statement, and I had a feeling she knew. Cataloging her outfit, I summarized how she looked both trendy and sophisticated. None of the sex goddess from the previous week, confusing me even more. It almost seemed like she wanted to impress someone.

Henry reluctantly left, and Fin worked her magic quickly, redoing my mess of curls, eye shadow, and bronzing. She stepped back, taking in my outfit before walking into my closet and coming out with something different.

"This."

Not arguing because, really, what was the point? I changed, slipping on the heels she handed me afterward. Taking a step back, she evaluated her work.

"Damn, I'm good. Okay, let's go."

Her nerves appeared to have returned, and I was even more curious now. It wasn't our birthdays, so what could be going on? Either way, I guess I'd have to wait as neither she, nor my brother, would budge as I pestered them on the car ride. I really fucking hated surprises.

twenty-four

. . .

sawyer

ASA PULLED up to a nice restaurant in town, making me even more confused. If we were just going to dinner, why was it such a secret?

Henry opened my door and took my hand in his. It was starting to get colder, and I was glad I'd grabbed my warmer jacket. Rhett had mentioned we'd have snow in about a week, if not sooner, and I couldn't wait. I loved the snow.

"Relax, Smalls. Whatever it is, I'm here. You got me."

Smiling at his reassuring statement, I realized he was right. Squeezing his hand three times, I walked in with him behind my brother and Fin. Asa was dressed in navy pants with a crisp white shirt. He looked really nice, and I realized I wanted to get a picture with him before the night was over. Assuming I wasn't being led to my death.

Too morbid? Well, you have two near-death experi-ences, and then we'll talk. Joking was the only thing that kept me from crying most days.

"Party for Walsh," he said to the hostess when we entered.

"Right this way, sir. Your guest hasn't arrived yet."

The maître d' lead us to a private room with a table set with five place settings. I was even more perplexed. Wait, who would… No!

"Asa… if I'm meeting who I think I'm about to meet, I'm strangling you," I ground out as I squeezed Henry's hand.

"Sorry, sis, but I figured it would be easier as a surprise so you wouldn't worry yourself to death."

"Because this is better?" I shrieked.

Removing my jacket, I started fanning under my arms as I paced back and forth. I was sweating and flushed—my skin felt on fire and not in the way I liked. Walking in circles now, I tried to control my breathing when Henry grabbed my arms, steadying me.

"Sariah, look at me."

"You just called me Sariah."

"I was trying to get your attention. Did it work?"

"Yeah. It felt so foreign, but at the same time like a pair of really comfortable pants, ones I haven't worn in a while, but when I put them on, it felt nice. Though, they don't really fit the same. Did that make sense? Part of me misses being her, but I'm not really her anymore, am I?"

"The best parts of Sariah are still in you, Smalls. Just,

now you're also stronger and fiercer. That is all Sawyer. You're a perfect mixture of all of you."

"Thanks, Henry."

"Any time. But for what?"

"For being you and always knowing what to say." I started to lean in to kiss him when gagging interrupted me.

"Yuck! Please, don't ruin my makeup job or wrinkle your dress. That was all heartwarming and everything, but I don't want to lose my appetite, so can we sit, please?" stated an exasperated Fin.

Flipping her off, I mouthed, "thank you." She always knew how to break up the tension, though, if she kept cock blocking me, we'd have words real quick. My hussy vagina would see to that, no doubt. She needed her daily dose of dick.

Sitting down, I had Henry on my left and an empty spot on my right that Asa had left open between us. I was starting to panic again when Henry grabbed my hand and squeezed. Just then, the door opened, and the maître d' led in a beautiful woman.

She talked to the man as she entered, not having noticed us yet, allowing me to take in every inch of her while I could. Asa was right; she was about my height, same blond hair, but more petite. She had that typical thin skater body I used to struggle with wanting.

She was dressed sophisticatedly in a dark green sheath dress and expensive heels based on their gleam. A strand of pearls hung around her neck, and diamonds dripped from her ears. Her hair was coiffed to perfection in an elegant updo. She was the picture of high class, and immediately I felt beneath her, unworthy.

At one point in my life, I would've fit that mold. But not now, not anymore. The past five years had taught me a different type of life. My jewelry was fake, my clothes knock-off, and my shoes borrowed. My makeup and hair, a pity gift from my best friend. Everything about me was less than.

We'd stood when the door opened, but at my realization, I sank into my chair, my head cast down. I couldn't do this. I couldn't witness the disappointment on her face when she realized what her daughter had become.

Henry was whispering something to me, but I'd tuned him out the minute I saw her. I was focused on her and her alone.

"Mom!" Asa's voice was full of love and genuine happiness to see his mom, and her responding voice indicated the same love for her son.

"Son! Oh, look at you. I swear you're still growing every time I see you," she gushed as they hugged. "Now, what was this surprise you said you had for me? You know I don't like surprises, Asa," she chastised, before landing on the girl standing next to him. "Oh, is this lovely girl, Fin?"

She pulled back from their embrace to take in Fin, a huge smile gracing her face. I was listening to every word, recording the sound of her voice in my mind, and memorizing her speech pattern and mannerisms to have it at my disposal for later, after she dismissed me. I knew it was going to happen. It was inevitable. I'd gone through this with several foster families and even one pre-adopted one. I was never chosen.

"Yeah, Mom, this is my girlfriend, Finley." At her name, he turned and smiled at Fin before finishing his introductions. "And Fin, this is my mother, Isla Walsh."

I watched their exchange closely, wanting to know what she looked like when she was happy. I wanted to savor this before it all went to shit. Fin blushed and her nerves earlier made sense now. She was meeting her boyfriend's mom.

This was a big deal, and I was happy for my brother and best friend. Just wished I'd been clued in so I could have avoided this disaster, or at least prepared more, brought a gift, perhaps, even fled the country. Any of those options were a possibility I'd been robbed to choose from. I was suddenly overcome with anger at them for not giving me a choice.

"It's so nice to meet you, Mrs. Walsh."

"None of that, give me a hug, dear. I'm so happy to meet you as well. Asa has done nothing but moon about you for the past year. I'm glad he finally got the nerve to make a move."

They embraced, and for the first time in forever, I was jealous of my best friend. She was hugging my biological mother as I sat on the fucking sidelines.

My mother was happy to meet her.

My mother even knew about her.

My mother was hugging her like the long-lost daughter she always wanted.

I couldn't deal with this. My anger clouded my real emotions, and I didn't want to feel this way about either of them, but everything was spinning out of control quickly.

Finley was speechless at the news Asa had told his mother about her, happily embracing her back. She'd always been a hugger, that girl. Tears tracked down my face as I took them in. I wanted that, but I felt so far away from ever having it. Henry was still trying to reassure me, but nothing he said penetrated my barriers. My emotional shields were up, too focused on the woman in front of me and the disaster that was looming to care.

It was a train wreck waiting to happen. Fin and Asa were the kinds of people who only saw the best, believed the best, and thought everything would work out. I'd been that way once too, but not anymore. Not now.

"So, was this my surprise?" She asked, but didn't wait for an answer before turning and looking at Henry and me. "And who are our other guests?"

She astutely observed us, taking in Henry first and then me. When she got to me, she stopped. Her face froze, and it was almost like looking in the mirror. There were slight differences, but minor. Looking back at me from across the table was an older reflection of myself. How Asa hadn't known shows the tricks our brains play on us.

Gasping, she grabbed her chest, her other hand covering her mouth as tears started to fall quickly down her perfectly made-up face. I was frozen in my chair. This wasn't the reaction I'd expected. No, I'd been prepared to book it out of there so fast it would put Usain Bolt to shame. Did she want to know me? I couldn't seem to move now, paralyzed to the spot.

"How?" she uttered that one word before fainting. Guess I had that in common with mommy dearest too.

Thankfully, Asa was quick on his feet and close enough to catch his mother, or our mother, before she made contact with the ground. He placed her delicately in the chair as he tried to stir her.

"Mom, Mom…" Gradually, she started to come around, blinking up at him as he hovered over her face.

"Asa, I had the strangest dream. I thought I saw your sister, but that can't be true. They told me she was dead," she mumbled softly in disbelief.

Her words gave me the strength I needed to stand up and make my way over to her. I was crying in earnest now, but I didn't care anymore. This was another relationship I'd been robbed of by Orson. One of these days, I was going to make him pay for everything he stole from me.

"Mom…" I breathed out, causing her to turn toward me at the sound.

"Abigail, is it really you?"

I was confused at first, but then the AA on the blanket clicked, and the memory of my mother telling me the name I'd been born with snapped into place. I simply nodded, falling into her arms, both of us a sobbing mess at this point.

Nothing else was able to pierce me as I clung to my biological mother. She smelled of roses, and her skin was soft. She felt safe and warm, comforting. Realizing I was probably leaving makeup marks all over her lovely dress, I finally pulled back, taking in her features this close.

"How is this possible, my baby girl?"

"I'm not sure you want to hear that story. It's not a pretty one."

At first, her face dropped at my words, and I hated it, but I wouldn't lie, not to her. Resolve filled her features, and I saw the strength she had in her. It made me proud, and I was filled with gratitude that not only did I get to call Victoria 'Mom,' but now Isla as well. Both of these women had overcome their circumstances, and I wanted that too.

I still had to dig more info up on the Draven's. But I knew, in my soul, my mom wasn't the bad guy, and neither was this woman. They were both victims of their upbringing, mere circumstances, not true intentions. What mattered, in the end, was who we were when faced with the truth. Did we blindly accept it, or did we push against it? I wanted to push the fucking doors open on the Council, and I think she would too.

"Maybe we should order, and then we can fill you in on all that we know, Mom?" Asa offered from the side. He was still holding her hand in his, and I realized he'd grabbed one of mine as well. Smiling at his suggestion, I untangled from the mother-daughter pile to walk back to my chair. Fin was there immediately to help fix my face.

Guilt bubbled up as I recalled the anger and jealousy I'd felt toward her earlier. I was a horrible friend. Now, I felt even worse for ruining her makeup job. Though the logical side of my brain pointed out she knew who I was meeting and kept it a secret, so I didn't feel too bad.

Somehow, the waiters knew they could enter then and took our drink and appetizer order. I had no clue what anything was, so I let them all order for me. To be honest, I was still in a daze. Realizing that I'd been ignoring Henry, I grabbed his hand under the table and squeezed. He leaned over and kissed my cheek, letting me know he understood. At least he'd been out of the loop too, so I wouldn't have to punish him later. But Fin, oh, that girl was going to get it.

Once the first round had been delivered, I started in on my history. By this point, I was good at condensing it and only mentioning the valid points without buckets full of emotions attached.

"And that's how I ended up here. Reconnecting with Henry and Fin, and meeting Asa. Quite frankly, it's been a whirlwind couple of weeks."

"I'm going to murder that bastard."

Taken aback by her words, I openly gaped at her. She was so fucking cool.

Once I'd recovered from the shock of her making that statement, I smiled wide at her. Mom, you have the right idea.

"Mother! This is not the place to be making death threats. Too many ears," Asa jested.

I wasn't sure at this point if Asa was joking or being serious, but it did offer us all some needed relief, as we broke out in laughter.

The waiters returned with our main courses, and again I wondered how they knew perfectly when to enter. It was like some *Beauty and the Beast* magic or some shit.

"So, what's the game plan to take these assholes down? And how can I help?"

I had to say Isla Walsh was not the woman I'd thought she would be. In fact, she was better. She was one badass classy bitch, and I hoped to be just like her.

twenty-five

. . .

elias

SAWYER AND HENRY had been out late the night before, and I heard from Rhett she had met her biological mother. I hoped it had gone well for her. She needed a win. Reviewing my schedule as I drank my coffee, I was surprised when Sawyer sauntered into the kitchen this early.

"Good morning, Sawyer. How was your evening?"

"Morning, it was informative," she replied around a yawn. Deciding to offer a peace offering, I held out a mug to her.

"Coffee or tea?"

She looked at me for a second, assessing me almost, weighing my sincerity.

"I'm afraid it's a coffee morning. Thanks."

I poured the liquid into the mug at her statement as she hopped up on the counter next to my day planner.

Lucky had followed her and retreated to his dog bed in the corner. He had a bed in most rooms, the big mooch. He was a creature of comfort, always seeking out the comfiest spots.

"Cream or sugar?"

"Both please, generous on the cream. I'm a fake coffee drinker," she faux-whispered, making me laugh at her statement. Adding her cream and sweetener, I stirred it before handing it to her.

"Thank you, Elias. This is really kind of you."

"Believe it or not, I'm a kind person. We've just had a rocky start."

Snorting at my statement, she took a long sip, moaning as she drank it down. Why did she have to be so sexy doing the most ridiculous things? And those noises, bloody Hell, woman.

"You can definitely say our start got off on the wrong foot, but I'm glad we're becoming pseudo friends. You're not so bad once you remove that stick stuck up," pausing, she tapped her chin in thought, "what's the word, oh, arse. Stick up your arse. Yeah, that."

"Ha, ha. You're so funny. I can tell you've been hanging around, Oliver."

I went back to reading my schedule, preparing lesson ideas, and jotting down some new ones in my planner.

"In all seriousness, though, you have loosened up. In fact, I think you've used three, maybe four, contractions this morning already! Progress, my friend!"

She shoved my shoulder in jest at her statement, laughing as she poked fun at me. I didn't seem to mind it, actually. It was… nice. As she drank her coffee, she started to look at what I was doing, watching me for a few minutes.

"Damn, dude. You need to teach me how to do that! I need to be more organized, and I've tried using one, but I forget it half the time and don't put things in that make sense."

Glancing up at her, I could see she was sincere and not poking fun at me this time.

"Well, I could help you if you'd like. I get great pleasure in an organized and balanced planner."

"Oh, that would be amazing! Thank you."

She jumped off the counter and surprised me by hugging me around the waist before she scurried off to God knows where. Just when I think I have her figured out, she takes a left turn, throwing me completely off.

I watched her walk out of the room, her shorts snug against her arse, and I was definitely enjoying this new development in our relationship where we could actually have a conversation without snipping at one another. It was nice.

"I think you've got something on your chin there." Came from behind me, causing me to spill a little of the hot liquid I was about to drink, on my tie. Turning to see who I owed for my clothing debacle, I found a beaming Soren.

"Whatever do you mean? We were having a conversation, that was all," I responded tersely, hoping he would buy it and drop it.

"Yeah, sure, bro. Keep telling yourself that. Denial is not attractive, just in case you care." He chuckled as he began to make himself some breakfast.

How he cooked on the stove bare-chested always surprised me. I would be scared of burning a nip or something. Focusing back on my diary, I made some marks to adjust some things to add in time for training. It had felt good the past few days returning to it, and I was glad to be getting back in it.

A sudden plop on the counter startled me out of my reverie to find a beaming Sawyer next to me. Confused, I looked down to see what she had dropped and found a journal and some pens. Oh, I guess she meant now. Okay, I could deal with this, I assured myself. Though, to be frank, I would probably reschedule my own funeral to have her smiling at me for once.

"How about we move to the table, so we have more room?"

"Sure thing, boss!"

Sawyer scooped up all of her belongings and set off for the table with a skip in her step. She still had on those tiny shorts, and with how the word 'boss' had sounded coming from her lips, I was glad the counter was there to hide my erection.

For the next twenty minutes, I helped Sawyer find a planning style that worked for her, set weekly goals, and organized her tasks and appointments. She was a quick learner and listened politely as I explained how to organize and prepare in the best ways. It was probably the best conversation we had ever managed, and it involved post-it notes and gel pens—her contribution, mind you.

"Wow, this makes so much sense. Thanks, Elias. I feel better, and like I can actually focus for once instead of trying to do a million things all the time but forgetting what I need to do."

My breath caught in my throat as she delivered me my first real smile. It was so warm, and it was directed at me. Fucking amazing. I think I stared at her for longer than was appropriate before I finally remembered to respond back.

"No problem. I'm glad I could be helpful. Using your new schedule, what time do you have free today to look through the yearbooks?"

A look of excitement displayed across her face as she turned her planner to today. "I'm free from about 1 pm to 3 pm. Does any of that work for you?"

I was distracted watching her, so I hadn't looked at my own schedule, but fortunately, I had it memorized. I did have something scheduled for that time, but I would move it for her, no hesitation.

"Elias?"

"Sorry, love. Yes, that time works for me. Want me to grab lunch, and then we can go through them here?"

"Great idea. I'm finishing a session before that, so I will be famished. It's a research date!"

My heart rate skipped at her use of the word date, and the joy in her voice. I tried to remain calm on the outside. She headed off in the other direction, and I pulled out my phone to reschedule my 1 pm appointment. Suddenly, I couldn't wait until lunchtime.

My alarm was going off, reminding me it was time to wrap up so I could grab some food for Sawyer and me.

"Alright, Clarence. That will be all for today. I think you are grasping your mathematics and science. Your struggle is still with English Lit, but I see improvement. Have any of the study methods we talked about helped?"

"Somewhat, I need to be better about using them consistently," he sighed. "Thanks, Mr. Turner. My parents are happy, at least with the improvement I'm making, which is good enough for me to keep skiing."

"You're most welcome. Now, if we can get your English Lit up, you will be set for college applications. I'll see you next Wednesday."

We both gathered our belongings before leaving the small library in the administration building. There were several tutor rooms available for use since we didn't have actual classrooms. I found it easier to migrate locations depending on the student's needs. Therefore, I found it wiser if I carried all of my teaching materials with me to be more mobile. Basically, I had a mini filing cabinet in the boot of my car.

Driving into town, I stopped at the cafe I knew had

great sandwiches and cake options. Not knowing which she would prefer, I had called in an order for the sampler. They had these amazing little cakes that almost resembled cupcakes with how they were arranged in tiny little cake pans. I was hoping they would win me some brownie points, to be honest. This morning had been pleasant, and I wanted her to see me as the guy I was, instead of the guy she had first met.

"May I help you?" the young girl at the counter asked. I think she was trying to flirt as she twirled her hair, blinking at me, but she was barely eighteen and so not on my radar.

"Pick up for Turner."

"Oh, yes. One moment."

She returned a few moments later, red-faced and bashful, and I couldn't make out why.

"Here you go. I added something extra to your cakes. I hope you like it."

"Um, thanks."

Not knowing what to say, I took the two boxes and left. This was part of the reason why I was awful with girls. I misread things or came off as an ass. Hookups were the easiest for me because the expectations were outlined from the beginning.

Parking in the garage, I unloaded the boxes and headed to the kitchen. Lucky picked his head up from the bed he was lying in, but didn't seem all that bothered I was home. *Thanks, dog, love you too.*

I took the food boxes to the conference room as I figured we would be more comfortable there. Plus, there was a whiteboard and smartboard, so we could project things if we needed to. It made sense for it to be our ground zero moving forward. We could leave things in here and lock them when others were over. I had been thinking about this for a few days and decided it made the best sense.

Dropping the food off first, I headed up the stairs to grab the box of yearbooks I had requested. There were two of them filled to the brim, so it would take me two trips. By the second one, I was a sweaty mess and cursing at myself for taking them up to my room in the first place. Taking off my tie, I started to unbutton my shirt, leaving only my white undershirt on.

Of course, this was when Sawyer walked by, causing her to stop and turn back, a curious look on her face.

"Is this a clothing optional research session? I don't think I got the memo for that. Also, it's not Sunday."

She was laughing at me, the saucy minx. Chuckling at being caught the moment my shirt was off, all I could do was spar with her. Leveling her with a look, I took a chance on myself to not fuck it up this time.

"Love, anytime you don't want to wear clothes, feel free not to. I've learned my lesson and will not dictate what you can or cannot wear. I happen to have gotten overheated carrying these boxes from upstairs. So, you see, it's because I was using my big strong muscles for you. I plan to keep this shirt on, though. I'm not sure you could focus if I didn't. It's for your own good, really."

Where the hell had that flirt come from? Waiting for

her to attack, I was surprised when she laughed at me but discreetly licked her lips. Did she like my comment? Was she thinking about being distracted by my chest? Interesting.

"Thanks for protecting my delicate sensibilities, Elias. So, what's for lunch? I'm starving." She entered the room, and I noticed my traitor dog was with her. I needed to admit defeat. He was clearly her dog now. I was only hurting myself at this point, trying to force the issue. I didn't need that kind of rejection every day.

"I grabbed a sandwich platter and cake sampler from the local cafe. They have a great selection. I got a bit of everything, since I wasn't certain what you would like." At my statement, her smile grew. I had noticed she'd been doing that more, but I wasn't sure what for. Sawyer was the epitome of an enigma wrapped in a puzzle.

"That's the cake box," I commented when she went to grab the pink box first.

"Perfect! I guessed correctly, then. I want cake first."

Well, okay then. She opened the box and began to look at the contents intensely. I went back to unloading the yearbooks by years into stacks on the table.

"Um, Elias?"

At her hesitancy, I looked up and noticed she seemed stuck between laughing and offended. How could she be offended by cake? Maybe I needed to rethink my attraction. Cake was life.

"Is the cake not to your liking, love? I thought I had a winner with the sampler."

"Um, it's not so much the cake I have an issue with. It's the naked photo of a girl that's taped onto the top of the box, that I'm not so sure about."

My brain faltered. What in the world was she talking about? Ambling around the table, I stood next to her to look at the apparently naked picture. She had to be taking the piss.

Clear as day, a very nude photo of the girl from the counter was taped to the top of the box. Guess that was why her face had been so red. Squeezing my eyes shut, I was trying to block out the image. I felt terrible for doubting Sawyer now. I really needed to quit seeing the worst in every situation when it came to women. It wasn't healthy.

"Ah man, I think she might have ruined cake for me. This is a travesty."

"Nah, it's just boobs, remember? I just wasn't sure if you knew it was there and were trying to prank me, or if you had plans to meet up with said girl later. But if you didn't know, and she slipped it in, then I'll help you out."

I was transfixed by her mouth as she spoke. She had taken one of the slices of cake and was eating it with a fork, but periodically, she would stop and lick the icing from the tines. Blinking, I tried to focus on what she said before I had gotten lost in her licking.

"You thought I had pranked you? Or that she was my booty call?" I asked slowly, trying to digest her comments.

"Yup. Rhett told me a story of you setting him up

and how you both mess with each other's stuff some-times. We've been getting along better, so I thought maybe that was your bridge—a prank war. No worries, though. The picture is gone, and the cake is edible. Now, where do we want to start?" she asked calmly as she walked around to the table, still eating her cake. Oh, to be that fork.

I stared after her, literally speechless at the events that had occurred in the past five minutes. I seriously did not understand the female brain—at all.

twenty-six

sawyer

RESEARCH WAS FUCKING BORING. I was not a fan. Flipping through another yearbook, I'd yet to find anything. It didn't help when I had no clue what I was even looking for outside of the name Abernathy. Turning the page loudly, I debated taking a nap right there on the table.

Tapping the pen, I wondered if Elias would even notice if I laid my head down. He was so in his element. I spent time just watching him work before I decided to try it. Slowly, I lowered my head down to the table.

"Don't even think about it," he said, not even looking up.

"How do you do that?" Glaring at him from across the table, I sat back up.

"I'm a tutor, love. You think you're the first disgruntled pupil I've had? What have you found?"

"Jack squat. This is pointless and painful. I thought it would be... I don't know, more montage like," I confided as I waved my hands all around.

"Montage like... I don't understand?"

"Oh, you know, when in the movies they have like a make-over scene or gathering information reel. They make it fun, and it goes by quickly, and they show you how amazing it was, and they find something. Like that... yeah." I snapped my fingers.

Staring at him, my brain caught up with interpreting my ramblings. I'd just admitted to wanting something amazing with him. Shit! Face flaming, I decided to distract. It was the only way, especially as he got a peculiar look on his face and started to ask me a question. Nope—not going to happen, buddy.

"You want—"

"I think you're up to double digits now on the contractions, mister! Way to go! I think that deserves a break and more cake."

He tilted his head at me like I was some complex problem he was trying to work out. Good luck—I still didn't understand me, and I *was* me.

"Sure, a cake break sounds good."

Hopping up, I scooped the cake box, now sans boob pic, and walked around the table.

"So, what's your poison? You ever thought how weird that phrase is?"

I was rambling again. Fucking hell. Elias kept looking at me, and I didn't like it. Nope, I did not. Shut up, vagina.

"Well, I'm partial to lemon and red velvet. Either one of those there?"

He kept staring at me, almost like he'd decided to wait me out or make me crack, more likely. His eyes peered into mine instead of looking for himself as I held the open box in my outstretched hand. He was testing me, the punk.

"Well…" I drawled, shaking the box under his nose. Still, no deviation from his whiskey eyes that were alight with mischief. Why did that turn me on? Realizing he wasn't going to answer, I gave in, the dickcheese.

"There's strawberry, chocolate, funfetti, and you're in luck because there does appear to be a lemon."

He was still watching me, the weirdo, so slowly I picked up the piece of cake, lifting it out of the box, and poised it in front of his face, ready to strike. Had he learned nothing about me? I never backed down. It was a strength and a flaw.

"How much you like it is the question?"

His eyes finally tracked the cake and grew wide. Moving back quickly, he put space between us, holding his hands out in front. Like that would stop me, fat chance.

"Now, I don't think we need to go that far, love."

"Oh, well then, I guess I get to enjoy it."

I brought the cake to my mouth, but just as I was about to lick the frosting, his hand grabbed my wrist, halting my movement.

"Not so fast, love."

Before I could even do anything, Elias took a giant bite of the cake. You know, the one I was holding mere centimeters from my own mouth. His eyes bored into my own, and for a quick second, I almost took a bite.

Stepping back, I'd let him have the cake, suddenly unsure where I stood. The moment had passed, and now we were stuck with a whole bunch of awkwardness. Dropping the cake into his hand, I walked back and picked up a fork to eat the strawberry one.

I avoided his gaze as I pretended to flip through pages. Just as I was about to close the book, a page finally caught my eye. Two girls stood side by side on the ice dressed in competition leotards. One had dark hair, Brazilian features, and my mother's eyes. The other had blond hair, short-statured, and it was almost like looking in a mirror—my biological mother.

"Holy shit."

Staring at the page, fork still held aloft, my brain was sputtering at what this meant or could mean. They'd known one another. For some reason, I hadn't made that connection when Aggie mentioned them at school together. Even more, they might have been close.

"Sawyer, what is it?"

Elias' voice surprised me, and I jerked back, knocking my head into his, which was now directly behind me. My momentum brought my fork up—you know, the one that still had frosting on it—and thereby smearing it all over Elias' nose.

"Ow," we both groaned, grabbing our respective heads.

Once the stars cleared from my vision, I looked up and saw nothing but pink frosting on the tip of his nose. Not able to hold back my laughter, I lost it. Laughing so hard, I rolled out of my chair and landed on the floor. Still forgetting I had a fork full of frosting in my hand, I managed to get it all over myself this time.

Elias came out of his head butt daze and joined in on the laughter. Of course, that was when someone walked by the room, stopping to see what all the commotion was.

"Um, everything okay in here?" Mateo asked, which, of course, only made us laugh more.

"Hey Mateo, want some cake? It comes with boobs!" I shouted. Clearly, I'd hit my limit. My mouth was running away from me, and no longer listening to what was good for me. My statement only caused Elias to laugh more and Mateo to be confused.

By this point, I was on my back, lying on the floor, snow angel formation style. Mateo took pity on me and walked into the room, offering me a hand to help me up. What took me by surprise, though, was what he said when I stood.

"Seems you've gotten yourself into a bit of a mess, Dulzura."

"That I have, though, you should see the other guy!"

"I'd much rather see you. How about I help you out?"

Before I could respond, Mateo licked the frosting off the cheek it had landed on. I was so shocked by his boldness, I stood still, mouth open, gaping wide at him.

Despite being stunned, his growing confidence was hella sexy. But my mouth, remember her bitchiness? I couldn't stop there. I think she and my vagina were teaming up. If so, I was in so much trouble. Heaven help me if my hand ever decided to join in too.

"Don't forget about Elias. He has some frosting too."

What. The. Hell.

Seriously, who let me out this morning? *Abort, abort, danger, Will Robinson.* Thankfully, they took my comment as a joke, and both laughed. If only they knew how sexy I found it.

"I'm good, Mateo, thanks. I do, however, like your method for Sawyer."

Fucking hell, he needed to stop, or I was going to forget I didn't like him.

"What did you find before our frosting snafu, Sawyer?"

"Oh, yeah." Turning back to the table, I grabbed the yearbook I'd been looking at.

"Oh, just a photo of my adopted mom and biological mom all chummy on the ice."

Elias smiled, and for a moment, I was scared of what he was going to say, looking that excited.

"Brilliant! That means we're on the right track! Let's keep going and see what else we can find."

Oh, fun, more research.

Fortunately, Mateo stayed and helped. By the time we left the conference room, which we now dubbed as HQ for Operation Toe Pick, we'd found four pictures that may connect us to the Council.

We still had a box of yearbooks to look through, too. For the first time since I started looking into my past, I felt hopeful that we'd found some real answers to who killed my parents and why.

"Stop fidgeting. It's going to be fine. I promise," Rhett admonished as we headed to his mom's B&B for dinner.

"But, what if they don't like me?" Worry laced my words as I fidgeted more with my necklace. This was the first time I was meeting the parents of someone I was dating—internal freak-out initiated.

"I like you, so they will like you. I even told them about us all dating, and they were accepting of it. I promise, it will be a good evening, baby."

At the thought they knew about me dating all of the guys, my heart raced with fear. Just, fucking great. Now, they were going to think I was a slut.

"Baby."

Rhett grabbed my face between his massive hands, stopping my spiral. His thumbs gently stroked my cheeks as he gazed into my eyes. Rhett's eyes were deep pools of emotion, drawing me in to trust what he was saying, and I wanted to surrender. Leaning forward, I placed my lips gently against his for a few seconds before pulling back.

"Thank you."

"Anytime, baby. I got you."

That he did, that… he… did.

Taking a deep breath, I pulled the door handle and got out of the car. We'd stopped on the way so I could grab some flowers. Rhett had told me it was unnecessary, but I really wanted to make a good impression on his mom and sister. Fin helped me pick out a dress, and I felt confident I was at least dressed "meeting the mother" appropriate.

Rhett didn't knock on the door, but walked right in. I didn't know why that stuck out to me; obviously, this was his home, of course, he would walk right on in. The smell of fresh-baked bread, apples, and pumpkin filled the air. We'd entered into the kitchen area. It was gorgeous, with its white cabinets and countertops. A woman worked at the stove and seemed to be singing to herself as she softly swayed back and forth while stirring.

"Mom, we're here."

At his voice, the woman turned, and immediately I saw resemblances to Rhett. Her smile was kind, and there were laugh lines around her eyes. She was much shorter than him, but still taller than me by a few inches. Her hair was lighter than his too, and her almost hazel colored eyes weren't as guarded.

Their physical resemblances were small, but there was something about her that made me instantly like her. Despite Rhett's prickly exterior most of the time, he exuded warmth, and I could tell he'd learned that from this woman.

"Son!"

Beaming, she walked over and immediately embraced him. Despite being shorter, she squeezed him tight, engulfing him in her love. A tear rose to my eye at their bond, but I squashed it down, now was not the time to get all weepy. Stepping back, she took a good look at him before turning to me. I didn't know what I was expecting, but her beaming smile wasn't it.

"And you must be Sawyer, the woman who has made my boy smile again."

Before I could even digest her statement, I was wrapped in her sugary smell and melted into her hug. Wow. This woman was a fantastic hugger. I just wanted to stay here and soak in her motherly comfort. Stepping back, she grasped my arms, peering into my eyes. At her swipe at my cheek, I realized the tear I'd been holding back a minute ago had managed to escape. Fucker—rogue tear alert.

"None of that, dear. Come, let's go sit. Rhett, can you finish the sauce?"

She took the flowers that somehow managed not to get smushed and placed them on the counter. Then she walked out with her arm around me, not even checking that he would indeed finish dinner or put those in water. I was kind of in awe of this woman. We walked over to a couch area and sat down. The room was homey and welcoming, and I never wanted to leave. Squeezing my hand, she brought my attention back to her.

"Sawyer, thank you for those beautiful flowers. It's so nice to meet the woman who has brought laughter back to my son. I know your relationship isn't typical, but I wanted you to know that as long as Rhett is happy, then I approve. He hasn't always let many people in, but when he does, it's for life. He's smitten with you."

She smiled kindly at me, but she had it all wrong. He made me feel that way. It had nothing to do with me. I was just happy she appeared to approve. She paused briefly, and I worried she was about to give me the "but" comment.

"Sawyer, I just have to ask, how do *you* feel about my son?"

Surprised she hadn't kindly told me to get out, I oddly didn't feel put on the spot or confronted. Instead, I could see her love for him shining through her eyes. She genuinely wanted to protect her son. I respected that. My blush gave me away long before my words, as it always did, but I didn't care. I would tell anyone who asked how I felt about Rhett Taylor.

"He's one of the most amazing people I've ever met. I know it probably sounds selfish that I'm dating more than one person, but it's more than that. We've all created a family, and together we're healing one another. Rhett… he doesn't see it, but he's the glue in a lot of ways. He brings us all together, encourages us, helps us communicate despite his own silence at times, and watches over all of us."

My heart was racing, and my blush only intensified on my cheeks. I couldn't believe I was admitting all of this to his mom, but she had that quality about her where you wanted to tell her everything. Her soft smile told me it was okay, so as I fidgeted with my necklace, I let my heart do the talking for me.

"Rhett has a way of being in the background making sure we're all cared for, never asking for accolades. He shines so brightly despite his attempts to hide. But I see him: the strength he has, the fierce protectiveness, the depth of his love for others, and this realness that exudes from him. He's taught me to be brave in our short time together, to ask for what I want, and that it's okay to be different. My heart has been hidden for so long, scared to feel real emotions again, but Rhett understood, and instead of pushing me, he's walked alongside with me the whole time. I—" before more words could flow from my mouth, she stopped me.

"Sawyer, nothing else needs to be said. It's clear you care deeply for my son, perhaps even more than you're ready to admit, but I think that should be for him to hear first. You truly are as amazing as he said, and I'm glad he's found you after everything. I fear you guys will face prejudice and judgment from the world, but never from me. I would be honored to have you as part of my family. Now, let's go find Rowan and eat before Rhett burns my delicious meal."

I followed her in a trance from the level of acceptance and emotions she'd dumped on me. Inside, though, my head and heart were exploding into a million tiny hearts.

twenty-seven

. . .

rhett

MOM HUGGING Sawyer was the culmination of my two worlds merging. It felt promising, giving me a glimpse of the future, and I was finally headed in the direction I wanted to go. I hadn't realized how stationary things had become, I'd just been spinning my wheels. Well, no more.

Turning the burner off, I removed the sauce from the stove and placed it on the hot pad mom left out. The bread was warming on the stovetop, and the pasta was ready. Looked like it was time to eat.

Walking toward the living room, I paused when I heard my mother ask Sawyer about her feelings for me. I felt like a creeper, but hearing her say those things about me lifted any fear or doubt that had remained.

Sawyer resonated within my soul. I'd never heard anyone describe me that way before; I almost thought she was talking about someone else. She saw all that in me? A sense of awe overtook me at how she viewed our relationship and the family unit we were creating together. Hearing them move, I backed up quickly to avoid getting caught eavesdropping, but unfortunately ran smack dab into Rowan.

"Ow, watch where you're going, you big oaf."

"I'm pretty sure you were the one standing behind me, so you can only blame yourself. Besides, creep much there, little sis?"

"Like you have any room to talk! I saw you listening in!"

"Ssh, here they come," I whisper shouted at her. Instantly, we both turned, smiles plastered on our faces, a picture of innocence.

"Ah, here you two are. Is dinner still edible, Rhett?" Mom asked, eying us suspiciously as she walked Sawyer to the table.

"What are you two up to, anyway?" She quirked an eyebrow at me but said nothing—at least I knew where I learned my facial expressions. Sawyer just smiled at me as she took her place. Rowan pinched me on my side after they'd passed, causing me to jump.

"Ow! What was that for?" I accused, rubbing the area.

"She's way too pretty for you! OMG. How did you convince her to go out with you?" Rowan jibbed as she walked by me, punching me in the arm and sticking her tongue out—so immature.

Rolling my eyes at her behavior, I waited until she

wasn't looking and chased after her. I grabbed her around the ribs and tickled her as we followed them to the table.

"Stop! Uncle, uncle. I give in!" Rowan laughed.

"Not till you say the magic words, pipsqueak."

"Ugh, fine. Rhett is the best big brother, and any sister is lucky to have him. There, you happy? Now your girlfriend knows how crazy you are," she retorted, her face sullen.

I didn't care because I liked how the word girlfriend had sounded and the way Sawyer's cheeks reddened. Rowan finally extracted herself from me and walked over to the table to introduce herself.

"Hi, I'm Rowan. The better sibling of the Taylors. It's nice to meet you, Sawyer."

Rowan gave her a hug despite towering over her seated, but I could see Sawyer's beaming smile over her shoulder. It was official. We all needed to hug that girl more; it was obvious she'd missed out on hugs over the years.

Grabbing the bread and bowl of pasta, I followed mom back into the dining area. She'd put the food onto platters while they'd introduced themselves. Sitting next to my girl, I turned in my chair to look at her. She'd been so worried, but I knew they'd love her just as I did.

"You doing okay, baby?"

"Yeah, you were right. They're great. Thank you for introducing them to me."

"Baby, I want you in every part of my life. You don't

ever have to thank me for that." I kissed her quickly on the forehead before turning back to the table. My mother and sister were both trying to busy themselves, but clearly had listened in on our conversation.

Clearly, we were an eavesdropping, eyebrow-raising, and exuberant hugging family. I think I was okay with that.

"It smells wonderful, Mrs. Taylor."

"Oh goodness, please call me Momma Bear or Rhonda. None of that, Mrs. stuff. Most of the guys call me Momma Bear when Rhett brings them by. It fits since he's such a grizzly bear on the outside but gummy on the inside."

I'd just taken a drink of water, but at my mother's statement, I sprayed it all over the table and, well, Rowan.

"Oh my God! Gross!" Rowan shouted as she quickly jumped up to get a towel. Sawyer laughed so hard she was crying, and I worried she might choke on her own drink she was attempting to swallow. When she finally managed, she beamed at me.

"That is the most amazing thing I've ever heard. I call him grumpy bear, myself. Glad to see I'm not the only one. You all are so my people." Sawyer managed to get out once she had her laughter under control.

"Har har, you guys are hilarious," I deadpanned as I cleaned up the table. If I wasn't so mortified by the comment my mom made, I would probably be more embarrassed by the spitting, but at this point, there was no room for any more humiliation. At least she hadn't pulled out the baby pics. I would need to hide those.

Once everyone had settled down and the table was cleaned, we started on the meal. We settled into a comfortable conversation as we all ate, and happiness filled me.

While I didn't want to keep comparing her to Molly, it'd never felt like this with her. Sawyer was quickly cementing herself in my family, just as quickly as she had in my heart. If someone wasn't trying to kill her, it would feel just like one of my favorite movies—just that one tiny detail.

sawyer

Dinner had gone wonderfully, and I enjoyed being around Rhett's family. His sister was sassy and bold, and I wanted to be her friend. She was a few years younger than me, but I could tell her illness had matured her. We had a lot in common, and I think she'd also get along with Finley.

We were sitting out on the back deck enjoying some brownie dessert Rowan had made, and I'd officially hit food coma territory. It was all seriously amazing.

"How come you can't cook this well, grumpy bear?"

The heated look he sent me set my insides on fire, but it was so not the right place for it!

"That's because he's too impatient for most things you have to cook. He's good at things he can make quickly, like the smoothies. But anything that requires time or details always ends up a burnt mess. I only let him finish the sauce tonight because it only needed a few minutes." His mother laughed, allowing all of us to join in with her.

"Mom, did you happen to look into those pictures and articles I asked you about?"

"Oh, yes, I did find a few things. It wasn't much, but I thought it might be helpful," Rhonda said as she jumped up to go back inside. Looking at Rhett, I questioned him with my eyes.

"I'd asked Mom if she had anything from her high school days. It would've been around the same time one or both of your parents might've been here. It was a small lead, but worth looking into."

"Thank you." I smiled, my eyes wanting to leak at his kindness. This guy, gah, he just continued to amaze me every day. I was too scared to admit my feelings, but my heart filled with warmth, and I was sure my eyes had hearts coming out of them.

Rhonda returned, handing Rhett a small folder. We both stood, taking that as a cue to leave. Everyone gave another round of hugs, and I relished in each one, squeezing them tight.

"Thank you for caring about him. He's the absolute best," whispered Rowan before she pulled back from our hug.

All I could do was nod and smile. What does one

say to that? It wasn't hard to care about Rhett Taylor. He *was* the absolute best.

We exchanged numbers, and I promised to let her know the next time we came into town for coffee. Her classes sounded interesting, and I looked forward to getting to know her more.

Hands full of leftovers for the guys and the folder, we headed back to the car. It had been a wonderful evening, and yet it was still early.

"They both really like you," he said as we pulled out.

"I really like them. Your mom and sister are amazing. I see where you get it from."

His smile was bright and full. It amazed me how he barely smiled a few weeks ago, and I'd set out to count them because they were so rare. Now, at least in my presence, it seemed to be his natural state. Whether or not that was because of me specifically, it definitely felt nice having one directed at you. I could get lost in his stare.

Once we were back at the house, we placed the leftovers into the fridge. The house was quiet. All I could hear was a faint shower running upstairs, but otherwise, it appeared to be a deserted Monday evening. I wasn't ready to end the night, though, and after that meal and the earlier revelations, I needed to do something.

"Want to start on the training you'd mentioned? Strengthening my muscles and seeing if you're able to do more with my injury?" I proposed.

"Baby, you, in a tight stretchy outfit doing fitness," he paused, his eyes scanning over me. "That will always be a yes. Meet you there in ten minutes?"

"Perfect." I beamed. He didn't realize it worked the same way for me with him half-naked. Drool's capital city was somewhere on his abs. I hadn't missed the heat in his eyes, either. Rhett appeared only seconds away from stalking toward me and taking me right there. Exercising was about to get hot—for an entirely different reason.

Jogging up the stairs, I quickly changed into some workout gear and pulled my hair up into a ponytail. I stopped briefly to pet Lucky on my way out. He'd taken to sleeping in my room throughout the day, so I left a blanket down on the ground for him to curl up in. He stretched before he followed me downstairs, so I figured he needed to potty.

Letting him out the backdoor, I breathed in the night air, loving how crisp everything in the mountains felt. Being away from a big city, the night air was clearer, and I could see the stars better. The sun was setting in the distance, and the picture it painted was lovely behind the mountain caps. Lucky finished his business and trotted back in all proper like.

Shaking my head at him, I swear sometimes he acted like such a prissy dog with all of his attitude. Secretly, it just made me love him more.

I could hear some bass pumping from the fitness room and knew Rhett had beaten me there. My little detour for Prince Lucky had put me behind schedule, but it was worth it to make sure he was okay. He'd truly become my little companion over the past month. I felt a little bad now that Elias wasn't such a dick, but I couldn't help it if I was just more lovable.

Pulling the door of the fitness room open, I found Rhett setting up some weights on one of the machines. An upbeat song playing on the speaker system, so I grooved to it on my way to him, making him chuckle.

"Ready to sweat?"

"Let's do it."

"Warm up your muscles, and then we will start with some circuits."

His bossy voice was incredibly sexy tonight, but I needed to focus. This training was important not only for my potential rebooted career but for my health and muscle development.

For ninety minutes, I did yoga, running, elliptical, and weight training. Rhett was focused and good at motivating me when I began to get fatigued. It was seriously the best workout I'd ever had. We were finishing with some stretches to increase mobility and cool down.

"I'm going to push. Try to breathe through it and let me know if it's too far. On three—one, two, and push."

His hands glided down my leg and pressed into my hamstrings. It hurt for a moment, but once I breathed through it, he was right; it was much easier.

"Good. Okay, now I'm going to draw it back. Next leg."

We followed the same procedure on my main muscles, stretching them and keeping them pliable. I thought it was my imagination at first, but with each new muscle, his hands would slip a little and briefly touch me in an intimate spot. He was doing it so slyly that it took me a while to notice—a little breast here, a slight graze on my core there, and a definite grab of the ass.

By the time we were on the last muscle group, I was panting for entirely different reasons than I'd been minutes ago. It looked like things were going to heat up, and I was so on board.

twenty-eight

sawyer

"HOW DOES THAT FEEL, BABY?" Rhett's voice had taken on a smoky purr that was not helping my current situation.

"Um-hmm."

His dark chuckle at my response told me he knew exactly what he was doing. Focusing on my breathing, I concentrated on my inhales and exhales instead of the slickness developing between my legs.

Rhett had apparently met his patience limit, though, because before I could exhale my next breath, he'd pulled me up to standing and grinded his hardened length against the curve of my ass.

"I think I have one more muscle to work out." His hand dipped into my leggings, and he quickly discovered how wet he'd made me with all of his touches.

"And here I thought you were focused, seems my stretching turns you on."

Words failed me as he plunged his fingers into me. Every time with Rhett was a new experience, and I never knew which version of him I would get, which made it exciting. Tonight, he was showing me his alpha male, dominant side, and I was not complaining.

"Ahhh, oh God, yes."

Throwing my head back, I reached up on my tiptoes to gain more height for him to go deeper. Rhett's other hand grabbed my breasts, squeezing, and it all felt amazing. Remembering his frustration with the sports bra, I'd worn the one that zipped in the front this time. A girl always had to be prepared in a house full of sexy men. Wanting to touch him, I turned around as much as possible with his hand down my pants until he pulled his hand out.

As I backed away slowly, I started to unzip the front a little at a time. Rhett watched me hungrily as he sucked the wetness from his fingers. Once I had the zipper all the way down, I shrugged the straps off and shucked my pants in the process as well.

His dark eyes tracked me the whole route I took, hungrily taking me in. It was so fucking empowering. Leaving on my undies, I turned, tossing my hair over my shoulder; I swayed my hips as I peeked over my shoulder and motioned for him to follow with my finger.

My come hither stare must've worked because Rhett shucked his clothes quickly and was upon me by the time I reached the weight bench. Inches from me, I stared at the sexy man before me as he fisted his monster cock in one hand. Gasping at the provocativeness, I momentarily paused at the desire evident in his eyes.

"What's it going to be, baby?" His voice was so thick with lust it rumbled.

"I've kind of had a fantasy of fucking on a weight bench. I don't really know why, but..." I shrugged, feeling silly for stating it now.

"Fuck yes," he growled, still fisting himself. I could see the bead of pre-cum now, and I wanted to lick it off as I wetted my lips.

"Though, I'm never going to be able to use it again without getting hard."

"Then I guess you'll just have to come and show me each time," purred out of me.

"Oh, baby, I don't think you know what you're agreeing to, but I'm good with this plan."

Rhett dimmed the lights and switched the music to Michele Morrone. If that wasn't setting the mood, then *dayum*. That guy's voice was sex on a stick. The music thumped through the speakers, and I pinched myself subtly to verify this was actually happening.

Bracing myself on my arms, I watched him walk back toward me, cock jutting out in my direction. He was such a hunky piece of man-candy. Licking my lips some more, I was so ready to have my world rocked. As the song said, "*I was going to feel it so strong.*"

Rhett dropped to the ground and pulled my ass

closer to the end, earning a squeak from me, but by the time his mouth hit my pussy, I'd already forgotten about it. He continued to devour me as I fondled my breasts, rolling my own nipples between my fingers. Might as well use them, since I had nowhere to put them at the moment. The bench part was skinny, so I only had room for my ass and back to perch on, but it was enough.

With one long lick up my center through the lace of my panties, I moaned so loud I was sure the whole damn house heard. Rhett started to slip them down my legs, leaving me completely naked on the bench. Before he returned to my center, I heard a sound but ignored it, too caught up in the moment. Especially once Rhett began to use his fingers and tongue simultaneously, pulling a long moan out of me. Just as I started to come on his tongue, I heard a groan followed by, "Fuck" too far away to have been Rhett.

Slowly, I lifted my head as Rhett continued to kiss his way up my torso. It was dim, but standing just inside the door was Elias with his tattooed chest bare and athletic shorts low. His chest was rising quickly as he focused on the scene laid out before him. The weight bench faced the door, so he had a great view.

My movement drew his eyes up, meeting mine across the room. We held each other's gaze for a long moment until Rhett nuzzled my neck and quietly whispered in my ear, "Let him stay, if you're okay with that."

His breath tickled my neck, and he punctuated his want with a bite to my earlobe. I wasn't sure what had overcome me next; it had to be post-orgasm thinking because I agreed. I wanted Elias to stay.

Licking my lips, I repeated the motion I'd made to Rhett just moments earlier. Let's see if those come-hither eyes worked twice in one night, and I beckoned him to come closer with my finger.

His face was frozen as he zeroed in and watched my digit. Rhett wasn't waiting, though, and began to suck my nipple into his mouth. Why was his impatience so hot tonight? He moved me back so he could straddle the bench as well. At his ministrations, my head rolled, releasing a moan from my lips.

Needing to feel Rhett, I moved so I could take him into my mouth. His dick was hard and leaking from the tip. Running my tongue up and down his length, I swirled the top before sucking him down more. Rhett grabbed my ponytail and wrapped it around his hand for some leverage. He wasn't forceful but used it to help set the pace as I sucked his rigid cock.

"Yes, baby. Fuck, that feels amazing. Your mouth is so wet and hot around me."

As I continued to pleasure him, I'd forgotten about Elias until Rhett pulled me back, not wanting to cum in my mouth. He then picked me up and turned us so that he was in my spot on the bench, now facing the door. But instead of me facing him, Rhett turned me in the same direction—reverse cowgirl. I hadn't ever been in this position before, so I was interested to see how it would be.

Straddling his legs backward, I slowly started to

sink down onto his length. This angle felt deeper, and I was a fan. Slowly, Rhett started to bounce me up and down on his cock, controlling me with his hands on my hips and thrusting up.

Throwing my arm up, I wrapped it around his neck to hang on. Blinking my eyes, I remembered Elias when they landed on him. He had followed my command and come closer. He stood next to the treadmill across from us, making the distance only about three feet apart.

I could make out the definition in his ab muscles as he watched our show. His tattoos were clearer too, and I could identify what looked like a swooping dragon breathing fire, a broken wing, and some script that appeared to be in a different language. Glancing up at Rhett, he considered me, searching my eyes; I hadn't realized he'd stopped moving.

"Are you sure you're okay with this?" he whispered to me in concern.

Staring at him for a minute, I realized that I was, because I was with him. Rhett made me feel both sexy and safe, and I trusted him to take me on whatever journey he envisioned now.

The lust in his eyes had magnified, and I could feel how taut his muscles were. Something about this turned him on, and I wanted to see what the outcome would be. The small part of me that wanted to tease and punish Elias had also awakened. Something about pushing his buttons to make him break his 'properness' made me feel wild at times, and this was apparently one of those times.

"I'm with you, of course, I'm okay."

My confirmation must've been the last thing holding him back as he finally kissed me. I hadn't realized that he hadn't since he'd been planting kisses all over my body, but until that moment, he'd yet to kiss me thoroughly on the mouth. For a minute, we just kissed one another, relishing in the passion brewing between us.

Slowly, he started to thrust again up into my wet channel. Pulling back from the kiss, I locked my gaze with Elias. He hadn't taken his eyes off of us. His shorts were tented, and part of me yearned to see what was underneath them. As Rhett began to move us faster, I joined in, undulating my hips. He leaned down and started to whisper dirty things in my ear, making me even wetter.

"Look at how much you're turning him on, baby. Feeling you around me while he watches us is so hot."

"Ahh, ohhhh," whimpered out of me as he began to tweak my nipple with one hand and rub my clit with the other. I was useless at this point as he played my body like a fiddle. My eyes were locked with Elias still, and I could see him watching Rhett's movements. Licking my lips, I drew his gaze there, causing him to lick his own.

Slowly, he began to rub the outside of his shorts against his hardened length to relieve himself. The act was incredibly hot, and I watched him touch himself. I started to move my hips more as my slickness increased around Rhett's monster dick. He filled me so full, and I was beginning to crave it.

"Fuck, baby. Watching him touch himself because of you is hot, knowing that our show is making him wish he was with you too."

Rhett pushed me forward, so I was now bracing my arms on the bench, and he could take my ass cheeks between his hands and fuck me harder. I watched Elias, and he seemed to become emboldened by my stare and slowly started to push his shorts down to free his dick.

The more he lowered his shorts, the more tattoos he revealed. The number of tattoos hidden under his suit, for some reason, was sexy as hell. It was like a secret map I got to discover. When he lowered his shorts all the way, I wasn't prepared for what awaited me. The tattoos traveled down his abs all the way to his hard as steel, beautiful, tattooed cock.

"Fuck," I moaned as I watched him begin to stroke it faster now that it was free. We continued to stare at one another, watching each other's movements as Rhett worked me over. My nerve endings were on fire from the stimulation being done to my body and the simple fact he watched us while touching himself. I'd never done anything like this before where I wasn't intimate with the second person too.

There was a level of danger present despite the fact Elias would never do anything to harm us, but the tawdry act of fucking while having a witness seemed so risqué, making it feel even naughtier.

Rhett must've agreed or felt my dripping wetness

because he suddenly began to grab my ass cheeks more and thrust into me with abandon. I focused on the show before me of Elias fisting his cock in his hand, eyes locked on me, my breasts, and Rhett's dick as it pumped in and out.

I couldn't take anymore, and I orgasmed hard from the erotic nature of it all. causing a chain reaction as both Rhett and Elias came in tandem. The room was full of groans and the smell of sex as we all returned back to the land of the living, having transcended during that orgasm, or at least I had. Fucking amazing.

twenty-nine

. . .

sawyer

RHETT PULLED ME UP, and I collapsed back against him, suspended on his chest, still impaled by his cock. Our breathing began to slow, and my eyes blinked open, not realizing I'd closed them.

"Where's Elias?" I croaked out, my throat hoarse. Rhett kissed my shoulder before moving me so he could slip out finally, but didn't answer me.

"Rhett?"

He exhaled slowly before looking at me. "He left right after, barely had his pants up before he bolted out the door. I'm not sure what he's thinking. That was the first time anything like that has happened between us. They don't really tell you how to talk to your friend after you've had a voyeuristic experience."

He had a point, but I felt worried. Things had felt good between us all day, and this had felt like a natural progression—even if it had been unfamiliar. I wouldn't have let him stay or seen me in this state if I wasn't there with him in those feelings. His avoidance made me face my own.

"Just when I started to like the guy," I mumbled under my breath, but Rhett still heard me based on the chuckle he let out.

We gathered our clothes and wiped down the machines and floor with cleaner before exiting the fitness room. Rhett and I might like to have sex in public spaces, but we were always mindful of others and cleaned up after ourselves—take that Judgey McJudgerson.

We didn't redress, so we walked straight into Rhett's shower after entering his room. My muscles felt languid and relaxed from both the workout and the incredible orgasms. Rhett was the best damn fitness trainer I'd ever met! That should be his tagline. I wonder if more sessions ended with an orgasm, how motivated people would be to workout.

We were both tired now and rinsed quickly before crawling into his bed. Rhett's room was like a cave, and I loved sleeping here. His bed was massive for his big frame, as well as being cold and dark. Before he even turned off the lights, I was out. Sleep a welcomed friend.

four days later

"Tighter. Pull your arms into your body more on that spin and extend out on that last one. Let's run it one more time and then call it quits."

The music restarted, and the two girls I coached took off again, practicing their scratch spins. We'd worked on these for the past two weeks, and the improvement in their progression was remarkable now. Working with committed athletes sure beat those bratty four-year-olds.

"That's it! Way to go, girls! Okay, that's all for today. See you guys on Monday, enjoy your weekend. Don't forget to do your strength exercises."

"Yes, Coach Sawyer! Thanks for today. I feel like I'm really connecting things. I'm excited about competition season." Brittany beamed.

"Yeah, same. Thanks! Have fun training with Coach Reyes. He's so dreamy," sighed a blushing Cindy.

"I will be sure to tell him that. Later, girls!" I chuckled, laughing to myself as they skated off. Though, they weren't wrong—Henry was dreamy. Sigh.

I began to warm up while I waited for him to finish his training with the speed skaters today. Gliding across the ice, the sound of my blades slicing the surface and the wind rushing past my face brought familiarity and comfort to me. You could do something so often and forget how it made you feel day in and day out. After my accident, I'd never take this feeling for granted again.

Picking up speed, I swished and glided, turning and practicing my step sequences into my layback spin. When I came out of it, I transitioned into a second spin, this one a scratch spin like the girls had been working on. It was a challenging transition because your equilibrium tended to be off from one spin to the next if you didn't spot correctly, but I loved the rush it gave me. Finishing my last turn, I posed in my end position. Breathing heavily, I was caught off guard at the sound of clapping from behind me.

Turning, I saw a very sexy Tyler leaning against the rails. A big smile spread across my face as I skated over to him. I hadn't seen him in several days, and I realized how much I'd missed him. We'd texted, but it wasn't the same. The other guys I got to see every day, even if just for small moments. They were always there and easy for me to access. Ty had the unfair advantage of not living in the same house.

I started thinking of a solution and realized that Elias was still ignoring me, so maybe I could convince them to trade places? Except that would be unfair to Elias to make him move, just so it was easier for me to have my boy toys closer. I'd already stolen his dog; it would add insult to injury to steal his room from him too.

I didn't even think as I leaned up and kissed Tyler on the lips when I reached the rails. It wasn't a very long kiss, but it had been initiated by me, which probably explained his shocked expression when I pulled back. Instantly, it morphed into a grin, and butterflies took flight in my stomach. Damn, I didn't remember having these before. But maybe I was just lying to myself.

There had to be a reason I kept seeing him all those years, right? If it was just friends with benefits, I should have gotten tired of him eventually. Perhaps in some ways, Josh was a buffer for me to keep it platonic and not cross into romantic feelings after the whole bet ordeal. Josh was indeed only a friend with benefits deal, or maybe even just a benefits deal. We weren't really friends and only occasionally hung out together outside our hookups.

"What are you doing here?" I asked.

"Well, I'm kind of dating this hot ice skater, and I hadn't seen her in a few days, so crazily enough, I missed her. You wouldn't happen to know if she's around, do you?" He started to search the rink acting as if it wasn't me he was talking about. Jerk, but it still made me laugh.

"Hey! Not funny!" I protested, slapping his chest playfully.

"Actually, I thought it was quite hilarious."

Shrugging his shoulders, I really wanted to punch him, but his face was just too cute, and I ended up kissing him again instead. This kiss he was prepared for, and it turned into more than just a peck. Despite the rail being between us, or me being on the ice even, the kiss was passionate, wild, and full of fire.

He pressed his lips firmly to mine, opening my mouth with his tongue, and we fell back into our kissing frenzy. His hands grabbed my hair as he took my cheeks into his hands, trying to pull me more into his kiss. Passionate and consuming, Tyler Matthews owned me in all the best possible ways. I could keep lying to myself, but it was clear as day.

It had always been real between us.

Denying it meant to deny part of my heart. I was tired of doing that.

Slowly, we pulled back and gazed into one another's eyes. His thumbs were casually caressing my cheeks in circles, sending shivers through my whole body. I was two seconds away from jumping this railing and having my way with him on the bleachers.

"Wow." His voice was filled with such awe, I hated myself for denying him this before.

"Wow, indeed. It was like comfort and passion mixed together for the perfect combination creating that. I'm sorry I was dumb back then, Ty. We could've had so many more years together."

"Ssh, Wildcat. I'm not. Those were great times we had, and I don't regret our journey at all. In fact, we probably would have messed it up back then and not be here at all. Nor would you have all these other relationships. Would you give those up just to have more years with me? I know I wouldn't ask you to do that."

He had a point. Part of what I'd always liked about Tyler. He never made you feel guilty for your feelings and always helped you see things differently. We probably would've fucked it up years ago, and I wouldn't want to lose the relationships I had now. The journey we all took to get here might've sucked, but it was the journey we all needed, so we became the people we were. It allowed us to appreciate this bond and be ready for it.

"You're right. No more living in the past. And that includes me being honest about things. Are you free for dinner tonight? There are some things I want to share with you... because I love you, Ty."

I might've been able to say the words out loud, but it didn't mean I wasn't freaking out about them. So, as I dropped that bomb on him, I skated off and began to warm up again. It was crappy of me, but it was the only way I was going to get it out.

Henry showed up a few minutes later, and we fell into our practice routine. Henry's choreography was incredible, and I loved skating with him. Our synchronicity and trust returned easily. Confidence I hadn't felt in years began to build in me, strengthening me. We finished an hour later, both breathing heavily and sweaty but smiling wide and feeling exhilarated. I looked over to where Tyler was, and Henry caught me.

"He's been there the whole time, you know. He never took his eyes off you. I wasn't sure of him at first. Scared you wouldn't need me anymore or something, I know, I know. It's stupid to think that, but hey, sometimes I'm stupid. But I like him, Smalls. He's a good guy, and I'm glad you're getting the chance to rekindle that. You deserve all the love and happiness you can fill your life with now."

"Thank you, Henry. I love you like crazy."

"I love you like crazy too. Now go, invite him over or something. I want to get to know him better if he's going to be a brother-husband or something."

Laughing at his statement, I kissed him before skating toward Ty, as Henry skated off the ice toward the locker room. When I was almost to him, a flash caught my attention in my peripheral. I turned to see what it was, but nothing seemed out of place. Assuming it was a weird light reflection, I continued skating to Ty. He hadn't left, so that had to be good, right?

thirty

tyler

I LOVE YOU. The words kept repeating in my mind as I watched her and Henry, or Rey—I wasn't really sure what he went by at this point.

They skated beautifully together, and it was amazing seeing a side of her I hadn't seen before. We'd skated together years ago, but nothing like this. They were fluid and synchronized, always anticipating one another's movement. Sawyer seemed lighter and freer in a way now when she skated that hadn't been there in the past.

Even if she hadn't dropped that bomb on me, I would've stayed to watch her. Since our kiss on the ice, the day I found her again, I wanted to be around her constantly. Unfortunately, with our hectic schedules and the fact something secretive appeared to be going on, it had been hard to find time together.

All the covert glances and the way she censored herself clued me in to the fact something was amiss. They might think they were sly or sneaky, but the tension from all the unsaid things had built to a noticeable level. Call it intuition or my training, but I knew when someone had a secret.

It was why I could believe everything Sawyer had said. She'd never had these feelings back in high school for me, or at least hadn't been aware of them. I'd always hoped for more, but it had never felt there, not like it did now. When I'd kissed her a few days ago, I'd felt it. Something had shifted with her, because now her heart felt open and this feeling made me want to shout it from the rooftops.

The situation wasn't how I expected our love story to go, but nothing with Sawyer ever was. My heart felt full and like all of my dreams were coming true. I was truly a sap at this point.

Watching her skate made me smile, and I knew I needed to tell her my secret too. To truly move forward and start something where we could grow, there needed to be a clean slate and a foundation of trust. I believed that down to my core.

The bond between her and Henry was solid, and I hoped to get to know all the guys better so I could have it too. It was what I loved about being on a team. Granted, that hadn't been there for me the past two years, but maybe with this family they were allowing me to be a part of, I could find a place to be accepted and valued. Despite what people might say, it was what we all wanted at the end of the day.

"That was amazing. I forgot how incredible you were to watch skate, but I've never seen you skate quite like that. It was otherworldly, Sawyer." Her blush made me feel good; I knew my words meant something to her.

"Thanks, we've been working on choreography to get back into the groove of skating together. I'm not sure I can do the jumps like I want, though. I boasted to Queen Bitch about being so much better than her, but falling on my ass really made me evaluate if I'm just kidding myself, you know? We haven't practiced them much with my recent near-concussion, so we'll see, I guess."

Her voice had faded as she spoke, and I realized she was worried about this and feeling ashamed and like a failure because of it.

"Even if all you ever do is dance on the ice, it was captivating and more amazing than some shows where they do jumps." Something I said sparked her eyes in delight, and she beamed at me. I was glad her smile was back. When Sawyer smiled, I swear I felt as if I could do anything.

"So, are you free now? Can we spend some time together?" Her exuberant nod was everything I'd hoped for, pulling a grin of my own.

"Yeah, let me grab my stuff, and I'll meet you out front."

"Can't wait."

Sawyer skated to the other side of the ice, heading to the locker room. Henry was leaving it as she got to the door, holding it open for her. Seeing she was in good hands, I made my way up front. Just as I was pushing open the doors, my phone beeped. I'd been avoiding it all day, and had a feeling this was coming. Dreading it, I turned it off, leaving it unread. Now was Sawyer's time. The rest could wait.

Sawyer exited the double doors a few minutes later, carrying her bag of skating gear and jacket. Grabbing her bag from her, I took her hand in mine as her cheeks heated more. Sawyer had never had me full-on, and I couldn't wait to show her the difference between friend Tyler and boyfriend Tyler. I pulled her along with me to the closest parking lot and walked up to my bike.

"No, way!" Sawyer exclaimed as we approached my baby. "Wow, she looks even better since I last saw her," Sawyer cooed, walking around the bike she was drooling over. I'd bought the Harley Fatboy my junior year and had slowly put it together as I saved up for the parts. She'd been there for part of it and probably remembered the off-color panels at one point before I had it repainted. Now, it was sleek and sexy as fuck.

"Yep, she's finally all finished. Ready to take her for a ride?"

"Hell, yes! I've missed my Velma and I'm still not sure if I'll get her back," Sawyer said, her voice full of melancholy.

"Was that the Vespa you were saving up for?"

"Yes! But with the accident, it went into the water, and well, yeah."

"Well, let's go for a ride and shake away all that."

I circled my hand in front of her face, making an exaggerated pout to distract her. When she perked up, it felt like I'd won the lottery. I handed Sawyer my extra helmet and assisted her with the strap. She smiled at me with happiness and my heart jumped. I looked at her bag quizzically and decided to try securing it to her back. It wasn't ideal, but it would do for the short journey.

Climbing on to my bike, I scooted forward to give her room. The moment she straddled the bike and wrapped her arms around me, I felt as if everything finally made sense in my life. All my choices, the hard times, and the good times led me to be the man I needed to be so I could be here, in this moment, with her.

It was everything.

Revving the engine, I pulled out of the parking lot and headed north toward the mountains. Her arms tightened around me, and I relished the feeling as we drove through the campus. The place I was taking her to wasn't far, but as the wind whipped around us, I felt her burrow her face harder into my back. Selfishly, I was glad it was getting colder if I got to snuggle with my girl more. Turning onto the dirt path, I slowed to avoid the holes. Coming to the end, I crawled the bike to a halt before kicking out the kickstand.

Turning my head slightly, I was careful not to knock

into her with my helmet. "How much time do you have until you need to be back? I should've asked that before we left, probably."

"I'm good until dinner, so a couple of hours, I guess."

"Perfect. Come on then, I want to show you something."

We took off our helmets, hanging them on the handlebars, and headed off in the direction I knew well. Grabbing her hand again, I linked her fingers with mine, loving the feel of our hands joined. They slid into mine like they were meant to be there, and I hoped it always would. I might sound like a love-drunk fool, but the girl I'd loved from afar for years was finally in my orbit, and everything was aligning for us. I wasn't going to take it for granted.

"I've been training at this school on and off for a couple of years. This is my second year as a full-time instructor, but Ollie had me help get on a few times for summer camps. I found this spot my second summer here, and it's been my favorite place to go since, and I want to share it with you."

The trail was easy to follow, and as we crested over the hill, I turned to see her expression when it came into view. The handmade sign bore my crooked handwriting, but the name stood out.

"Wildcat Falls," she whispered, as her hand lifted to her mouth.

"I found this little offshoot of a big waterfall and the natural spring here. It's so unknown since it's small and doesn't really exist, so I got to name it. Welcome to Wildcat Falls."

Her hand hadn't left her face as she took in the small little waterfall and hot spring that was surrounded by trees and nature. I'd even set up a hammock, so I pulled her over toward it.

"It's beautiful, Ty."

"Not as beautiful as the girl it's named after."

"I have no words. It's so peaceful. Thank you for sharing this with me."

"I hope to share everything with you moving forward."

We were laying back in a sitting position on the hammock, turned toward one another. Her eyes held some tears, but they weren't falling. I hoped they were happy ones. Grasping her face, I placed a gentle kiss on her cheek. I needed to get this out before I chickened out.

"Sawyer, there's something I need to tell you. Well, a couple of things."

"Okay, should I be nervous? I've kind of had my fill of surprise news."

"That makes me curious, but I want to get this out. I don't think you need to be nervous. Okay, here I go. First, you would've had a lot more dates Senior year, but I punched anyone that talked about you, and eventually, they all stopped. I'm sorry, I shouldn't have done that."

I cringed, waiting to see what she would say. Her

laughter rang out in the secluded area, helping to settle my nerves.

"Okay, that's not too horrible. I feel like that isn't all, though, is it?"

"No, just a few more things." Taking a deep breath, I prepared myself to say them.

"The guy that I kind of have a crush on, he's, well, um, he's one of your roommates, and I don't know how you feel about that. He doesn't think of me that way, but I felt I should be honest with you about my feelings."

"Okay, I'm good with that. Henry and Soren have their own relationship, and I love being with them both and separately. Can I ask who?"

I debated but eventually stuck with my original answer and shook my head no.

"I'm not trying to hide it, but if something ever developed, I think I'd want him to know first, you know?"

"I can respect that, and if something ever changes, just talk to me. I'm not going to stand in the way if you both have feelings; I just don't want it to be kept a secret from me."

"That's reasonable, and I accept that, but I doubt anything will ever come of it. I just didn't want to have any secrets from you." Taking the biggest breath I could, I released it slowly as I geared up for the big ones. She squeezed my hand, and the encouragement gave me the courage I needed.

"Okay, the next two are going to be the hardest to

hear. Do you remember that year I was gone for a few weeks, on and off?"

Her face scrunched up in thought before she answered. "For your hockey things?"

"Sort of. Apparently, my family is involved in this weird secret agency, and it's all by family legacy. So those weeks I was gone, it was to go to training camps to learn how to do all these weird spy-like things."

Her face started to drain of color the more I talked, and I felt as if I'd just royally fucked it all up. Shit. How did I fix this?

"What's it called? This secret agency?" Her voice was flat, devoid of emotion, and I didn't know why. Scrambling, I tried to spit it out quickly to remove that look from her face. I hadn't expected this reaction, not for this one, at least.

"It doesn't really have a name it's called—" before I could say anything, my phone went off again, cutting me off. Sighing, I pulled it out and silenced it, but now Sawyer's face was filled with fear.

"Is it called the Council?" she whispered out.

Quirking a brow at her, I shook my head no, and to my relief, she relaxed, head falling to my chest.

"No, it's just called the Agency."

Her head popped up at my words, and she mouthed the words, almost like she was tasting them out on her tongue.

"The Agency. Oh my God! Tyler, we have to go back to the house, now!"

She pulled my hand and heaved me back to the

bike. It was some weird Herculean strength she was pulling off. Part of me was relieved we were leaving since she appeared to have forgotten I had two things to tell her.

I hadn't gotten to the worst one yet. The one I was afraid she wouldn't be able to get over—sleeping with Adelaide Aldridge.

thirty-one

. . .

READING while Rey played around on his guitar was my new favorite way to read. Well, Sawyer being here would make it better, but I probably wouldn't get much reading done then. It was hard enough with one sexy distraction.

We had another book club date to discuss the second book in the series we'd started—*Destiny Rising*. This book had me on the edge of my seat the whole time. It was action-packed, and I was almost at the end. I feared the cliffhanger I could feel building, but it would hurt so good.

Ever since Rey had played for us the other night, he'd been more open to playing around us now, and I was a huge fan. He would get in these zones at times, and I could stare at him unashamedly, watching him work out a chord or lyric. His passion for music was more apparent now and made perfect sense to me. I hoped he did consider a career writing songs, and maybe now he could also skate with Sawyer.

Swiping another page on my kindle, I was completely engrossed in the bookworld the author had created. I lived for that moment when the world stopped, and it was just you and the words. Anything seemed possible in that time and space.

I was so entranced I hadn't noticed Rey had stopped playing until I felt his weight pressing down on me as he straddled my waist. I'd been lying on my back with the kindle propped on my chest. Peeking over it, I saw him smiling cheekily at me.

"Can I help you?" I loved the guy, and at any other time I would so be right there with him, but I literally had two chapters left in the book, and things were intense.

It was a common misconception that it was okay to interrupt people when they were reading. It was, in fact, not okay. This relationship might be doomed.

"Nope. I'm just going to stare at you while you read. This just happened to be the best seat available."

"Humph." Well, at least he wasn't going to talk to me; I guess I could deal with that.

Focusing back on my book, I fell back into the world and this giant tree they were climbing. Man, I really wanted a giant squirrel to snuggle with. I bet Rhett was like that. Hmm, I wonder if he would snuggle with me, just once, you know, just to see?

Twenty minutes passed, and I was closing in on the

last few pages. I could feel the anxiety building in me, wondering how this would end. Slowly, I started to feel Rey's hands move up and down my legs. It was subtle at first, and I ignored it, but the more I ignored it, the more insistent he became.

Fucking hell, I was about to yell at him to give me five minutes to finish when the sneaky bastard started to brush along the outside of my gray sweatpants in one particular area. That part of me had no interest in reading and was climbing its own tree toward Rey's hands. I was still trying to tune him out as I read these last pages, but the rest of my body disagreed. Traitor.

When he pulled the waistband of my sweatpants down and pulled out my hardened cock, I was done for. Sorry CJ, but Rey's mouth was all consuming as he wrapped it around my dick and began to lick and suck me.

Giving in, I dropped my kindle to the side of the bed and saw a small hint of a smirk on Rey's face. I vowed right then to get him back for this, but later, of course. He already had my dick in his mouth, and it would be cruel to rob him of that. I was considerate, after all.

"Fuck, Rey. I want to be mad at you for making me miss the last few pages, but damn that feels good," I moaned.

Now that he had my attention, he began to suck and lick with more enthusiasm, playing with my piercing and sending waves of pleasure through me. Grabbing his locks in my hand, I yanked to apply slight pressure. His deep moan echoed my own, sending vibrations around my dick. It wasn't long after that I was cumming down his throat.

He looked up smugly at me, feeling proud of himself. I couldn't be too mad about it. Damn him. I'd still find a way to return the favor, though.

"It's a good thing you're so good at that, and I love you."

Pulling him up by his shirt, I kissed him deeply. Kissing Rey never got old, and each time felt like the first time. I hoped it always felt this way. He pulled back after a few minutes; love and happiness evident on his face.

"We better go downstairs and start dinner. Sawyer should be back soon. Then, we can have some real fun."

"Fine. Just," I paused, folding my hands together in the praying motion, "for the love of all book readers out there, please let me finish these pages. Then, I will be all yours." I begged, causing Rey to roll his eyes, but he did let me finish before we headed downstairs.

I wasn't sure if it was worse knowing the ending now or before, though. Damn you, CJ Cooke! You sucked me in and left my heart on that cliff. I hoped I could start book three after that doozy of an ending. It was a feeling of exhilaration, and that always meant a great book to me.

"What do you want to make tonight?" questioned Rey.

"Hmm, what about chili or a stir-fry?"

"Oh, chili sounds good! It's just starting to get cold, so it will be nice."

"Chili it is then!"

We set about getting the ingredients. Rey followed my instructions as I busied myself around the kitchen, getting it all put together. We'd just finished adding everything when Sawyer rushed in with Tyler. I was glad she'd brought him, I wanted to know him more, and he had the disadvantage of not living here. I wondered what we could do about that.

"Hey, sweet pea! How was your day?"

I snagged her as she walked in, wrapping my arm around her waist, pulling her, and apparently Tyler to me. I didn't care, though; he could have a hug too. As I pulled her in more for a kiss, he dropped her hand. I was able to spin her out to Rey then, and he gracefully caught and dipped her for his own kiss.

"Wow, if that's the 'welcome home' you get each day, I've been missing out!" joked Tyler, causing us all to erupt in laughter.

"Only for the pretty ones." Sawyer chortled in a teasing voice as she snuggled under Rey's arm.

"Oh, then I definitely qualify," Tyler fired back. He pulled her hand and twirled her into him this time, and then kissed her himself.

"Why is it so hot seeing her kiss him?" Rey whispered to me. He'd walked over, leaning into me and the familiarity we had around one another now was my favorite thing—just being with him, small touches, and acceptance.

"Because it is. It doesn't have to make sense. It just does; that's all that matters."

"Hmm. I like that. It just does."

We continued to lean against one another as we watched them kissing in the middle of the kitchen. It felt kind of creepy after a while as they seemed to have forgotten we were there, but it was also hot, so I wasn't going to stop it.

"I feel like we need some popcorn," Ollie whispered as he walked in from the other side of the kitchen. A laugh spilled out of me, reminding the two kissing they weren't alone, as they reluctantly pulled apart.

"Ah, man. It was just getting good," fake whined Oliver, causing Sawyer to stick out her tongue at him.

"Um, sorry," Sawyer apologized to the room.

"No apologies needed. We all enjoyed that." Sawyer's checks reddened.

Her blush was going to kill me. Something about it always made me want to lay her down and fuck her hard.

"Who's home? Tyler told me something I think we all need to hear." Tyler glanced down at her weirdly, but it clued us all in on what the subject matter must entail.

"Just Elias, I think," Ollie answered. Sawyer's face brightened even redder at that, and I wondered what that was about. Interesting.

"Okay, well, maybe let him know. What's the ETA on dinner?"

"20-30 mins, probably. Just needs to simmer."

"Perfect. I'm getting really good at condensing this now," she stated with purpose as she led us all out of the kitchen. We trailed after her as she bypassed the living room and ended up in the conference room. Looked like we had a new location for our family meetings.

She unlocked it, and I realized it was getting real if we had an official room. Walking in, I noticed all the stuff sorted in the room. We all took a seat around the table to see what the new development was.

"Normally, we have these discussions, it seems, in the living room, but I figured it would be easier to tell you here since it's now our HQ for Operation Toe Pick." We all sat up a little, even Tyler, who had a confused look on his face. Anything with a title meant business. "Tyler, there are some things about my past I've been learning. Things I've never told anyone... until I got here."

We all scanned his face closely as she told her tale. Since we didn't know how he played into this, I think we were all watching to make sure he wasn't a threat. Thankfully for him, he appeared surprised in the right spots, upset in the others, and angry at the end. She summed it up in about five minutes, and I realized she was right; she had gotten good at condensing.

"So, when I mentioned an agency, you thought I was going to say the one that killed your parents?" Tyler asked as we all held our breaths.

"Exactly. But then you said, and I hope it's okay to share this, but at this point, we're all in this together," Sawyer rushed out, "but when you said 'the Agency' I realized it might be the same one—"

"That's been recruiting me," Ollie finished for her. Tyler turned, and a look of shock crossed his face as he viewed Ollie.

"Yes! But that's not all. Ty's story tickled a memory, and I realized it was part of the message my dad had said to me. I think… I think someone from the Agency helped us escape. Guys, this is huge! We just might have inside connections for once and be a step ahead of them."

At her disclosure, we all sat shocked, having forgotten that part. This was major.

"Holy fuck."

I wasn't sure who uttered it, but I concurred 100%. Holy. Fuck. Indeed.

thirty-two

. . .

MY HEART WAS RACING at the realization we might finally be heading somewhere. When Tyler had started talking at the falls, I was scared another of my guys would be connected to the Council, and I didn't know if I could cope with it. It was all starting to feel a little too coincidental, and that everyone was in on the conspiracy. But that only happened in romance novels, right?

Ollie and Ty regarded each other with new eyes and how they might be more connected. We needed to meet this Agency guy. He could be the lynchpin in connecting me to my parent's murderers.

"Ty, do you know people in this Agency?"

"Yeah. There are a few agents here, actually, and I've known some of them my whole life, including my dad. I just didn't know at the time they were part of this whole secret 'take down the bad guys' club. I'm not supposed to tell you about it, but I'm not going to live my life that way or start a relationship built on lies." His words warmed my heart, and I knew we'd find a way this time to be together.

"I'm glad you trusted me. You might have just given me the decoder key to this crazy puzzle."

"You might not be as far off as you think…" Ty trailed off as he stood up, walking over to the whiteboard. We'd started to tape some of the pictures up to make flow charts with how things connected. Elias was really good at organizing information. So far, we had Draven and Abernathy connecting, as well as my two moms, and Latimer.

Tyler pointed to a picture I'd found the other day. It had Abernathy in it, but I didn't know who the other people were.

"I recognize this guy, but I don't remember his name. But this one has a few Agency people in it."

He was pointing at another one I'd found that had my adopted mom in it. Shock struck me, and I sat back in my chair. So, it must be true; my mom was on the right side. Silent tears filled my eyes as an unknown weight lifted from my chest.

"Wildcat?"

Looking up, I found Ty kneeling in front of me with a look of concern on his face. "That woman, she was my mom, and I'd recently learned her family was potentially connected to the Council, and I just couldn't understand how she could be part of it. So, you just gave me some clarity, that's all."

"I'm glad I could give you that. We can all work to piece this together. We got this, Wildcat. We'll make sense of it together." He squeezed my leg, smiling at me. I liked the sound of his promise.

"Thank you, Ty. Did Elias ever respond back?" I asked, looking at the other guys. "He's really good at piecing things together," I admitted.

"I texted him earlier, but he left it on read. He's been kind of MIA all week. I don't know if he even came out of his room today or not. He's a ghost." Henry shrugged as he flipped through some of the yearbooks on the table.

Interesting, I wasn't the only one who hadn't seen him. He was clearly ignoring me, and I hated it. I'd come to begrudgingly enjoy his company, the tension even playful when we weren't at each other's throats, and we had great conversations. The other night had been amazing, but now he made me feel dirty, and I didn't like it. In fact, the more I thought about it, the more pissed I was getting. He should be acting like a fucking adult, not hiding out in his room.

Deciding we'd all go through this more later, we headed back to the kitchen. Dinner was ready, since Soren had kept popping out to check on it. We all scooped some up into bowls and gathered around the table.

It was comfortable, and I was happy we were spending time together. Especially with Ty, as I wanted all of them to get to know him better. Mateo and Rhett got home halfway through the meal and joined us. It was the kind of meal I'd always wanted growing up, with laughter being the main ingredient.

It was around that table I think I fully grasped what Rhett had seen from the beginning. We weren't just lovers or friends. We were a group of people bonded together, who genuinely cared about one another and could depend on each other to be there. Elias' presence was missing, and I felt the gaping hole more than I wanted to admit. He wasn't just hurting me though, he was hurting all of us.

I wasn't going to let that stand because this was something that needed all of us. It was too special to destroy over some hurt pride or embarrassment. Fueled by righteous indignation, I left the room quietly and made my way up to his. This wasn't something I needed to do in front of a crowd, but it was something I needed to do now.

Hands clenched down by my side, I barged into his room without knocking. I wasn't going to give him the chance to deny me; I just hoped he wasn't doing anything embarrassing. Thankfully, he was hunched over his desk, working on something or pretending to, for all I knew. At my entrance, he looked up, startled to see me. A flash of shame crossed his features, fueling my anger.

"No. You don't get to do that. Not to me, and not to them. You're acting childish, Elias. Hiding away, running from your feelings. Fucking. Grow. Up. We were connecting, and we shared something I thought at the time was special. But this…" I waved my hand around, "the way you're acting, the looks you're giving me now. That has ruined anything we shared that night because you were too chickenshit to confront your own damn feelings."

Breathing heavily, I realized how upset I truly was. The indignation had transitioned into genuine hurt. I held the tears at bay. He didn't deserve them. Elias wasn't even trying to contradict me. He just sat there like the whipping boy, taking what I was saying.

"You and me—we're done. I deserve better than to be ignored, to be treated like one of your fucking booty calls. Fine. I can deal with that. But it's not okay for you to ignore *them*—the guys who are supposed to be your brothers, your family. They haven't done anything to deserve your isolation or silent treatment. They're missing you, and you're too busy licking your wounds to even realize how much you mean to them. For the sake of them, I will act cordially with you. I won't pick any fights. You're basically a piece of furniture to me now. You look nice and have a function, but I don't have to sit there. So, grow a fucking pair of ovaries and get over yourself."

With that, I turned and walked out. I waited until I was past Mateo's door before I let the tears I'd sworn not to cry, fall.

Quietly, I shut my door and turned music on in my room before heading into my bathroom. Rotating the taps, I set it on the hottest I could get it. Stripping out of my clothes, I felt I needed to get all the grime and shame he'd made me feel off. I made sure the overhead fan was on before stepping into the scalding water. I couldn't even enjoy the shower heads as the tears leaked from my eyes.

Feeling overwhelmed and just so done with everything, I drew in a breath and screamed bloody murder at the top of my lungs for a solid minute. Every muscle in my body tensed, and I poured my grief out in that scream. Once I was done, I collapsed onto the shower floor, letting my tears mix with the water as it ran down the drain.

Every thought and feeling I had for him washed away with the water. The action itself gave me the physical representation I needed for them to be washed clean from me. Clarity was a heavy thing, and Elias was a great reminder I couldn't have it all.

There were always going to be sacrifices, and I wouldn't be enough for some people, or I'd be too much for others. I would never fit into his world. I wasn't anything like Adelaide, and I never would be. It was better we knew that now, before our hearts had gotten involved. At least I was trying to pretend mine hadn't.

My insecurities poured out of me on the tiled shower floor as I sobbed for my broken heart. Once I had thoroughly beaten myself up for not being something I never could be, I stood up, wiped my eyes, and washed the last bit of self-hate off. Drying myself, grief and heartache were written all over my face, but for once, I saw it for the strength it was.

No one came to my room while I was in the shower, indicating my sound barriers had worked. Part of me felt like seeking out one of the guys, but I didn't need them to comfort me about another guy. Something about that just felt wrong.

Besides, I wasn't a damsel. I didn't need a prince to save me. I was a fucking Queen, and I could save myself. It was time I reminded myself of that.

thirty-three

. . .

elias

I WAS BEING A WANKER; I knew it too. Every fiber of my being was yelling at me to talk to Sawyer, to check on her, to just bloody do something. But instead, I sat at my desk while the first girl to ever see me for more than my family name walked away, taking my broken heart with her.

When I had come home, I'd planned on facing her, finally. I had run out of the fitness room like a coward after one of the most intense and intimate moments of my life. Each morning, I pushed myself to say something, anything. But the longer I went without saying anything, the more space between us grew, and I'd dug myself so far down in the hole I just didn't see a way out anymore.

Sawyer was wrong, though. The guys didn't miss me or need me. It was clear Sawyer was the one we all needed, even if I didn't want to admit it. I was barely tolerated by anyone other than Rhett. I had been a good friend once, but this past year I had turned into someone I didn't recognize anymore. I didn't like who I had become, but how does one erase a year of heartbreak?

Though, as I felt the loss and pain of losing Sawyer, it was apparent I hadn't even loved Adelaide. My pride had been hurt more than my heart, but I used it as an excuse to be the vile man I had become. My life had been on a specific trajectory, a course set out for all the men in my family. When Adelaide threatened that, instead of seeing it for the blessing it was, it had soured my insides.

I could blame her all I wanted, but I was responsible for myself and who I became at the end of the day. I had chosen wrong, wasting my time and life with bitterness. And now, I was letting the best thing that had come into my life walk away because I wasn't worthy.

It was better this way.

She would come to see that. Feeling empty inside, I returned to the journal I was poring over.

Research was my solace, and through it, I could always find the right answers. Sawyer had given me her mom's journal after discovering it was written in a cipher. More and more was pointing to her mom not being what she first appeared as. For Sawyer's sake, I hoped it was the right side. That girl needed some good news in her life.

A couple of days ago, I had reached out to a contact

from boarding school who was now at MIT and could help with the key. The further I dug, the more holes I uncovered. It felt as if I'd spent as much time jumping through hoops as I had trying to discover anything useful.

If it hadn't been clear before now, it was becoming glaringly apparent this was beyond anything we had anticipated. We were talking global reach. Just the small amount I had been able to figure out was already scaring me shitless.

A knock at my door pulled me from the journal. I closed it and hid it under a binder, not really sure why, but I just felt I needed to for some reason.

"Enter."

"Why are you pushing her away?" Rhett demanded as he barreled his way into my room.

"Well, hello to you too, Rhett."

"Cut the shit, Elias. That night we shared something. But instead of talking about it and figuring out what it means, you're up here hiding. I don't get you, man."

The big brute crossed his arms as he leaned against the wall. His glare was intense, and I knew I was disappointing him. Hell, I was disappointing myself.

"What's there to get, Rhett? We shared a moment. It didn't mean anything."

The words tasted sour on my lips—wrong, even. But I didn't know what else to say, or how to say it, more accurately.

"If you believe that, then you're not the guy I thought you were."

The words pierced me deeply, ringing true as he walked out the door. Something in me shattered at that, and I wondered if I would ever be whole again—or even if I deserved to be.

My phone pinged a few hours later, and I was excited to find it was my contact finally getting back to me. I'd been hiding in my room all night, scared to face anyone and feeling inadequate. This was something I could do, something manageable I could contribute.

> **Flyman3405:** I was able to crack the cipher with the computer. It's one of the most complex ciphers I've ever seen. Whoever used it has connections. We're talking MI6, CIA type of connections. Be careful.
> **Flyman3405:** I also found this *pic attached*. Thought it might lead you somewhere.
> **Tutorguy2308:** Thanks, mate.

While I waited for the pic to download, I started to read the journal he had been able to decode.

Sept 1992

I'm glad I was able to come to this school. I see improvement every day. My instructors are excellent, and I've met the best mentor—Aggie. I've even started to make friends with a few girls in the house. I think a boy may like me, but I'm not sure if I like him. He hangs around with Billie Bellamy, and that guy gives me the creeps.

So far, I've been safe. No one appears to know who Dad is. I would be run out of school if they ever did. It's nice to be away from them, from the family. Here, I can just focus on skating.

July 1993

Skating is going amazing, and I feel confident I will make the Olympic team. I can't believe it. Still seems like a fairytale. Alek keeps sending me gifts. He makes me uncomfortable. I don't want to be mean, but it's starting to be excessive. His friends are horrible as well. Billie Bellamy is the biggest bully. I saw him push a kid down the stairs the other day because he was a higher rank than him.

Samson and Isla continue to be good friends to me. I hope they get married someday. They make the cutest couple. Logan gets all tongue-tied around me. I kind of like it.

There is a rumor that they are shutting down the school side of TAS and making it exclusively a sports training school. That would be awful. I love that it's free and open to all the kids in the area as well. I hope the school board and the student council find a fair resolution.

Oct 1994

Someone knows who my father is. They are threatening to hurt my friends if I don't do what they want. I want to tell Aggie, but I don't want to draw her into their fight. I don't know what to do.

Aug 1995

I told Logan tonight after he kissed me. I couldn't hold it in anymore, and everything came pouring out. He held me while I cried and said he would keep me safe. I don't think he understands the real danger I'm in. I don't want to leave him, but I may have to in order to keep him safe. Is this what my life has become? Always having to hide who I am in order to keep those I love safe.

May 1996

Tonight, after the end of school expo, when all the alumni and donors are here, I'm making my escape. It's now or never. I have to do better this time. I can't keep anything from this life. I have to shuck it all, or they will keep tracing me. I can't live that way. I will miss my friends, but it's better this way. One day they will understand.

I decided to skip forward some to see if things change. It sounded like the school was run differently back then. I found a date for after Sawyer would have been born, as I didn't want to read too much about her adoptive mom's past without her consent. I was already pushing my luck as it was.

December 2001

Everything is falling apart. They keep coming for us, or perhaps me. I've never hated my family as much as I do now. They cannot ask this of me. I won't do it. We had a deal. She's just a child. Brian is in contact with someone. He won't tell me who, but I trust him. He's a good man and has been the one good thing I've found at this company.

Coming here was meant to be a compromise, but they keep asking for me to push things each time. But this... this is too much. I can't. I've learned from last time. I won't get found. Not this time. There's a family that is undercover in my dad's organization that can help me. They will not take my baby. I would give my life for her. This legacy ends with me.

Bloody hell. Sawyer would have so many answers with this. At least I was able to do that for her. I was about to turn another page when my computer dinged that the file had been scanned. Clicking on it, I was speechless for a minute.

Fuck. Fuck. Fuck.

Immediately, I printed out what the cipher had decoded and placed it in the journal. I started packing a bag and grabbed my computer and passport. At least I knew Lucky would be taken care of.

Pulling out a pen and paper, I wrote a note for Sawyer, Rhett, and one for the guys. She deserved more, and it was weak and cowardly of me to do it this way, but if I was leaving... I might never get to return.

At least this way, she had a truth she could live with. That was the only thing I could offer her now—the truth.

thirty-four

. . .

sawyer

THE SWEAT DRIPPED from my brow as I counted out the last eight count of the dance move I'd been working on for the past hour. It seemed counterintuitive to get sweaty when I'd just taken a shower, but let's be real, that shower wasn't to clean my outside, but my insides. Dancing helped me center and focus on the rhythm.

It honestly felt like I was constantly running around with my head cut off. Sometimes it was like I'd taken on too much—training, teaching, and dating multiple guys. Not to mention trying to discover who killed my family, finding a twin, and meeting my biological mother. It was a lot.

When I allowed myself to accept it was, in fact, a lot of shit and I was handling it as best I could, it didn't seem as overwhelming. Anxiety was a real bitch. She preyed on your vulnerable moments and made you doubt everything.

Accept the good, brush away the bad. That was my new mantra.

Grabbing a towel, I headed to my room and wondered if anyone had even noticed I was missing. Shit. There was anxiety's friend, doubt, lurking about. Both you fuckers can go suck a big toe. Didn't you hear me earlier, doubt? I was a Queen, and I owned my shit.

Feeling that my thoughts were properly chastised, Lucky and I made our way back to my room. I wasn't focused on my surroundings, so I was taken aback at first when I entered.

Leaning against the big cuddle chair was the canvas Rhett gave me on our first date. Over the past weeks, we'd added some dried flowers from the garden and wrote in the song lyrics to the *Sound of Music*, but that was all we'd added. So, when he'd asked to take it, I hadn't thought anything of it. In the chaos of my life, though, I'd forgotten.

Gasping, my hands lifted to my mouth as I took it in. The canvas was almost entirely covered now; only a small section in the top right corner was empty. Rhett had filled it with sketches and odds and ends from the things we'd done over the month? Few weeks? It had blurred altogether, but now, I could remember every one of those moments when I looked at the canvas.

Mateo and I in the hammock talking. Soren and Henry cooking in the kitchen. Ollie laughing. Lucky sitting in my lap. Rhett and I kissing. Me skating. Elias and I working together on my planner. Meeting Rowan and Rhonda. Cake frosting, a post-it, part of a pasta box, and some grass added dimension to the canvas. It was breathtaking and encapsulated all of us so well. Even a small section looked like Ty, Ollie, and Rhett at a bar with a coaster.

"Do you like it?" a voice asked hesitantly from behind me. Turning, I ran and hugged him hard. My head buried in his abs. I was so moved by his gesture I wasn't even focused on that for once.

"It's perfect. I love it. Thank you. I had no idea you were so talented. Why aren't you doing more with it?"

His face reddened at my praise. Too bad, Grump, you do something sweet, then you have to deal with the compliments. That was just the way it went.

"It's nothing. Just something I like to do in my spare time."

Deflect much there, Rhett?

"Uh, uh. I don't buy it. What's the real story?"

"How do you do that? See beneath the layer?"

He honestly looked astonished I was asking, that I even cared. I swear if I ever met that Molly chick, I would have words—very strong words. I mean, I would like to punch her, but let's be honest, I would end up hurting myself more than her. It was safer to just use my words. Even then, it was fifty-fifty if I embarrassed myself or not.

"Because it's you, and I want to know everything about you. Because I care about you and want you to achieve everything you can. Because you're talented, and no matter how much you deny it, your work doesn't lie."

"Baby, I hope you know I'm never letting you go."

Why did that send my heart racing? I guess because doubt whispered, they would all get tired of me and leave at some point, as everyone else had. But here he was telling me the opposite. I think I'd been waiting my whole life for someone to say that to me—in the not creepy way, of course.

"Good, because I don't ever want to be apart from you either, grumpy bear."

He bent down and kissed me gently but in a meaningful way. He pulled back, and his eyes held so much emotion that I was swimming in his chocolate orbs, coating myself in his love. I wrapped it around myself, fortifying me. I didn't need him to save me, but there was no doubt he made me stronger.

Saving yourself didn't mean you had to do it alone.

"Goodnight, baby." He left so much emotion unsaid, probably sensing I wasn't ready for it yet, but I could accept it and recognize his feelings were real for me.

"Goodnight, Rhett." I watched him leave, shaking his ass as he walked out, I knew he did it on purpose, but when he had an ass like that, I wasn't going to complain. I'd just stand here and drool.

"That was sweet," came from the direction of my bed, causing me to scream.

"What the fuck!" Jumping, I swirled and promptly fell on my ass. How I skated on the ice some days amazed me.

"Are you okay?" Soren asked as he jumped up off the bed he'd apparently been watching me from.

"I'm fine. You just gave me a heart attack. How long have you been there?" I shook my head. Dumb question. "Never mind. Obviously, longer than me. My brain has officially decided to go offline."

I stood up after untangling myself and made my way over to him. Lucky was snoozing already in a dog bed. I wondered when that had gotten there and by who?

You think after I had someone bug my room, I would be more aware of it, but I rarely spent time here. Despite my first impressions of wanting to spend all my time in here, I rarely was, in fact, in my room.

When I was close enough, Soren reached out and grabbed my waist, pulling me to him. He had stopped at the foot of the bed when he realized I'd managed to get myself up.

"Hey."

"Hey, yourself."

"I kind of missed you, so I figured I'd wait for you and see if you were free. I was hoping to spend some time with you. Is that okay?"

"So, okay. I'm glad you're here. I could use a good cuddle."

"Oh, well, then I'm going to cuddle the shit out of you, sweet pea. But first, may I make a suggestion?" He scrunched his nose up all cute, and all I could do was nod at him.

"Maybe, take a shower? You stink!"

"Hey! Not cool, jerk." I laughed as I slapped his chest playfully. "Just for that, you can't join me and have to watch me undress on the way to this shower that you think I need."

"Besides not getting to shower with you, I don't see how this is a punishment for me."

Sticking my tongue out at him, which was becoming a habit, I decided to make it as torturous as possible. And by torture, I meant not sexy at all. As I stripped, I made the most ridiculous dance moves known to mankind.

The sprinkler, the Dougie, the running man, the cabbage patch, and the end move was none other than the chicken dance. His rolling laughter as he clutched his stomach, tears streaming down his face, told me I'd gotten one over on Soren. High-five self!

My shower was a quick one, and I made my way back out to my room, ready to spend some time with Sor. I was surprised he was still alone, lounging on the bed. I'd gotten used to him and Henry being together nowadays. I had to admit it was nice, though, as I hadn't had much alone time with just Soren. I took my brush to him again and gave my best cutesy, pouty face.

"Give it here, sweet pea."

"Yes!"

Jumping up on the bed, I handed him my brush as I sat in front of him. He began to brush my hair in smooth strokes, and it was so soothing. It reminded me of the first time he'd brushed my hair and how different this time was.

"I was just thinking how crazy it was last time you brushed my hair. You know, when I gave you a nosebleed."

"Holy shit, I think I'd blocked that out. No sudden movements then."

"Ha, Ha. Soren?"

"Yes, Sawyer."

"How are you doing, you know, with everything? Because I feel like I'm constantly on a roller coaster, and depending on where I am on the ride determines my mood for that moment. It's exhausting."

I hadn't realized that until I said it, but it was true. Emotions, like everything, had a balance. I felt I constantly teetered on the highs and lows these days.

"I feel that way some days too, but I think it helps that I've not had any major bombs dropped on me. Discovering Pamela was connected hurt, but it didn't change what happened. But you've been getting hit with new things every day, and sometimes every hour, it seems. The fact you're sitting here asking how I'm doing just shows me how strong and resilient you truly are, Sawyer. You do realize that doing okay doesn't mean you have to have it all together, though, right?"

"Oh, it doesn't? Well, no one shared that bit of info with me. Thanks to whoever slept in on that day and forgot to tell me," I sassed.

"See, you still have humor. You still have light. You still have hope. You're doing fine, Sawyer. There's no right or wrong way. Well, I guess there is a wrong way. Mass murder would be bad, but you get what I'm saying. There isn't a how-to manual on how to deal with finding out your entire life was a lie. There's not a pamphlet, and the guidance counselor isn't going to be able to help you map out your decision tree. The only one who has the answers for you, is you. Trust yourself. You've gotten yourself this far, don't start doubting now. But it doesn't mean you have to do it alone anymore, either. Lean on us. We all want to be part of your life."

"Thanks, Sor. I needed to be reminded of that. It's nice not doing this on my own. Rhett proved that as well. But it's like I get wet, and it erases my brain."

"Oh, when you get wet, huh?"

"Perv. But yes, I guess that wet works too!"

He finished brushing my hair, pulling it over my shoulder, and kissing the soft spot there.

"Will you stay with me tonight? You did promise me cuddles."

"I was hoping you'd ask. Come here and let your cuddle monkey take care of you."

"Oh my God, I am not calling you that!"

"Why, not! It's an adorable name."

"No, Chilly Willy is adorable."

We laughed as he pulled me back into his body. My head fit under his chin as I rubbed his now bare chest. He'd taken his shirt off while I was in the shower. I traced his muscles as I slowly began to drift off to sleep.

I wasn't positive, but I could've sworn I heard Soren whisper, "Can I keep you? Always and forever, sweet pea."

thirty-five

. . .

sawyer

DAMN, I was having the best dream. It was so vivid and felt so real. I needed to have these types of dreams more often.

"You're not dreaming, Sawyer."

Opening my eyes, I found a smirking Soren between my legs, feasting on my slick core. Giving in to the dream that wasn't a dream, I threw my head back with a low moan. My throat felt tender today, and I realized it was from the screaming in the shower last night. Hopefully, no one would ask me why I sounded like a chain smoker. I didn't want to lie.

Focusing back on what was happening below the sheets, I felt Soren's tongue flick up my center that was already so wet. Damn, he gave good head. Fisting my hands in his hair, I yanked him up to me. I wanted to enjoy this and get in on the action. Kissing him briefly, I tasted myself on his lips. The naughtiness of the act turned me on more.

I pushed him back against the bed and turned so my rear was facing him and my head was closer to his beautiful cock. Every time I saw that piercing, I wanted to lick it. So, since I was in licking range, I did. Running my tongue up his shaft, I swirled it around the piercing, biting it a little as the cool metal rolled over my tongue.

"Fuck, Sawyer, that feels good. Good thinking, babe."

With that, he pulled me closer to his lips, and then we were both giving and getting pleasure—good ol' sixty-nine.

Soren began to push a finger in, causing me to moan around him. He apparently liked that, as he moaned back into my cunt. The vibrations did feel amazing, so I did it again. Except, his vibrations kept going. Fucking hell, what was going on? Did he have some kind of magic vibrating tongue? How did I not know about this?

"Ahhh, fuck, Sor. What is that? It feels amazing."

"I can't reveal all of my secrets. But... do you like it?"

"Uh-huh. It feels incredible."

"Good. Now get back to pleasing me, woman!"

"You're lucky I like your dick, or I'd edge you soooo —" the rest of my sentence was cut off by the embarrassingly loud moan that escaped me.

"What was that you were saying?"

Two could play that game. Increasing my speed, I took my hand and started to fist the base of his dick as I made my way down. Twisting and sucking interchangeably, I fondled his balls and felt them start to tighten. Slowing down, I began to lick him like my favorite lollipop. Slow, long licks, up and down, made Soren a panting mess. He was so distracted he wasn't even focused on me anymore.

Taking control, I scooted down and turned as I straddled him, impaling myself on his very hard cock. That seemed to have gotten his attention as he sat up, pulling me closer to him. At this angle, we both groaned out in pleasure. Slowly, he rocked his hips up as I rocked mine. We naturally found a rhythm together as our moans combined.

What had started as a fuck frenzy a moment earlier had slowed to an intimate encounter. We'd pushed one another toward orgasm just moments earlier, but as we stared into one another's eyes, it was clear it had transformed into this beautiful exchange between two people. Leaning in, I kissed him passionately as I swirled my tongue with his. Together, we twisted them around one another in a dance we both knew all the moves to.

Wrapping my arms around his neck, I pulled him incredibly close to me, needing to feel all of him. Soren palmed the globes of my ass cheeks in his hands, squeezing them as he used them for leverage to pull me tighter onto him. Every inch we could, we tried to eliminate space to be fused together.

His piercing rubbed me in all the best places, and I was about to combust. My breasts brushed against his chest, making my nipples pebble against his hard planes.

Dropping my hand, I found my clit and stroked it in tandem with his thrusts. Soren made long and deep pumps, joining our two bodies together, setting off a long, languid orgasm. My head fell back, causing my hair to brush against his legs. I felt him grab me tighter as he found his own release. Somehow, we just managed to have the most beautiful sex I'd ever had.

No, that wasn't right. We'd made love.

Peering into his eyes, we stared at one another, searching for the answer we both had on our hearts but unsure what words to use. Something like acceptance, or perhaps agreement, flashed in his eyes. Brushing my hair behind my ear, he caressed my cheek with his thumb.

"That was magical, Sor."

"I agree, sweet pea. I've never experienced anything like that before. We were perfectly synced. Is that what it feels like to skate with Rey?"

"I've never thought about it that way, but I guess in some ways, yes. But this was beautiful in its own way, Sor, because it was you and me. We laid ourselves bare before one another. I honestly don't know if I've ever been that vulnerable before."

I held his gaze for a moment, needing to feel the honesty in my own words. Everything with him had hit me out of nowhere. I hadn't expected it.

"Thank you for giving me the courage to be vulnerable. That feels kind of weird to thank you, but it's because of who you are that I can be like this. You make it safe. Am I making sense? I don't think I'm making sense. See, I get wet and lose all brain functions."

"It makes sense, sweet pea. We found our safe place in each other, something we've both needed for a long time."

Damn, that was beautiful. Kissing his nose, I hoped to always be that for him. We laid down, cuddling spoon to spoon, and things felt okay today. That was the thing about depression and anxiety, wasn't it?

Some days could feel great and happy, and then other days, you wondered what the point was to it all. Having these reminders that things could be safe and loving was the foundation I needed for those other moments when I questioned. I think we all needed that, a landing place to come back to.

I guess your parents were meant to be that for you at first. As a kid, you knew no matter what happened in your life, they were there for you. Giving you the confidence to spread your wings. But what happened when you had shitty parents or, like me, they were taken from you?

Made sense why so many people struggled with this; with no foundation, we had nowhere to build—nothing like deep thoughts first thing in the morning. Snuggling under Sor's arm, I kissed the part of it right in front of me.

"What was that for?"

"Just because I can."

At that, he kissed my shoulder, "Well, just because I can."

Giggling at him, I was about to say something cheesy when my door burst open. Why did I even shut it if no one ever knocked? Lucky barked at the intrusion, and I'd honestly forgotten he was in here since he wasn't on the bed. Looking up, I thought it would be one of the guys, most likely Henry.

But nope.

Standing in my doorway, looking shocked, eyes open, mouth hanging wide, was none other than my best friend. Though at this rate, I was starting to question that title. The girl needed to learn to knock. Finley stared at us, and all I could do was roll my eyes. She better be glad it was just Soren. Finally, she seemed to come out of her stupor, covering her eyes, and started screeching at us.

"Ew! Please tell me my brother is not somewhere under those blankets."

Tossing a pillow at her head for being a dumbass. I got out while her eyes were covered and threw Soren's pants to him. I snagged his shirt and put it on.

"Don't ew me, Finley Amelia Reyes! Yes, I just three named you. Get over it. You stormed into my room, be prepared to see nakedness. I'm not ashamed of my sex life, so if you don't want to see it, perhaps knock next time. Especially since I happen to like to see your brother naked."

I couldn't help but tack on that last line. Payback for her interrupting a special moment with Sor. That was the thing about best friends, wasn't it? You loved them but also took pleasure in torturing them—tit for tat and all that.

Gagging sounds came out of her mouth at my mention of Henry. Which apparently was his alarm clock, because a moment later, he came stumbling in, rubbing his eyes.

"Hey, sis. What's got you here so early?"

He squeezed her to him and kissed her cheek. Despite her earlier gag, she melted into his embrace. They really were great siblings. I hoped Asa and I could be that close someday.

"Well," stated Finley before turning back to me, "I was coming to drag this one out of bed. I decided that it's Saturday and we're all going skiing! The first real snow fell overnight, and we're getting first dibs on the fresh powder."

We all instantly perked up. Skiing could be fun. Happy chattering started as we devised a plan to get everyone up and out of the house as quickly as possible.

I'd been hoping to go skiing for a while, so this was the perfect excuse to blow off everything else for the day. After last night, some distraction would be nice. Hopefully, I could avoid Elias as well. Despite what I'd said, it was still going to hurt to see him and know nothing would ever happen between us. Fickle bitch, my heart.

"Fin, you're in charge of coffee and texting Ace and Chloe. Soren and Henry, you're on breakfast duties and securing transportation. I'll wake up everyone and get us all moving." We all started to move out of my room before I remembered I was only half-dressed.

"On second thought, Sor, can you wake Elias on your way?"

No explanation, just a question. Thankfully, he only quirked an eyebrow before nodding. Having that disaster waiting to happen removed allowed me to head toward the other rooms on this floor.

It was a snow day, time to go play!

thirty-six

· · ·

KNOCKING on Mateo's door first, I heard a sleepy 'come in' muttered. Entering his room, I found his curly hair mussed, a bare chest, and tight boxer briefs displaying his scrumptious ass sticking up in the air as he stretched out on his bed.

I was instantly drooling. Hmm, maybe I should've given this job to someone else because I think I was about to get distracted. Scratch that, definitely going to be distracted.

Sitting casually down on the edge of the mattress, I stroked the hair off his forehead. Matteo suddenly pulled me down next to him on the bed, eliciting a squeak out of me.

"What do I owe this early morning wake up to?" rumbled a sleepy Mateo.

Damn, his voice was pure honey first thing in the

morning. Kissing his lips, I quickly drew back before being pulled under his spell. Mateo was the most dangerous at times.

Unassuming and innocent, you never expected to have your vagina bamboozle you into giving him everything. Because I so wanted to give him everything. Heart, soul, and body all on a platter, ready for him to take at his will. Fucking dangerous.

"It snowed."

His eyes opened more at my statement, blinking as I came into focus.

"It snowed?"

"Yep, meaning…"

"Fresh snow."

His smile at the announcement wasn't helping me stay focused and only reinforced my dangerous assessment earlier. Mateo's grin was infectious and I couldn't help smiling just as big back at him. His love of skiing showed through then, and I knew that while he had a mishap this past year, he would be back to competing soon. It was inevitable; it was just as much a part of him as skating was for me.

"Uh-huh. Feel keen to give me some lessons?" I waggled my eyebrows in exuberance, hoping to entice him into those lessons he promised.

"I would like that very much. When are we leaving?"

"As soon as we're all ready. I'm in charge of waking everyone."

"Well, that might have been a bad choice." He smirked.

I laughed because he wasn't wrong.

But really, could you blame me? My boyfriend was practically naked and all sexy sleep looking; it wasn't really my fault.

Leaning in, Mateo kissed me passionately, and I was about to say, "fuck it" and explore that more, when I remembered his smile at the fresh snow. Pulling back with great effort, I kissed him once more on the lips before crawling over him. Just because I was using restraint didn't mean I couldn't have some fun torturing him.

"Damn. You didn't have panties on either? You're killing me, Dulzura."

"See you downstairs!" I squeaked, not able to look back, or I might never leave his room. Sexy Mateo was lethal. Especially, when his accent came out with his rolled Rs on Dulzura instantly setting fire to my vagina.

Managing to escape fairly unscathed, I shut his door and took a big gulp of air before heading to Ollie's room. I probably should've gone and put on pants at this point, but apparently, I liked living on the edge. Or I was crazy? Yeah, that was more likely.

No response on his door when I knocked, so I eased it open slowly. Ollie's room was dark, and I could make out his shape under the covers. Quietly, I tiptoed to the bed, deciding it was time to get some payback. From what exactly at this point, I wasn't 100% sure, but it seemed appropriate, nonetheless.

When I was a few feet away, I took a giant leap, pouncing on him. His resounding 'oof' as he grabbed then rolled us, so he was pinned over me was not what I was expecting. Especially, when I realized it wasn't Ollie at all on top of me.

"Ty?" I squeaked.

"Good morning, Wildcat. Based on your question, I'm guessing you thought I was Ollie."

"Well, you are in his bed." I laughed.

"Very observant."

He turned my head, and there, laying on the other side of the bed was a sound asleep, softly snoring, Ollie.

"Oh."

Kissing me quickly, he rolled off me, so he was no longer pinning me down. Instead, he pulled me toward him, encasing me in his arms. Damn, all these cuddles were terrific. I should wake them all every morning. It would so be worth the early alarm I would need to set to make my rounds. Hot damn, I had a lot of boyfriends!

"What brings you pouncing on Ollie at stupid o'clock?"

"Snow."

"Snow."

"Did someone say snow?" mumbled out from a still sleeping Ollie.

"Yep, fresh snow." That had Ollie opening his eyes.

"Ski day?" His voice was hopeful, and all I could do was nod my head enthusiastically, yes.

"Ski day!" he shouted. Ollie jumped out of bed at

my proclamation and started making some fist-pumping dance moves around the room.

In only his boxers. Very tight, snug boxers that highlighted his substantial morning wood.

At my notice, I couldn't help but giggle. I think my brain was malfunctioning, actually, because seeing Oliver Windsor, star hockey God, practically naked with his abs and leg muscles on display and sporting some very impressive manhood was anything but funny. It was downright sexy as hell, causing me to stealthily wipe at some imaginary drool to make sure it was just fictional.

At my giggle, Ollie looked down, noticing his own morning erection, and just shrugged his shoulders.

Shrugged. His. Fucking. Shoulders.

Oh, to be a guy and have no shame about that. Why did women get so bent out of shape over this stuff? Had to be the patriarchy making us feel bad for our sexuality. Deciding to take a page out of his book, I sat up and started cheering him on.

"Woot! Go, Ollie, Go, Ollie! Get it!"

Ollie took my attention and started hip rolling and gyrating for us. It was hilarious and sexy at the same time. A perfect Ollie representation if I ever saw one. At the end of his impromptu dance, he winked and made his way to his bathroom. Ty had sat up behind me, leaning his head on my shoulder, watching the dance show with me.

As Ollie got to the bathroom door, the cheeky bastard pulled down his boxers and bared his ass cheeks to us all casual like. Fucking hell, those were some buns of steel.

"You got some…" Ty pretended to wipe up the drool, but I didn't care. Oliver was a sexy man, and I had no guilt in enjoying the view—especially when he invited me to look. Turning, my brain started to fire off at an alarming rate as pieces clicked into place.

"It's Ollie, isn't it?" Tyler turned to me, shock and some fear on his face only cementing my assumption. "It's okay. I get it. I won't say anything." I kissed him gently and felt him relax around me.

"Somewhere in all those years that I was pining for you, my friendship grew with him. I'd admitted senior year my attraction to guys, but I never acted on it. When I got to college, it wasn't as taboo, but I never really connected with anyone. One night, Ollie and I stayed up talking, and I realized how close I'd become with him. How much I relied on him and how, with a simple smile, he made my day. I was basically head over heels for him by the time I realized it, but I seem to keep giving my heart to straight guys."

He seemed sad about that, and it hurt my heart a little. I could understand wanting something and having it just out of reach. Tyler was my oldest friend outside Henry and Fin, and I knew him on a level I didn't even know them. Tyler knew me as only Sawyer. He knew the hard things I'd had to deal with and how difficult high school had been for me. We had a bond forged from broken hearts, boredom, and lack of parental supervision.

"Ty, you will never know if you don't say anything. I'm here for you, whatever you decide." His smile was sad, and I just wanted to hug him, so I did. Pulling him to me, I held him tight for a few minutes. Letting go, I was happy to see some of the sadness in his eyes had disappeared.

"Thank you."

"Anytime, Ty. I have to ask, though. How did you end up in bed together? Maybe it's closer to reality than you think?" He guffawed at me, but something seemed to stick, as he didn't seem as hopeless.

"After dinner, we all played video games. It was late after, so Ollie suggested I just stay over and not have to drive home. He mentioned he had a king bed and we would both have enough room. It's not like you're thinking."

"Sure, yeah, that's totally believable. I cuddle with 'just my friends' too. Actually, I do, Fin is a cuddler, but that's beside the point! Ugh. Never mind. I'll see you downstairs."

Kissing him, I climbed off the bed and exited the room quickly, trying to outrun my embarrassment, but his laughter trailed after me. *Glad I could entertain you, punk.*

One more to go. I was seriously reconsidering this whole wake-up call duty. Unfortunately, or maybe it was fortunate, because the wetness between my legs increased with each bedroom wake-up call I made, Rhett was already awake. He was working out in the fitness room, doing his morning exercises. Leaning in the doorframe, I watched him for a few minutes.

What? The man was doing squats! Once he made it to the wall, he stopped to grab some water and noticed me there.

"Hey gorgeous, want to get sweaty with me?"

His flirting was horrendous, but it worked for him. I think if he was too smooth, the female population wouldn't be able to deal and would spontaneously orgasm at the sight of his eyebrow game. Still, he gave me tingles every time.

"Actually, there's snow, so we're rounding everyone up to go skiing."

At my statement, his smile widened. Suffice to say, this house was a fan of the fresh snow ski trip. I'd learned despite Rhett not being here to train in an area, he was an avid fan of all things winter sports and, according to Soren, was actually pretty advanced at some of them. It didn't surprise me. Rhett was the type of person to put everything into something, especially when he was passionate about it.

"See you upstairs in twenty minutes," I sing-songed as I blew him a kiss, knowing if I entered that room another inch, I wouldn't be leaving it anytime soon.

The memory of our last tryst there had a sting to it now that I hated—damn you, Elias. Why did you have to turn something beautiful between us all, into something that now made me hurt all over? I was really going to have to rein it in to not punch him in his stupid hot face today.

thirty-seven

. . .

mateo

"YOU'RE DOING GREAT, Sawyer. Just balance your weight and use your hips to propel your movement."

We were on the bunny slope, or as close to one as the school had here. It was an elite training school; they assumed everyone on the slopes had a basic knowledge of skiing. Thankfully, Sawyer was picking it up well and seemed to be enjoying it. Some of the others were snowboarding, a few were on more demanding routes, and a few were with us on this easier one. All in all, it had been a fun morning.

"Ready to go down the hill? You know how to stop and fall. Everything else is gravity and momentum." I laughed.

She looked adorable in her borrowed ski gear. Finley apparently was an avid skier and had brought extra over to the house, saving us a trip into town to get Sawyer some.

"Yep! As long as you go with me, I think I'm ready."

Her cheeks were windblown, and I could barely see her with the goggles, but she'd never looked more beautiful than she did now, doing the thing I loved. Snow, all around with the mountains in the backdrop, painted the perfect landscape for the day.

"I'll be there, Dulzura. I won't let you fall."

With that, I gave her a little push to propel her momentum. She started down well, and I got the bonus of watching her from behind as I trailed her. Swishing through the snow, I was feeling the exhilaration of speeding down a mountain at 40mph. There weren't very many students out this early since it was barely 7 am on a Saturday. Hence, the ones who were skiing were on the more challenging terrains being ski students themselves. Fresh snow was one of the best things for a skier. It was our kryptonite.

Sawyer and I were almost at the bottom of the hill when some random person swerved over into her path and clipped her ski, causing her trajectory to go off course. My heart jumped up into my throat as I tried to reach for her; thankfully, she remembered how to properly fall and turned her skis into an X before falling down on her butt. Stopping next to her, I sprayed snow toward the asshole who had almost caused a disaster.

"You okay?" I asked. "You handled that perfectly." I reached down to help her stand. Trying to calm my nerves, I sucked in a big breath so I wouldn't panic Sawyer with how badly that could've gone.

"Yeah, I think so. They scared me, but my instincts took over. I remembered what you said, and it just clicked for me."

Her smile at herself for handing it well was cute, causing me to place a kiss on her lips to seal it.

"Your reward for listening to your instructor."

"Oh, there are rewards, are there? Well, in that case, what kind of reward do I get for going again and not falling this time?" Sawyer flirted.

"Well, if I told you the reward beforehand, you might not work as hard, so you'll just have to do your very best and then see what you get. I promise you will like it."

"Of that, I have no doubt! Come on then, let's go back up! I have a reward to earn."

Unhooking her skis, we made our way over to the ski-lift. From the corner of my eye, I saw Bitchclaide and her minions whispering off to the side. The random skier who had swerved into Sawyer wasn't so random after all. Looked like Bitchelaide had her trusty side-kick, Ashley, do her dirty work. Rage filled me at her pettiness and taking liberty with Sawyer's life. I wouldn't allow that to stand. Bitchelaide had just made me her enemy.

Herding Sawyer around so she wouldn't have to deal with her today, we found Asa and Fin waiting in the ski lift line. The three of them started talking as I formulated a plan to get back at the bitch. One thing about being quiet, people didn't always expect you to say a lot in conversation, so you could tune things out easier. It also meant the things I thought in my head were far more diabolical than anyone ever realized.

I might watch Disney movies like they were going out of style, but it didn't mean I wouldn't stand up for my family. Focusing back on our friends, I was able to shake off the rage for now and enjoy my time with Sawyer. For the first time in my life, I felt entirely accepted for who I was and not what I had to offer. It was freeing in a way I could never have imagined.

The whole morning was an absolute blast, and I didn't remember the last time I had this much fun, just skiing. It was nice, and I decided I wanted to do this more—have fun. I just wished we had all been there. I didn't know Elias well, but he was part of our family, and I found I missed him. Maybe I should step outside my comfort zone and see what was going on with him? I could do that for him *and* for us.

We'd stayed out on the slopes for a few hours, but we were all tired and decided to head back to the house around 10 am. Everyone had been up since about five thirty thanks to Finley's early wake-up call, but it had been worth it, even if we were all yawning now.

"I think hot chocolate, followed by naps is in order," suggested Ollie. A chorus of "yes" rang out through the kitchen, where we'd all gathered upon our return. The mudroom was full of our discarded snow attire, and we now all sat around the massive kitchen island in our thermals. Looking around the room, I noticed Elias was still missing.

"Does Elias know we're home? Why didn't he come skiing with us?" I questioned, deciding to get to the bottom of this.

"Not sure. He didn't answer when I knocked or called him this morning. I left him a note, but it doesn't look like it was found." Soren shrugged.

Looking over, I saw the note on the fridge was left untouched, with nothing below it in response. Odd. This was all very bizarre and out of character for him. Thinking back over the week, he'd been more withdrawn since Tuesday. In fact, I think I'd only seen him in passing a few times, but nothing in the past two days. A spike of fear went through me. No, this couldn't be happening.

"Did you actually go into his room? See him?" I asked calmly, but something in my voice must've given me away because instantly, everyone stopped their conversations and turned to me, paying close attention.

"What is it, Mateo?" Sawyer asked hesitantly, her lip between her teeth in worry.

"When was the last time anyone actually saw or spoke to him?"

"I did last night after dinner. It wasn't a, um… it wasn't a good conversation," mumbled Sawyer, her face looking crestfallen.

"I spoke with him around 8 pm, probably. Told him to stop being an ass," Rhett also replied.

"So, no one has seen him since last night? No texts? Nothing?"

Everyone pulled out their phones to check at my question, but all their heads shook 'no' as they pocketed their phones. The color drained from my face, and I didn't think. I just took off running for the stairs. Maybe I wouldn't be too late.

Please, don't let me be too late, I chanted in my head over and over.

At the top of the stairs, I paused for a brief moment at his door before entering as I panted, gathering my breath. Carefully, I pushed open his door, fearful of what I might discover. I was expecting to find an unconscious body, instead what I found was almost worse.

His room was completely empty.

The air even appeared disturbed when I'd opened the door, indicating no one had entered in hours. The bed was meticulously made, and I could still make out the vacuum marks on his carpet. Lucky's bed looked to be missing from the corner, but nothing else seemed amiss right away.

Looking around closer, I spotted his bag was also gone. A few schoolbooks and texts were missing from the vast pile he typically had. I wasn't in his room a lot, but having to walk past it multiple times a day, my brain had cataloged the information. I had just made a sweep of the room when someone else entered after me.

"Whoa. He's gone?"

"At least he didn't off himself," mumbled someone behind me, followed by a grunt.

"Hey, that hurt," Ollie said clearer, indicating he had been the one to make the comment.

"Good. That was insensitive to say. This could be serious, and suicide isn't a joke," Sawyer said, reprimanding him. My fierce little protector, that one.

"What does this mean? He just left? No notes or anything?" Her voice trembled, and when I turned, I saw tears brimming in her eyes.

Sawyer was blaming herself, but that wasn't fair. Whatever had occurred, Elias had chosen to leave. This was his doing, whether right or not, Sawyer wasn't responsible. I hoped she understood that part when she wasn't so flooded with emotions.

Rey pulled her into his arms, and she went easily, taking his comfort. It was moments like this, when I felt out of my depth, and was thankful we were in a group relationship. We each got to excel at what we were good at and could lean on the others for the things we weren't. There was no pressure to feel we had to meet every need, and I learned from watching each of them how to improve on the things that were new to me.

The support of the guys was just as wonderful for me as it was for her. Though I didn't feel anything for them romantically, their friendship and love gave me the family bonds I'd craved my whole life. I was open enough now and secure in my sexuality, despite being new to it, to admit I loved these guys in a platonic way.

While I'd been pondering this, Rhett had stormed in. He didn't appear to be handling this well and seemed almost as gutted about it all as Sawyer. I'd never seen the quiet mountain so full of emotions before. If steam could come from someone's nose, I think it would've right then from Rhett's. He clenched his fists open and closed before turning and stomping down the stairs.

"I'll go check on him," Soren offered before heading out.

Rey held Sawyer as she cried. Ollie and I stood in the room, glancing around and wondering what this meant. Was this because of the relationship? Or was it something more sinister? Did the Council have something to do with this? Things were escalating if that was the case, and I worried we weren't prepared to handle this. Would we even be able to survive this in the end?

I desperately wanted the answer to be yes. I'd just found this family, these friends, and I wasn't letting anyone take them from me. Not without a fight.

If they wanted to bring this to our door, then we would just have to be ready for them. I think it was time we went on the attack and showed them just how strong we were as a unit. The kid gloves were off—time to play, assholes.

thirty-eight

. . .

rhett

PACING BACK AND FORTH, I struggled not to punch anything. How could he do this? Why wouldn't he say goodbye? Pure gut-wrenching pain filled my body. Why did he leave?

Memories of Molly leaving me without even a word slammed back into me. Feelings of my father leaving me and having to pick up the family mantle swarmed me.

I couldn't do this. I couldn't.

Falling to my knees, my chest started to burn as I clawed at it, and I realized I wasn't getting air. Tugging at my shirt, I attempted to get it off me when I remembered to breathe. Sucking in a breath, I was flooded with oxygen as my body filled with relief at having air back. A tear fell and hit the floor, the splash magnified in the silence as I watched it.

Something about that image broke me, and I lost it. Needing an outlet for my pain, I pulled back my arm, preparing to strike the floor in a punch. My momentum was stopped before I was able to release my rage and sorrow. Seething, I gritted out between my teeth, "Let. Go."

"No."

"Let. Go."

Even as I repeated the command, I knew it wouldn't be followed. Why would anyone listen to me? My anger and guilt slammed into me hard. Elias had left because of me. I had pushed Sawyer too far, pushed him too far, and now he was gone—hurting us both in the process. It was all my fault—my depravity ripping apart anything good.

Just another person in a long line leaving me. They would all leave me eventually, and I'd be stuck in this town trying to keep it all together. I didn't realize my arm had dropped until I felt arms around me, holding me tight in an embrace.

"It's okay, big man. It's okay. Ssh."

Soren squeezed me tight, and I realized the pressure was helping me to breathe. The tears fell fast as I sobbed on the floor of the fitness room. My heart was breaking in the place a few days ago, it had felt the fullest.

I didn't notice I'd shifted at first, but the softness of his shirt, the beat of his heart, the smell of his skin eventually permeated my brain, and I began to ground myself in his presence as my sobs petered out.

Soren was rocking me as he squeezed me tight in his arms, or as much as one 6ft guy to another 6ft guy could. The thought of what we looked like crouched on the floor of the fitness room sent a laugh through my tears in a weird hiccup sob/laugh combo.

"Whatever you're thinking, it's not your fault, man. We're assuming one thing when it could be something different. Until we know the facts, we shouldn't jump to conclusions. That being said, Elias made his own choice; we don't have to like it, but we have to accept it because it was his to make, his. But most importantly… we're not going to leave you."

The last part was stated with such conviction, I had to assume I'd voiced that part out loud. Something about how he said it, though, soothed me.

"I say that out loud?"

At his nod, I exhaled, sitting back on my haunches. I kind of missed his hug, though. I didn't see Soren that way, but there was something to be said about another man hugging you just for the sole purpose of supporting you. Not everything had to be sexual, and that bond between guys was powerful. Too many things got corrupted because the world wanted everyone to fit into a box.

"Thanks, man. I needed that hug."

"No problem, Rhett. Anytime. You know that, right?"

"Yeah, I'm starting to see that."

"You know why this relationship with Sawyer works?"

"Because Sawyer is one in a million."

"Well, yes, that is true. But it works because we all believed you when you told us it would. You came in that night spouting off all these things about being a family, a unit, and how we all trusted one another and could be successful together. *You* did that, Rhett. We don't say this enough to you, but you're the glue, dude. Our mother hen, in fact. We all feel safe because you make it safe for us. Let us do the same for you. It doesn't all have to be on your shoulders. We let you do it because you're awesome at it, and it's second nature to you, but it doesn't mean you have to be the only one. It's not your responsibility to make sure we're all okay, but you do it. So, let us do it for you."

Soren's words sat heavy in my heart as I thought them over. I'd never realized it, but what he was saying was true. I needed to protect everyone. It made me feel worthy to take care of others, and I wanted to be worthy for them.

But I didn't let anyone take care of me. His appreciation and notice of how I contributed to our family bolstered my confidence in myself. It felt nice to be recognized for something and respected for it.

"Thank you, Soren. I don't think I realized how much I needed to hear that. You're right. I don't ask for help. I want to change that, I do. I'm scared I pushed Elias away."

Fear filled me, and I felt myself on the edge again, teetering. It wasn't as scary this time, though, because Soren was here with me. I didn't have to face the storm alone. I'd worked so hard to create a family, but I hadn't truly realized I had it. I was pushing myself to obtain something without enjoying it when I reached it. Which was fucking mental.

The relief I felt at that acknowledgment was tremendous. How long had I been unconsciously taking on the weight of the world? I needed to do better. Starting with taking better care of myself. Which meant dealing with shit instead of hiding it, even if it scared the crap out of me.

"Why do you think you pushed him away?"

"This is kind of awkward to say, but there was a, um, moment. Let's call it that. But a moment between Sawyer, Elias, and I. And ever since that night, he's been avoiding us both. Last night I questioned him and pushed him to accept what he was feeling toward her. When he didn't and told me it didn't mean anything, well, it hurt. I might have lashed out in anger because I told him if he believed that, then he wasn't the person I thought he was."

"Was anything you said untrue or mean? Because it sounds like you were actually a good friend and pushing him to confront himself. Kind of like how I just did with you, and you didn't push me away."

He had a point. Thinking about it, I recognized Soren was right. I hadn't been mean or unfair. I had pushed him as friends should when we were asses. The difference between Elias and I, though, was that I was willing to hear the truth. Elias hadn't been.

"Can I ask a personal question?"

"Come on, Rhett. We just shared a man hug and a good cry. I think we're beyond having to ask if it's okay at this point."

Laughing, because he wasn't wrong. When someone saw you at your most vulnerable moment, what else was there to hide? Nothing. That was the beauty of vulnerability.

"How, or when perhaps, when did you know, you um, had real feelings for Rey?"

"Why I declare, Rhett! Are you hitting on me, big man?"

"Hilarious. But if I did like you, Soren, you wouldn't stand a chance. I'd have you falling in love with me before you even knew what was happening. I have years of romantic comedies on my side. If I'm in, I'm all in. I'd hit you so hard with the feels you would be professing your love to me in a musical number. So no, I do not like you that way, dude. Just answer the damn question, please." I huffed, glaring at him.

"Fuck, Rhett. I think I just came a little from that speech."

Giving him my patent eyebrow raise, I was about to resort to punching him. I was still owed a good punch since he'd stopped me. With us still sitting on the floor, I could reach him easily if needed. My look must have communicated this as he finally answered and carefully moved out of my reach.

"Sorry. I said I would be here for you and then I go get all weird. Though I have to say, I'm a little jealous you don't like me that way after that speech. Sawyer, and I'm guessing Elias, are lucky."

I couldn't help but chuckle at him as he steepled his hands to think about my question. Even when he annoyed me, he was still my good-natured brother.

"Hmm… it's hard to say when I knew I liked Rey. I think the better question might be when I realized I was attracted to guys because that was before him. The obvious clue was getting hard thinking of a guy, or seeing a cock, I guess."

Soren stretched out his legs, bracing himself back on his arms as he looked up at the ceiling, almost like he was sorting through his memories.

"With Rey, it was more about always wanting to be with him. Missing him when he was gone and feeling happier when he was in the room. Sometimes now, when I'm sitting there with Sawyer and Rey, I wonder how I got so lucky, you know? They are my moon and sun, and I hope I get to spend a long time loving them both."

Soren was pretty poetic when he tried. His calm demeanor and easy-going personality made it easy to spill your secrets to him. I never realized how important that was to have.

His reflection gave me something to think about, though. I didn't know if I felt that way about Elias. He was my friend, and I cared deeply for him. But I didn't feel the same way I did about Sawyer, with him, at least not yet.

The other night had been one of the most incredible

experiences of my life. Was that from just the kinkiness of it, the explicitness and tawdriness? Or was it because it was with Elias? Maybe I would need to have another experience with someone in the room, and then I could compare and contrast the feelings. Shit, I sounded like Elias with my lists and research methods, only making me miss him more.

"Thanks, Soren. That actually helps a lot. I'm not sure if it's that way with us, so I appreciate the feedback. I guess it's time to go see if we can figure out what happened with our runaway."

We both got up and started toward the door. Before we made it out of the room, Soren turned back toward me, a pensive look on his face.

"I enjoyed the hug too. If you ever need another platonic hug, I'd be there for that."

Well, when you were given that type of invitation, there was only one thing to do.

I pulled him into a platonic hug and took comfort in the arms of my friend. I think Soren graduated from the Rhonda Taylor school of hugging because he was excellent at it. Breaking apart, we headed back upstairs—time to find my best friend. There was a sparring session I couldn't wait for in our future—his face, my fist. It was so on.

thirty-nine

sawyer

HENRY HELD me as I contemplated what this meant. I couldn't believe Elias would just leave like that. At the first sign of conflict, he ran. It said a lot to me about his character, if I was being honest. The more I stood there thinking about it, the more pissed I got at him. This was precisely what I'd been talking about with him. You know what… screw him! He'd get no more tears from me.

Pulling away from Henry, I hardened my resolve. This was the last time I was going to feel upset over Elias Turner. He wasn't the person I thought he was, and I didn't need him in my life if this was how he treated people. It should've been evident when I found out he'd been engaged to the Queen Bitch we weren't compatible. My first instinct was correct; he was a douchecanoe.

"Elias has made his decision. I'm not going to chase him or sit around and pine over his departure. We've had a great day, and I'm not letting him ruin it. Now, didn't someone mention hot chocolate?"

The guys all looked at me with varying degrees of emotions, but I didn't care. I couldn't. I'd said I was done last night, and I meant it. He didn't get to make me feel this way when he wasn't even brave enough to face us.

Leaving the room, I ignored the face Mateo was giving me. Out of all of them, he seemed the most distraught. Whether with Elias or me, I wasn't sure, but I didn't like how it made me feel, thinking he was disappointed in me. I just—

Nope. Stop that, brain. Just a whole bunch of fucking nope.

Pulling out the cocoa mix, I got to work making hot chocolate. The guys trickled in one by one from upstairs. Rhett and Soren still seemed to be missing. Fuck, I hadn't even thought about how Rhett might be feeling. Elias was his best friend, and because of me, he'd left. Shit, if Elias ruined what we had together, I would never forgive him.

The milk started to boil, so I began to divvy it up between the mugs I could find. Ollie grabbed some marshmallows and whipped cream from somewhere overhead, and I smiled in thanks. No one said much of anything as we grabbed our drinks and sat around the table in silence. We were one morose bunch.

Fuck this shit. I needed to do something, pronto.

"That's it. I'm making an executive decision. It's sleepover night. Gather the gang, put on your PJs, and we're going to spend the night playing games and watching movies. None of this sad shit. If he didn't have the ovaries to tell us he was leaving, then he doesn't deserve our sadness."

"Why do I feel like I'm missing something? How do you know it wasn't the Council?"

Mateo finally spoke the words that had been playing on his mind. I thought about it for a minute but decided it wasn't the Council. It couldn't be. Right? No, this wasn't how they played things. They've always come after me. What would they want with Elias? Nothing. He was just a tutor.

This was all him—his choice to leave. I debated how much to tell them when Rhett beat me to the punch. His face was red and puffy, but I didn't see any hatred toward me in his eyes. He held them as he spoke to the group.

"This was Elias. He's running from facing things. What that pertains to is between Sawyer, Elias, and I."

"Um, hello? I thought this was an open communication relationship. Why are you being so fucking cagey?" Ollie demanded.

"It's not—"

Before Rhett could explain his evasiveness, code orange detonated. Sometimes, I swear it has a monthly quota it had to hit because I'd been doing so well.

"For crying out loud. Rhett and I fucked while Elias jerked himself off watching us. He ran off, scared, and quite frankly, I'm over it. I'm done talking about this. He's clearly made his decision, and it's not us. If we don't rank high enough on his list to even get a fucking goodbye, then I'm glad it never went further." I semi-shouted to several stunned faces. Taking a drink of my hot chocolate, I avoided looking at them, worried I would see accusations.

"Sawyer, you can't mean that," Rhett whispered, drawing my attention to him. His face looked so sad, and I realized something else was going on with him, and I would need to check-in.

"I do. Last night, I told him he didn't have to be with me but he owed it to you guys to be here and that I would be civil because he was important to you. And what's his response? He fucking leaves. He left his dog, he left his students, and he left our family. So yes, I'm not going to wallow in this. There are too many other things going on that rank higher. This is why we need to have this sleepover. A night of fun will do us some good."

I wasn't sure whether it was my tone, the comment about our weird sexual experience, or just pure brain overload, but no one said anything as they stared at me. Rolling my eyes, I pulled out my phone and started messaging Fin, Tyler, Chloe, Ace, and Asa.

ME: Sleepover party. Attire-PJ's. Food-Junk. Activities-General Mayhem. Time to party, my friends!

Ty: Fuck, Wildcat. I have that away game

tonight. I'll be thinking about you, though. Send me pics!

Chloe: Woo! I'll be there

Fin: Yes! M&M time!

Ace: I'm glad I still get an invite after our last convo. There is something I want to talk to you about more. Thank you, this is just what I need. I'll bring snacks!

Asa: Cool. I have something for you from Mom as well.

It still felt weird to think of Isla as Mom, but a warm sensation coated me as I thought about her and Asa. I really hoped we could make up for the time we'd lost and bond. I'd forgotten about Ty's game and felt like a jerk rubbing something else in his face he was missing out on. Ace, well, I didn't know where we stood, so it would be good to talk and possibly clear the air with whatever was going on there. I had a feeling it was more than him just liking one of my boyfriends.

Happy with the responses, I looked up from my phone to see none of the guys had moved. They all had a look of dumbfoundedness on their faces. Seriously, it was like they'd just found out the pizza girl didn't want to have sex with them or something. Rolling my eyes, I decided I didn't have it in me to explain anything else.

It might have seemed callous and cold of me, but people leave. They always did; my life was a prime example.

You could sit around and mourn the destruction and

chaos they erupted in their wake, uprooting everything. Or you could just get over it. I chose to get over it. 'The heroes were the ones who stayed.' Veronica Mars taught me that.

Pushing back my chair, I rinsed out my mug and placed it in the dishwasher. Not even looking back, I walked out of the room. They would have to learn, and me holding their hand wouldn't help. Besides, I had a sleepover to arrange.

rey

Sawyer was acting cold and distant, and it concerned me. It was obvious she cared about Elias, but was protecting herself by closing off her emotions. Her expression was eerily similar to the one that had stared back at me in the mirror for years. She was firmly in the land of denial and stationed at the capital city of stubbornness. She wasn't going to budge unless something drastic happened.

"Is she going to be okay? Am I the only one who thought that was freaky?" Ollie asked, staring after her.

"I'm not sure, dude. I've never seen her shut down her emotions so quickly. One minute she was upset in the room, and the next, she acted like he was just some stranger on the street," Mateo replied in a concerned tone. Shaking my head, this was where my history with Sawyer was an asset.

"That's not it at all. She shut herself down because she cares too much. Sawyer is hurting, but her history has taught her to push it aside. If we don't do something about this, we'll lose the Sawyer we know and fell in love with."

Pushing back my chair, I took my now cold hot chocolate to the sink and dumped it. I just needed to find the right thing to trigger her emotions. I hadn't realized I'd been washing my mug for several minutes until Soren softly took it from my hands, turning off the water.

"We'll figure this out together. Come on. I think we all need to talk." Pulling him into a hug, I held him for a moment, drinking in the comfort he offered so effortlessly.

"Thank you," I mumbled before kissing him on the cheek. Walking out of the kitchen together, I realized the guys were no longer in the dining room. How long had I zoned out?

"Rhett's room. Come on." Sor answered before I even had to ask. He pulled me downstairs, and I followed willingly because there was nowhere I wouldn't go with him.

When we got to the bottom of the stairs, I saw the rest of the guys in Rhett's room scattered about. It felt kind of wrong having this conversation without her, but I also knew she wouldn't hear anything we had to say at this point. She had her walls sealed as tight as Fort Knox.

"How can we fix this?" Rhett asked immediately. Direct and to the point, as usual, he didn't mess around. I admired that about him, honestly. Blowing out a breath, I voiced what I had been thinking earlier at the sink.

"It's not going to be easy."

They all nodded, ready to accept what I had to say, filling me with confidence. Part of me felt relieved, and I realized the beauty of this relationship. It wasn't all on me, and we trusted each other to use our strengths when needed.

"First, we go to the slumber party…"

The faces around the room ranged in emotions from stoic, to curious, to accepting as I detailed out my plan.

It would either work, and we would get Sawyer back, or it would backfire, and we would all lose her. In some ways, we already had, even if they didn't realize it. At least this way, we had a shot.

forty

finley

ASA'S KISSES felt like ice cream on a warm day—sweet and satisfying. Thankfully, he hadn't hated me for dropping the bomb he had a twin sister who happened to be my best friend. Things since that day had been good between us, and when he introduced me to his mother as his girlfriend, I about fainted. Everything was coming up Finley.

We went back to my room after skiing and had a fun day of relaxing and cuddling. Sawyer's text about the sleepover had woken us from our cat nap, so we decided to watch a movie until it was time to head over to the house. That had quickly evolved into an intense make-out session. I was not complaining.

He pressed his body down harder, rubbing against my core. A moan escaped me, encouraging him to keep going. I wrapped my legs around his waist and pulled him into me even more as I rocked up. His little moans of pleasure filled me with desire.

Despite things being great, he'd seemed hesitant to move too fast. I could appreciate it, but I also wanted to get down and dirty with the boy who had my heart. We'd been having foreplay for over a year, and I was suffering from a mad case of blue ovaries.

Yep, that was right. Blue. Fucking. Ovaries. It was so a thing.

Finally, his hand started to trail up my shirt, tracing along the bare skin. Chills erupted over me in anticipation as his thumb brushed against the outside of my bra. Moaning, I rocked up into him more as I rubbed my clit against his hard cock. We both still had our jeans on, but the friction was enough to feel fucking fantastic.

Unfortunately, that was when my phone decided to blare from across the room. Motherfucking shit stain. Just when it was getting good.

Asa froze and pulled back, asking me what I wanted to do with his eyes. He was practically sitting up now, and the lust was leaving him the longer our bodies weren't melded together.

Might as well answer the damn thing; it wasn't like we were going to be getting back to that hot session right now. Besides, it had to be someone important, right? Who else would fucking call these days? No one. Unless it was work-related or a death in the family, my phone did not ring. If anyone ever wanted to know what anxiety sounded like, it was the telephone ringing.

Rolling off the bed, I grabbed my phone off my

dresser, barely managing to answer it before it went to voicemail.

"Hello?" my voice came out in a croak.

"Hi, I was given your number to call for help in getting, um, some, you know, information?" a small female voice asked from the phone.

Shit. I hadn't received one of these calls in a while. I was mostly out of the hacking game, but I would dip my toes back in to stay fresh on my skills every now and then. Yeah, I had a hard time believing that myself too.

Mouthing to Asa, "I'm going to step outside." I pulled the balcony door open and stepped through. Grabbing a blanket, I wrapped it around my shoulders as I sat down in the Adirondack chair. Fortunately, the overhang kept the snow from them.

"Codeword."

"Oh, um. Monkey Balls," the caller whispered to me. Why were people so embarrassed to say that? Cracked me up every time.

"This is 0BL1V10N. How can I help you?"

The caller proceeded to drop a humongous bomb on me. Holy. Fucking. Shit. Why did I keep having to find out these secrets? I sat in the chair for a few minutes until I could no longer feel my face or toes. Bundling up, I walked stiffly back into the room.

"Everything okay, Fin?"

"Yeah. It's great."

"Are you sure, babe? You look like you just saw a ghost."

That was one way to put it.

sawyer

It had been about three hours since I declared we were having a sleepover. I'd spent part of it resting alone and the rest setting up our party space. I was finishing up the last touches in the media room. I had blankets, pillows, movies, games, beauty care, and a Polaroid camera to capture it all spread about the room.

A couple of drinks and snacks were out, but I was hoping the others would bring the good stuff. I'd hung some fairy lights in the media room and had some other random lamps scattered for ambiance. I wanted this to be the best sleepover party ever. Besides, I had several years to make up for. The guys had been distant since earlier, but I was trying not to let it bother me. Tonight was about connection and friendship. No relationship drama was allowed.

Chloe and Ace were the first to arrive. Ace wore some crazy getup that was more for looks than practicality based on the barely-there fabric. Chloe was in a unicorn onesie, and I realized I had definitely met a friend for life in her. When she saw my similar fox onesie, very girly screams accompanying jumping and clutching fingers ensued. It was epic. I think I just had my first girl crush.

"Oh my god, I love your outfit! How cute is this!"

"Same girl. I love that we both went full onesie!"

"You know it!"

"What are we going to do with this one?" I joked, pointing to Ace behind us. Linking my arm with hers, I pulled her over to a spot she could drop her bag. Ace responded by sticking his tongue out and posing in a warrior pose. I was guessing he was dressed as a gladiator with the tight man spanks and a cape. He had a sword, but I wasn't sure where he planned to put it. My questioning look finally made him cave as he made himself a drink.

"I'm Spartacus!"

"You realize I said PJ party and not BJ party, right?" I sassed, causing him to spew some of the soda he'd just drank.

I'd decided to let the tension go between us for the night. I needed some good friend time more than I needed answers. As Chloe and I chuckled at Ace with soda dripping down his admittedly nice abs, I realized I had made the right choice. It was nice having a break. Especially when the guys were acting weird and broody.

Finley and Asa arrived next, looking all cuddled up. I ran and jumped on my brother's back as they were putting their stuff down. Thankfully, he had good reflexes and didn't fall forward.

"Hey there, little sis, happy to see you too," Asa teased.

Exuberance filled me, and I kissed his cheek before

sliding off his back. I was looking forward to spending time with him tonight. I wondered what twin shenanigans we could get into. Sounded like fun to me!

"I put the box from Mom in your room. She said she wanted you to have it. Don't look at me though, I have no clue. That woman is a mystery most of the time."

I debated going and seeing what it was, but I wasn't confident I could handle it at the moment. I had already cried too damn much, so I decided to wait until tomorrow. After all, I had deemed it a no tears night, and I planned to stick to it.

"Did you see any of the guys when you were up there?"

"Nope, where's my brother?"

"If I knew, I wouldn't be asking you now, would I?"

"Good point. Trouble in paradise?" Fin jokingly asked, and I just shrugged in response. Honestly, I had no clue. I didn't think so, but they had avoided me all afternoon, so maybe they were done with me. I took a big swig of my drink, hoping to cover any sadness I might've displayed just then.

"Hey, everything okay?" Fin grabbed my arm and pulled me away to a private area.

"Yeah, it's fine. It's just the crap with Elias kind of exploded everywhere, and I guess they didn't like what I had to say. It is what it is, but tonight is for fun. So no relationship drama. Come on, if it's just going to be us, then let's get this party started."

Dragging Fin toward the others, I was momentarily surprised when all the lights went completely dark.

"What the—" before I could finish my sentence, music began to start up over the speakers. Instantly, I recognized the song as none other than the 2000 pop hit, "Bye, Bye, Bye" by *NSYNC. The lights came up a moment later, and standing there at the bottom of the room in tight jeans, bare feet, and naked torsos were my boyfriends.

They began to lip-sync to the song and dance along to the iconic moves. Henry was in front, with Soren to his right and Rhett behind him. To Henry's left was Ollie and then Mateo behind him. They were actually dancing well and synchronized to the dance moves. At first, I laughed along with the rest of the room to their dance number, but gradually the words started to filter through, and the bottom fell out from under me.

"Life will be so much better when you're gone… I want to see you out that door, Bye, Bye Bye."

Were they fucking breaking up with me in song? In front of my friends?

Not only had they just devastated me, but they ruined *NSYNC for me! That alone was a crime punishable by death. So much for no relationship drama. Fucking Hell.

Slowly, as they entered the song's climax, I began to back away, fading into the background. No one noticed; why would they? Once I was clear. I turned and casually walked the fuck out of there. Message. Received.

rey

Part one of my plan to break through Sawyer's barriers was performing one of her favorite childhood songs. Convincing the guys to lip-sync and dance had been more challenging than I'd anticipated. Still, they'd all agreed eventually, even if it was reluctantly.

We spent all afternoon practicing, and I was impressed with the moves some of them had. Mateo was actually a pretty skilled dancer when he let go of his embarrassment. We finished the song, slightly breathless and sweaty, and I looked around for my Smalls, our girl. The lights glared down on us, making it hard to pinpoint anyone. I couldn't find her.

"Smalls?" I called out.

The room was silent, and I didn't understand what was going on. Looking at the other guys, they didn't seem to know either based on the shrugs and looks of confusion.

I blamed the fact I was facing the opposite direction for my inability to stop what happened next, but let's face it. I was a lover and not a fighter. I wouldn't have been able to defend myself even if I had seen it coming.

"You asshole!" was shouted before a fist connected with my face.

In my confusion of the shout, I'd turned and directly ran into Asa's fist. The pain took me by surprise as I fell backward into Soren. By twisting, I'd given him direct access to my jaw. Ouch. Thankfully, Soren managed to keep me from hitting my head on the floor.

"Asa! Henry! What the hell!" my sister screamed out, echoing my own thoughts. What the hell, indeed. I felt like I was missing something to have garnered such an intense reaction from him. Guess he really hated boy bands.

Rubbing my jaw, Soren helped me stand on my own, and we faced off with a seething Asa. Rhett was rumbling behind me like a jet engine and was seconds from throwing punches himself, it seemed. This had all gone horribly wrong.

"How dare you do that to her!"

"What are you talking about, bro?" Ollie questioned, confusion heavy in his voice.

"What am *I* talking about?" Asa's incredulous look was plastered all over his face, and I still had no clue where his anger was coming from or where Sawyer was. Looking around the room, I saw various states of anger and disappointment etched on the others' faces.

"Where's Sawyer? Why is everyone mad?" I managed to finally get out as pain rang through my jaw with each word.

"Henry… that was cruel. I'm not even sure I can look at you," Fin finally responded. Screwing up my face and forgetting it hurt again, I welcomed the pain this time to help keep my head clear, so I could think.

"I honestly don't know what any of you are talking about. Can you just tell us so we can get to the bottom of this, please?"

Maybe the pleading tone would get us somewhere. Ollie, Soren, Mateo, and Rhett stood with me as we waited to hear what we'd done that was so horrible. I'd honestly thought she would like the number. It used to be her favorite guilty pleasure.

"You seriously don't understand how breaking up with your girlfriend in a room full of people through a song would be considered an asshole thing to do?" Chloe finally responded.

It was the first time I'd heard her say so much. It took me a minute to process her words.

"Break up? What the fuck are you talking about?" Rhett roared, clearly having understood her quicker and setting off Soren, Mateo, and Ollie as they voiced their own questions.

"That wasn't what this was!"

"Why would we break up?"

"Are you guys pranking us?"

Staring at Finley, I tried to process the events of the night: Asa's anger, Finley's disappointment, Chloe's statement and belief we'd broken up with Sawyer in a very public and humiliating way. When the lightbulb went off, all the air was sucked out of me.

"FUCK."

Everyone stopped and turned to me at my utterance. The color drained from my face, and I felt dizzy. Stumbling back, Soren caught me again as I tried to figure out how to fix this; I had to fix this. We hadn't meant it that way.

I wasn't focused on the lyrics, just the dance moves and the iconic feeling of it all, trying to remind her of a time when things were fun and straightforward. A time where she had been happy and free and hadn't needed her barriers. Not this, no, the opposite of this.

Quietly, I whispered the words that had just torn my world fucking apart.

"Bye, bye, bye…"

forty-one

sawyer

IT WAS cold as the wind whipped around my face. Somehow, I found myself walking down the middle of the road in the snow, clad only in my fox onesie. Couldn't say I was making the best decisions today.

I was so fucking numb. Everything seemed to have gone topsy-turvy. Had I misinterpreted everything? Was I deluding myself into thinking they cared about me?

The cold seeped into me more, but it was hard to decipher if it was the wind or my emotions at this point. Pulling my arms tighter around me, I braced myself against the freezing gust blowing through me. I was attempting to convince myself it was only the wind cutting through me that was chilling me to the bone.

The administration building loomed in front of me, and I decided to head there. Best to get out of the cold; I was heartbroken, not stupid—no sense in dying of hypothermia.

Pulling at the door, I was relieved to find it was unlocked. Shuffling in, my socked footie bottoms left a watery trail in my wake. I glanced around the corridor and took in my surroundings. It was dark, and most of the offices appeared to be locked up. A seating area came into view, so I shuffled my wet feet toward it. My PJs didn't provide much warmth, and despite being out of the cold, my body was still shivering.

Curling up on the sofa, I pulled my knees up, making myself into a ball as small as possible to maintain my body heat. Lying there shaking from the frigidness with my teeth chattering, I thought about how drastically the night had turned.

I'd managed to drift off to sleep when I heard voices. I hadn't expected to stumble upon people, so I was startled awake, being pulled from the unconscious state I'd slipped into. They echoed down the hallway, sounding louder than they probably were. Pulling myself in tighter, I hid in the shadows of the couch corner to avoid being seen.

A man and woman were arguing, and as they drew nearer, I could make out some of their conversation. One of the voices sounded eerily familiar, and I realized with absolute clarity that it was that woman, Squawky —the one who'd offered me the job.

"He will be at the expo and expects a certain audience to be available to him. If you cannot make this happen, then you will not like the consequences, Ms. Pekins. Do I make myself clear?"

"Of course, Mr. Morano. We value Mr. Abernathy's contribution to our school and aim to please him when he's on campus. Please, let our office know if there is anything else we can do to make the Council's stay better. The board is here at your disposal."

"We will see. He hasn't been happy so far with efforts to avert the Agency or the girl. You're skating on thin ice."

The man's voice gave me chills, and I instinctively pulled my body in more, drawing in memories of trying to hide from monsters long ago. My body was shaking again, but not from the weather this time—fear.

Their footsteps sounded off in different directions, and I waited as I counted to five hundred before I slowly got up from my hiding spot. Creeping around the corner, I decided to get back to the house. Whatever awaited me there had to be better than here.

It was stupid to come out alone. People were after me, and I'd just given them a perfect opportunity to find me vulnerable. I needed to face the relationship stuff and deal with whatever it was. I'd yelled at Elias for acting childish, and yet when shit got tough, I did the same. Perhaps, I owed him an apology. It wasn't okay what he did, but I could've given him more time or listened to what he had to say.

Wounded pride intact, I slowly began to make my way along the dark hallway. The creep factor had multiplied after overhearing that conversation. When I got to the corner, I braced myself to peek around when a hand from behind covered my mouth.

Instinctively, I started to bite down on the finger and prepared to head butt the person when they whispered, "Ssh, tiny dancer."

The memory engulfed me, letting go of my bite and I swam in the memories of the past.

"Why can't mommy and daddy see you, Brave Heart?" I asked the man who visited me in the gardens when mom and dad were at work. The housekeeper, Ms. Maple, was supposed to be watching me, but around this time of day, she tended to fall asleep, and my three-year-old self enjoyed the adventure of traipsing the gardens by myself.

My friend knelt down to my height, brushing my braid over my shoulder. I was wearing a frilly purple dress, and I both hated and loved it. It was frilly, but mommy didn't get mad when I got dirty, making them bearable. They were easier to move in, and I was always making up dances and performing for my mommy and daddy, and of course, Brave Heart. He was my protector and would rescue me from dragons.

"Because, tiny dancer, only you have the power to see me. You have a special heart and eyes that make me visible to you and lets us fight the dragons together. Do you have any magic dances for me today?"

Nodding, I started to show him my latest dance, and he clapped and grinned at my twirls. Laughing, we would run around swinging our arms, fighting off the bad guys. Brave

Heart said my love was the cure, but I never really under-stood what he meant.

Hearing the housekeeper calling for me, I knew it was time to return back to the house. My time with my friend was over. He pulled me in for a hug, holding me tight before brushing a kiss over my forehead.

"Be strong, tiny dancer. You are capable of great things. I will make sure of it," he whispered before letting me go.

"Bye, Brave Heart. I will miss you! Until our next adventure!"

"Until our next adventure."

He handed me a daisy, and I skipped off to show Ms. Maple my new flower. On the breeze, I heard a barely-there whisper, "I promised her I would."

The next day we ended up moving in the middle of the night, and I never saw my garden friend again. Eventually, my brain convinced me he really was only imaginary.

"Brave Heart?" I trembled as the memory connected and his smell registered with me. He was the one who'd saved me from the crash. It seemed my childhood imaginary friend wasn't so imaginary.

"Yes, tiny dancer. Ssh, he's still close by."

His hand dropped with the knowledge I wouldn't scream as he watched over my head at something. I took the opportunity to take him in; familiarity and memories bleeding together, overlapping what I'd forgotten, or assumed were my made up imagination.

"You saved me…" At my whisper, he looked down

at me. I'd already put the pieces together, but part of me wanted him to admit it.

"I've been saving you your whole life, Abigail."

"That's not my name."

He looked down again, a little annoyed this time, perhaps at my continued distraction, but I didn't care. Rather, I did, but this was just as important.

"I promise I'll explain everything. We just need to get out of here first, okay?"

Searching his eyes, I could tell he meant what he said and wasn't just trying to get me to go along with him, so I nodded. Appeased, he grabbed my hand and pulled me back the way I'd already come, except instead of turning into the alcove with the couch I had hidden on, he turned down a different hallway.

Several turns later, we exited the building through a service door, and I was completely turned around from where we were. Attempting to gather my bearings, I was taken aback when he opened a car door and shoved me in. Rude!

I probably should've been freaking out right about then; he was practically a stranger who'd just shoved me in a random car. But we had already decided I wasn't making the best decisions tonight; what was one more?

The memories of a little girl made me want to trust him. He had been my first friend and protector, and I had this overwhelming feeling I was safe. It didn't have to make sense; it just was.

Brave Heart slid into his seat, shutting his door

quietly behind him as he started the engine. The lights stayed off as we circled the parking lot until we were back on the road away from the building. Once we appeared to be clear, he finally began to talk.

"I'm not sure what happened tonight, but running off on your own, barely dressed, was stupid. You can't do things like that, Sawyer. Fortunately, I happened to be in the area when my contact told me you'd gone rogue."

Wait, contact? Was I being watched?

"I know, okay. I already berated myself on how stupid it was to leave before you got there. I didn't think at the time. I just reacted, and my flight instincts kicked in. I was halfway to campus before I even realized what I was doing. I promise I didn't intentionally put myself in danger," I said, not sure why I was explaining myself to him, but it felt important he wasn't disappointed in me.

He exhaled slowly, almost like he was calming himself before he spoke again. "I'm sorry, you're right. That's unfair of me to barge in here and start making demands. You do usually make better choices, and I shouldn't hold this one infraction against you."

His words didn't bring me the comfort he probably intended. In fact, it only made me realize how unfair I had been to the guys. Fuck a duck. I had royally screwed up and made a mess of things. Facepalming emoji had returned.

"Thank you for saying that, but I don't deserve it. I

need to do better, be better. I'm never going to take the Council down if not."

Something about my proclamation made him swerve off the road a little before righting it. Squeezing the door handle, I was trying to regulate my own breathing as flashbacks assaulted me. If I could manage to not ever get in a car again, I so would—my track record being what it was and all.

"I'm sorry. What did you just say?" his voice was steady and devoid of any emotion as he stared straight out the windshield. His knuckles tightening on the wheel was the only sign he was irritated or upset.

"That I'm going to make the Council pay for what they did to my family, to my parents. They can't get away with this."

Laughter flooded out of him, causing me to tense at his reaction. Okay, he was starting to officially piss me off now. I pinched myself to make sure I wasn't dreaming.

"Why is that so funny? I'm starting to think I should have named you, Sir Asshole," I mumbled, which unfortunately only caused him to laugh more. Fucking, great. My imaginary friend was bonkers.

"You actually did once. Can you imagine a three-year-old saying that? It was hilarious. I'm sorry, I don't mean to laugh at you. It's just that you have no idea what you're in the middle of, sweetheart."

"Don't call me that. I'm not your sweetheart." He exhaled deeply again, and I couldn't help the smirk that formed on my lips at the knowledge I was frustrating him. Something about that made me happy.

"Listen, there's a lot more going on. Here is what I can tell you, but you must discover the rest yourself. It's the way it has to be. Yes, I'm real and not imaginary like I made you believe. It was just easier. I'm sorry. Yes, I saved you from the wreck. I had met with your dad before that and was following at a distance. Yes, the people after you are dangerous. Yes, you should take these threats seriously."

He paused and let me digest the info dump he just gave me. Everything I'd assumed a few minutes ago, he confirmed, but I wasn't feeling as smug about it anymore. Nodding to him, I indicated I understood what he was saying.

"Listen to me closely on this. You are so strong, Sawyer. Stronger than I think you even know. I've watched you struggle; I've watched you give up, and I've watched you overcome. I don't know what's going on in that house, and quite frankly, I don't want to know the details. But you guys need to work your shit out because you're going to need each other. It's not a coincidence all of you are here at this school right now. I've been orchestrating this for years; for you to meet the right people who will be able to help you."

What the ever-loving flip? Orchestrated? Panic started to claw at me, but he continued talking, so I shoved it down, for now. We were going to need to circle back to that tidbit of information.

"I'm sorry I had to do it that way, but it was necessary. Trust in the bond you have. It's real despite what you're thinking right now. I can't fabricate that. Yes, I put you together with the guys in the hopes you would have all the pieces you would need to succeed. What you've created with them is all you and better than anything I could've done. Trust that. Your connections are genuine and the most important thing."

He spoke of trust as if it were easy. I wanted to believe him, but everything felt overwhelming, and I wasn't sure I wanted to. Denial was more manageable at times.

"Do not, and I repeat this, do not go up against your father yet. I know what you overheard, and I know you think you can make some type of play. Don't. It won't end well. Find the journal Elias had of your mother's. It's important. It will give you the last pieces you need to figure this all out. You're not going to like all the things you discover, but remember you had to lie to people for five years on who you were; longer than that actually, you just weren't aware."

My mind was racing. How was I going to remember all of this?

"Your trust will be tested, and how you manage it will be of utter importance. It could be the difference between winning and losing. I believe in you, tiny dancer. You always were my best-kept secret."

Swiftly, he kissed my forehead, and he was out of the car before I even managed to get my seatbelt off. It was then I realized we were in the driveway of the house and he'd actually driven Ollie's, or maybe Ace's car. I hadn't been in either of their vehicles, to honestly tell. Slowly, I stumbled out and looked around, but he'd vanished. I never figured out how he did that—crazy magician with that freaky spy shit.

Walking in a daze toward the front door, I was surprised when it opened, and what seemed like the whole house poured out from it. I was too exhausted to deal with any more of this tonight. Asa's arm went around me, and I let him lead me through the door. He and Fin were fussing over me, Ace and Chloe following quietly behind them, looks of concern on both of their faces.

Glancing back as we climbed the stairs, I saw five pieces of my heart staring at me from below. Disparaging grief was etched on all of their faces, confusing me. Just as I turned the corner, I swear I saw a tear fall from someone's eye. But when I blinked, all I could see was the hallway.

Turning back into my brother's embrace, I let them take care of me, too weary to fight tonight. It felt good, actually, to have people wanting to look after me. When we walked into my room, my eyes instantly landed on the canvas in the corner. The remaining blank spot was no longer empty. Now, it was etched with the words. "I love you."

Gasping, I drew my hands to my mouth, tears falling fast from my eyes. But… he would've had to complete this before their song. Asa and Fin stared at me, trying to work out the reason for my tears as they glanced from me to the canvas like a ping-pong match.

I didn't stop to tell them. I didn't stop at all.

Racing as fast as my damp, socked feet would carry me, I ran down the hall, flew down the stairs, and catapulted myself straight into their arms.

We collapsed into a heap on the floor, a conglomerate of arms and legs, making a giant octopus. Tears stained my cheeks, and my sobs wracked my body, covering any other sound. I couldn't even hear what was being said, but each time someone came near me, I smothered them in kisses.

'Sorry's' poured out of me and the others, and we all sat there in an entangled, weeping, sorry mess. And I wondered if I had ever felt happier?

We would be okay. We would be strong.

At some point, we managed to stand, and we all piled into the media room and ended up having the sleepover I'd wanted all along. Surrounded by my friends and family, my dog, and the men I loved, I was cocooned in what mattered most—love.

forty-two

sawyer

WHISPERING WOKE me the next morning. Looking around the media room, it was hard to make out faces in the dark. It was the perfect place to have a dog pile of people with all the pillows and bean bags, though. However, I regretted basically sleeping on the floor as my body was stiff and sore from skiing the day before. The floor hadn't helped things at all. Scooting out from under the arms around me, I detangled myself from the blankets before standing.

After my evening walk in the snow, I'd changed out of my fox onesie and had gone to sleep in one of Rhett's shirts, a pair of my old sweats and fuzzy socks. I'd wanted to be comfortable, and nothing made you feel more comfortable than a good pair of fuzzy socks. That was my philosophy anyway, and I was sticking to it.

Stepping over bodies as I made my way out of the

room, I was careful not to trip over anyone. Fin and Asa were the whispering duo in the corner. It looked intense, so I just left them to figure out their stuff in my search to find a bathroom.

Deciding to just go upstairs and get dressed, I headed to my own. That was the wrong choice, though, as I was frantically doing the "don't pee" dance by the time I made it there. Finally relieving myself, I walked back into my room and found Lucky curled up in the cuddle chair. Guess he'd sought refuge here when we all fell asleep.

A few of my shirts were tossed over the chair, along with a blanket. I swear, that dog was a comfort hog. Always found the softest places to sleep. Climbing in the chair, I curled up around him and gave him some cuddles and love. Reaching back, I pulled the blanket from under me to cover us, deciding to take a little snooze right here. I was surprised when something sharp dug into my back after shifting the blanket.

"What the hell…"

I reached back to grab the offending object, only to come in contact with a journal—my mother's journal. Sitting up, I flipped it open, and a few envelopes fell onto my lap. These weren't here before. Looking them over, I noticed one was addressed to me, one to Rhett, and the other one was to the guys. The neat script across the white surface made my heart race. *Elias.*

Tearing open the letter, I devoured the words and then reread them several times as I attempted to digest their meaning.

"Baby, what's wrong?"

Glancing up, I found Rhett standing in my doorway, but at the sight of my tears, he walked in, crouching down in front of me, waiting for me to answer.

"Elias, he um, he left us letters after all," I managed to get out.

The relief on his face melted my heart. In my grief and pain, I'd forgotten to check on him. Rhett was missing his best friend. I was selfish to think it only affected me. Placing my hand on his cheek, he leaned into it, briefly shutting his eyes as he relished my touch.

How I thought this man was breaking up with me in a song, I had no idea. His love was clearly written on every inch of him—for me, for the guys, for his family. It was part of who he was, and I was dumb for not recognizing that sooner. Maybe I'd gotten a concussion, after all?

No, that was an excuse. I'd messed up, and I needed to accept the consequences of my actions. That was the thing about regret; you never knew until you did, and doubt had a way of making us believe the most blatant lies.

"I'm sorry. I—"

"Ssh, baby. It doesn't matter. I'm sorry too. There were many mistakes made by all of us yesterday, but what's important is us. What we are now and what we are moving toward. We all have things we need to work on—that's just life. We just have to remember we have each other while we do it."

Kissing him briefly, I took his solid belief about us

and wrapped it around me. I wanted to have that same assuredness he did. Rhett picked me up and sat back down in the chair with me in his lap. Lucky wasn't impressed with this disturbance if the glare he gave us was anything to go by. He stood up and readjusted himself, huffing when he plopped back down, causing us both to chuckle at him. Gah, he was adorable.

"What does your letter say?"

Handing it to him because I was still digesting the info to speak it, I relaxed back into his embrace as he read the words Elias had left me.

Dear Sawyer,

There are so many things I owe to you, but most importantly, I am genuinely sorry for my cowardice. You were correct that I was indeed hiding. But it is more than you could possibly know. I grew up going to boarding schools, never having a real family bond. My parents and siblings are distant strangers to me, but the expectations and demands are very real.

I came to TAS to escape some of that. On the pretense I was here to finish my dissertation for my doctorate, my family approved. What I found here was beyond anything I had expected. I have had heartache, but in the grand scheme, that seems minor compared to now.

The guys and I have always been close. They were there for me last year after things with Adelaide erupted. It was the first time in my life I relied on someone, depended on someone. Most importantly, I found a real best mate in Rhett. Having people in my life who did not want some-

thing from me but who truly cherished me for the person I am is foreign to me. I sometimes forget the people in this house, this family, do not operate as the outside world does.

I lied to you today—to you and Rhett. I thought if I denied what I was feeling, what we all experienced, then we could just brush it under the rug. I have never had to face those types of emotions before and, in essence, was unprepared for what I felt. In that inexperience, I ended up hurting two people who mean a great deal to me. For that, I am sorry. I never meant to make you feel tawdry or anything other than the brilliant woman you are. Because you are, Sawyer. You're bloody brilliant.

The day we met in the kitchen, I royally placed my foot in my mouth and unforgivably offended you. But somehow, you did, you forgave me. Despite being some of my worst behavior, that encounter was one of the most exhilarating moments of my life. In actuality, every barb and insult traded with you since then has been.

I know that must sound odd, how my poor behavior can make me feel more than anything else. But love, it is not the behavior I enjoy, but the woman I engage it with. You have lit a fire within me, Sawyer.

Sometimes we are like a brushfire, destroying everything in our wake. Other times we are like an inferno of heat between us, capable of melting an ice cap. Whether we are trading insults, tasting cake, or even bloody tedious research (your words), I have felt more passion, more of the man I have always wanted to be.

Hurting you tonight was the lowest I have ever felt. It is no excuse, but I was scared. Scared of what it meant, fearful of how I might get hurt again, but mostly I was afraid of facing the truth. The truth of who I am with you, but worse, without you. The reality of what this meant for my life and how it would irrevocably change my path. The truth of the role I may play in your story, love. I'm afraid it's not pretty.

I have decoded your mother's journal, and looking through it, I realized a lot of things. I hope it gives you the answers you seek. It showed me what I needed to do.

I hope you will forgive me again someday and that we can relight the spark I let blow out. Even if that never happens, I have been made a better man because of you.

Part of that is why I have to leave. There is something I must do. I hope you will understand someday. You have given me back hope in my life, and for that, I will be eternally grateful.

I am sorry I could not say goodbye to your face, but I never seem to get out the words I need to say. Please take care of Lucky, though to be fair, he is practically your dog already. I know he will be well looked after.

If I return to TAS, I hope my choices will be some first steps in redeeming myself. You deserve nothing less, love. I'm sorry I ever made you feel that. Your heart is a masterpiece and the most beautiful symphony I have ever heard.

Wholly yours,

Elias

forty-three

. . .

rhett

READING the words Elias wrote to Sawyer filled me with an extreme amount of conflicting emotions. On the one hand, I was glad my best friend had finally taken some action and was beginning to make waves for himself. However, a larger part wanted to know where I stood with him. What hadn't he told me about his family? Would I ever see him again? Why hadn't he trusted me enough to say anything before?

It was all feeling too much, and I needed to quit chasing anxiety. I supposed I could start by opening my letter. At least then I might have some answers to the questions running circles through my mind.

Sawyer must've sensed my hesitation. She grabbed the potential bomb out of my hand, opened it, and began to read it out loud when I didn't stop her. Relief washed over me, and I pulled her closer as I leaned back in the chair. I could do this; I could listen to her read.

Dear Rhett,

Thank you for reminding me of the man you see me as. I seem to have gotten lost and fallen off track here lately. I don't want to be that fool any longer. So, much gratitude.

You have been the best mate I could ask for. The best mate I've ever had, in fact. You probably don't know that, but it's true. Your friendship is one of the most valuable things to me. I'm sorry I didn't cherish it as I should have. Hopefully, my actions will show you the man I see you to be and the faith I have in you. You are one of the worthiest men I have ever had the pleasure of knowing. I only hope I can become half of the man you are someday.

I have to leave now to make things right. There's something I must do… and it might not bring me back here. The risk will be worth the reward in the end. I hope. It's my way of proving my own value in this relationship. To show our family I can be counted on. You taught me the importance of that. Thank you for showing me the way.

Protect our girl and remind her always of how special she truly is. Love her deeply for both of us until I'm able to do it right. Because I so want to do it well. I finally understand what that means. You have shown me what it means to have real courage.

There are things I would like to talk further with you about, and if I make it back here, the first pint will be on me. I'm not running, and hopefully, that has become clear because I don't want to run anymore. If my plan works, then I will have evened out the playing field in her fight. It's bigger than we all even imagined.

I know you will protect them all. I have no doubt in you, mate. I'm lucky to have met you and call you my brother.

Until we meet again,

Elias

Sawyer briefly checked with me before continuing to read the next one.

Fellas,

I have been a right bastard the past couple of days, and for that, I apologize. You blokes have been the best friends I have ever made. My behavior has created undue stress and a volatile living space, which wasn't fair to you all. I vow to make it better, and to do that, I need to leave. I have a way that might help us all. Sawyer and Rhett can explain more. I'm hopeful that it will give us a boost against our enemies. To do this, I have to do something I have been avoiding for a while, but it is time. I finally understand my purpose in this family.

My return is questionable, but know that you lot have meant more to me than anyone. Thank you for accepting me as I am, stodgy rules and all. For the love of all that is holy, do not microwave water. I will feel it in my bones if you do. Please, save me from this misery.

Until we can share a laugh and a pint, make sure to take care of one another. The bonds we have forged are extraordinary and need to be protected. I have a feeling they will serve us well in our fight ahead.

Elias

"Wow," Sawyer uttered when she'd read the last one. Turning into my embrace, her eyes searched mine. Hiding nothing from her, I let her see all the anguish and confusion I felt. Things with Elias and I were skewed now, and I didn't know how I felt about it all. His view of our family and me was validating, but there was this unresolved sadness I had no idea what to do with. At least he hadn't left because of what happened. That burden lifted off my shoulders and I instantly felt the relief.

"How are you feeling, baby?"

"Probably about the same as you. Confused, hurt, relieved, sad, and possibly hopeful. I want to be angry at him for leaving like he did, but I'm glad to know he didn't just leave. I want to know what he is doing and how dangerous it is, though. I want to shake him for being so stupid and not telling me any of this to my face. Part of me wants to punch him and then kiss him. I want…" she trailed off as her tears started to fall, burying her head in my chest.

"I know, baby, I know."

I smoothed her hair down as she cried. Every time I saw her tears, it pained me, and I just wanted to solve her problems, but that wasn't the type of girl Sawyer was. I had to remember the strength I was attracted to needed space to be cultivated by her. If I stifled Sawyer, she would only grow to resent me and stop being the woman I'd fallen in love with.

Holding her close, I poured what I could into her with my hug and presence. I offered her my strength and love. Her tears slowed as she lifted her head and kissed me softly.

"I love you, Rhett."

"I love you, Sawyer."

Nothing else needed to be said. We would figure it out together. We all would.

tyler

The hockey team had returned late last night from the game, and I hadn't wanted to interrupt the sleepover, but my anxiety was riding me hard. Not hearing back from Sawyer since her text that afternoon, I felt something was off. Hopefully, I was only overreacting, but I wouldn't know until I saw her. Living outside in a different house was becoming more and more of a disadvantage. I wondered if I could request a new housing arrangement?

Pulling into the driveway, I noticed Ollie's car was in the middle of it, almost as if he'd just stopped it there. This didn't help my anxiety, so as I parked my bike, I jumped off before removing my helmet and ran up to the front door.

My fist pounded against it as I frantically rang the doorbell. Neither appeared useful, as they both went unanswered, making my anxiety spike even more. Finally taking off my helmet, I started calling people, but no one answered those either. Shit, this wasn't good. Trying the doorknob, I was shocked when it opened easily of its own accord. Fuck! This was bad, so bad.

"Hello?"

When no one called out, I decided to check Sawyer's room first and ran up the stairs. I scanned the rooms as I went, finding they were all devoid of people. My heart raced more with each step I took. Sawyer's door stood ajar, and the morning light filtered out through the door frame as I approached. All the other rooms on the floor had been closed, but not this one.

My pace slowed, uncertainty filling me for what I might find. Centering myself, I took a deep breath and walked into her room. Nothing looked amiss from the one time I'd been in there. There was a box on her bed, but everything else appeared tidy and organized. Turning, I decided to search through the rest of the house, when the sound of the shower running surprised me.

Not stopping to think due to worry, I opened the door and walked in. The steam surrounded me at first, making it difficult to see anything until my vision cleared. The sight that was revealed instantly set my blood racing for an entirely new reason, my cock hardening in my jeans in response.

Sawyer stood under the showerheads being sprayed from all directions. The water rolled over her body almost seductively. It was the most erotic scene I'd ever witnessed. When I noticed her holding one of the showerheads between her legs as she groped one of her breasts, I was stripping my clothes off faster than I could process.

It had been a few years since we'd slept together, but this week had felt as if no time had passed between us. Opening the shower door, I tried not to scare her when a moan slipped out of her.

"Fuck, Wildcat." Her eyes lazily opened at my comment and took me in appreciatively.

"Ty." My name was uttered in a moan, sending tingles through me. Fuck, I wanted her to always say my name that way.

Her eyes pleaded with me to answer her call. Leaning down, my lips crashed into her as I took her mouth in a hungry kiss. My hands roamed over her wet skin, mapping out her body in fond recollection. Her moan through the kiss encouraged me to take more.

Withdrawing the showerhead from her, I replaced it with my fingers as I began to stroke her soaking wet center. Needing her closer, I picked her up, and she wrapped her legs around my waist. This height allowed me to enjoy both her breasts and pussy simultaneously. Lowering my mouth to her taut nipple, I sucked and nipped the peak. My fingers were plunging her deep and fast as she continued to ride them, seeking out more friction.

"Sawyer, condom?" I finally managed to get out.

Pausing, she pulled back and looked strangely at my question before returning back to our kiss. I needed her to tell me where they were so I could give her what we both really wanted.

"Yes," she moaned when I felt her climax around my fingers.

Breaking the kiss, I pleaded with need this time, "Condom, Wildcat. Where are they?"

She shook her head, and my face dropped. Fuck, she didn't have any, and I wasn't in the position to go rooting through the other guy rooms for one. I started to put her back on her feet to remove the temptation of slipping into her wetness mere inches from my rigid dick. However, when I began to lower her, she tightened her legs around me, not letting me set her down.

"Wildcat, I don't have any. I need to remove the temptation because you are way too tempting…" trailing off, I was caught up in her wet body in my arms, "Fuck, you're so sexy." Giving in, I dropped down to her breasts to have my meal, causing me to almost miss her words.

"Don't… need."

Snapping my head up, I looked at her, unsure of what I had heard.

"Say that again, Sawyer." Seriousness laced my words as I waited to make sure I understood what I didn't need.

"I'm on birth control… guys, clean… no other sex."

I took her disjointed statement to mean I had clearance to land where I'd been dreaming about.

"Are you sure?"

"Fuck me, Ty. Remind me how you own my pussy," she purred.

Not wanting to stop now I'd been given the green light, I moved her back some to impale her on my straining dick. The moment I entered her wet heat, a thousand sensations exploded, and I felt surrounded in pure bliss. I had to hold myself back from exploding right there.

"Fucking hell, Wildcat. You feel better than I remember."

"Mmhmm, Ty."

She was hardly able to get the words out before I started to move in her. I was holding her in the middle of the shower, her legs wrapped around me as I fucked her standing up. It was the type of thing out of a porno. I could make out our reflection in the mirror, and it was sexy as hell.

Lifting her ass with my hands, I moved her body up and down on my hard cock. Her breasts rubbed against my chest with each move, and I felt like I was in sensation heaven. Her small moans filled me with incredible need and satisfaction, knowing I was pulling that from her.

When I looked toward the mirror again, I was surprised to find Rhett standing there clad only in his boxers. He appeared to be in shock at first as he stared. I was too far gone to stop at this point and didn't really know what the rules were, so I just kept fucking my girl as he watched. Plus, it wasn't exactly a foreign concept with us.

"Wildcat, we have an audience."

"Hmm." She turned her head at my words until she spotted Rhett.

"Are you okay with it? You know I find it hot," she whispered in my ear. Her voice and words were turning me on, even more, proving how okay I was with it.

"Fuck, yes."

My words seemed to be the permission Rhett needed, and he soon started to stroke himself through his boxers. Realizing I had more than likely stolen his shower based on his half-dressed state and the towel and shampoo he was holding a minute ago, part of me felt guilty. But the other part of me couldn't be bothered since I was the one currently fucking Sawyer.

Moving her up and down, I was pulled back to the giant of a man when he pushed his boxers down, and his massive cock sprung free. If I needed verification of my bisexuality, the sight of his cock cemented it for me as I found myself salivating at the sight of that monster. Instantly, I was jealous that Sawyer got to enjoy that.

"Damn, Wildcat. You're one lucky girl to get to ride that beast. How are you not walking funny?"

Her eyes lit up with amusement as I continued to use her body to push her up and down on my own rigid shaft.

"Maybe you can watch next time," she purred.

"Fucking hell, I'm going to come if you keep talking about that."

The little wildcat only smiled wider at my statement. She started to add to the movements herself, pushing our pace and friction higher.

Turning slightly, we were both able to watch Rhett now. He leaned back casually against the sink as he stroked his mammoth cock, eyes fixed on us. Not just Sawyer, but *us*.

Something about that spurred me on, wanting to put on a good show for him. I felt my climax building as I began to fuck Sawyer with everything I had. Our skin smacking together, the sliding of the water off us, the steam, and our moans all combined to heighten the arousal in the room. Sawyer's climax smacked into me as she tightened around my dick, her head tossed back on a low moan.

I flicked my eyes back over toward the mirror and locked eyes with Rhett before he moved back to her. There wasn't any heat in our eyes for each other. It was purely physical lust for what was occurring with Sawyer.

Returning to her, I gave into the sensations riding me and felt my balls draw up as tingles raced down my spine. Cumming inside her blew my ever-loving mind as everything emptied out of me.

After that intense workout, my arms were jelly, but it had been the best damn arm exercise I'd ever had. I kissed Sawyer full of passion, lips and tongue twirling, before I placed her feet back on the ground.

Rhett must have come when I had because he stepped into the shower with us at that moment. It was awkward, at first, but we'd just shared an orgasm together; what else mattered after that?

Sawyer pulled him down for a kiss as well, and I had to turn away before I got turned on again. We washed away the evidence of our fun, and I could appreciate the novelty of this massive shower, as we all had our own showerhead and room to do so.

My first group shower and bareback experience were not how I'd imagined this morning ending. I had to say it was much more satisfying this way. It would've been even better if Ollie had been part of it.

Sawyer's words kept replaying in my head, and I was contemplating finally saying something. The scared part of me was urging me to just wait and see if something organically occurred.

But whatever happened, I had Sawyer, and that was what mattered the most.

forty-four

. . .

rey

AFTER EVERYONE HAD WOKEN UP, we had a late breakfast together, and then Rhett and Sawyer shared the letters with us. Fortunately, Chloe and Ace had taken off first thing, meaning the remaining people were family and firmly in the trust circle.

Sawyer updated us on the conversation she overheard with Ms. Pekins, the admissions counselor, and someone called Mr. Morano. She informed us how she had learned that her and Asa's biological father would be attending the expo from him.

"I had no idea he was coming," Asa replied, when she was done.

"I thought we could do something, but Brave Heart said not to," Smalls mumbled.

"Brave Heart? Is Mel Gibson suddenly on campus?" Ollie joked.

"Oh, uh. Did I not mention him? He's, um, well, he's hard to explain." Smalls stumbled over her words, slightly cringing, causing us all to be more interested now.

"Ugh, fine. Sorry, it's just kind of embarrassing." Her face reddened, and I leaned closer.

"Wait, wasn't that your imaginary friend? I remember you crying about not getting to see him and wanting to go back to your garden," recalled Finley in thought, tapping her lip.

"Uh, yeah. That'd be him. Turns out, I wasn't a loon. He's real, after all. I just forgot to ask his real name in the hustle of him saving me last night. He's the one who rescued me from the crash too, and while he didn't say it, I think he works for the Agency."

Sawyer looked to Ty and Ollie, but neither appeared to know who Brave Heart was based on their mutual shrugs.

"There is an agent on campus; maybe it's him," Ollie offered, and Ty agreed.

"What did he say?" Rhett asked, getting back to the point.

"Basically, there's more going on than we know, and I need to discover it for myself. Um, hmm," she paused, glancing up as she sorted her thoughts. "Something about the journal, I think, connecting dots or something. It kind of all ran together with the emotional mess of yesterday. The last part I remembered, though, because it was about all of us. He said…" she glanced around at all of us, "he said we weren't put together by accident, and to work out our shit because we would need one another because we couldn't underestimate the Council."

Clearing her throat when she finished, we sat there digesting her words. How far-reaching were these two organizations, and what part did we all have to play in them?

I was curious how much he might've played in her forgiving us last night. I didn't necessarily trust this guy, but I might owe him a giant thank you for bringing her back safely. Especially, if he got her to soften and listen to us. Deciding in the end, it didn't matter because we were back on track, and that was what we needed to focus on.

"So, we've all somehow been selected to form a unit?" Ollie asked the question which was going through all of our minds.

"Yeah, or something along those lines. He made it clear that our bonds were real and all organic. So, as much as it creeps me out thinking someone has been playing puppet master, I can't really be angry for the end result of having met each of you."

Hearing her say that helped settle my own feelings of distrust that had popped up. Nothing like feeling as if everything in your life was arranged—cue the heebie-jeebies.

"Have you looked at the journal yet?" asked Finley.

Smalls shook her head no, and weariness settled on her shoulders. She was dealing with too much.

"No, not with everything this morning, and Henry

and I have practice starting at noon, so it will have to wait unless someone wants to take a crack at the cipher code."

"I wouldn't mind looking at it if you're okay with that," chimed Mateo. At her nod, he looked excited to have something to do, and I was glad she accepted help. We would need to make sure we watched her and made sure she was taking care of herself.

"What is everyone else up to today?"

Everyone went around and shared our plans like a family. It gave me the warm fuzzies. Once we all knew what the plans for the day were, we dispersed to start the day.

Smalls and I headed to the rink for training. As I continued to think of the group we'd made, I realized how much fuller my life felt. I didn't just have one friend and my sister anymore; I had a whole group of people who I cared about and two people who loved me.

Rebelling Reyes might've seen his last day. It was hard to be a rebel when you were happy. I would take that over being a poster boy for ice skating any day.

"Henry, I had a thought the other day and wanted to see what you might think." She had an anxious look on her face, and I wasn't sure where she was headed with this, so I just nodded.

"Ty actually mentioned it after our practice. As much as I've been hoping, and as much as Rhett has helped with my strength training, I need to face the facts. I just can't take the physical labor on my knee doing jumps." Smalls looked very disappointed and afraid she was going to upset me as well.

"Smalls, I don't want you to push yourself. We can do what is safe. I'm just happy to skate with you again. It's brought back a part of me I've missed."

"That's great, Henry, and I'm glad you think that, but I might have a solution to not do jumps and yet keep skating competitively." Sawyer seemed really excited now, and I couldn't wait to see what put that look on her face.

"I'm listening…"

"What do we both love as much as skating?"

"Soren?" Scrunching my face, I tried to figure out where she was going with this.

"Well, yeah, but think broader." She giggled.

"Tacos, Fin, cuddles…"

"Seriously, Henry!" She laughed louder. "Dancing! We both love dancing, and you've become some hotshot choreographer now. Why don't we switch over to ice dancing instead? It incorporates our love of dancing and takes away the jumps. We still have lifts and partner stunts, but more focus on program development and artistry, which we both excel at. I don't know why we didn't do this sooner." She smacked her forehead. "Oh yeah, well being away from one another for five years. But you get my point!"

Laughing with her, I thought about her proposal, and she was right. It did fit us better. It was the perfect solution.

"Brilliant. I know just the song to start with and a tricky lift I want to do. Let's get started."

Three hours later, we were a sweaty mess, but exhilarated. The happiness we felt for accomplishing the moves far outweighed the soreness. Ice dancing had similar elements, but there were some new components we had to work out, such as twizzles, dance spins, and dance lifts. In pair skating, we were a unit, but our elements were mostly individual, and we could skate on the ice at a distance.

In ice dancing, we had to be within two arm lengths of one another at all times and have more contact with the ice overall. Our lifts couldn't be higher than the male partner's head and every movement was part of a dance sequence—the fluidity, the timing. It all had to paint the picture of grace and poise. Pairs skating was gymnastics on ice, whereas ice dancing was ballroom on ice.

"That was amazing. You really are an incredible choreographer. The musicality of your moves blows me away, Henry. I'm so excited about this now."

I spun her around once more, loving the feeling of her in my arms again. Our spins and lifts were integrated now, continually touching and assisting one another in both. It really was the perfect transition for us as partners.

We fit one another in a way I never could have replicated. Maybe it was her "Sawyerness" or our shared history together. Perhaps it was that I loved her and trusted her implicitly, or maybe it was just that we had been destined to skate with one another. Some partnerships were just meant to be, and Sawyer and I, we just *were*.

Skating with Smalls would always be my favorite thing because it was us. No other reason was needed. Dipping her like some old school romantic, I swept her up as I skated.

"This was the best, Henry. I'm so happy. Thank you for being you."

I looked at her, love shining in my eyes. "Smalls, I once told you that kissing you was all my favorite things wrapped up together, but skating with you is transcendent. I didn't understand that at sixteen, and when my parents kept pushing me to find new partners, it was why it never worked. Because when we skate, the earth moves around us. For four minutes and thirty seconds, the only things that matter are me, you, and the ice. That freedom, the creativity and power that is connected to us is what makes us great."

"Always so poetic, Henry Alexander. I hope you know I love that about you. Now come on, let's hit the showers and possibly the steam rooms before we head back."

At her statement, she winked before skating off. Oh, I was so there for whatever she had planned in her dirty little mind.

Chasing after her, I'd almost caught up to her when the Ice Queen stepped out onto the ice. So much for the reprieve from her bitchiness. It had been pleasant not dealing with her shit while she licked her wounds. Guess that was over with now.

Now that she knew Sawyer and I were skating together, she'd increased her badgering of us guys in the house. She dated Elias the year before I began teaching here, but I was present for the very toxic fallout and her never-ending attempts to get every one of his roommates into her bed. Sawyer had become an even bigger reason for her to want to bed us all. She disgusted me, and I hated being in her presence.

"Well, well, if it isn't Slutyer and Rey. Saw your practice the other day. If you want to trade up to a real ice skater, you have my number." She skated off like she believed I would actually call her. She was delusional.

"If there was ever anyone who fit the word cuntstain, it was her. She is so fucking vile. I feel like I need a shower just from being within six feet of her. She's like a contagious virus you don't want anywhere near you," Sawyer said. Her whole body shudder was fun to watch, but I reciprocated her feelings on the matter.

"That is a great way to describe her. She makes me gag every time I see her. Come on, let's head to the showers while she's out here."

Stepping into the locker room, I recalled the night Soren and I shared a shower. Granted, it was the same night as Sawyer's accident, but before I knew that information, it had been a great time.

We gathered our belongings and transferred them to the lockers by the showers. We'd seen too many high school movies where the mean girl stole your clothes, and you have to walk around school naked. While that wouldn't be too big of a deal, it was October in Utah… cold. Best to not chance it.

Giggling, I chased Smalls into the waiting shower as we quickly washed up. Pulling her naked body flush with mine, I kissed her deeply.

"You know, Soren surprised me after training one night in the shower. It was very stimulating. I do have a fantasy… I wonder if you would indulge me."

"Oh, do tell." She nipped at my bottom lip, pulling a groan from me.

"Better if I show you."

Shutting off the water, I wrapped a towel around her first and then one around my waist before I pulled her across the way to the sauna. It might be cliche, but I had a naughty fantasy of doing it in a sauna, and today I was making it happen.

As soon as the door closed, I pushed her back against the door as I attacked her mouth. Sweeping my tongue in, we twisted around one another, devouring each other. Nipping at the bottom of her lip, I lifted her up. Deciding to go full fantasy, I walked toward the risers and sat her down before releasing her towel to pool around her. Taking my own towel, I folded it before sitting it on the bench.

"So, this is your fantasy, huh? How did you imagine it?"

She was leaning back on her elbows as she watched me. Fisting my cock, I walked toward her, enjoying the view she was providing me.

"Well, the full effect would also involve Sor and more time. But I think we have time for the prelude before Ice Queen returns."

Her eyes tracked my hand on my dick, and she started to rub her own hands over her breasts. Beads of sweat and condensation pebbled on her skin, and I wanted to lick them off her one by one. I was going to need to revisit this place when we had more time and privacy. I was getting images of all kinds of kinky shenanigans I wanted to try.

Picking her up, I sat down on the towel as she straddled me. Face to face with Smalls was my favorite position. Hearing her moans and watching her enjoyment increased my own tenfold. She knelt for a second as she took my cock in her hand and rubbed the tip through her folds. We didn't need foreplay today; we were both turned on and ready.

Sinking down on me slowly, she braced herself on my shoulders as she acclimated herself to my girth. Each time I entered her, I never wanted to leave. Pushing her hips down, I felt her bottom out, accompanied by a long moan. Grabbing her ass cheeks between my hands, I squeezed them as I helped her start to bob up and down on me. Her breasts were eye level as she pushed off my shoulders to give herself better momentum.

Kissing down her neck, I sucked and nipped along her collarbone, the top of her breasts and nipples. We were fucking with such force the bench began to shake with each thrust. Our moans were rising as we both chased our orgasm. Squeezing her ass tight, I propelled her down as I thrust my dick up. Her arms wrapped around my head, bringing me to settle between her breasts. Fucking nirvana. Removing one hand from her ass, I slid it forward to rub circles around her clit.

"Fuck, yes, harder, Henry."

Her commands urged me to thrust up harder, shaking the bench harder in the process. Concern over it detaching from the wall was the furthest thing from my mind. Pressing my lips firmly against her, I poured all of my emotions and lust into the kiss, challenging her to take my everything. With one last thrust, I held her hips down on me as I felt myself coming deep in her.

Continuing to rub her clit, I pinched it at the same time as I gently nipped her nipple, sending her over the edge.

"Ohh, ahh, yes, Henry."

Her pussy tightened around me as her muscles spasmed, holding my dick in a viselike grip, sending tendrils of pleasure through me as my toes curled.

"Fuck, that was hot."

Laughing at her ill-timed temperature joke, we quickly cleaned up and jumped back under the water in the shower to rinse off.

Last night there was a moment I'd thought I lost one of the most important people in my life again. It made me appreciate even more how fleeting life was and to cherish the small things. I felt transparent and freer than I had in a long time. Part of that was Sawyer and Soren being in my life, but I still had to believe in their love, accept their love, and be able to give them love back. Validating myself in the battles I faced and overcoming them was just as important to remember.

Life was hard enough; I didn't need to spend it at war with myself.

forty-five

. . .

TAKING A DEEP BREATH, I knocked on Mateo's door. Things hadn't felt right between us since we discovered Elias was missing, and I needed to check-in with him. Dating multiple guys was challenging at times, but it was part of the reward for connecting and caring for people. The benefits outweighed the cost, and that meant being there when they needed me.

Remembering he had headphones in last time, I pushed his door open slowly. Privacy was important, so I didn't want to violate it, but I also didn't want him to think he wasn't as significant as what was going on. Unfortunately, his room was empty, with no Mateo to be found.

Deciding to check the patio since I'd found him there once, I headed down the stairs. Lucky was trotting along with me and had officially become my shadow when I was home. I loved it, and he was just so cute and loved all my cuddles. Music poured out from HQ, catching my attention, and I veered there to check it out. It sounded like the music Elias had been playing in the gym, the aggressive classical one. Was he back?

Peeking in through the crack, I didn't know why I was so nervous. Possibly because I didn't know how to feel after his letter. I was still upset, but he'd also laid his heart bare for me, and I had to acknowledge the courage it took.

It didn't help that he thought he might never return. Did I want to get all hopeful about something that might never develop? No, I didn't. I couldn't waste time playing the "what if" game. I'd just have to see how things played out if we saw one another again. There were relationships here which needed my attention now.

Seeing the dark curls and glasses through the crack, I was happy to find who I was searching for. Mateo didn't notice me when I pushed the door open more. He was bent over, reading the journal and making notes in another notebook. I could tell where he'd added more pics and notes to the whiteboard. It was starting to look like a proper crime scene investigation. Hopefully, it wouldn't actually turn into that.

Morbid? Perhaps. Reality? Looking likely.

Lucky betrayed my presence, yet again, when he bounded into the room, seeking out Mateo. I think Lucky wanted us to make sure we always knew he was there. He was an attention whore at times. Chuckling at

Lucky's energetic bounds into the room, Mateo gave him some pets before looking up and spotting me.

"Hey, Sawyer." His soft smile gave me hope that things were still okay with us.

"Hey, Mateo. Any luck?" Moving into the room, I took a seat next to him. He adjusted his glasses slightly before he responded.

"There's a lot of info here that I think you'll find interesting. It will give us some good insight into the Council and maybe even the Agency."

"Whoa, that's amazing. You must have been working hard to crack that cipher."

"Actually, that was Elias. He left the key, and I've been reading through finding names and places to connect."

"Elias? Wow, I guess when he said he decoded it, I thought he meant...," I shook my head, clearing my thoughts. "Actually, I don't know what I thought. It wasn't this level, though."

Sitting back, I was again unsure how to respond to this info. Could I forgive him for his shitty behavior because of all the good things he was doing? Yeah, I think I could. Forgiveness didn't mean I forgot, but I didn't have to hate him either. He would still need to redeem himself to me. Just because I forgave him didn't mean I trusted him implicitly. That would take time and effort.

"Cliff notes version?"

"There are a lot of connections to both organizations throughout the history of the school. I bet there are more, even now. It might not be as "open" as we were led to believe. There appears to be one head position that runs the Council, voted on after so many years. I can't work that part out yet, or your mom didn't know. Under him are the council seats, or really companies. Each company then has its own people. The trickle-down effect is hard to track, as well. The school does seem to be some sort of breeding ground, leverage, bargaining chip? It's hard to say at this point. The school is a pinnacle piece, though, so your father was right in telling you to start here. I think the school board might work as a mini council within these walls."

"Well, damn. Guess that explains Squawky's comment last night about being at their disposal. Any info on what the Council does or how they operate?"

"Not too much, but I'm only about halfway through. I'll keep digging."

"You're the best, Mateo. Thank you, so much, but don't feel like you have to spend all your time doing this. I appreciate your help."

"Of course, Sawyer. If I can help, I want to. Especially if it will keep you safe." Leaning in, I kissed him gently.

"You're the sweetest. I don't know how I would do this without you."

"Oh, I'm sure you would be fine. But I appreciate you saying that."

"Don't do that—no dismissing compliments. I don't throw around words. Do you trust what I have to say?"

"Of course, absolutely, but—"

"Er, nope. Anything you say right now after that but will just dismiss the first part."

"Sawyer, I'm not trying to do that. I just… I guess I don't see myself the same way. That's all." He ducked his head, hiding his eyes. Touching his cheek, I lifted his face.

"You don't have to see yourself that way, yet, as long as you believe I do, okay?" He smiled softly and nodded.

"I was looking for you because I wanted to check in. A lot happened yesterday, and I don't know. I guess at one point, it just seemed like you were disappointed in me, and I hated that feeling."

Mateo looked torn and like he wasn't sure how to answer my question. My heart sank because it solidified my belief that something was wrong.

"Ah, okay. Well, I'm just going to get out of your hair then. Thanks for looking through the journal."

Getting up from my chair, I walked around the long table, cursing it for stopping me from making a dramatic exit. Seemed I was becoming an expert on that, as well as losing boyfriends. At this rate, they would all be dropping like flies by the end of the week.

mateo

Panicking, I jumped up and flew across the table like some slick guy in a movie. It didn't work out quite as well for me, though.

First, I didn't slide. So instead, my momentum resulted in me skidding, creating some weird table burn and skeet sound.

Second, all the things I had on the table flew off and scattered everywhere. Amazingly enough, in that process, I'd managed to propel a tape dispenser in Sawyer's direction, hitting her in the back of the head.

"Ow?"

She turned around, a look of pure confusion plastered on her face at my awkward attempt to stop her. Meanwhile, I was half hanging off the table, cringing from the burn on my lower back, but unable to move for fear the whole table might collapse. Shit, this was bad.

"Ugh. That was meant to work out way better and be badass. Sorry, I didn't intend to throw tape at you."

"Are you okay?" Sawyer asked, walking back into the room. A look of concern now etched across her beautiful face.

"Yeah, just an epic fail here."

"What were you going to do if it hadn't been a failure?" Her arms crossed, she looked at me, needing to hear the things I'd been holding back.

"I was hoping to make some dashing move, demonstrating my prowess and convincing you I was worthy."

"Worthy? Why would you think I thought you weren't worthy?"

The cutest look of confusion reflected back at me, and I had to accept she was honest earlier. Her arms dropped to her sides, opening up her body language. I'd misread things. Hanging my head, I took a deep breath.

"I thought you were disappointed in me, that you thought I was weak with how I responded yesterday with Elias missing. I guess I just assumed a lot of things and thought you were realizing the error of your ways and moving forward without me."

"Oh, Mateo."

She moved toward me, wrapping her arms tight around me.

"Honey, I've never been upset with you or disappointed. I love that you thought of things differently. It showed your compassion and understanding. We all needed that to show us it's not always about us. I'm sorry if I gave you the impression I didn't care. Honestly, I thought you were disappointed with me because I had closed myself off."

Chuckling, because it seemed we had both wasted a lot of time assuming. Typical. Pulling back, I brushed her hair away from her face. Kissing her on the nose, cheeks, forehead, and then her lips. I'd gained more confidence in kissing her whenever I wanted, touching her and exploring her, and reassuring myself that this was real.

"How about we finish this journal together? I'll go and grab some snacks and drinks, and then we can tackle it." She peered up at me with such hope shining through her eyes. I would say yes to just about anything she asked of me.

"That sounds like a plan I can get behind."

Sawyer returned a few minutes later with some fruit, crackers, and cheese. She had some tea as well and encouraged me to try some. She fixed it for me, and I didn't hate it. Maybe it was something else I could get behind.

We spent the rest of the afternoon deciphering the journal and laying out the Council hierarchy, possible Agency connections, and the school's position. What wasn't clear was the why.

What did the Council have to do with the school, and what did they want?

After dinner, I debated going back and working more on decoding the journal. I enjoyed puzzles, and it made me feel useful. But as I headed to HQ, Rey grabbed my arm and dragged me into the living room with the other guys. They'd been inviting me each week to hang out and play video games with them, but I'd kept declining.

I couldn't really say why, other than I felt they were

only being nice to include me, but the more time I spent with the guys, the more I realized how false that was. I was quickly becoming friends with Rey and Sor, too. It felt nice to have actual friends, and it made me miss my first friend, Samuel. Things between us had been weird ever since—

"Mateo, think fast!"

My thoughts were cut off at Ollie's shout. Looking up, I barely caught the soda can as he tossed it my way. He cringed when I fumbled with it, but fortunately, I maintained it, and no soda erupted all over us.

"My bad!" mumbled an apologetic Ollie.

"It's cool. I, uh, got it. Uh, thanks."

Nodding at him, he took a seat while he waited for the game to load. We were playing Mario Kart so four of us could play at once. With Tyler called away to deal with a discipline issue, it was just the five of us here. The last place person had to sit out after each round, and we rotated in. It was fun, and we all seemed to match equally skill-wise, getting equal playing time.

I was still sad that Elias was gone, as I hadn't gotten to know him well, but he seemed like someone I would mesh well with based on our personalities. I was surprised at how comfortable I felt with Rey and Soren, and I could see Rey quickly becoming my best friend outside of Sawyer. She had cemented herself in my life regardless of what happened romantically. I was finding myself having feelings I didn't know how to process.

"I need a break," Rey exhaled as he threw down his

controller. He blew out a breath and got up off the floor to join me on the couch.

"Hey, man. Do you want to play in my spot? I need a breather. My thumbs have that 'I've been smushing buttons on a controller for hours' feel to them."

"Ah, man. I hate that. Then your thumbs feel all numb." I chuckled out in response.

"Exactly. See, you get it!" We both laughed then, the easy silence comfortable between us.

"You doing okay, though? I know yesterday was pretty rough?"

"Yeah, I mean, it was hard, but with everything going on, I think I'm doing as well as I can. I'm trying not to be a perfectionist for once. Which is hugely freeing."

"That's great."

"Yeah, it is." I relaxed back into the couch, at peace.

We watched Ollie whoop Soren, and Rhett in the next round before they called a timeout to grab some snacks. As the three of them went into the kitchen, I decided to use the moment to my advantage.

"Hey, Rey?"

He'd thrown his head back on the couch, eyes closed, appearing to be resting, but at my question, he peeked an eye open to regard me.

"Hmm?" he sleepily murmured. Well, crap. I had the worst timing.

"Um, never mind. It's not important." Instead of going back to sleep, Rey sat up, fully alert now.

"No, I'm listening. What is it?"

"Well, I just wanted to share something I enjoy that I've never really told anyone. I'm trying to step out of my comfort zone." I shrugged. Dropping my head, I picked at a loose thread on the couch.

"Ah, did a certain blonde have anything to do with this?"

"Yea and no. I came here to make my own decisions for once and stop being so scared, so part of it is doing that. She definitely gave me the shove to take the first step."

"She does have that effect." At his comment, we both smiled at each other.

"Yeah, that she does."

"Well, I'm all ears. Whatcha got?"

"So, on the buses traveling from one event to the next, I had a lot of downtimes. Somewhere along the way, I developed an obsession with Disney movies, and I'm in the official fan club and everything." I took a deep breath, exhaling it. "Rey, I'm a Mousehead."

I stared at him, watching his expression. Fearing his laughter, I wasn't prepared for him to smile.

"That's awesome. I love it. Next movie night, let's all watch one. I think the guys would be down for that too, you know."

"Yeah?" I grinned, relief spreading through me.

"Yeah."

I felt silly for how right Sawyer had been. These guys were real friends and wouldn't make fun of me, at least not in a mean way. Friends still joked with one another, but it always came from a place of love and not hate. That was the important thing I'd forgotten. The guys returned a few minutes later, setting down some cookies, crackers, and hummus.

As we all dug into the spread, I found myself enjoying the camaraderie as well as joking and encouraging one another. For the first time in my life, I wasn't scared to trust people, care about them, and feel accepted for who I was, scars and all. Now in my real life, I finally felt the magic I'd always envied in Disney movies—complete acceptance and belief.

forty-six

. . .

LYING on my stomach in the middle of the bed, I tapped my pencil against my planner in thought. After dinner, I'd moved up here since the guys were having their video game extravaganza. I was trying to be mindful of making sure they still got their friend time. It was important for us all to have that time outside of our relationships.

I hadn't wanted to go back to HQ for fear I might've started throwing things. The number of secrets now was making me batty. Looking at what I'd written, I went over all the things I'd discovered about my mom, Kyla Brennon, or better known as Victoria Draven. I wasn't sure what to call her anymore.

Her father was Nicholas Draven, CEO and owner of Draven Tech. Her mother was a Brazilian model that died when she was eight. She didn't talk much about her family in her journal, and what little she had wasn't favorable. Her entries were mostly focused on her time here at TAS.

She had been friends with my biological mother, Isla, explaining the photo I'd found with Elias. Aggie was her mentor, which we already knew. Still, it was interesting seeing her relationship from her perspective on the pages.

She dated a few people, some coming across as creepy. Her most significant relationship here was with someone named Logan. Then there was a gap, almost as if in the years she was missing, she didn't write or want to have any of that info on paper.

It picked back up when she was sent to work at Latimer, and that was where she met my father, Brent Harris/Scott Brennon. That was a surprise to me as they never mentioned my mom actually worked for Latimer, just that he'd introduced her to dad. The details around her going to work at Latimer Shipping and what she did there were vague, at best.

The most surprising thing was discovering Victoria was engaged to be married but refused and went to work for Latimer in exchange. Basically, it was all a jumbled mess, and keeping track of it all gave me a headache.

Turned out the Reyes' were a plant, as my father stated, but reassuringly, not for the Council. Or maybe they were, but they were double agents? That part was confusing, and I think we would only know the real answer if we asked them. They had been instrumental in helping my mother at some point, as she spoke of them as being trustworthy.

Someone would have to start talking soon and quit with the subterfuge because I was at my limit for secrets. The next one just might kill me.

Feeling exhausted from the emotional drain and craziness of it all, I decided to have a 'pamper me' night. What that pampering entailed, I was still trying to decide. Fortunately, it didn't look like I would have to do it alone.

"Knock, knock. Earth to Sawyer?"

Looking up, I found Ace at my door. Casually, I closed the planner and journal as I got up to greet him with a hug.

"Hey! Did we have something planned, and I forgot about it?" I asked, worried I'd forgotten something. I bit my lip between my teeth as I waited for him to respond. I wasn't even sure what day it was, to be honest. Everything was muddled in my head, overloaded with keeping all the conspiracy theories straight. I was literally relying on everyone else to tell me where I needed to be.

"Nope! But I figured you could use some chill time. We never got around to all the fun pampering stuff last night, and I still owe you that talk. How about we do those now?"

"It's like you read my mind! Let me just go grab it. I think most of it's still in the media room, honestly."

"I'll go. You get changed and ready. Time to unwind, girl!"

He kissed my cheek before leaving, and I was grateful he'd stopped by. I had missed spending time with him lately, and I hoped we could clear up whatever weird tension there was.

I needed to get better at balancing my life, but it seemed as if my schedule was constantly out to get me. Seriously, I think it had meetings with the pens, and they conspired to add things instead of taking them off—the fuckers.

This downtime I had tonight was with no expectations, and strangely, it was exactly what I needed. I was tempted to text the girls, but I felt selfish and wanted to spend time one on one with Ace. Plus, it would be easier to have our "talk."

Changing into some comfy clothes of leggings and a long shirt, I pulled my hair up into a ponytail. I never could do those bun things; I always ended up looking like a demented cat or something. Exiting my closet, I started to toss pillows and blankets on the ground. I selected some fun music just as Ace returned.

"Let's get this party started!"

Laughing, we dove into the goodies I'd put together and began our pamper fest. Toenails painted, face mask on, and eyebrows shaped, I was feeling like a new me. There really was something to be said about self-care. The laughter helped too.

"You should have seen his face when I kissed him! He looked torn between shock and turned on and wasn't sure where to land," Ace said before pulling the face he referred to in his story.

Laughing, I was trying not to spew the soda I'd just drank, but it went up my nose instead.

"Ow, ow, it burns!" I half laughed and screeched as I waved my hand in front of my face. Thinking for some reason that would help stop the burn.

"Funny, that's what he said later that night!"

"Oh my god, Ace. You're horrible! I just can't with you."

Laughing more, I stood up to grab something to clean up the soda mess that had dribbled down my face. I was drying it in the bathroom when I heard raised voices through the door. Rushing into my room at the commotion, I was surprised to find a disgruntled Tyler staring down Ace. His face was panicked and stricken as Tyler threatened him in a low voice I wasn't unable to make out.

"What's going on?"

"Sawyer, I can explain," Ace pleaded as tears filled his eyes. Looking back and forth between Ty and Ace, I didn't like what I was seeing. Seeking Ty's face, I hoped he would tell me what the hell was going on.

"Ty?" His face fell at my words, almost as if he knew this would hurt me and didn't want to be the one to do it.

"I think it would be better to hear it from him," Ty uttered before walking over and wrapping his arms around me from behind. He rested his head on my shoulder, offering me his own strength like a shield. That didn't bode well.

Fucking hell, I just wanted one night to pamper

myself without being hit in the face with another secret. Strengthening my own resolve, I reminded myself how strong I was and that I could handle this, no matter what. Looking Ace head-on, I was ready.

"Tell me."

"I… you… it wasn't meant for you to find out this way. I was actually trying to build up the courage to tell you tonight. I guess I should have tried harder. I'm not just here to be an instructor, Sawyer. I was recruited three years ago to work for…"

Everything seemed to hang in the balance as I waited for those last words.

"… the Agency. You were my first assignment."

"So that day you approached me?"

"It was to make contact, yes, but then I genuinely liked you and I wanted to tell you. I told my handler I didn't feel right about deceiving you, but he told me I'd be replaced if I couldn't control myself. I couldn't let them do that. I cared for you already and wanted to be the one to keep you safe. I've been running interference, and I've already staved off two possible attacks. I promise I was going to tell you."

Coldness enveloped me as his words penetrated my mind. My instincts were failing me, and instead of fight or flight this time, my body chose the third option—freeze. I could see his mouth moving, I could feel Ty's arm around me, but nothing else seemed to be making it through.

I… just… felt… cold.

"Sawyer, please, say something."

His voice should've made me feel sympathy, something, but I was too far removed. In a monotone voice, devoid of any emotion, I responded.

"Thank you for telling me, and I guess saving my life. But, I think it would be best if you leave. I can't deal with this right now. I'm not saying I forgive you, I just… yeah. Give me some space, please."

Nothing else needed to be said as he picked up his belongings, watching me the whole time. I said nothing as he came and stood in front of me, placing something between my hands. I just stared blankly at him.

He turned one last time at the door, but when I still didn't respond, he finally left. When his footsteps faded down the stairs, I didn't have to say anything for Tyler to turn me and pull me into his chest. Limp noodle, frozen to the spot, I faded into the background, allowing myself to become one with my surroundings.

tyler

"Sawyer, are you okay?"

She was staring at my chest, but she was unmoving. Shit. Maybe I should've waited to say something, but when I came in here and saw Wallace Benedict III sitting on my girlfriend's floor, I lost it.

We'd gone through training together and were acquaintances. I knew instantly when I saw him, he wasn't here because he was friends with her; no, this screamed Agency, and I was angry at myself for not anticipating it, for not looking into who was on campus. Thinking back, he'd been here that first night I came by the house, but in my excitement to have found Sawyer, it didn't register.

"It's fine, Ty, but I just want to be left alone."

Her voice was back to being that creepy monotone where she sounded like a robot. She pulled away and started to pick up the stuff she had out around the room, effectively ignoring me. Fuck!

Running my hands through my hair, I knew I needed to do something. Walking out of the room, I started knocking on doors as I made my way down the hallway; maybe some extra help would be a good start.

No one answered until I got about three doors down to Oliver's room. I momentarily paused as he answered the door, sleep bedraggled, and all. Hell, he looked fine rolling out of bed.

He was shirtless, sweats low on his hips, barefoot, and his auburn hair was rumpled all over the place. Damn, he was too sexy. He was rubbing his eyes clear of sleep, and I just wanted to be the one to do it for him. Shaking myself out of the stupor, I remembered the state I'd left Sawyer in and how I needed help.

"Ollie, I need your help. Something's wrong with Sawyer."

At her name, he perked up and focused on me.

"Where is she? What's wrong?"

Instantly, he moved from the door, looking for me to

lead him to the danger. Fucking hell, it was hot to see him respond that way to her. Clearing my throat, I stalked back to her room and found her frozen in a kneeling position, holding something in her hand.

"Sawyer, it's Ty. I've brought Ollie. What do you need?"

"He's gone. People always leave," she mumbled.

"Ssh, Wildcat. I'm here; Ollie is here."

"Ollie?"

"Yeah, pretty girl. I'm here. What have you been up to? Do I need to dance for you?" Ollie joked as he swaggered into the room.

Sawyer looked up finally and licked her lips when she noticed him. Yeah, Wildcat, me too. He was too delicious for his own good, that cocky fuckboy swagger, though—he owned it.

"I guess that's a yes," Ollie replied to himself when she didn't respond.

He started to roll his hips, and I had to admit Sawyer wasn't the only one mesmerized. His next move was some TikTok dance, or maybe it was a Fortnite one? I knew it was a viral one, but not being familiar with either, I was clueless. Whatever it was, it made Sawyer laugh, and that seemed to be the trick to cracking the detached state she'd been in.

Ollie continued to go from one move to the next and even had some Saturday Night Fever moves in there at some point. I pulled her onto my lap as I sat on the floor, and we watched and laughed as Ollie entertained us for the next fifteen minutes.

This was the boy I'd fallen for many years ago. The kind hearted guy who would do anything for someone he cared about, even if it meant making an ass out of himself. I didn't remember when he started being the cocky guy. Perhaps it was at college, or maybe just when I wasn't around. It just wasn't who I saw him as, and I was glad he appeared to be losing that person more and more.

When Ollie finished, we both clapped for him as he did some elaborate bow. He squatted down in front of us, directly across from me, hands placed on his knees.

"There's the smile I love to see. Are you going to tell me what happened to make it go away so I can go and punch it in the junk?"

Her smile dropped some, and I wanted to yell at him for reminding her, but then she started to talk, and I realized what he was doing. Ollie was so much smarter than he portrayed. He made you feel comfortable and okay to just be.

"It's nothing. Just a typical day in Sawyer-ville."

"Bullshit. Try again."

"Ugh, why do you have to be such a pain, Ollie?" she groaned.

"Ugh, why do you have to be so stubborn, Sawyer?" he mocked. "Fine, how about a question game? Each one I get right, you have to tell me a truth of my choice." She rolled her eyes, but nodded. As I said, he was a freaking genius.

"Fine, what's my favorite food?"

"Easy, whatever is being made for you unless there are peppers."

Her face must've meant he was right. Surprisingly, his question wasn't the obvious one I assumed he would ask.

"Sawyer, what're your favorite things about Ty?"

We both seemed to be momentarily shocked at his question as she turned a little to peer up at me.

"He sees me, all parts of me," Sawyer whispered as she stared into my eyes.

"Hm, I thought you'd say his butt. But I agree with you and raise you his unique ability to make you feel like you matter."

Glancing up, I was amazed at what Ollie said about me but was cut off before I could respond back.

"What's my favorite color?" Rolling his eyes, Ollie answered again, quickly.

"Purple. What's your favorite sexual position?"

She went quiet for a moment, and I thought she wouldn't respond until she did, surprising us both.

"Hmmm. Maybe reverse cowgirl. Okay, how about, what's my favorite season?" She was leaning forward now, engaged in this game they were playing.

"Trick question, you love both fall and winter. Who in the house have you had sex with?"

Glancing at Ollie, I was upset he asked that question as it wasn't really any of his—

"Four. You have to use your imagination to figure out which ones. What's my favorite type of animal?"

"Domestic or wild."

"Wild."

"I'll do both. Wild, dolphin, domestic, baby goat."

On and on they went, and I was amazed at how many Ollie was getting correct. They inched closer and closer each time, almost like they were instigating the other one with the question.

Just before Ollie asked his next question, they were mere millimeters apart, lips practically touching. I sucked in a breath because it was hot and beautiful. The tension must've built too high between them, because the next thing I knew, Sawyer was propelling herself into Ollie's lap.

Well, okay then.

forty-seven

. . .

sawyer

LAUNCHING MYSELF AT OLLIE, I attacked his mouth with passion. This kiss had been a long time coming, and I was tired of waiting. We'd been holding ourselves back from truly giving in to our feelings, and quite frankly, it was dumb.

Ollie had proven himself to me and shown me the type of person he was, down to his core. Fuck, he was willing to go against his family for me. Why hadn't I jumped him the moment he said that? I was a fucking idiot.

Too much grief, doubt, and fear had consumed me since the day I'd lost my parents, and when I was almost killed, again, mind you, it was like a part of me slipped back into survival mode.

Everything kept piling up on me from discovering my true identity, my imaginary friend becoming real, and even Elias leaving the way he did. All of it was chipping away at my ability to cope, to manage things. Discovering Ace's secret identity hurt, and for a moment, I wondered if I knew anyone. I'd slipped into the dark place of my mind where fear bred.

I was fucking tired of fear.

As soon as Ollie made me laugh, a light switched on, chasing away the shadows, dusting away the cobwebs, and illuminating the truth. We all had secrets to bear. Every fucking one of us had something we were either too ashamed to admit or too afraid to say, but it was there.

I wasn't innocent either, considering I had been lying to Ace the whole time I knew him. How could I be angry with him when he was doing his job? At least he'd kept me safe. I owed him a big fucking thank you at the least, a hundred coffees at the most.

Life wasn't black or white, and I needed to learn to live in the gray. Starting with showing Ollie how much he meant to me.

His lips were softer than I expected as his mouth consumed me. Ollie put everything into his kiss just as he did everything in life. He might come off as the cocky jerk, but I'd started to see it as his passion. When he committed to something, Ollie dove in at full force. His hands were in my hair, his lips firm and soft, his tongue seeking as we ravished one another. It was the kiss to end all kisses. While I didn't want to think about his previous sexual partners, I had to admit, the boy had skills.

My whole body tingled as he swirled his tongue around mine, offering the perfect pressure. It was a dance set to a perfect tempo, and I was lost in it as my head filled with stars. Pulling back, Ollie nipped my lip before sucking it in between his. The sensation sent a shiver all the way down to my clit. It was like a fucking live wire.

Moaning, I tried to move closer to him. When I'd jumped the last bit of space between us, I'd managed to land half on the floor and half on his lap. Adjusting myself, I was able to fully straddle him now. My hands began to roam, and I realized what my brain hadn't noticed earlier—Ollie was bare-chested. Running my hands over the planes of his muscles, I salivated at the definition he had. Pectorals were severely underrated muscles. Holy hell, his were amazing.

Trailing my hands up to his wavy hair, I mussed it up as I twined my fingers in it. Ollie's hands began to explore my body as his deft fingers lifted my shirt over my head in the process. Told you the boy had mad skills.

Pulling my shirt off, I spotted Ty sitting awkwardly behind me, watching. Our moment in the shower with Rhett had been incredible. And with our history, I knew he wasn't against group situations. I wondered if his hesitation was more to do with who. Turning my head, Ollie started to leave kisses and love bites down my neck with the access. Locking eyes with Ty, I beckoned him to come over. Cautiously, he crawled on his knees toward us, hesitant to get too close.

"Quit acting so scared, Ty. I'm not going to bite, unless you like that," Ollie flirted.

At his remark, I felt his smirk against my skin. Seemed cocky Ollie was out to play, and I was here for it. My deep moan gave me away with what I thought of that idea.

"Seems our pretty girl here likes that idea."

Ollie continued to nibble down to my breasts, pulling sounds of pleasure from me as I rocked on his lap. Ty finally scooted in behind me, and as I looked at him, I prayed the need in my eyes was unmistakable.

"Please, Ty. I want you both. I *need* you both."

Pure want poured out of me, and I must've been convincing enough as Tyler finally gave in to his own lust, kissing me firmly on the mouth. His hands landed on my hips, and he rocked up against my ass as he settled his hard as steel cock between my cheeks.

Elongating my neck, I offered it to Ty as Ollie continued his feast on my breast. Despite this being my first time with them together, they coordinated well and anticipated one another's movements. There was something to be said about guys familiar with one another before you took it to this level. It seemed to cut some of the awkward discomforts as you tried to figure out how to just be naked with another individual.

My bra was soaked through from Ollies sucking, and the fabric kept rubbing against my pert nipples, sending me into sensation overload. Ty unhooked it with nimble fingers, allowing Ollie even closer access to what he was seeking.

"Fuck, yes," breathed Ollie as he finally captured the peak in his mouth. Starting to rock more on his lap, I ground myself against him as I felt two hard lengths bracketing me. Their echoing groans matched my movements of back and forth.

"Wildcat, I think it's time to get you out of these pants."

Nodding, because words were too hard to form at the moment, I lifted my ass up some as Ty dragged down my leggings and panties in one swift move. Ollie assisted with my legs from the front, and I was suddenly completely naked between them.

"Holy shit, that was awesome. High-five dude! That's what I call teamwork," Ollie chuckled.

If his face wasn't so cute with how that had worked out, I think I would have punched him. Still, his enthusiasm was contagious, and we soon found ourselves all relaxing and settling into the dynamic more.

"Not to sound weird, but you've done this before with another dude, right? So I'm just going to defer to you."

"It's not all that complicated, Ollie. Just do what feels good and please Sawyer. The rest always sorts itself out."

"Speaking of the pleasing Sawyer part, can we get back to that bit?" I asked.

"Oh, is someone feeling neglected? Nope, we can't have any of that."

Before I could respond to Ollie's snark, he stood with me in one movement. Whatever leg routine these guys did, it clearly worked, because damn. Every time they lifted me with such ease, it melted my insides to liquid goo. Ollie resumed kissing me with everything he had as he effortlessly carried me to the bed.

"Damn, that's hot," whispered Ty in awe as he watched us.

Pulling apart from Ollie, I was trying to see if it was just our movement or something else. Ty was standing there, eyes affixed on Ollie's ass, and that was when I realized he'd magicked his pants off somehow as he had carried me.

"Damn, that is hot," I stated back, conspiringly smiling with Ty.

He shook his head in laughter at me as he began to strip. I knew this would be hard for him with his feelings, but I was hoping it would help him either do something about them or be happy with the relationship they had. I didn't want anyone pining for someone. If I could have my heart's desire, I wanted them to as well.

My back hitting the bed brought my attention back to Ollie. His eyes were intense as they stared at me, and it was the most serious expression I'd ever seen on him.

"Hey, I'm not going to change my mind or regret this. I want to be with you, Ollie. I see you for the man you are, cockiness and all, and you're someone I desperately want in my life."

"I knew I would win you over eventually. The Oliver swagger—" cutting him off by squishing his lips together, I was trying to save him the hassle of digging his own grave. My hussy vagina was already locked and loaded, and she was ready to go.

"Let's just leave it at that, shall we? Now, stop your gabbing and kiss me some more, dammit!"

Ollie smiled wide before planting kisses up and down my body in slow and purposeful caresses as he worshipped me. Each one left me wanting more, and I was a panting mess by the time he reached the area I wished he'd been all along.

I'd lost track of Ty as Ollie ravished me in kisses, so when the bed dipped above me, I bowed my head back to see Ty kneeling over me as he fisted his cock in his hand. He was watching Ollie as he feasted on my core like I was his favorite cookie.

When he saw me watching, Ty smiled down and inched closer, teasing me with the head of his cock on my lips. Not able to get good traction with my head upside down, I beckoned him to move to my side, which he willingly obliged.

Now with more access, I was able to lick around his head as I took the tip into my mouth, sucking for any drops of pre-cum as I flicked my tongue into the slit. His hands settled on my head, and he gently directed me at his pace. Soon I was moaning along with him as Ollie's tongue magic showed my pussy lips what it had been missing out on.

I was so wet at this point that Ollie's fingers were gliding in and out with ease, creating a sucking sound. I felt embarrassed about it until both Ty and Ollie moaned at the sound and sight of me coating Ollie's fingers. Ty started to move deeper into my throat until he felt my gag reflex trigger and then pulled back. Looking down, I could see Ollie was transfixed as he watched Ty and me.

Pulling Ty out of my mouth with a pop, I sat up, needing more friction. Moving us into a similar position as we had been on the floor, I straddled a now naked Ollie. Getting a good look at his dick for the first time, I took in his length, thickness, and how it curved a little. I was happy to report he manscaped, but I could tell the carpet did, indeed, match the drapes. Smirking at Ollie as I straddled him, he winked in return.

The transformation in him since he'd shared his secret had been significant. Ollie seemed lighter, freer.

Rocking back and forth on his erect dick, I soaked him with my wetness. With each pass over, I hit my clit with the tip of Ollie's cock, sending tendrils of pleasure through me. The next pass through, he grabbed my hips as I was about to hit my clit again and surged up in me, filling me wholly.

My back arched at the force, and I propped myself against Ty as Ollie began to thrust up in me. Ty cradled me in his arms, giving him access to my breasts. Kissing me upside down, I was smug as fuck to think my version was even better than Spiderman's iconic kiss. Mary Jane got a kiss. Well, Sawyer Sullivan got kissed by one guy while also being fucked by another. Pretty sure I won, MJ.

Ty's fingers distracted my thoughts as he began to

pinch and twist my nipples and moved his other hand down to my clit.

"Fuck, bite-size, your pussy is swallowing me whole and coating me in you. I think I'm in heaven, Ty, am I in heaven?" joked Ollie, a moan escaping him at his words.

His thrusts were quick but deep as he used my hips as leverage to move me. Ollie surged up in me, rubbing me against Ty's dick in the process with each movement. Twisting, I was trying to reach Ty's dick so I could stroke it.

"Shit, that feels good. I can feel your fingers on my dick, too," moaned Ollie to Ty.

Ty paused for a second, but then he almost started rubbing me even more viciously. I wasn't complaining, as all my love buttons and erogenous zones were being hit.

Ollie must've realized I was struggling to get in a good position for both of them because before I could even suggest anything, he was twisting me around and slamming back into me from behind. Ollie hit me deeper from this angle as he began to pick up more speed, his balls slapping my clit with each thrust. Peering up, Ty was fisting his dick as he stared lovingly down at me.

Lowering myself down to my elbows, I took him back into my mouth, able to do so with more ease now. They soon found their rhythm, and we were all beginning to peak as I felt my own climax rising. Ty gave me his old signal we'd developed years ago to warn me if I didn't want to swallow by tapping my cheek with his fingers. I was in the zone, though, so I continued to suck him down as he plunged into my mouth. Moments later, his warm cum erupted down my throat, and I moaned around him, licking it up.

He withdrew himself from my mouth once he was done, and Ollie took the opportunity to draw me back up to him. Wrapping his arm around my torso, his hand snaked up between my breasts to tilt my head back toward him to kiss. His tongue swished around mine, tasting all I had to offer. The fact he didn't balk at Ty's cum in my mouth encouraged me that things might develop more.

Pulling back, he stared deep into my eyes as he continued to impale me on his dick. I was taken aback briefly when I felt a wet tongue licking up my juices until I realized that Ty was joining. He must've been laying under me on the bed, because by Ollies' moan, he was feeling the effects as well.

"Holy shit, that feels amazing."

He let go of me, and I fell forward, bracing myself on Ty's legs as Ollie began to drive his cock into me harder. His balls had to be slapping Ty in the face based on his position. Yet, neither commented, so I soon forgot about it as I enjoyed the sensations being sent through my body. When Ty sucked on my clit a moment later, my orgasm crested, sending shock waves through my entire body, curling my toes and causing my whole body to shake from its strength.

My orgasm triggered Ollie's, and he soon followed

me over as he moaned deeply, holding my hips to him tightly as Ty continued to lick us from below. Ollie pulled out slowly, and I imagined Ty's tongue dragging along the length of his cock as he did. My imagination was very pornographic, so I hoped it was accurate.

Before I could move to get up, Ollie dropped down and began to lick up both of our cum from me with Ty. How they fit two mouths down there was lost to me as I fell into a second orgasm from their ministrations.

"Ahhh, fuck. Oh my god," I howled as my brain went blank.

When I'd apparently been cleaned up, they moved away, allowing me to fall onto the bed in a heap of contented ecstasy. Ollie started to move off the bed, but I wasn't having it.

"No, both of you stay, please." Evidently, it had been the right thing to say as they both smiled at me with love in their eyes.

"I'm going to grab some clothes and clean up; I'll be right back, bite-size. I promise. Ty, you want some clothes?"

"Ugh, you're going to keep calling me that, aren't you?" I whined. Ollie just ignored me, as he waited for Ty to respond.

"Uh, yeah. Thanks, man."

Ollie walked out as he answered, grabbing his discarded pants and holding them in front of his junk. There wasn't much left to hide at this point, so I guess the guys didn't mind walking around practically bare for all. I wouldn't say no to it, either. Turning to Ty while Ollie was gone, I wanted to check in with him.

He had moved off the bed and was grabbing me a shirt to slip on. He always took such good care of me; how did I not see it before? He dropped it over my head and kissed me on the nose and forehead. His love for me was evident and made me feel all warm inside.

"Thank you, Ty. I love you."

"I love you too, Wildcat. I don't think I'll ever get tired of hearing you say it, though."

"Good, because I don't plan to stop. How are you feeling after that? You doing okay with everything?"

"Yeah, I am."

He brushed my hair back behind my ear, and I tucked in next to him as the exhaustion finally took me under to the land of sleep. It wasn't what I'd intended for my pamper fest, but it definitely got the job done.

forty-eight

. . .

elias

THE CHAUFFEURED car rolled to a stop outside a massive stone mansion, and I braced myself for the shit show I was about to enter. I had left here four years ago; hopeful I wouldn't have to return. My family had wanted one specific path for me, the one expected of me as an heir.

My father was Sir Richard Fitzroy—icon and billionaire extraordinaire. My father's entire name was pure irony. The etymology of Fitzroy was "son of a king," and the name was given to the illegitimate children of royals. And well, his 'dick' often resulted with him in precarious situations, such as between the legs of his secretary—my mother, Mia Turner. Real original there, dad, having an affair with your secretary.

However, the most sardonic part was how he must've subconsciously seen his name as a challenge or rite of passage. I wasn't sure if it was an honor or shame to be the bastard child in my family. Somedays, it felt like both.

For the most part, I had been allowed to ignore the Fitzroy side of my heritage and all the bullshit titles associated with it. I had been able to live by my mother's surname, Turner, in the world, helping to hide my family legacy outside the elite circles.

My tragic story started with my mother's death when I was a young child. After the funeral, all my belongings were packed, and I was sent to live with a father I didn't know. After discovering her pregnancy, my mother left her job, hoping to shield me from the life she knew I would be cast in if not.

My father hadn't known about my birth. After her cancer diagnosis, my mother wrote several letters and contacted an estate lawyer. They were to deal with her affairs upon her death. At her diagnosis, my mother had known she didn't have much time left and did the best she could to provide for me after. I often wondered how different my life would have been if I hadn't lost her at the age of four.

Upon receiving his letter, my father sent for me, and I left New Jersey behind for Connecticut. At first, I was excited to learn I would have siblings. I'd always wanted them and had hoped to have moments like the ones I'd watched on TV come to life. However, my siblings were much older and mostly ignored me due to their age. Despite being a bastard child, my life hadn't been difficult. I was provided for with the best care, given superb educational opportunities, and had access to anything I ever wanted—materialistically speaking.

When I started school, I'd been sent to the same boarding school all Fitzroy's attended in London. "It was the family way." I spent the bulk of my holidays and years there. While I was often lonely and desiring real connection, I had been excused from all the obligatory family bullshit melodrama.

I wasn't bullied or made to feel different from my siblings, and in truth, I was given more freedom to be my own person. I often wondered if my siblings resented me to some degree for it. I received all the benefits of the name without the strings. Or, at least, I thought there were none.

When I graduated top of my class, my father took notice, much to my siblings' annoyance. Sir Richard might be a philandering wanker, but he was a bloody brilliant businessman. When he saw an opportunity to gain more power, more leverage, or more anything really, he took it. He exploited any weakness he found to get what he wanted. Sir Richard had ventured out on his own, stepping away from the traditional role he was groomed for from his family lineage. In some ways, I admired him for that.

Using his trust fund, my father started a conglomerate with his schoolmates. It had grown into the mega-corporation it was today. Exousia Corp had ties in several sectors from Automotive, Oil and Specialty Chemicals, Banking & Finance, Media, Technology and Communications, Infrastructure Project Development,

Commercial Trade, and Real Estate. There was not much they did not have their fingers in. It was scary how much of the world was controlled by a few men when you thought about it.

"Mr. Turner-Fitzroy, welcome home," the footman voiced to me as he opened my door. Smiling tersely, I headed up the steps and through the door as I prepared myself for the pretentious bullshit I had grown to hate.

"Mr. Turner-Fitzroy, your father and brother are waiting for your arrival in the west wing," the butler at the front entrance announced once I'd stepped foot into the door.

"Thank you, Seamus," I replied as he took my coat. Nodding in the butler's direction, I headed toward my father's study. Seamus had worked for the family for years and had always been kind to me. But I never forgot who his true boss was, and it wasn't me.

Quickly, I made my way to the study. My father's arrogance had no bounds, as he surreptitiously had his study placed in the west wing to make him feel as important as the United States president. Despite our ties to the British Monarch, the corporation had offices worldwide, and my father had chosen to run his office in New York.

His relationship with his family had always been strained once he'd deviated from living the life of a Duke or something, in the countryside of England. Relocating to New York had been the escape he wanted, effectively cutting himself off from his lineage. He was a self-made man now and didn't need the title to open doors. This was my father's one weakness.

The family home was located in Greenwich, Connecticut, a mere forty-five minute drive from New York City, and two hours north of where I'd lived the first years of my life, New Jersey. The Connecticut home was where I'd grown up when I wasn't away at boarding school, but I had no real memories here. It was just an overly large house with too many ghosts. It was empty and devoid of what made a family a family. And after being at TAS, I understood what that was now.

This place was not that—not even close.

My footsteps were silent as I made my way down the hall. Photos of long-forgotten ancestors and his business associates lined the walls. It was ostentatious and gauche, and I cringed every time I traversed it to my father's office—nothing like the eyes of rich men cast on you to feel judged the whole length of the hall. I wouldn't be surprised if it was a deliberate tactic on my father's part to unsettle his opponents.

Knocking on the open door frame, I entered once my father looked up from his desk. His salt and pepper hair was neatly combed, his beard trimmed, and his eyes calculating—always calculating. His starched white shirt drew a sharp contrast against the dark leather chair he sat in. The rolled-up sleeves allowed his Patek Philippe watch to shimmer in the afternoon sun. He spent more on that watch than most people spent on their cars. It was all about status and appearance in his circles.

"Elias," my father acknowledged. No hint of emotion in his voice to clue me into his feelings. My brother leaned against the wall near a side cart that held decanters of whiskey and bourbon. Whether he was getting one and stopped at my entrance or had purposefully stood there was unclear. Either was likely, as he was always attempting to intimidate me.

"Father. Tomas." Nodding to both, I took a seat in the wingback chair positioned in front of the large cherry desk.

"Elias, to what do we owe this pleasure? Last I remember, you were paving your own path and didn't need the Fitzroy money or title. So, why are you here?" the eldest of my half-siblings questioned. Tomas was nearing forty, married, and had two bratty children he never saw. It was likely he had followed in dear old dad's footsteps as well and had a mistress, or two. He had never been a fan of mine, and subsequently, we had not gotten on well when he was around.

His sneer at me and my choices made my blood boil, and I wanted to smack it off his elitist face. Briefly, the image of Sawyer doing just that if she were here made my lip lift up a millimeter before I staunched it. I couldn't allow my emotions into this room. They would only use it against me, and I couldn't afford any disadvantages at the moment.

Tomas continued to sneer at me as I stared blankly at him. He was set to take over as CEO at one of the Investment and Banking companies when our father retired and, consequently, became more arrogant since it was officially announced for the end of this year. It wasn't like the rest of us were lining up for it, so I had never understood what he felt he had won—until now.

Nevertheless, he had lorded over the rest of us. He was the most insufferable of the lot. I was fortunate he had been out of the house when I arrived, being twenty years my senior; otherwise, I was confident my experience would have been much different.

"Some things in my circumstances have changed, and I wondered what the price might be for a favor."

My father observed me. He hadn't been an awful dad, despite my attitude toward him. He just hadn't been present. He had no interest in attending recitals or sporting events. Sir Richard preferred his children to be out of sight as long as you didn't bring shame to the family name. He was ostentatious, self-centered, and more focused on being a successful businessman than caring for a grieving boy.

He had provided for me in every way he knew how and never treated me differently than his other children —much to their dismay. While I had craved a better bond with him, I could never fault him for the life he gave me. It was better than most in his situation would have chosen to do.

At graduation, my father had approached me with an offer. He wanted me to head up one of the offices and take Fitzroy as my surname. That wasn't on my five-year plan, so I had declined. He allowed it but told me one day I would need him and what the cost would be. I knew coming here would fundamentally alter everything I had worked for over the past eight years. I no longer cared.

"Seems you finally have something you care about enough to sully yourself with us. Or should I say, someone?"

He steepled his hands as he looked me over. I didn't deny what he was saying. I was confident he would be aware of everything going on in Utah on some level. It wasn't like him to leave an opportunity of attack open or vulnerable. The mere fact the broken engagement hadn't made it past the tabloids screamed my father had gag orders at the newspapers—it was easy when you owned most of them.

"The alliance between our family and the Aldridge's was a huge loss when the engagement fell through. Their ties in Russia would have been very advantageous for our family and company."

Dread filled me as he talked. What had my engagement meant to him? Had it all been some duplicitous ploy all along? This was becoming more sinister with each piece of information I learned, and I didn't like the direction this was headed. It wasn't going to end well for me. That was becoming glaringly obvious. Suddenly, everything I had believed and known was pulled into question. Had I any choice all along? Or had everything been some elaborate ruse to give me the illusion of freedom, only to have me always end at the same outcome? The outcome my father wanted from the start.

"When you denied your lineage to the Fitzroy name,

I told you that one day you would need me. Do you remember what I said the cost would be?"

Anxiety spiked despite having known this was the course I would have to choose. I knew the cost would be steep when I came here. Nothing in my family came without strings. I just hadn't expected to learn my whole life had been some elaborate chess match with me always ending here. Doubt that my plan would even work filled me. If this was the inevitable conclusion all along, would I be able to even effectively execute my plan?

Sawyer's face filled my mind. Her eyes filled with passion, fire, and sadness. Her body moving over Rhett's cock sensually, moaning as she came. The way she stared at me, asking me not to hurt her. If anyone in my life deserved to live without fear, to be happy and hopeful, it was Sawyer.

Perhaps my whole life had been an elaborate sham, but it didn't matter now. I was already here; the plan was set in motion. It was too late to stop now. I would have to see it through and just outsmart the grandmaster in the process. It would be the ultimate chess match.

Besides, she was the Queen, and I, her reluctant knight. It was time I asserted myself, picked up my shield, and proclaimed my true intentions. Sawyer was worth any sacrifice.

"I remember, and I am ready to take up the family mantle. I realized it was the correct course for me," I avowed resolutely.

My father's smile should've creeped me out at my acquiesce, but everything in me had retreated.

"Then it is settled. You will return to the fold immediately. No more dissertation, no more tutoring, and especially no more fighting. You return to the family and play your part."

Shit, as he laid out the terms, it was apparent I hadn't been as clever as I thought if he knew about my fights. Panic crept up at the realization I'd underestimated my father. The picture that had been downloaded on my computer flashed through my mind, strengthening my resolve. I had to do this. I was the only one who could. It wasn't just Sawyer at risk anymore either.

"Understood."

His grin grew wider, effectively freezing my insides. I couldn't have emotions anymore. Not here. Not if I was going to survive and succeed in my plan.

"Wonderful, I look forward to seeing what you will contribute to the family, son. You start tomorrow morning, where I will make the announcement at the Tuesday board meeting. Welcome aboard to Exousia Corp."

He held out his hand, and no part of me wanted to touch him, but I had to play the role he wanted. Reaching out, I shook it firmly before making my way out of the room. I didn't miss my brother's glare or my father's triumphant gleam. Things were not as they had always seemed. I used to think my father was at least a decent man, despite being a crappy father. Not anymore.

The picture was the key we had been missing.

A school club picture, probably long forgotten, depicted my father shoulder to shoulder with six other individuals. At the bottom, it was labeled, "the first meeting of the Aldridge C.O.U.N.C.I.L chapter."

We had been off the mark from the beginning. It was larger than we ever imagined. We thought the Council was some organization bent on world domination. Instead, it was a term for a sinister group of people— seven watchmen sitting in their lofty towers. Though, to be fair, they probably still wanted world domination— nothing like an acronym to scream evil intentions.

And it wasn't the only one.

Chapters had to mean there were more out there. The magnitude of this was mind-boggling and had led me to make the choice I did. We couldn't do this on our own. Not even if we had the help of the Agency. It was clear they hadn't been able to take them down all these years; why would they be able to now? They wouldn't. We needed something to level the playing field.

Nothing in my life was what I thought anymore. But I was going to find out, and in the process, I would find a way to protect the people I had come to love. If that was all I would have in life, it would be enough to know they were safe.

That would be the legacy I would leave in life and, hopefully, bring some cleansing to the Fitzroy name. If not, at least I would leave the Turner name clear.

Reflecting on the photo, fear filled my veins at the repercussions this would have on our group. No one was safe.

At the bottom of the Picture: (names in Alphabetical order, from right to left)
Abernathy, Bellamy, Draven, Fitzroy, Hawthorne, Latimer, Rothchild
"Council of many, the voice of one, the goal of all."

forty-nine

. . .

sawyer

THE BEGINNING of the week flew by with training practices as we prepared for the expo this weekend. Henry and I had been burning the midnight oil every night, either in the rink or dance studio.

It was Thursday, and Charlie was coming in today. I was excited to see him. I couldn't believe it had been around six weeks since I'd left Iowa. So much in my life had changed in that time frame. We hadn't made any more progress on the research and were at a stalemate for the time being as we waited for Brave Heart to get in touch. We had a bunch of names and ideas, but nothing concrete. It was infuriating to feel like it was at the tip of my fingers, barely out of reach.

We still hadn't heard or had any contact from Elias, unless the guys were keeping secrets. Based on the level of trust we all had now, I doubted that was the case.

Secrets were the death trap of any relationship, especially in ours. We had made a commitment to be honest and open with one another; it was the only way we could all move forward. Life had a funny way of throat punching you when you least expected, though.

"What time's Charlie arriving?" Fin asked as we finished up our lunch.

We were both making efforts to find time to connect more lately. Since the reveal, we hadn't hung out with Ace or Chloe, and I had to admit I missed them both. It wasn't fair to Chloe, but I couldn't see her right now and not think about Ace. And that was something I just couldn't deal with currently with my training load. Maybe after this weekend, we could all grab a coffee and invite Rowan along again.

Fin had been quiet all lunch, and it felt like something was going on with her, but she was being pretty hush about it. That thing about secrets, yeah, I didn't like it. I had a bad feeling something was going to blow up in our faces. This overwhelming feeling of responsibility weighed on me to be there for everyone, or something terrible would happen. Needless to say, the little sleep I was getting this week hadn't been restful.

"His plane lands this evening. Henry and I are picking him up after practice. You and Asa should stop by for dinner. I think Soren's going to make something yummy. Plus, I'm excited about you meeting him."

"Me too. I feel like I already know him."

"Speaking of knowing… are you ever going to tell me what's going on with you? I've been trying to give you time to tell me, but at this rate, we'll be eighty," I stated sternly. Her sheepish face only proved my gut instinct.

"It's nothing. There's so much other stuff going on that I wanted to take care of this myself. It's something to do with my old hacker persona. I still get requests for things on the white hacker site. You know, using my skills for good now."

"That sounds like you need help, Fin! Even if I can't do anything, I can be a lending ear. A problem shared is a —"

"—problem halved. Yeah, yeah. Your mom used to say that all the time."

The comment made us both recall Kyla Brennon and her words of wisdom she would bestow upon us. I wondered how different my life would've been if my mom had shared more about what was going on with more people. Maybe she would still be alive.

"I promise, it's nothing. Just someone I'm helping out. If it gets too much, I'll come to you first."

"You're so stubborn, Finley Amelia! Ugh!"

"Back at you, Abigail Sariah Sawyer! Oh my god, all of your names make A.S.S. I am so calling you that from now on!"

"Ha ha, so funny. Why are we best friends again?"

"Because everyone else is lame."

"Oh yeah, there is that."

We both laughed at our statements as we pushed aside the things we were avoiding, or at least Fin was avoiding.

"How are things with my bro? I saw you guys having a heated conversation the morning after the sleepover, and I forgot to mention it."

"Oh, that, yeah, it's just a difference of opinion on a matter. I would tell you, but we promised not to discuss our sexual lives with one another's brother."

Gagging, I stuck my tongue out at her. Something about her statement felt off, though, as if that wasn't the whole truth, and she was using it as an excuse. Fin was being cagey, and I didn't like it.

"Are your parents coming to the expo?"

"Uh yeah. I think so. At least mom is. Joy. Joy. Henry hasn't told them about you being resurrected and all that. Figured it was best until we knew their full role in things. Mom's bugging me about meeting Asa, but I want to still have a boyfriend after this weekend, so I'm trying to find a way around it."

Laughing because it was plausible with her mom. Sofia Reyes was feisty and had the potential to scare anyone away. With her intensity, though, came a vast ability to love and push her children to excel. She was a brilliant woman, and I had fond memories of her despite the grief her children often spoke with about her.

The bell rang, indicating the lunch hour was closing, so we gathered up our trash and headed out of the cafeteria with the students. Hugging Finley goodbye, we parted ways and headed in separate directions. I had one session before practice with Henry. It was dance class today, though, so at least it wouldn't be a long day of skating. My knee was improving, but I always had to be mindful of it and not push it too far. Several nights this week ended with me and an ice pack.

The ice dancing was going wonderfully, though, and I was excited about our change. We should've done it years ago, honestly. We were always on that cusp with our peers in pairs, but I think we would've excelled in the ice dancing category straight away. Dance spoke to us both in a way that translated well on the ice. At least now we had this option. It was giving me renewed hope.

Entering the building for the dance studio, I saw Adelaide and her minions in the lobby. I skirted around them in an attempt to avoid them. I wasn't in the mood to deal with her shit today, or any day, really. She seemed to always be lurking now, waiting to toss jeers my way to see which stuck.

"He keeps texting me, and I feel sorry for him. Apparently, he thought things would be different, but it's still the dead fish sex he's getting. I'm debating giving him another shot, but he would have to get tested first. No telling what diseases she has. Can you imagine?" I heard her shout.

Her words grated on me like nails on a chalkboard. I didn't know who she was talking about, but I knew it was all bullshit, whoever she was making it out to be. It was clear she was referring to me, though, as she continued to get louder. I really needed to learn to keep my mouth shut, but I guess I was just over living my life that way.

Silence could be just as deadly as the bully. It was the silence that allowed the bully to prosper in the first place.

"Adelaide, your obsession with me is getting old. I get it, I'm hot and amazing, but you're just not my type. You know the whole cold bitch thing doesn't work for me. So how about we drop the pretense and move on? Sounds great. See you around, never."

Walking away, I was feeling confident about my jabs at her. Cockiness really wasn't a good look on me. I should've learned that one from Ollie.

"How cute. But no, I'm not in any way infatuated or obsessed with you, as you like to claim. But could you give a message to one of your 'boyfriends?' Tell Tyler that it was a one-night stand and I don't date hockey players, so he can stop sending me nudes."

"Funny. Ty wouldn't touch you with a ten-foot pole, but sure, I'll let him know that he's free from Satan's clutches. I'm sure he'll be relieved."

Walking off, I was beating myself for responding. I didn't want to deal with her shit. When I got to the door for the stairs, she volleyed one last comment before the door slammed closed. The slamming was a perfect representation as she so clearly eviscerated me, shattering my heart in the process.

"If that's true, then how do I know he has a star-shaped birthmark on his right butt cheek? Hmm."

"First position, demi-plié. Second position, demi-plié."

I was on autopilot as I ran the students through warm-up exercises, thankfully they were muscle memory to us by this point in our training. I trusted Ty, I reminded myself. This seemed like I was missing something. There was some truth to what she said, but no way did I believe it was the full truth.

She did know about his birthmark, so she saw him in some state of undress at some point, but was it what she was alluding to or something innocent? Fortunately, the other dance instructor, Chris, took over after warm-ups, giving me time to think. Moments like these, I was glad these classes were dual taught.

Shaking myself off, I brought my focus back to the present. A couple of the girls and guys showed real promise and were progressing really well. Some of the other students were from different sports but needed an elective to take. I was curious which hockey coach had pitched for them to enroll in dance to increase their flexibility. It sounded like something both Ty and Ollie would do.

The thought of Ty reminded me of Adelaide, and the momentary calm I had, faded. Deciding the only way to get out of this funk was to dance it out, I chose some hard beats for today's lesson.

"Okay, today we're going to let the music move us and dance out emotion. Musicality is important for skating. Can you feel the beats? Can you manifest your body to represent the emotion? Well, let's give it a try."

We all started to groove, and I soon lost myself in

the rhythm and beats. There were six of us in class, so we had enough room to spread out and feel our own dance. Surprisingly, they all got into it, and I saw some freedom come through some of the students who'd been struggling with technique. Chris even seemed to be enjoying himself. Guess I wasn't the only one feeling stressed and confused.

By the end of class, I was a sweaty mess, but I felt better, lighter. The smiles on the students' faces communicated they had to—score one for the emotional dance release.

"Great class, Coach Sawyer. I really enjoyed it," Aaron, one of the hockey players, said on his way out.

"Yeah, it was awesome."

"We should do that once a week!"

"I don't know what led to that change in the lesson plan, but I think it was a success. Fun class today. Looking forward to seeing you skate at the expo this weekend," Chris stated as he packed up his belongings.

"Oh yeah. Thanks. I'm glad it worked out. See you around."

I felt awkward now, like I'd shown my hand or something. But it had been needed. My head was clearer, and I knew what I needed to do. Pulling out my phone, I texted Ty to meet me at the ice rink. That was the thing about secrets. They only blew up on you if you kept them. I wasn't going to let Adelaide poison my relationship.

fifty

. . .

sawyer

THE MUSIC WAS ALREADY PLAYING as I made my way into the rink. I was hoping it was Henry and not anyone else, not sure I would be able to restrain myself from punching Queen Bitch this time.

"You've gotta do eight rotations, Jill. Starting from the entry of the spin to the exit of the spin in order to get full points. The side-by-side spin is the first time they see your synchronization, so you have to be together. Let's try it one more time, and then it's a wrap for today."

Leaning against the rails, I adoringly watched Henry in his element. It was kinda hot hearing his bossy voice. He had a passion for his students, and while I knew this wasn't his dream, he was good at it. The stupid boy was good at a lot of things.

Which reminded me of book club with Soren the

other night for book two in our series. If every book club was going to end with orgasms, I would definitely meet my reading goal for the year. Henry had popped in my room as we were wrapping up, and well, things escalated quickly.

It wasn't my fault some authors wrote mega-hot sex scenes, leaving me all hot and bothered. Some of them were better than porn. The guys were definitely reaping the benefits of my book addiction. Lost in my haze of sexual lust, I didn't notice Ty had entered until he wrapped his arms around me from behind.

"Hey, Wildcat. What do I owe this midday text to? Hmm." I tried not to tense up. I didn't want QB in my head or messing with things, but my heart was still a fragile thing, and no matter what I said, it didn't listen and was shielding itself.

He turned me around when he felt me tense, concern radiating in his eyes. I searched his face for something, for what I wasn't sure, but the love in his eyes shone through, softening me.

Relaxing, I pulled him to me as I wrapped my arms around his torso. It didn't matter. QB was just that, a bitch. I wouldn't let her destroy anything in my life. I know that even if it was true, it was before me. I couldn't hold it against him. He squeezed me back as he dropped his head to my hair, breathing me in. "Everything okay?"

"Yeah, just wanted to see you. I miss you. We really need to figure out a way for you to move in with us.

Fancy changing your last name? Or pretending to be Elias?" I joked.

"Is that your way of proposing to me? If so, the answer is yes!"

"Tyler Sullivan. I like it. It's got a nice ring to it."

"Oh, I would so be the best bride! I do look hot in a dress."

"I'm sure you do, but I think I would want to wear the dress for our make-believe wedding."

"Oh well, I guess that's fair. It doesn't have to be make-believe, you know, but I'll leave that for another day. Now, are you going to tell me what's really bothering you?"

"It's nothing. I ran into QB, and she made a comment, and I was letting it eat away at me, but seeing you reminded me it didn't matter. I know what we have is strong. My doubt just needed to be bitch slapped back to her hidey-hole."

"Ah, I'm guessing she made some comment about me sleeping with her. Worst mistake of my life. That's what I get for getting drunk at a party and not having my standard discretion available. She was horrible, that much I do remember. Laid there like a limp noodle. When I came to, I booked it out of there so fast. I meant to tell you—"

"Ssh. It's fine. Thank you for that image, though. Now, I will never be able to get that picture out of my head. I really need some of that brain bleach." Shuddering, I looked back up at his smile. It was clear as day, this boy loved me.

"Henry and I are running through our program. Can you stay? Then you could go with us to pick up Charlie."

"Oh yeah? Charlie's coming in tonight? Sounds perfect, Wildcat. I love you."

He kissed me softly and full of promise. Leaving him sitting on the bleachers, I went to lace up my skates. QB had thrown a Hail Mary, but like all of her cheap shots, in the end, it was an incomplete pass. Trust was something you couldn't buy, and she hadn't ever learned that.

She could keep coming at us, and I assumed she would, but each day we became stronger. That kind of strength was foreign to her and something she would always misunderstand and underestimate. Bring it, Bitch.

tyler

Thankful my idiocy hadn't bitten me in the ass by never getting around to telling Sawyer about Adelaide, I sat down to watch her and Henry skate. I'd been trying to find a way to tell her, but it always seemed like something else more important was going on than clearing my conscience. I was glad it was out there now. Henry finished his lesson and skated over to where I waited.

"Hey, Ty. You hanging out?"

"Yeah, hope that's okay. Sawyer invited me to stay and then ride with you guys to pick up Charlie."

"Of course, man. I'm excited to chill. Does she have any idea about tonight?"

"Not as far as I could tell. She's more focused on Charlie and, well, Adelaide, or as the house calls her, Voldemort, she tried to stir up some shit today, apparently."

"What? That bitch. Everything okay?"

"Yeah, she's good. Thankfully, Sawyer didn't fall for the trap, and we talked and cleared the air. A piece of my history I wish I could scrub from my memory." I shuddered.

"Guess that means you're officially one of us. I swear she's hit on all the guys in the house. So, you're in good company. She's a piece of work. I don't know how Elias stood her for over a year when they were engaged."

"Yeah, I think she hypnotized me or something, so maybe she has some kind of voodoo magic that pulled him in, but once she revealed her true face, the spell broke."

"It wouldn't surprise me. She's pure evil, that one." He did that full-body shudder Sawyer had done a few moments ago, and I couldn't help but laugh at their similarities at times.

"Hey, so I know I'm like this new guy coming in, and there's this shared history she and I have outside of everyone else. I don't want it to seem like I'm stepping on any toes or trying to assert myself over anyone. I don't even know if that makes sense, but I'm just happy to have connected with her again and feel honored to be included in what you guys have going on."

"Thank you for saying that, man, but you have nothing to apologize for or whatever. I should thank you for being there for her when I couldn't. You're in all her best memories of those years, man. That speaks volumes to me about your character, and I'm honored to get to know you. Wow, I feel weird saying that, but it's honestly the truth. I hope we can be as close as brothers."

"Ah man, you're hitting me in the feels." I grabbed my chest to break up some of the weird emotional shit we unwillingly opened up, causing us both to laugh, dissipating the awkwardness. Thank god.

Sawyer came out rescuing us as well, and they began to run through their program while I watched. They were as synchronized as ever, and it was like watching one skater in two bodies. The music crescendo and their dance fit perfectly with the music. I didn't know what anything was called, but I could appreciate the beauty of the program. Sawyer moved like liquid around Henry, and they effortlessly predicted and anticipated one another.

I was so transfixed, I didn't even feel my phone vibrating at first. Pulling it out, I saw my father was calling. I'd been dodging his calls for over a week now; I couldn't put it off any longer. Getting up, I walked around to the front lobby so I could hear him over the music.

"Hello, Dad. How are things going?"

"Oh, you finally remembered to answer your phone. How nice," growled my father.

"I know. I deserve that. Things have just been… intense."

"Well, I imagine so. It's not every day you meet back up with your high school girlfriend."

"Ah, so you've heard."

"Of course, I've heard Tyler! What I don't like is not hearing it from you, but from another agent."

Hanging my head, I knew I'd screwed up, but I had been too worried he was going to ask me to do something I hadn't wanted to do, so I had avoided him instead.

"I'm sorry, Dad. I handled it poorly."

"Hmph. Do I finally get to meet this girl, since you never introduced her to me when you were in high school?"

"Of course, dad. I would love that, actually."

"All's forgiven then. I'll be there this weekend for the expo, but I won't be in until Saturday. I reserved a car and a room, so you won't need to worry about picking me up. I know you have a game that morning. There is some Agency business I need to discuss with you while I'm there, so let's make sure we make time."

"Sounds good. I'm looking forward to seeing you. Mom coming too?"

"She's not sure yet. Your sister might have some recital, so she's waiting to see. I'll see you Saturday, son. Love you."

"Love you too, Dad. Bye."

We hung up, and I felt guilty for avoiding him for so long. My parents were good people, and I should've trusted he wouldn't ask me to do anything I didn't want to. They never had before, and even with the Agency, it had always been my choice.

Walking back into the rink, I saw they were finishing up, so I stayed leaning against the rails. They finished their last move in some spin dip that had Sawyer across Henry's leg. They were both breathing heavily after almost an hour of practice, but the smiles on their faces were radiant as they looked at one another.

If I didn't know Sawyer loved me, I would be jealous of their connection. Instead, it actually made me happy, and a little turned on if I was honest with myself. Anytime I saw her with one of the other guys, it was arousing to me. They pulled apart and skated toward me, and I was thankful the guard rail hid my erection.

"So, what did you think?" Sawyer asked hesitantly.

"It was incredible. You guys are going to be the hit of the expo. I don't even know half of what you did, but I couldn't look away."

"Yes! That is the look we are going for. Let us go change and freshen up, and we can head to the airport." She kissed my cheek as she walked by, leaving me with a, "Thanks, Ty."

"Yeah, thanks, Ty," Henry mocked as he walked by, acting like he was going to kiss my cheek too.

Shoving him away, I chuckled out, "You wish you were so lucky, dude," making everyone laugh.

They sauntered off once they had their skate guards on, joking the whole way. I never thought I would have friends as great as this group and the sense of belonging that accompanied it.

fifty-one

· · ·

oliver

I WAS STRESS BAKING, but nothing seemed to quell the thoughts running through my head. At least, the apple tart I'd just finished smelled delicious. It joined the banana bread and cinnamon rolls I'd made, as well. Breakfast tomorrow would be lit! Now, I was finishing off the icing for Sawyer's cake, and I would officially be out of things to do in the kitchen. Shit, maybe there was—

My thoughts were cut off as Soren sauntered into the kitchen, looking like he'd just woken up from a nap. He scratched his head, making all of his hair more mussed and sticking out in every direction.

"What's up?" he yawned.

"Just baking."

"Uh-huh. You only bake this much when something is bugging you. Spill."

Exhaling, part of me was relieved he'd asked and knew me well enough to notice my behavior, even if the actual talking would be awkward.

"How did you know… I mean, how could you… ugh. How did you know when you had feelings for Rey?" I finally managed to get out in a jumbled, stuttering mess. Soren's laughter rang out around the kitchen, making my face flame with embarrassment. Well, I hadn't expected that response.

Pouting a little, I turned back to the sugar fondant roses I had wrapped chocolate-covered strawberries in. It was quite genius, and this cake was going to be epic.

"Sorry, it's just I hadn't realized I'd become the bi-curious go-to guy in the house. I had this conversation with someone else recently too."

That piqued my interest, who else was questioning things? Maybe Sawyer had a magic vagina, and once you had a taste of it, you started becoming sexually fluid and curious. Though, I didn't think I could blame my confusion on her. And as cool as a magic vagina would be, I think it had more to do with the fact she made it okay to be yourself, allowing your feelings to be open.

What that entailed for each person, I thought, was different. Thinking back, it did seem to have helped us all grow closer as well. Who knew, maybe she really did have special vagina juice, Lizzo style. I couldn't wait to make fun of her for it.

"I've never really thought about guys sexually before, but this whole relationship dynamic is making me wonder things. How do I know if it's a sexual attraction or just sexual lust in the moment kind of thing?"

"Hmm, that's a good way to put it. I guess for me, it's always been about who I connect with and find sexual based on their personality or who they are, regardless of gender. Rey found it was more of needing a deep emotional connection before he was aware of his feelings. So, I guess you need to ask yourself if those feelings are only present during sex, then it's probably just sexual exploration or lust-driven. If you find your-self thinking about this person outside of that, and it's not always sexual, it might be actual feelings. The best advice I can give you is just to talk to the person."

"I think that was the solution I knew, but was avoiding admitting it to myself out of fear."

"You know, I once read a quote about fear. It can either mean 'forget everything and run' or 'face every-thing and rise.' You're a badass hockey player, Ollie. You scream at fear in the face and make it your bitch daily. I have absolute faith in you that you can do this too. Hell, you're willing to go up against your family. Surely, being honest isn't as scary as that? Just talk to him. What do you have to lose?"

When he put it that way, he made it seem so simple. Jerkwad. But like a helpful one.

"Thanks, Sor."

"No problem. I'll just take one of these delicious looking cinnamon rolls as thanks."

He grabbed one and shoved it in his mouth before I

could say anything. Lucky's barking alerted us that people were entering the house. A look of panic flashed across Soren's face when he realized he was only half-dressed. I'd never seen him run so fast as he booked it upstairs with a cinnamon roll hanging out of his mouth.

Quickly, I hid the cake in the fridge and washed my hands. Drying them, I hurriedly put away all of my ingredients. I was wiping down the counters when I heard them entering the kitchen from behind me.

Turning around, I was greeted by my beautiful girlfriend and my oldest friend. Both were making my heart race at that moment when they saw me and smiled. Their smiles alone were enough to send me into cardiac arrest, affirming what I rapidly had to admit to myself—I was falling for them both.

"Ollie! I want you to meet one of your biggest fans. This is my Charlie. Charlie, Oliver Windsor."

She skipped over to me at her introductions, hugging me tight around the waist. She pointed to the older man who'd followed her, Ty, and Rey into the kitchen. He looked to be in his sixties, with graying hair and a staunch look that would give Rhett a run for his money. His eyes looked kind, and I could tell he cared a great deal for the girl in my arms. That was enough for me.

"He really is your biggest fan. We watched all of your games from college and pro. I think he's a little star-struck," Sawyer fake whispered the last bit to me, making Charlie sport a wry grin. Okay, I think I would like this guy.

"Sir, it's nice to meet you," I stated as I reached out my hand to shake his.

"Oh no, not another one of you calling me sir. Charlie will do."

His shake was firm and assuring, and I could see why Sawyer respected him. He had a sense about him that made you want to tell him all your secrets, as well as undying loyalty.

"Where's Soren?" Rey asked, right as Soren slid into the kitchen ala Tom Cruise style from *Risky Business*. Fortunately for Soren, he was dressed in more than just his underwear and white shirt. Though, that might've been funny to watch.

"I'm here. Sorry, I fell asleep after class. Dinner will be starting shortly!"

We all laughed at his antics and started to help him get things ready for the surprise dinner while Sawyer gave Charlie a tour. She had picked up Lucky, and they were both oohing and aahing over him as the sap soaked it all in.

Soren and Rey pulled out food to cook, and Ty set the table. Despite him not living here, he'd fallen into our dynamic quickly. Mateo walked in a few minutes later and began to get stuff out for a drink station. We were all working together seamlessly, and it made me understand how we could have this type of relationship.

Soren had been right; I really had nothing to lose but fear of the unknown. I had to trust in our connection and ask the scary things; otherwise, what was the point of having something special if I couldn't treat it as unique?

Gathering my courage, I walked over to Ty as he was finishing up his task. He looked up from placing silverware down, giving me a soft smile. My heart flip-flopped from that simple gesture with a resounding echo, making me fall headfirst into the 'actual feelings' camp of the equation.

"Hey, Ty. Could we, um, talk for a moment?" I desperately hoped the wobble in my voice wasn't noticeable.

"Sure, let me just finish this."

He placed the last of the silverware before turning to me to lead him out of the room. I debated where I was going to take him and decided to head to my room. At least there, I knew it would be private. Shutting the door after he walked in, I started to pace back and forth as I tried to figure out how to say things.

"Everything okay, Ollie? You're starting to freak me out."

"I'm not really sure what things are, and that's what's confusing me. I have to admit to hearing you talking to Sawyer the other day about you having feelings for someone—"

"Oh, it's nothing. You don't—"

"Let me finish, please," I cut him off this time. Clearing my throat, I started again. He sat on the edge of my bed, his own nerves now on display. Wringing my hands, I pushed myself to step out of my comfort zone.

"It got me wondering who it was, actually. And then the other night with Sawyer, it was mind-blowing! Like, wow! And I've never felt anything like that, and it got me thinking about things I never thought about, and it's all just become a big mess, and I'm not sure what's going on with me."

I stopped and turned to face him once I'd blurted all of that out in a typical Sawyer code orange fashion. His face was frozen as he stared at me. Crap on a cracker!

"Ty? Say something, you're freaking me out, and I've already met my quota for a freak-out today. I baked four things, for crying out loud!"

"You… like me?" I couldn't make out his emotion to tell if it was a good or bad question.

"I think so? That's kind of what I wanted to talk to you about. To see if I imagined things or if I was just way out in left field. But if I've read this all wrong, then just file it away as Oliver's rambling."

Slowly, he stood from where he was sitting on the bed and drew near. His hands were outstretched, almost as if he was afraid to approach me.

"Ollie, I want to make sure I understand what you're saying. Are you stating that you're confused about your sexuality or that you may have feelings for *me*?"

"Aren't they the same thing?" I scrunched up my nose in thought.

"No, they're very different in my book."

Thinking about it, I realized it must be like how

Soren had explained it, and that was what he was referring to.

"You, Ty. I'm sorry if that makes you uncomfortable, and if I'm not that for you, then I will push these feelings away and get over it, but I had to say something, I guess. I'm trying to be more open and real and not the cocky boy persona I used to distance myself from people."

"What if *I like* the cocky boy?"

He'd walked closer to me, our toes touching. We were about the same height, so I looked straight into his eyes when he spoke.

"Huh?" My brain was dead. I couldn't process anything with him this close to me.

"What if the person you overheard me talking about was you? How would you feel about that?"

His voice was soft as he asked me, and my mind faltered on the words. Everything disappeared as I stared into his eyes. Wow, he had nice eyes. This was crazy pants. How had I never noticed him before? Was I just following the footsteps of the other guys? How would I know? Licking my lips, my breath started to come in quickly. Was this happening? Was I bi-sexual? Wait, Soren had said not to label myself and to just focus on my feelings.

"I think it would make me happy because I seem to get excited when you look at me, and the thought of you liking someone else made me want to punch something."

"That makes me happy to hear because I've been scared to tell you, Ollie."

"You have? For how long?" He blew out a raspberry at my question, and the air ticked my face a little.

"College, I think? It's hard to say when things changed, but I never thought I had a chance."

"Have you ever been with a guy before?"

"No."

"So, you're just as clueless as me about this stuff?" I laughed.

"Yeah, basically." We smiled at one another, and I felt the anxiety lift from my body.

"Sawyer figured it out the other night and said she was cool with it, but I understand if you want to talk with her about what this means."

"Yeah, I think that would be smart. I'm not in any rush, but it felt like I had to say something or my mind was going to explode. I can't imagine how you've managed this for a few years." Chuckling some more, we awkwardly stared at one another, not sure where to go from here.

"Should we hug it out or something? I feel like we should hug?"

So that's what we did. Ty and I shared a man-hug, and it was the best man-hug I'd ever had.

We walked downstairs and joined the rest of the group. Dinner was almost ready, and it looked like the surprise birthday dinner was going to be a success. The rest of the guys in the house were home too. Everyone was hanging out in the kitchen, and I saw Rhett's mom and sister walk in. Perfect, now to surprise the birthday twins!

"Have no fear, the party is here!" I announced as we walked into the room, causing everyone to burst out laughing. I felt more at ease now and back to my regular joking self.

I introduced Ty to Rhonda and Rowan, and Ty and I ended up chatting with Charlie about hockey. Finley texted me she was close, so I casually walked to the door, giving the guys the signal that the surprise was about to happen. Sawyer still appeared clueless as she chatted with Rowan.

Right as I approached the door, the doorbell rang. Well, that had worked out perfectly. Come to think of it, hadn't I told Fin not to ring the doorbell?

Opening it, I was shocked at who stood on the other side. It wasn't Finley and Asa. This surprise dinner just took on a whole new meaning of surprise. It was about to get a whole lot more interesting.

fifty-two

. . .

sawyer

MY TWO WORLDS were colliding in the most amazing way. Charlie was laughing with Ty and Ollie, and they were getting along great, and it made me feel all warm and fuzzy.

"How you doing, baby?" Rhett asked as he came up behind me. All the guys liked wrapping me in their arms from behind, and I was a fan. It was like being enveloped by a bunch of grizzly bears, all warm, cozy, and safe.

I sounded like a fucking Hallmark movie these days, but my hussy vagina was happy with all the sex she was getting, so at least she was quiet for once. My Altitude Delirium had seemed to settle as well, so that was a relief. I didn't think I could take any more symptoms, or men. Leaning back, I relaxed in his embrace.

"I'm perfect. Charlie's here, and he's meeting all of

you. All my favorite people are in one room; well, they will be once Fin gets here." I grinned upside down at him as I tilted my head back. Even upside down, his smile was just as gorgeous. He kissed my nose before I righted myself.

As much as I tried to not think about Elias, I would find him popping up in my head from time to time. Probably more now than he ever had when he was just down the hall. Things felt so unsettled, and I hated it, as much as I didn't want to admit that.

I wanted to see him and talk to him face to face to figure out where we stood. He said a lot of pretty things in his letter, setting my heart on fire, but he also left a lot of things unsaid. I was finding I didn't deal with uncertainty well. This constant emotional whiplash was just too extreme.

"Your mom and sister seem to be enjoying themselves. I'm glad they were able to come over and get away from the B&B for a bit."

"Yeah, me too. They seem to be getting along with everyone. I've been bad this year about having them over and I know they miss the guys. Rowan won't stop talking about getting coffee with you again. She had fun when you girls went out the other day. I'm glad you're becoming friends. I don't think I realized how lonely or isolated she must have been feeling."

That made me feel good, I liked Rowan a lot. We met up with Fin after I had texted her earlier in the week. It had been a lot of fun, and like I'd anticipated, she got on smashingly with my besties.

It was weird being at the coffee shop without Ace and Chloe, especially Ace. He had become such a good friend to me, and I was missing him the more I thought about it. I understood his situation and had already forgiven him, but I just didn't know if I was ready to see him. I hadn't been at the beginning of the week.

It looked like I would have to figure that out real soon, though, as Ollie walked back into the room. I hadn't realized he'd left, so seeing him with his guests took me by surprise.

Ollie looked really uncomfortable, and I didn't understand it until I saw not only Ace, but also Brave Heart. I really needed to figure out his name. It was eerie how everyone stopped as they walked in and stared, the chatter dying down as we all took in the visitors. Pulling myself from Rhett's arms, I approached the two uninvited guests.

"Uh, hey. It's kind of not a good time. I wished you would have called first or something."

"I kind of did, but you've been avoiding me all week, Sawyer, so I figured this was the best option. I didn't realize you had company, so for that I'm sorry. But this is important," Ace answered.

He glanced to Brave Heart as he spoke, almost like he was referring to him, but Brave Heart just stared at us all, hands in his pockets as he took in the crowd. It clicked then that Brave Heart must be the handler he'd spoken of. Really, it didn't surprise me once I thought about it. Nothing was coincidental, after all.

"There's been a situation, and it's time we read you

all in," Ace informed us. That finally seemed to be the cue Brave Heart was looking for as he clapped Ace on the shoulder.

"You're doing great, wunderkid. It looks like you all were about to eat. Do you have enough for two more? I'm famished!"

Just as he finished, Asa and Fin walked in carrying balloons. The balloons threw me as I stared at their message.

Happy Birthday.

Shit! Did I forget someone's birthday? I would need to write everyone's down in my planner pronto! Opening my mouth to make apologies, the room turned to me, and they all yelled, "Surprise!"

What the what? Blinking, I stared at them as the dates finally started to click into place. But wait, it was October 8th. Asa took pity on me and walked over, throwing his arm around my shoulders.

"We wanted to do a surprise dinner now since our first birthday together is the day of the expo. We can do something more formal with Mom after, but I wanted to celebrate our reunion. By the look on your face, I take it birthdays haven't been a big deal for you either?"

"Um, no. Not since…" swallowing, I tried to gain control of my emotions.

"Yeah, that's what I thought. So the new tradition is going to be… see who can surprise the other first! Great, well, I would say let's eat, but it looks like we have some additional guests?"

Everyone was trying not to watch us as we talked,

but their stares were heavy with concern. I decided I wanted to enjoy the thoughtful celebration they had prepared for me regardless of who the guests were. Brave Heart stood off to the side, observing us all. At my glance, the cocky jerk started to rub his stomach.

Scoffing at him because it seemed I collected the grumpy ones, I went and grabbed two more place settings. We were going to need a bigger table at this rate. Dinner was a tense and quiet affair as we all ate despite it being a birthday celebration.

The food tasted wonderful, and we all quickly scarfed it down. I would wager a bet that it had to do with Brave Heart, who had yet to introduce himself to anyone.

He settled himself right in, though, and acted oblivious to all the stares as he hungrily ate the cheesy chicken concoction Soren made. Rhonda was trying to engage Charlie in a conversation. However, he had clammed up even more at the newcomers' arrival. He almost appeared to be sending death stares from across the table.

It was the most uncomfortable meal ever, and that included the one where I had baited Elias and gone too far on my rant about women's rights. When the last plate had been cleared, we all awkwardly looked to the only one who appeared to be enjoying himself, Brave Heart.

"Brave Heart, spill it. We've been held in suspense long enough." His smirk at me made me want to punch him and wipe that look off his face. I was really starting to doubt my judgment if I had once considered him my friend.

"It might be best if we all head to your HQ."

His use of our code word had me stiffening. How much did this guy know? The others of us in the know at the table swallowed loudly as we looked at all the people gathered. Rowan and Rhonda didn't know my history, and neither did Charlie. I wasn't opposed to telling them, but I didn't want to put them in a position to get hurt.

Rhonda must have sensed all of our unease at his statement and started to make an excuse for them to leave. That woman was one of a kind with how she could read a room.

"Dinner was lovely, but I think it's best if we head back to the B&B."

"Nope, Mama Taylor. You and little Taylor are included. You too, old man."

Brave Heart scooted his chair back and made his way to HQ like he fucking owned the place. Charlie bristled at his comment, and I hated he was feeling offended. This wasn't how I wanted to tell him things. I hated Brave Heart right then for forcing my hand at this.

"Charlie, I… I wanted to tell you in a different way. There's so much going on." Cringing, I felt like I had let him down.

"Listen, Sawdust. It's okay. There's something I wanted to tell you too, but it looks like neither of us gets that option. So just know that… that I love you, okay?"

And with those words, he walked off, officially melting my brain and heart with his words. Not caring about Brave Heart's commands, I took off running and wrapped my arms around Charlie from behind before he made it into the room. He clasped my hands in the front as I squeezed him.

"I love you too, old grump." I let him go, and he walked in without turning around, but I swore I'd felt wetness hit my arm before he did.

Rhett and Asa had stayed back with me. It was nice to feel I had people who genuinely cared about my emotional wellbeing.

"I'm okay." Neither had to say anything; the concern was written all over their faces. "Let's go see what this crisis is. And here I thought we would get through a whole week without one for once," I joked sardonically.

The yearbooks, the journal, and some of the things Rhonda had given us were stacked in the middle of the table. Other notes and pictures we'd been connecting were taped to the whiteboard on the far wall. On the other one, we had started making a flowchart of the Council hierarchy.

Brave Heart was standing by the whiteboard and looking it over when I walked in. There was only one chair left with all the additional people, so Rhett took it and pulled me into his lap as he sat in it. It was like Brave Heart had eyes in the back of his head because as soon as my butt hit Rhett's leg, he turned and began to address us all.

"I am Agent B. You may not call me Brave Heart unless you are that girl right there. She's the only one who has earned that privilege. What I'm about to tell you is classified information. From this point forward, you are all brought in on our investigation. You're all involved in some way or another, whether you knew it or not. Someone in your life, family, or friends has connections in some way to the Council or the Agency. I see that you've started to put some pieces together here, but let me shed some light for you."

He started to pace in front of the board, hands in his pocket as he continued to address us. I almost felt like I needed to get my notepad and take notes. Would there be a quiz?

"The Council is corrupt, and they will use whatever they can to get the leverage they need, to get what they want—absolute power and domination. It's comprised of seven seats with a representative from each family who is currently on the Council. The Council has been around a long time, but each new reign is allowed to choose how they will operate. This current seven, they have been in power for almost thirty years, and every seven years, there is a vote whether they remain in power or a new Council is elected."

Doing the math in my head, I'd wager this was year twenty-eight, meaning a new Council vote was on the horizon. Something about that sent chills through my body. Brave Heart kept pacing in a perfect formation, back and forth, back and forth. It was making me dizzy.

He had been focused on the direction he was walking, with us almost as an afterthought to his tale. Stopping, he leaned over the table, placing his hands firmly on it as he stared us all down.

"There is a head Council member who is elected by the other chapters from the seven. To remain in power, the current seven must prove why they are the most powerful. The other chapters can place a bid to be selected as a possible Council candidate. It is unknown what they must do to get the bid, but you can guarantee it isn't legal. The current leader of the Council seven is Alek Hawthorne. He is the deciding vote if there is ever a tie on any decisions. He is the most powerful overall and a very dangerous man."

We were all on the edge of our seats now as he filled us in on the organization that had created such turmoil in my life. As he began to name the other members, he clearly looked around the room, watching everyone's reaction. He was fishing for something.

"The other seats are held by Abernathy, Latimer, Bellamy, Fitzroy, Draven, and… Rothchild." At each of the names we knew, he looked casually at the corresponding connection. But at the mention of Rothchild, he looked at Rhonda, causing her to gasp and confusion in the rest of us.

"What is it, Mom?" Rowan asked in concern, but Rhett had tensed, his arms tightening around me. He recognized that name. Tilting my head up, I saw the stricken look on his face and knew it wasn't anything good. Brave Heart was apparently ready to move on after he had dropped his bomb. He was starting to piss me off even more. This was a game to him, but it was our lives.

"The Agency was created as a counterbalance to the Council. Families that wanted legacies to mean something good and to stop the corruption from spreading joined together. There are four of those families in this room, not including me. Ace and Ty, you've already discovered. Reyes, your father, has been an agent with our organization and friend to Victoria Draven or, as you knew her, Kyla Brennon. He helped her escape and cultivate an identity. He was on the inside of a subsidiary for Draven Technology for several years."

At the mention of their father's role, Henry and Fin seemed to exhale that their parents weren't on the wrong side of things like we'd first assumed. My mother's journal had started us in that direction, but it was comforting to have concrete proof the people I'd grown up with hadn't been out to kill my parents or me.

"And our last mystery line is none other than my very own mentor, Charlie Smith. How did I do, Chuck?" Brave Heart stood at the front, grinning manically, as he lifted up and down on the balls of his feet.

Now it was my turn to freeze. What. The. Fuck. The declaration out in the hall now made sense. Slowly, I turned to where he was sitting. It was hard to see him through the water someone had filled the room with— what a weird thing for someone to do. Blinking, I managed to shift the water around some and could see him mildly more transparent through the water film filling my eyes.

"Charlie?" I whispered. He was glaring at Brave Heart, but at my word, he turned and looked at me, his face stricken.

"It doesn't change anything, Sawdust. I'm still me. I've been retired for years. Everything we had was organic. I wanted to tell you this weekend. You had finally started to figure out some of your past, and I hadn't wanted to put you in more danger by being connected to me, so I kept quiet. I'm sorry I didn't tell you sooner. Please…" his voice trailed off. His remorse was evident, and he appeared burdened by my sadness, but it didn't matter because my heart was breaking inside.

Like I said, nothing was coincidental.

Apparently, nothing in my life was even real, and it had all been staged from my fucking birth by one organization or another. I was getting really sick of everyone else deciding what my life was going to be like. Fuck that shit. I would just have to make it real fucking clear I was the goddamn Queen in this house. Firm in my decision, I pushed back and climbed out of Rhett's lap, despite his hesitancy to let me go.

"It's okay, grumpy bear. I'm done sitting on the sidelines. It's time he listens to me."

At my words, he let go, and I strode my 5'2" ass right up to Brave Heart and punched him right in the fucking throat.

That's right, I fucking throat punched that bitch. Granted, I'd been aiming for his face, but I was short, and his throat was about all I could reach without a chair. It worked out, though, because I didn't hurt my hand as bad this time.

As my fist connected with his throat, I swear the room erupted in applause. Whether that was only in my head was debatable.

Coughing and spluttering exploded out of Brave Heart as he doubled over, holding his throat. He looked at me in such a state of shock, unsure what to make of me. Good luck with that one, buddy. Underestimate me again, and next time I would aim for your balls. Once he had stopped coughing, I let all my sass flow.

"I've had enough of you coming in and dropping people's truths like some form of sick entertainment. I did have it right the other night; you are an asshole. You should have stayed imaginary because all you've done since you became real is make things worse. So, I'm taking back the reins, buttmuncher. If you're staying, it's on my terms. Sit down and shut the fuck up. I have an organization's destruction to plan."

He stood up once he caught his breath, and part of me was upset my punch hadn't caused him more discomfort—a small sick part that I would deny if you ever asked. He started to slow clap, and I wanted to punch him again. Seriously, what was with this dude? I didn't remember him being so pompous before.

"Finally, ladies and gentlemen, the real Sawyer is here! It's about time you quit standing on the sidelines, tiny dancer. It's just there's one more issue I came here tonight to share."

"Fucking hell, what else?" I groaned, rubbing my temples.

"A student is missing, and her partner is making claims she's being blackmailed by a staff member."

"Who?" Henry whispered, his face already draining of color. Ah, fuck, what was it going to be this time? Agent B, or whatever you wanted to call him, had the decency to look Henry in the eyes to answer him.

"Jill is missing, and Phil is making the blackmail claims."

"Fuck," someone shouted, and it mirrored my thoughts exactly.

Fuck, indeed. I guess I wasn't going to get to have a fun birthday celebration now. Seemed we had a mystery to solve while also navigating all these grenades he tossed at us like we were fucking minesweeper or something. I had a feeling it was going to be a late night.

fifty-three

· · ·

rey

MY HEART WAS RACING. I'd just been with both of those students earlier in the day for practice. I was so distracted by everything going on I hadn't followed back up with Phil. I felt like a complete jackass. He'd broken down and told me about the pressure he was feeling from his dad and some arrangement his father and the director made. It had seemed suspicious, but he hadn't wanted to talk more in-depth about it then. I thought waiting for him to be ready was the right call, and with everything that happened afterward with Sawyer, I'd pushed it aside.

"What more can you tell us about the students?" Smalls asked. She knew them too, and I could tell she was shaken by the news.

"Jill went to meet a friend but appears to have been abducted on her way there. They found her car on the side of the road, doors ajar, with the keys still in the ignition. Her friend called the dorm monitor when she never arrived at the cafe and couldn't get a hold of her by phone. Her location services have been shut off, and her phone keeps going to voicemail, likely also shut off and left elsewhere. Around the same time, Phil was meeting with the headmaster to report the skating program director as blackmailing Jill with inappropriate pictures."

"Wait, that doesn't make sense," I muttered. Something wasn't adding up. Soren squeezed my knee in support under the table. It barely registered as I thought through things, attempting to put all the pieces together.

"Why bring us in now? Why tell us these things and include everyone?" Smalls demanded of him. Her arms were crossed, and she stood with so much attitude in her small stature you would think she was 6ft instead of just over 5ft. Her fierceness brought a momentary smile to my face as I watched her standoff with Agent Asshat.

"Always the perceptive one, tiny dancer. The Agency feels now is the right time. That's the reason. They deem it so, and I do as told. Simple as that."

He folded his arms and leaned back against the wall, way too nonchalantly for me to actually believe he was nonchalant.

"There's something you're not telling us," I concluded, causing him to turn toward me. His smirk grew, but there had been a fleeting flash of panic in his eyes. There was a more significant reason he was here, more to this story than he was sharing, and even to what was going on currently. I think the agent had a separate agenda or a secret he was keeping. Filing that away, I made sure to not forget this nugget. I observed him, watching what else he might say without words.

"Ah, young Henry, always seeing more than meets the eye. Well, you got me. There is one other thing. Let's just call it a perfect moment of opportunity to hit the Council where it hurts. Oliver, your uncle and brother will be attending the expo this weekend. It would be an excellent opportunity to reconnect and start to infiltrate them—"

"No way! He's untrained and a civilian. You can't send him in undercover like that. It's a death threat waiting to happen, and you know it," Tyler shouted. He stood, hands fisted on the table as he glared at the Agent.

"Tsk, tsk, Tyler. You don't make the decisions. And while I think your little display of overprotection is cute, it's unnecessary. Oliver is free to make his own choices, and part of that is doing what I tell him to do. He and I have a deal." That didn't sit well with Smalls, or me either, as she was the next one to jump in.

"You're crazy. You walk in after all this time and start making demands of us. I don't think you understand how we work. The people in this room are my family. To me, that means something. So, before you start putting us in perilous situations, how about you discuss it with us like adults and get our feedback? As far as I know, Ace is the only one who is actually on your payroll and, therefore, the only one you can truly boss around. So, get that through your thick skull, you dimwit!"

She was breathing hard, face red, her hands fisted at her sides in what Fin called a power pose. It was definitely working for her. Soren leaned into me, apparently also noticing what I had.

Whispering, he asked, "Is it wrong that her fierce voice gets me hard every time?"

Trying not to laugh, I avoided looking at him as I casually shook my head, no. Because he wasn't wrong. Going all fierce mama bear on Agent Asshat and protecting her family made Smalls both endearing and sexy as hell.

"Has anyone ever told you how cute you are when you do that?" quipped the Agent. Wrong thing to say, dude! Abort, Abort.

"Why I oughta—" before she finished, she kicked her leg up in a perfect *attitude*, knocking him right in the family jewels by surprise. This time, he did go down.

A collective "ooh" rang out from the guys in the room as the Agent rolled around on the ground clutching his manhood. His face looked purple now, and I think he was either struggling to breathe or trying to not throw up. Bet that would be the last time he ever underestimated a dancer. They could kick your ass and look graceful while doing it.

"Listen up, Buttercup, I don't think you heard me. You do not have any say here. You may nod, you may offer advice, but you do not get to tell us what to do. Not when it comes to me, not when it comes to Ollie, and not when it comes to any of the people in this room. I've been listening and respected what you had to say because you knew my father and saved my life a couple of times. But I am not a child anymore. So, you can either get up, join us in a discussion about how we, as a group, want to tackle this problem, or you can leave. Your choice."

The Agent had stopped groaning on the floor, and the look of awe on his face wasn't the one I expected. He nodded before wobbling and stood up. He sat down after that and quietly kept his mouth shut.

Seeing Smalls take charge was the epitome of her growth since being here. She had always been feisty, even as a teenager, but there was a grace about her now, a quiet strength, and belief in the people she cared about. It was amazing watching her trust others to be there for her. It proved how much stronger she felt if she didn't even hesitate to speak for everyone, knowing we would back her without question.

"I meant what I said. We all get to be part of the process. That also means that there are some things about me I should share…"

Smalls filled in the few people in the room who hadn't known her history. Mama Taylor and Rowan had tears in their eyes at her tale but seemed to finally connect why we all cared about destroying a council.

When she finished, Mama Taylor stood up to give her a hug, holding her tight for a few minutes. It was precisely what Smalls needed, though, because after that, she held her head up high as she addressed the entire room fully, taking on her role as command.

"Okay, now that we're all up to date, let's brainstorm and think about a solution that works for us, not because that's what we were told to do." We all agreed and spent the next hour going over the topic at hand. When we all felt satisfied with the risks we were taking, we settled on an action plan.

"Too bad Elias is missing this. He loved a good brainstorm," mumbled Rhett.

"Where do you think I learned it?" Sawyer joked, trying to distract Rhett from the missing housemate and whatever bomb the agent had triggered earlier.

"Okay, Agent man. What do you think of our plan?" Sawyer asked. As much bravado as she had earlier, she seemed to desperately want his approval. Almost as if he were a parental figure to her. I guess it made sense somehow, but he was kind of an ass, so I didn't really want her caring what he thought.

Agent Asshat had sat there quietly, hands steepled throughout the entire discussion. Quite frankly, I was impressed at his ability to remain quiet. Surprisingly, everyone had something to add during our action phase, from Rhonda to Mateo. Each person took her statement seriously and offered up their thoughts. Finally, he looked up at Sawyer, her lip between her teeth while she waited for his answer.

"Your plan has merit, but there are some flaws."

Smalls deflated a little at his comment, and now *I* wanted to punch him.

"Okay, what would you suggest?"

"You have too many players and variables in place. You need to simplify it. You can't control everything, so maximize what you can control, or your plan will fail before you even start."

"That's actually helpful, thank you."

"Shall I share the rest of the plan the Agency came up with and see how we might integrate them?"

"Uh, yeah. Sure, that would be okay."

"Ollie was to meet with his brother and uncle. He was to make it known he's been thinking about finishing his internship for the company this summer. When they ask what changed your mind, Ollie, you simply state, 'it's time I got serious,' and 'that family is important.' That gets us an in at Latimer and a man on the inside."

At her nod, he continued.

"Next, while everyone is at the expo, we have a group that will search the rooms of the known Council members present. It is unlikely they will have any info on them, but it's also a chance to plant new bugs. Our tech department has developed a practically untraceable bug that is unseen and can pass any device sweeps they might perform. This may get us a lead on where the girl is being held."

"Wait, you think the Council is behind Jill's abduction?" I interrupted with my question.

"Wasn't that obvious? They are bad people. This is

what they do. This is what they tried to do to you, Abigail." He looked at her even though I'd asked the question.

"I told you already, that isn't my name. We will swing back to Jill. Continue." He sent a sharp look at me, almost as if he was pissed at me for her being mad at him. You're on your own there, pal.

"The riskiest part will be the finale. Sawyer, you will be revealing yourself to the Council. The ones who thought you were dead will now know you are very much still alive. This includes Abernathy. But we hope to play this off that you still have no clue about anything. Including that he is your father, and Asa, your brother. You both haven't shared that with anyone outside this room, so we have that on our side."

He grabbed the bottle of water off the table and took a giant swig as we all waited for him to continue. Now that he had the floor, he was milking it for all he was worth. Once he drank half of the bottle, he finally continued.

"To pull this off, you will need to control your emotions and maintain you have no idea about anything. At the dinner, after the expo finale, you and Reyes will be introduced to the alumni. We need them to invite you to join a 'secret school alumni tour.' That is where we will find the most info on their organization and how it works. Minimal risk, and we can start training for interrogation skills if you feel that will be helpful. There will be agents around at all times, and you will never be alone with any members. Believe it or not, we do care about your safety. We wouldn't put you in any situations where we didn't control the level of risk. You've been an important part of this from the beginning to them. We want to know why."

He had moved from his slouched position during his monologue to bracing his arms on the table in front of him. He spoke to her the whole time as if he finally understood she was the one he needed to convince.

"It still seems risky," she answered.

"It is. There's not a risk-free plan. We may lose people. They aren't good people, but we may also uncover some valuable information on how to bring down the organization and save a young girl's life."

Well, when he put it that way, it sounded selfish to not do it. Smalls seemed to agree and slowly nodded.

"On one condition. We're all included in *all* plans moving forward, you're open with us about information, and you promise to protect everyone in this room. Especially those who are only involved by association even if... something happens to me."

A couple of gasps rang out, but she held eye contact with him. She wouldn't let this lie and needed to know the people she cared about would be looked after. She'd figured out they wanted her for something, so she was using it for leverage. Smart girl, my Smalls, even if I wanted to shake her for leveraging her own life.

"Agreed," he finally answered.

We had a plan, but it felt like one made by a toddler with crayons. I wasn't confident we would all come out of this unscathed, and that thought terrified me.

fifty-four

. . .

sawyer

"SAWDUST, CAN WE TALK?" Charlie asked as he approached me. Everyone else had started to pack up and leave HQ. It was close to midnight, and we were all exhausted.

I'd avoided looking at him since I found out he knew more about my past than he'd ever let on. On the one hand, I was pissed. But he had kept me safe and given me a home. I hadn't exactly been open with him either, but he was the adult at the time. I was spinning out and didn't know where I was going to land. Everything seemed to come back to this catch-22.

How could I be upset with people not telling me who they were when I did the same?

Short answer, I couldn't. Not really. Especially, if their role had been to keep me safe.

Taking a deep breath, I prepared myself for this

conversation. The guys all gave me looks to see if I wanted them to stay, but I shook them off. This needed to be between us. When the last person had left the room, Asa shut the door behind him. Collapsing in the first chair I saw, I turned to Charlie, waiting him out this time.

"Sawdust. I didn't know who you were at first. When Samson called me—"

"Samson?" I muttered. The name sounded familiar, but I couldn't recall why.

"Yeah, Agent B, or as you call him Brave Heart. His first name is Samson." Nodding at his explanation, I rolled the name around in my head while he continued.

"He told me someone important to him needed a stable place to live. You were already working at the rink at that point. I didn't want to listen to him. I was done with that life; it was why I returned back home to the rink to spend my days with Martha. So, I told him, no."

"But—" he raised an eyebrow to let me know if I was patient, he would get there, so I snapped my mouth shut, letting him tell me at his pace.

"Then, one day, you were working, and I realized how sad and alone you seemed. I could hear my Martha's voice urging me to do what was right. That perhaps I could use a companion as well. So, yes, technically, Samson put the idea into my head, but it was my decision in the end. Our interactions have never been fake or forced. Please believe me." His eyes bore into me, his face open.

"Why didn't you tell me then?" I dropped my eyes, picking at the table. It hurt, even if I believed him.

"Because I was scared of losing you, Sawdust. I'm not good at communicating my feelings, but you've always felt like the daughter I never had. When you told me you were coming here, I was scared shitless because I knew it would be dangerous, but also that you might find out and hate me."

"How long have you known about my past? My parents?"

"I didn't know. Samson tried to tell me once, but I told him to butt the hell out. I didn't need to know, and if I did, you would tell me." I wanted to believe him, and I felt he had no reason to lie to me anymore. "So, you have a brother, a twin even? How do you feel about it?" he asked.

"Yeah, it's been pretty crazy, but finding him has been great. I'm still trying to get to know him, but in some ways, we've just automatically clicked. I even met my biological mom, Isla. My biological father better hope I never meet him alone since he was the one who gave me away."

"Gave you… Wait, when he said Abernathy…" Charlie trailed off, a look of horror mixed with hope covered his face as he waited for my answer.

"Yeah, Orson Abernathy is my biological father."

"Abernathy," he whispered. Nodding, I watched him, hoping he would explain more.

"Oh, my dear girl." He dropped to the floor in front

of me and started to cry all over my lap as he held me to him.

"Charlie?" I'd never seen him this way before, what was I supposed to do? I patted his head, hoping it would help. After a few minutes, his tears dried, and he lifted his head.

"Sawdust, I've been looking for you for what feels like my whole life, and in the end, you found me."

"What are you talking about, Charlie?" I murmured, my voice shook at the level of the emotion from him.

"You were the last case I'd been tasked with. The Agency had gotten a tip that Abernathy was making a play to take the open seat. He was connected to the other members and had a good chance of winning it. I knew he would do something drastic, as it was the only way. There was a rumor he was to sell one of his babies. When I made it to the hospital, it was to Isla's mournful scream. I searched and tried to find connections of who he'd given you to, but in the end, it drove me to early retirement when I was unable to find you. I realized I couldn't live the rest of my life, fighting an enemy I couldn't see."

I wiped the tears as he spoke of his heartache. If only we had actually trusted one another years ago. We were here now and could still mend this. I needed it too. The pain had taken on a life of its own, and it no longer belonged here. We were all grieving from something the Council had taken from us, we'd just never known.

Once he collected himself more, he continued,

almost as if he needed to purge this secret from himself, unable to bear the weight of it any longer.

"I couldn't be part of something that harmed children, even if not directly. The Agency had changed as well, and I didn't have the fight I had initially. It was also around the same time Martha suffered her third miscarriage. I decided to stop trying to be something I wasn't—a hero—and returned home. It ended up being the smart choice, as Martha was diagnosed with cancer a few years later. I got to spend as much time with her as I could have asked for. I never stopped looking for you, though. There was a moment when I met you that I wondered, but your cover story was so thorough I dismissed it. Guess I trained Samson better than I thought."

He laughed at that. Charlie's story was just as sad as mine was. Both of us had the people we loved taken from us too soon. The Agency hadn't told him who I was all along. That was kind of cruel when you thought about it. They were supposed to be the good guys, but I was starting to wonder where they actually fell on the line. Seemed like they were only centimeters on the side of good.

"No more secrets, okay? From now on, you and me, we're family, and we tell each other things. Okay?"

"Okay. Family."

I did the only thing I could do after that. I hugged the old grump. Seems Mama Taylor had rubbed off on me after all.

The next day was hectic as we prepared for the expo to put our plan into action. The rumor about Jill and Phil had circulated amongst the students quickly. It seemed they were going with a lovers' quarrel between Jill and Phil, and the director had stepped in, a love connection developed, and then Phil created a plan to get them separated.

The rumor mill was stupid, but it was almost better they didn't know the actual truth. Phil had left the program the same evening he'd made his allegations after his parents showed up. No one knew if he'd intended that or not, or who even called them. The school was being quiet with the details on the administrative front as well, and only told us, "It's an unfortunate event and is being looked into."

For some reason, that didn't fill me with confidence.

The board was still "investigating" the claims, but after I learned that the board was just a mini council, I didn't have hopes for that either if something truly was going on with the director. He creeped me out, that was for sure, but I didn't know if that was because he was just creepy or an actual predator. I warned all the girls to stay clear of him, though, just in case.

We met with Samson at lunch on Friday to go over "interrogation" techniques that basically summed up to "don't say anything." Great advice, dude.

I continued to struggle with Samson and sometimes felt he pushed my buttons on purpose, but I wasn't sure the reasoning behind it. The part of me that remembered his friendship as a child felt connected and drawn to him, making me instinctively trust him and seek his approval. At one time in my life, he had been my only friend and had saved my life.

But every time he opened his mouth, I wanted to punch him again. I did like that he flinched each time I walked past him. That was funny and made me feel proud of myself. Little ole me took down the big bad agent. Ha!

Now, it was Saturday, my birthday and the expo. Happy 22nd birthday, self.

Asa and I were to meet Isla this morning for breakfast. She was excited to see me again, and I had to admit, I was too. I wanted to ask her about her friendship with Victoria, my adoptive mother.

"Happy official 1st birthday, twin!" I beamed as my brother opened the door of his car.

"Happy 1st birthday, sis! Come on, I'm starving."

"Hey, did you ever open that gift I left for you the night of the sleepover?" Asa asked, as we pulled up to the diner.

"What are you talking about?" I looked at him curiously, not remembering what he was referring to.

"I put it on your bed. It was a gift Mom had sent with me. It was in a small bag. You didn't see it?"

I shook my head no; thinking back to that morning, I vaguely recalled something on my bed. But with the journals and that hot shower sex with Ty and Rhett, I didn't remember anything being there when I got out.

"Huh." Shrugging because there wasn't much we could do now, I got out of the car and walked in with my brother. Isla was already seated this time, so we walked over to her booth. Asa scooted in across from mom, so I decided to sit next to her.

"Abigail! Oh, shoot. I mean, Sawyer? What do you want to be called, hun?" Laughing because it was funny when you thought of all the names I had.

"Sawyer works."

"Sawyer it is then. Happy birthday, you two. I can't believe I get to spend it with both of you this year. I never…" she trailed off as tears started to form.

"Thank you. You missed the most delicious cake that Ollie made us. It was four layers with chocolate-covered strawberries hidden in the icing! It was epic! I think I had a sugar coma for a whole day!"

"Oh my gawd, do not remind me of that cake. I think I'm still dreaming about it," Asa added. We all laughed, helping to dissolve the sadness of this being our first birthday together since our birth.

"So, how are you?" I asked Isla, hoping for some easy conversation to get to know her better. Thankfully, she took it and regaled us with her week and what project she was working on.

I discovered she ran an organization that helped single women get back on their feet in domestic violence situations. She was amazing, and I was happy I had this chance to know her. After a yummy breakfast of pancakes, Isla asked how I was feeling about skating today.

"I'm feeling good. Henry and I are prepared, and I think it will be a big hit."

"I can't wait to see you skate. Gosh, it's been ages since I've even stepped foot on the ice."

"Speaking of skating, I meant to ask you how close you were with Victoria Draven?" Her face drained of color at the name.

"How do you know that name?" she stuttered out in a hushed whisper.

"She was my… adoptive mom." Shock filled her face, and I realized she hadn't known. Why I kept expecting the worst from her, I didn't know, but I was glad I kept being shown how amazing she really was. She was just as in the dark with the secrets as we had been. How many secrets would it take before we all shattered from the pressure?

"I can't believe this. Did she know you were my daughter?" I shook my head because while mom had known to contact Aggie, she hadn't ever mentioned Isla, so I didn't think she knew.

"We were the best of friends. As close as sisters, really. She had warned me away from Orson on several occasions, but I wasn't thinking clearly after Samson had disappeared. Samson was my true first love. He attended the regular school at TAS, and we dated for over two years. I thought I would marry him, but he broke up with me out of the blue one day. It broke my heart, and during that time was when Orson swooped in. Victoria told me not to trust him, but when she vanished as well, I felt alone, and Orson was there. He asked me to marry him a week later, and I accepted. Things were okay at first, but after a while, I saw what everyone had said."

Isla was lost in her memories, but it made me wonder what happened. Why did Samson leave her if he loved her? Fuck. Was it the same Samson? It wasn't a common first name. What were the odds there were two? As I said before, nothing was coincidental anymore.

"How did you meet Orson? Did he attend the same school?" Asa looked curiously at me, trying to figure out where I was going with this.

"Oh, he had, but he was older than us. He'd already graduated from college and was starting his business when I graduated high school." She took a drink of her tea, and I smiled, imagining her and Victoria sharing tea as young girls.

"So how did you meet, if he was older?"

"Oh, Orson was Samson's older brother." Fucking hell. Brave Heart was my biological uncle.

Spraying my orange juice all over the table, they both turned to me as I coughed up the burning sensation. OJ up the nose, I did not recommend it.

"You okay, sweetie?" she softly rubbed my back, and it was everything I had been missing. Melting into her touch, I nodded as I got myself under control. Samson and I would be having words. That you could bet on.

We finished up our meal and hugged, and she promised to find me after the ice show. As she was walking to her car, she turned back, a question on her face.

"Sawyer, you never said how you liked the gift?"

"Oh, um, it seems to have gone missing. I don't remember seeing it. I'm sure it just fell off the bed or something." If I wasn't mistaken, her face grew tight at the mention of not knowing where it was.

"Of course, well, let me know when you do find it, dear. It was a family heirloom, and I thought it would be nice for you to have it."

With that, she walked off to her car, her steps a little quicker than before. Shit. Why did I feel like it wasn't okay if I couldn't find whatever she had given me? Something else to add to my ever-growing to-do list.

Sending a questioning look to Asa, he shrugged, and we got into his car. It was time.

Time for the plan to fall into place or blow up in our face, you know, great odds either way, really. I was going to get some damn answers if it killed me.

fifty-five

. . .

finley

I'D BEEN anxious since Thursday, and I couldn't hold it in anymore. I was about to do something foolish. Picking up my phone, I debated who I could call. Sawyer, Asa, and my brother would all kill me. I needed support. Deciding to try Rhett, I was surprised when a girl's voice answered.

"Hello?"

"Uh, I was trying to get a hold of Rhett. Is he there?"

"Finley, is that you?"

"Rowan?"

"Hey, girl! Yeah, it's me. Rhett left his phone here earlier when he stopped by."

"Oh, that makes sense. Hey, do you happen to be busy? I need help with something."

"Sure. What do you need?"

"Can you meet me on campus before the ice show?"

"Yeah, I can do that. I was going anyway, so I'll just get there earlier."

"Perfect, thank you! I'll send you the meeting place."

"Sweet. Okay, see you in a bit. Bye."

"Thanks, Rowan. Bye."

Hanging up, I logged into my computer to send the last message. I had been going back and forth all week with this hacker. When Jill had called me to help her wipe some pictures off a phone, I had assumed an ex was harassing her and told her no problem. Now, I had a sinking suspicion it was more nefarious than that, and I had inadvertently wiped away any evidence to be used against the director, or even the Council.

I had been looking for a way to connect it back to him and find Jill, and I think I finally had a lead. I just needed a lookout during the ice expo to break into his office. Everyone would be busy and occupied, so it was the perfect opportunity to get the leverage I needed. I was confident it would work.

> **0BL1V10N**: I can make the exchange tonight. Do you have the girl's location?
>
> **CH405**: If you give me the files, I will provide you with the location. You know how it works, babe.
>
> **0BL1V10N**: Which is why I'm asking. I'm not going to risk my neck if you can't deliver.
>
> **CH405**: Oh, I can deliver. If you ever took me up on my offer, you would know that.

0BL1V10N: These games we play are growing tiring. I'll text you the meetup location.

CH405: One day, you will admit your undying love for me.

0BL1V10N: In your dreams.

CH405: Every night while strangling the monkey, baby.

0BL1V10N: I'm going to ignore that, Chaos. Later.

CH405: You can't deny our chemistry, Oblivion. One day you will see that. Later.

Shaking my head, I hated to admit I had a smile on my face. Chaos was always flirting with me, but it never went any further. I had known him for a few years, and while he joked about meeting, we never actually went through with it. I had quit holding onto that hope long ago.

Especially now that I had Asa. He was real and unique. Even if he was still holding out on me in the sex department, I found myself falling in love with him. Packing up my stuff, I headed over to map out the best spots at my location. My skills were a little rusty, but it was like riding a bike, right?

sawyer

"Are you ready, Smalls?"

"Yeah, I'm ready. I'm always ready when it comes to skating with you."

Leaning up, I kissed him gently. We might be trying to infiltrate a corrupt Agency, but it didn't mean I couldn't stop and enjoy the small things. In fact, it meant I should do it even more.

"When this is over, I want to take you away somewhere with Soren? What do you say?"

"I think that sounds wonderful. We could all use a getaway."

"Well, if it isn't my two favorite skaters. I can't wait for you to wow us. You guys are on deck. The last skater is finishing up," Director Donnelly said as he waved us through.

After the info the other night, I couldn't help but look at him with a more scrutinizing gaze. Unfortunately, it wasn't like there was a pedophile creep stamp they all got, so you could check for it. The government should look into developing something like that.

Henry grabbed my hand and pulled me away from the creepy director, and we headed out onto the ice. This was the part I loved—the build-up, the anticipation, the excitement. All the hard work and training hours led to this. This was where my soul was happy.

"Now, closing out our program, are reunited partners, Sawyer Sullivan and Henry Reyes, two of our very own

instructors! Thank you for coming out for our Fall Semester Alumni Expo! Don't…"

Tuning out the overhead announcer, I spotted a few faces in the crowd, but it was hard to really see too many people with the lights. We skated out onto the center and got into our first position. He stood behind me, arm wrapped around my front, holding my hand. We counted our breaths as we waited for the music to start. In and one, in and two, in and three… and then we were off.

He spun me into a twirl, and we started to skate side by side, arms and feet moving in sync in a twizzle, just as we had practiced a million times. Pulling me toward him, he extended me out in front of him as I grabbed the edge of my skate and held the position.

He pushed my hand using the momentum, and I went into a low spin, coming up into a backward spin. We joined again and started to do one of the new lifts as he twisted me around his body. We were as fluid as liquid, moving and bending together, aligned with the music.

We continued to skate around the rink, joined together and dancing, always in tune with one another. Skating with Henry was as easy as breathing. All I had to do was listen to my heart and follow.

Pulling my arm, he tilted me upside down as I grabbed his waist and kept my leg straight in the lift before he set me back down on the ice into a side-by-side spin. We were nearing the end now and had one more big lift to pull off.

Pulling me in, we skated fast to build up momentum before he lifted me by my hands over his head as I did a split in the air, then tumbled over his front, wrapping my legs around him as we did a joint spin.

It was technically an illegal move for ice dancing, but since we were showing off for the alumni, we had decided to keep some of the moves. We would need to change our whole routine moving forward if we pursued competing.

Keeping my center, I tracked the spot I had picked out a month ago to still have my equilibrium when we came out of the spin. Something shifted my focus on the last spin, and I swore I saw Elias for a brief second, but when I looked again after the spin, no one was there.

Focusing back on the moves, we skated, shifting our feet and going into our last turn before he pulled me in and dipped me over his leg; my arms were thrown out wide, safe in his arms.

Grinning wildly, the adrenaline after skating a clean program ran through us. Which is why I guess he did the next thing and kissed me on the ice in front of the whole stadium. Welp, that cat was officially out of the bag.

Hello, gossip mill, you have new fodder to spread.

Laughing, we skated off together to the applause, and I sent a prayer to whoever would listen that everyone else was getting on okay. Part one of our plan was officially in play.

oliver

"Nephew. How interesting to see you here. I thought you despised us, going so far as to even change your last name? So, tell me, why should I believe your message that you've changed your mind?" My uncle studied me, his tumbler swishing in his hand.

Tilting my head, I gave him a serious look. "You could say I've had an awakening. I'm tired of living this mediocre life, and I'm ready to embrace the future I was meant for."

Uncle Jayce regarded me with a calculating gaze, but I knew what my face showed. If there was one thing I could do, it was to present to people the version of me they wanted to see.

"Hmm. Interesting. Does this have anything to do with your new roommate? The hot little piece of ass?" I wasn't surprised he knew about Sawyer. I just hoped he didn't know more than I wanted him to know.

"Hmph. You could say that. I realized I wanted to stand out, and it was time I quit eating with the servants, and time I started dining with the royals. I'm ready, Uncle."

"I'm happy to hear that. It was hard on your father when you turned your nose up at the family legacy. Your brother, Sebastian, will be here shortly. We can talk about details with him. I think I have the perfect test for you to prove your family loyalty."

"Of course, Uncle. Whatever it takes."

He turned from me and watched the skaters on the ice. Rey and Sawyer would be next, and I was both nervous and excited for them. I didn't want to see my uncle's reaction when she skated out; I was afraid I would punch him, ruining everything. But I was looking forward to seeing my bite-size on the ice. Ty kept giving me a hard time about having watched their program, and I was a little jealous he'd seen them skate already.

"Little Brother!" boomed a loud voice behind me. Turning, I took in Sebastian, my oldest brother. He had taken on more responsibilities within the company and was now primed to take over for Jayce when he retired, since our uncle didn't have any heirs.

"Bash. How are you? Maureen and the kids?" He gave me a big hug before pulling back. Despite not seeing him for years, he at least appeared happy to see me for once.

"They're good. But let's talk about you. What's this I hear about you leaving Uncle Jayce a message about changing your mind? Are you finally going to accept your legacy, little brother?"

"It looks that way. We're going to talk about it after the last show."

"Oh, this is going to be fun." He rubbed his hands together, an eager look on his face.

I wasn't sure I agreed with him. Sawyer and Rey

skated out, and I watched my uncle for any sign of recognition. He kept his face blank, giving nothing away. Halfway through the program, my uncle's guard, Leon Rojas, approached him.

"Sir, there's a situation. You're needed downstairs."

Fuck, this wasn't good. I was to keep them occupied and in this box. Besides, since when was there a downstairs in the ice rink? Thinking quickly, I interjected myself.

"Sounds like a good learning opportunity. What do you say, Uncle?" He observed me for a brief second before nodding. Bash laughed, clapping me on the back as we headed out of the box.

"Your first time below is going to blow your mind."

Fucking hell. What had I gotten myself into? This wasn't part of the plan. Checking my pockets, I felt the minuscule bug and pulled it out and carefully attached it to my uncle's belt as he walked in front of me. Hopefully, that was good enough.

We walked down a back hallway, and then to a door marked 'private'. I had never noticed this door before. My uncle and brother walked up to the door where they placed their thumb and had their retinas scanned. Shit, this wasn't good.

"Oliver. As a Latimer, you're already preprogrammed. Go ahead. It grants you entrance."

Stepping up, it scanned me, and as he said, it beeped and allowed me in. Walking down the stairs, I wasn't prepared for what laid below the hockey rink. This was bigger than we realized and it was all taking place right here under our noses.

I guess it finally made sense what the connection between the Council and the school was. It truly was their breeding ground. Elite athletes, the finest specimen in the world, all for them to groom and blackmail for a chance to achieve their dreams. I think I was going to be sick.

Hardening my resolve, I straightened my spine and walked into that room like the Latimer I was pretending to be. It was the performance of a lifetime, and I had a feeling that all of our lives depended on it. No pressure, right?

epilogue

· · · ·

elias

"ELI, hurry up! We're going to be late to meet with the alumni Daddy wants us to schmooze."

Fucking hell, I was in agony. Adelaide stomped her foot like a two-year-old, and I almost lost it. This was pure torture, and I wasn't sure how much longer I could put up the charade. When they requested I reconnect with Adelaide to meet with one of the other families, I was appalled.

My father ensured me it was necessary and that after this meeting, I could fuck her, dump her, humiliate her, or any other act I chose. I just had to get through this first. I honestly didn't know if I was going to make it.

Her voice grated on my nerves, and I was positive I would chip a tooth before the night was over. I hadn't expected to be back on campus this soon, much less this way. I was nervous about running into any of the people I had come to know as family. It wouldn't look good, but there wasn't anything I could do about it now. I was here, I was with Adelaide, and I had to pretend to like her. I was screwed.

"Ah, yes. Mr. Fitzroy and Ms. Aldridge, the Abernathy's will see you now," stated the doorman.

Who had their own fucking doorman for an ice hockey box? Apparently, Abernathy did. Walking in, I prepared myself to come face to face with the man who had sold Sawyer off. Who I wasn't expecting to see sitting there was Rhett. Bloody Hell, just what mess did I walk into?

His eyes rounded at me, but his face gave no other emotion. Seemed like we both had some explaining to do after this. He was sitting next to two people I didn't know, and it would be impolite for me to walk over there, so I would have to wait until I could make my way across the room. For a school hockey rink, this box was spacious and currently held about fifteen people. It was like a whole different social hour up here.

Adelaide pressed her fingernails into my arm when I wasn't giving her enough attention. Turning to her, I grinded my teeth before speaking to her. "Hands off, or I will tell everyone here how you cheated at the Olympics."

Her face went wide in fear, and she lessened her grip. Dear-old-dad had been at least forthcoming with some information to help me. We made our way around the room, and I was getting closer to Rhett and Abernathy, finally.

"Mr. Fitzroy. It's so nice to finally meet Richards' youngest heir," said Orson Abernathy, who I recognized from his picture.

"It's a pleasure to meet you as well. My father holds your business in high regard and is excited about this new opportunity you have for him. Perhaps, we can set up a time to discuss it further this week?"

"Of course, I will have my secretary send over the details. It's in poor taste to talk business here, so enjoy the food. I'm going to greet the rest of my guests."

He slipped off, and I noticed how he grazed Adelaide's ass as he did. She turned, looking at him almost as if she was interested. I'd felt sorry for her at first, as no woman should have their ass grabbed without consent, but it seemed she was all for it—even more reason to disentangle myself from her.

Stepping away, I was finally able to make my way to Rhett. I nodded, and he followed me to a somewhat private corner.

"What are you doing here?" I asked, narrowing my eyes at him.

"I was just about to ask you the same question," he retorted. He seemed angry, and I realized how shitty it was of me to cut off all communication. I figured it was easier that way, but I had been wrong, so wrong.

"Look—" before I could finish, his phone went off, and he pulled it out to glance at the text. His breathing stopped, and just before he dropped the phone to the ground, I grabbed it from him. The text displayed chilled me to my bones.

Soren: They're gone. Finley and Rowan. They've been taken.

To be continued….
Read on for some bonus scenes

afterword

Whew… that was a ride! You doing okay? I hope so, and thank you for hanging in there with Sawyer and the gang on this journey. For me, book two was more emotionally raw and vulnerable as it showcased the emotions we all carry daily. Grief isn't linear, and it doesn't just go away over time. How could it? Whether it is the loss of a person, dream, or identity, it was an integral part of us that we now have to learn to live without. That's hard. Hopefully, Sawyer and the guys resonated with you as you learned more about their stories and who they are.

Trauma also has a lasting effect on us and can alter how we react and perceive things. What I love about these characters is that they show us it's okay to feel happy and sad at the same time. That we can doubt and still try to trust others. The important part is that we try, that we realize we aren't alone, and we find support in those around us. It's so okay not to have it all together; very few do.

You're probably cursing me out for that cliffhanger. It's okay, go ahead, you can cuss me out! Lol. I didn't set out to end it that way, but the story led me there, and I had to follow it. This book, in particular, took on a life of its own in certain parts but led me to some of the most beautiful chapters. Rhett's breakdown, the N'Sync debacle, and Sawyer meeting Brave Heart were all times where the characters went rogue on me! The outcome was simply beautiful, and now I can't imagine it any other way.

Let's talk about Tyler… He was the first curveball this book threw at me. For days, I kept seeing him and Sawyer reuniting, but I was fearful of listening to it. I'm sure some will think I'm just adding, as Elias stated, "anyone with a penis," but that's not the case. Tyler had a story to tell and was needed in the family. I see that now, and I hope you do too. Plus, I just love the dynamics between him, Sawyer, and Ollie.

So many things came to light in this book. What are your theories? Who is your favorite? What was the biggest reveal to you? I want to hear from you and know these things, so please think about joining my readers' group on Facebook and joining in on the fun.

Can't wait for you to read the third and final book for Sawyer and her guys and see how it all ends. Are you on pins and needles already? Because I am!

acknowledgments

First, thank you to all the readers who have taken a chance with a new author and picked up and read this book. If you're reading this, then I hope that means even more so that you have enjoyed, or even perhaps love this series! You guys simply are the best and make it all worth it. So thank you from the bottom of my heart.

Two ladies, in particular, have become my ride or die and have imprinted on my heart. Cat, you have held my hand through it all and made sure I listen to my own voice instead of the haters. Thank you for being my friend and saving me from all the "thats." Em, you have reassured me through it all when I worried it was all garbage and are always there even when I'm needy. Whether it's to read something for the hundredth time to check my tenses, bounce ideas off of, or assure me I can do it, you're always there, and I appreciate that so much. I can't wait for all the journeys we three will take.

To all my beautiful beta babes, Shawna, Becki, Lin, and Marla, you guys rocked and helped me make this story better. Your encouragement and thirstiness were the push I needed to keep going and get those edits done! So thank you for loving these characters and their story. I can't wait for you to read the next one to see how it all ends. I will try to add more steam for you! Love your thirst.

Thank you to all the ARC readers who took the time to read this book and review it. Your excitement and encouragement to read this book have meant the world to me. Especially on those sleepless nights when I wonder if anyone even cares, so thank you! I look forward to seeing your reviews and theories.

There are so many others who have made an impact on my journey as an author. From late-night messages, helpful advice, and words of encouragement, it has all helped me get to where I am today. So thank you for taking the time to help a newbie. I genuinely believe that we can all be successful and help one another. It isn't a limited thing, so bullying and hate have no legs to stand on. I'm glad that I have found my tribe of people. If you're someone who is thinking about writing or new to the genre, reach out to others, reach out to me, basically just reach out! It's so much harder on your own, especially when you don't have to!

My husband—there aren't enough words to describe how much your support and love mean to me. Thank you for encouraging me and being my biggest cheer-leader. I know the late nights I'm up writing, the count-less hours spent doing book-related things, or my obsession with these characters at times hasn't been easy and a shift from our normal. And you never complained… okay, not much at least, but you knew this was something I needed to do. So, thank you for giving me the space to have the freedom to try something new and follow my heart.

Lastly, to my fur baby Lucky. You are my whole heart. May you live on in the hearts of readers forever as they fall in love with you as much as I am.

If I've forgotten anyone, know it wasn't intentional. The end of a book is a magical and bewildering feeling, and some days I don't even know which way is up. So if I've forgotten to thank you, know that I do appreciate you! Thank you for being on this journey with me.

also by kris butler

beauty and the cleats

#baseball #standalone series #heartfelt

The Cleat Retreat (Blake's prequel)

The Pitch Slap (Blake's book, MMFMM)

No Balking Way (Bryce's book, MMF)

Whiff it Real Good (Ledger's book, MM)

lux brumalis (completed)

#hockey #girlboss #nonbinary sibling

3 guys, no MM

Penalty Box

Dead Lift

Breakaway

the council series (completed)

#figure skating #secret past #dark elements

7 guys, lots of MM with bi-awakening

Damaged Dreams

Shattered Secrets

Fractured Futures

Bosh Bells & Epic Fails

The Council Boxset

the order duet (council spinoff)

#secret agency #spy + hacker games #fashionista

4 guys, light MM (in book 2 at the end, and bonus)

Stiletto Sins

Lipstick Lies

The Order Duet Omnibus

dressed to kill shared world (standalone)

#female assassin #quirky & curvy #twins

4 guys, no MM

Raven

f*ck steal kill (standalone)

#morally gray #bestie unalivers #sassy

3 guys, biawakening, (FF in Joy's chapter)

F*ck Steal Kill

dark confessions (completed)

#mafia #therapist #foster kids + dogs #tattoos

5 guys with MM

Dangerous Truths

Dangerous Lies

Dangerous Vows

Reckless (Cami's Novella)

Relentless (Nat's Novella)

Dangerous Love

Truth Lies Vows Love: The Complete Series

tattooed hearts duet (completed)

#tattoos #penpals #music #curvy fmc

3 guys with MM

Riddled Deceit (Part 1)

Smudged Lines (Part 2)

Open Road (Road trip Novella)

Tattooed Hearts Completed Duet

music city diaries (tattooed hearts spin-off)

#motorcycle club #age gap #TW #cam girl

4 guys, no MM

Beautiful Agony

Beautiful Envy

Beautiful Unity

vacation romcom

#romcom #social media experiment #besties

3 guys, no MM

Vibing

sinners fairytales (standalone)

#Rapunzel retelling #dance #TW

3 guys, no MM

Pride

about the author

Kris Butler writes under a pen name to have some separation from her everyday life. Writing has become her second love, providing a safe place to normalize mental health through her characters. Kris enjoys writing emotional books with flawed characters, sassy heroines, and all the book boyfriends she loves to drool over. You can find her at home most nights reading with her husband and furbaby, trying to maintain her nerdy sock collection, or playing tabletop games with her friends. Kris loves to talk with readers about her books, even if it's just them yelling at her for that cliffhanger. If you enjoyed her book, please consider leaving a review. You can find her in her reader group or on social media.

Join my newsletter
Join my reader group
Check out my website

www.ingramcontent.com/pod-product-compliance
Lightning Source LLC
Chambersburg PA
CBHW072033190726
48294CB00005B/1248